HALLOWED

NEW YORK TIMES BESTSELLING AUTHOR
CYNTHIA HAND

HALLOWED

First published in Great Britain 2012 by Electric Monkey, part of Farshore
This edition published 2026

An imprint of HarperCollins*Publishers*
1 London Bridge Street, London SE1 9GF

farshore.co.uk

HarperCollins*Publishers*
Macken House, 39/40 Mayor Street Upper, Dublin 1, D01 C9W8, Ireland

Text copyright © Cynthia Hand 2012
Cover illustration © Palinlineart 2026

The moral rights of the author and illustrator have been asserted

ISBN 978 0 00 878591 8

Printed and bound in the UK using 100% renewable electricity
at CPI Group (UK) Ltd

1

A CIP catalogue record for this title is available from the British Library

All rights reserved. No part of this publication may be reproduced, stored in a retrieval system, or transmitted, in any form or by any means, electronic, mechanical, photocopying, recording or otherwise, without the prior permission of the publisher and copyright owner.

Without limiting the exclusive rights of any author, contributor or the publisher of this publication, any unauthorised use of this publication to train generative artificial intelligence (AI) technologies is expressly prohibited. HarperCollins also exercise their rights under Article 4(3) of the Digital Single Market Directive 2019/790 and expressly reserve this publication from the text and data mining exception.

Stay safe online. Any website addresses listed in this book are correct at the time of going to print. However, Farshore is not responsible for content hosted by third parties. Please be aware that online content can be subject to change and websites can contain content that is unsuitable for children. We advise that all children are supervised when using the internet.

For Carol, my mom

When men began to increase in number on the earth and daughters were born to them, the sons of God saw that the daughters of men were beautiful, and they married any of them they chose.
—Genesis 6:1–2

PROLOGUE

In the dream, there's sorrow. I feel it over everything else, a terrible grief that chokes me, blurs my sight, weighs down my feet as I move through the tall grass. I walk among pine trees up a gentle slope. It's not the hillside from my vision, not the forest fire, not anyplace I've seen before. This is something new. Overhead the sky is a pure, cloudless blue. Sun shining. Birds singing. A warm breeze stirring the trees.

A Black Wing must be nearby, *really* nearby, if the raging grief is any indication. I glance around. That's when I see my brother walking beside me. He's wearing a suit, black jacket and everything: dark gray button-down shirt, shiny shoes, a striped silver tie. He gazes straight ahead, his jaw set in determination or anger or something else I can't identify.

"Jeffrey," I murmur.

He doesn't look at me. He says, "Let's just get this over with."

I wish I knew what he meant.

Then someone takes my hand, and it's familiar, the heat of his skin, the slender yet masculine fingers enfolding mine. Like a surgeon's hand, I once thought. Christian's. My breath catches. I shouldn't let him hold my hand, not now, not after everything, but I don't pull away. I look up the sleeve of his suit to his face, his serious green gold-flecked eyes. And for an instant the sorrow eases.

You can do this, he whispers in my mind.

1

LOOKING FOR MIDAS

Bluebell's not blue anymore. The fire has transformed Tucker's 1978 Chevy LUV into a mix of black, gray, and rusty orange, the windows shattered by the heat, the tires missing, the interior a sickening blackened twist of metal and melted dashboard and upholstery. It's hard to believe, looking at it now, that a few weeks ago one of my favorite things in the world was riding around in this old truck with the windows rolled down, letting my fingers trail through the air, sneaking glances over at Tucker just because I liked looking at him. This is where everything happened, pressed against Bluebell's beat-up, musty seats. This is where I fell in love.

And now it's all burned up.

Tucker's staring at what's left of Bluebell with grief in his stormy blue eyes, one hand resting on the scorched hood like he's saying his final good-byes. I take his other hand. He hasn't said a lot since we got here. We've spent the afternoon wandering through the burned part of the forest, searching for Midas, Tucker's horse. Part of me thought this was a bad idea, coming out here again, looking, but when Tucker asked me to bring him here I said yes. I get it—he loved Midas, not only because he was a champion rodeo horse, but because Tucker had been there the night Midas was born, watched him take his first shaky steps, raised him and trained him and rode him on practically every horse trail in Teton County. He wants to know what happened to him. He wants closure.

I know the feeling.

At one point we came across the carcass of an elk, burned nearly to ash, which for an awful moment I thought was Midas until I saw the antlers, but that was all we found.

"I'm sorry, Tuck," I say now. I know I couldn't have saved Midas, no way I could have flown carrying Tucker and a full-grown horse out of the burning forest that day, but it still feels like my fault, somehow.

His hand tightens in mine. He turns and shows me a hint of dimple.

"Hey, don't be sorry," he says. I loop an arm around his

neck as he pulls me closer. "I'm the one who should be sorry for dragging you out here today. It's depressing. I feel like we should be celebrating or something. You saved my life, after all." He smiles, a real smile this time, full of warmth and love and everything I could ask for. I tug his face down, finding all kinds of solace in the way his lips move over mine, the thump of his heart against my palm, the sheer steadiness and strength of this boy who stole my heart. For a minute I let myself get lost in him.

I failed at my purpose.

I try to push the thought away, but it lingers. Something twists inside me. A sharp gust of wind hits us, and the rain, which was drizzling on us before, starts to come down harder. It's been raining for three solid days, ever since the fires. It's cold, that kind of chilly damp that passes right through my coat. Fog rolls between the blackened trees.

Reminds me of hell, actually.

I pull away from Tucker, shivering.

God, I need therapy, I think.

Right. As if I can picture telling my story to a shrink, stretched out on a sofa talking about how I'm part angel, how all angel-bloods have this purpose we're put on earth to fulfill, how on the day of my purpose I happened to bump into a fallen angel. Who literally took me to hell for about five minutes. Who tried to kill my mother. And how I fought him with a type of magical holy light. Then I had to fly off to save a boy from a forest fire, only I didn't save him. I saved my boyfriend instead, but it turns out that the original boy didn't need saving, anyway, because he's part angel, too.

Yeah, somehow I have the feeling that my first visit to a therapist would end with me in a straitjacket getting comfy in my new padded cell.

"You okay?" Tucker asks quietly.

I haven't told him about hell. Or the Black Wing. Because Mom says that when you know about Black Wings you're more likely to draw their attention, however that works.

I haven't told him about a lot of things.

"I'm fine. I'm just . . ." What? What am I? Hopelessly confused? Completely screwed up? Eternally doomed?

I go with: "Cold."

He hugs me, rubs his hands up and down my arms, trying to warm me. For a second I see that worried, slightly offended look he gets when he knows I'm not telling him the entire truth, but I stretch up and give him another kiss, a soft one, at the corner of his mouth.

"Let's never break up again, okay?" I tell him. "I don't think I could handle it."

His eyes soften. "It's a deal. No more breaking up. Come on," he says, taking my hand and leading me back to where my car is parked at the edge of the burned clearing. He opens my door for me, then runs around to the passenger side and gets in. He grins. "Let's get the heck out of here."

    I love that he says heck.
    I've totally had enough of hell.

It's a different girl this year, sitting in the silver Prius in the parking lot of Jackson Hole High School on her first day of class. First off, this girl's a blonde: long, wavy gold hair with subtle tints of red. She wears her hair in a tight ponytail at the base of her neck, and on top of that she's crammed a gray fedora, which she hopes will come off as cool and vintage and will take some of the attention away from her hair. She looks sun-kissed—not tan exactly, but with a very definite glow. But it's not the hair or the skin that I don't quite recognize as my own when I peer into the rearview mirror. It's the eyes. In those large blue-gray eyes is a brand-new knowledge of good and evil. I look older. Wiser. I hope that's true.

    I get out of the car. Overhead the sky is gray. Still raining. Still cold. I can't help but scan the clouds, search around inside my own consciousness for any hint of sorrow that could mean there's a bad angel lurking, even though Mom said Samjeeza's unlikely to come after us right away. I injured him, and apparently it takes a while for Black Wings to heal, something to do with the way time works in hell. A day is a thousand years, a thousand years a day, something like that. I don't pretend to understand it. I'm just glad we don't have to hightail it out of Jackson and leave my entire life behind. At least for the time being.

No bad-angel vibes, so I look around the parking lot hoping to see Tucker, but he's not here yet. Nothing left to do but head inside. I straighten the fedora one last time and start for the door.

My senior year awaits.

"Clara!" calls a familiar voice before I even make it three steps. "Wait up."

I turn to see Christian Prescott climbing out of his brand-new pickup truck. This one is black, huge, glinting silver at the wheels, the words MAXIMUM DUTY stamped onto the back. The old truck, the silver Avalanche that used to be permanently parked on the edges of my visions, burned up in the forest too. That was not a good day to be a truck.

I wait as he jogs over to me. Just looking at him makes me feel weird, nervous, like I'm losing my balance. The last time I saw him was five nights ago when we were standing on my front porch, both of us drenched with rain and smeared with soot, trying to work up the nerve to go inside. We had so much craziness to figure out, but we never ended up doing it, which, I confess, is not Christian's fault. He did call. A lot, those first couple days. But whenever I saw his name light up on my phone, part of me always froze, the proverbial deer in the headlights, and I wouldn't pick up. By the time I finally did, we didn't seem to know what to say to each other. It all boiled down to: "So, you didn't need me to save you." "Nope. And you didn't need me to save you." And we laughed awkwardly as if this whole purpose thing was some kind of a prank, and then we both fell silent, because really what is there to say? I'm sorry, I blew it, it looks like I messed up your divine purpose? My bad?

"Hi," he says now, sounding out of breath.

"Hi."

"Nice hat," he says, but his eyes go straight to my hair, like every time he sees me with the correct hair color it confirms that I'm the girl from his visions.

"Thanks," I manage. "I'm going for incognito here."

He frowns. "Incognito?"

"You know. The hair."

"Oh." His hand lifts like he's going to touch the obnoxious strand of hair that's already sprung loose from my ponytail, but instead closes into a fist, drops. "Why don't you just dye it again?"

"I've tried." I take a step back, tuck the runaway strand behind my ear. "The color won't take anymore. Don't ask me why."

"Mysterious," he says, and the corner of his mouth quirks up into a tiny smile that would have melted my heart to butter last year. He's hot. He knows he's hot. I'm taken. He knows I'm taken, and yet here he goes smiling and stuff. This irritates me. I try not to think about the dream I keep having this week, the way that Christian seems to be the only thing in the entire dream that keeps me from completely losing my mind. I try not to think about the words *we belong together*, those words that used to come to me over and over in my vision.

I don't want to belong to Christian Prescott.

The smile fades, his eyes going serious again. He looks like he wants to say something.

"So, see you around," I say, maybe a little too brightly, and start off toward the building.

"Clara—" He trots along after me. "Hey, wait. I was thinking that maybe we could sit together at lunch?"

I stop and stare at him.

"Or not," he says with that laugh/exhale thing he does. My heart kicks into high gear. I'm not interested in Christian anymore, but my heart doesn't seem to have gotten that message. Crap. Crap. Crap.

Some things change. Some things don't, I guess.

Everybody notices my hair. Of course. I was hoping that they'd notice in a quiet way, a few whispers, some gossip for a couple days, then it'd blow over. But I'm two minutes into first-period French when the teacher makes me take off the hat, and then it's like a nuclear blast. "So pretty, so pretty," Miss Colbert keeps saying, an eyelash away from coming right up and stroking my head. I stick with the story that Mom and I came up with earlier about Mom finding an amazing colorist in California this summer and paying some astronomical fee for her to transform me from orange nightmare to strawberry fabulous. Saying all that in high school–level French while pretending I don't speak the language perfectly is an especially fun part of the morning. I'm ready to go home before nine a.m. Then I duck into AP Calculus, the bell rings, and it's like the whole fiasco starts all over again. *Your hair, your hair, so pretty.* Then again, in third period art class, like they could all start drawing me and my amazing hair.

And fourth period, AP Government, is worse. Christian is there.

"Hi again," he says as I stand in the doorway gawking at him.

I guess I shouldn't be surprised. There are only around six hundred students at Jackson Hole High School, so the odds are in favor of us having a class together. Tucker's supposed to be in this class too, last time I checked.

Where the—*heck* is Tucker this morning? Come to think of it, I haven't seen Wendy either.

"You going to come in?" Christian asks.

I slide into the seat next to him and rummage around in my bag for my notebook and a pen. I take a deep breath and let it out slowly, roll my head from one side to the other to try to release some of the tension in my neck.

"Long day already?" he asks.

"You have no idea."

Right then, Tucker breezes in.

"I've been looking for you all day," I say as he claims the desk on the other side of me. "Did you just get to school?"

"Yeah. Car trouble," he says. "We have this old crap car that we use around the ranch, and it wouldn't start this morning. If you thought my truck was junk, you should see this thing."

"I never thought Bluebell was junk," I tell him.

He clears his throat, smiles. "How about that? We're in a class together, you and I, and I didn't even have to bribe anybody this year."

I laugh. "You bribed somebody last year?"

"Not officially," Tucker admits. "I asked Mrs. Lowell, the lady in the office in charge of scheduling, real nice if she could get me into Brit. History. At the last minute, too, I mean like ten minutes before class started. I'm friends with her daughter, which helped."

"But why . . . ?"

He laughs. "You're cute when you're slow."

"Because of me? No way. You hated me. I was that yuppie California chick who insulted your truck."

He grins. I shake my head in bewilderment.

"You're crazy, you know that."

"Aw, and here I thought I was being sweet and romantic and stuff."

"Right. So, you're friends with Mrs. Lowell's daughter?

What's her name?" I ask with mock jealousy.

"Allison. She's a nice girl. She was one of the girls I took to prom last year."

"Pretty?"

"Well, she's got red hair. I kind of have a thing for red hair," he says. I punch him lightly on the arm. "Hey. I kind of have a thing for tough girls, too."

I laugh again. That's when I feel the surge of frustration, so strong it wipes the smile right off my face.

Christian.

This kind of thing's been happening lately. Sometimes, usually when I least expect it, it's as if I'm allowed access into other people's heads. Like now, for instance, I can perceive Christian's presence on the other side of me so keenly that it's like he's boring holes into me with his eyes. I don't get what he's thinking in words so much as what he feels—he notices how natural it is for me to fall into this easy conversation with Tucker. He wishes that I would joke around with him that way, that we could finally speak to each other, finally connect. He wants to make me laugh like that.

Knowing this, by the way, totally sucks. Mom calls it empathy, says that it's a rare gift among angel-bloods. Rare gift, ha. I wonder if there's a return policy.

Tucker looks over my shoulder and seems to notice Christian for the first time.

"How you doing, Chris? Have a nice summer?" he asks.

"Yeah, fantastic," answers Christian, and his mind suddenly retreats from mine into a wave of forced indifference. "How about you?"

They stare at each other, one of those high-testosterone stares. "Amazing," Tucker says. There's a challenge in his voice. "Best summer of my life."

I wonder if it's too late to get out of this class.

"Well, that's the thing about summers, isn't it?" says Christian after a minute. "They have to end sometime."

It's a relief when class is over. But then I have to stand at the doorway of the cafeteria and decide what to do about lunch.

Option A: My usual. Invisibles table. Wendy. Chitchat. Maybe some awkward talk about how I'm dating her twin brother now, and maybe her asking about what exactly happened out there in the woods the day of the fire, which I don't know how to answer. Still, she's one of my best friends, and I don't want to keep avoiding her.

Option B: Angela. Angela likes to eat alone, and people usually give her a lot of space. Maybe, if I sat with her, they would give me a lot of space. But then I'd have to answer Angela's questions and listen to her theories, which she's pretty much been bombarding me with for the past few days.

Option C (not really an option): Christian. Standing casually in the corner, deliberately not looking at me. Not expecting anything, not pressuring me, but there. Wanting me to know he's there. Hopeful.

No way I'm going in that direction.

Then the decision kind of gets made for me. Angela looks up. She tilts her head to indicate the empty seat next to her. When I don't hop to it, she mouths, "Get over here."

Bossy.

I go over to her corner and sink into a seat. She's reading a small, dusty book. She closes it and slides it across the table to me.

"Check this out," she says.

I read the title. "*The Book of Enoch*?"

"Yep. A really, really, ridiculously old copy, so watch the pages. They're delicate. We're going to need to talk about this ASAP. But first—" She looks up, then calls loudly, "Hey, Christian."

Oh. My. God. What is she doing?

"Angela, wait a second, don't—"

She waves him over. This could be bad.

"What's up?" he says, cool and composed as ever.

"You're going out to lunch, right?" Angela asks. "You always go out."

His eyes flicker over to mine. "I was considering it."

"Right, well, I don't want to mess up your plans or anything, but I think you and me and Clara should have a meeting after school. At my mom's theater, the Pink Garter, in town."

Christian looks confused. "Um, sure. Why?"

"Let's just call it a new club I'm starting," says Angela. "The Angel Club."

He glances at me again, and yep, there's betrayal in his green eyes, because obviously I've gone and blabbed his biggest secret to Angela. I want to explain to him that Angela is like a bloodhound when it comes to secrets, virtually impossible to get anything by her, but it doesn't matter. She knows. He knows she knows. Damage is done. I glare at Angela.

"She's one too," I say simply, mostly because I know Angela wanted to spring it on him herself, and it makes me feel better to ruin her plans. "And she's crazy, obviously."

Christian nods, like this revelation comes as no surprise.

"But you're going to be there, at the Pink Garter," he says to me.

"I guess so."

"Okay. I'm in," he tells Angela, but he's still looking at me. "We need to talk, anyway."

Awesome.

"Awesome," says Angela cheerfully. "See you after school."

"See you," he says, then wanders out of the cafeteria.

I turn to Angela. "I hate you."

"I know. But you need me, too. Otherwise nothing would ever get done."

"I still hate you," I say, even though she's right. Kind of.

This whole Angel Club thing actually sounds like a great idea, if it can help me figure out what it means that Christian and I didn't fulfill our purpose, since my mom still isn't exactly forthcoming on the subject. Angela's stellar with research. If anyone could uncover the consequences for angel-blood purpose-failure, it's her.

"Oh, you know you love me," she says. She pushes the book at me again. "Now take this and go eat lunch with your boyfriend."

"What?"

"Over there. He's clearly pining for you." She gestures behind us, where, sure enough, over at the Invisibles table, Tucker is chatting with Wendy. They're both staring at me with identical expectant expressions.

"Shoo. You're dismissed," says Angela.

"Shut up." I take the book and tuck it into my backpack, then head to the Invisibles table. Ava, Lindsey, and Emma, my other fellow Invisibles, all smile up at me and say hello, along with Wendy's boyfriend, Jason Lovett, who I guess is eating with us this year instead of his usual computer-games pals.

It's weird, us having boyfriends.

"What was that all about?" asks Wendy, peering over at Angela with curious eyes.

"Oh, just Angela being Angela. So, what's on the Jackson High menu for today?"

"Sloppy Joes."

"Yummy," I say without enthusiasm.

Wendy rolls her eyes and says to Tucker, "Clara never likes the food here. I swear, she eats like a bird."

"Huh," he says, eyes twinkling, because that's not his experience with me at all. Around him I've always eaten like a horse. I slide into the seat next to his, and he scoots his chair closer to mine and puts his arm around me. Perfectly G-rated, but I can almost feel the topic of discussion shift in the cafeteria. I guess I'm going to be that girl who holds her boyfriend's hand as they stroll down the halls, who steals kisses between classes, who makes the moony eyes across the crowded cafeteria. I never thought I'd be that girl.

Wendy snorts, and we both turn to look at her. Her eyes dart from me to Tucker and back again. She knows about us, of course, but she's never seen us together like this before.

"You guys are kind of disgusting," she says. But then she scoots her chair closer to Jason's and slips her hand in his.

Tucker smiles in a mischievous way I know too well. I don't have time to protest before he leans over for a kiss. I push at him, embarrassed, then melt and forget where I am for a minute. Finally he lets go. I try to catch my breath.

I am *so* that girl. But being that girl has its perks.

"Ew, get a room," Wendy says, stifling a smile. It's hard to read her, but I think she's trying to be cool with this whole best-friend-dating-my-brother thing by acting completely nauseated. Which I think means that she approves.

I notice that the cafeteria has gone momentarily silent. Then suddenly everything starts up again in a flurry of conversation.

"You do know we're now officially the talk of the town," I say to Tucker. He might as well have taken a marker to my forehead and written PROPERTY OF TUCKER in big black letters.

His eyebrows lift. "Do you mind?"

I reach for his hand and lace his fingers with mine.

"Nope."

I'm with Tucker. In spite of my failed purpose and everything, it looks like I'm actually going to get to keep him. I'm the luckiest girl in the world.

2

FIRST RULE OF ANGEL CLUB

Mr. Phibbs, my teacher for AP English, which happens to be—thank God!—my last class of the day, immediately gets us started on our first "College English" assignment, a personal essay on where we see ourselves in ten years.

I take out a notebook, click my pen to the write position. And stare at the blank page. And stare. And stare.

Where do I see myself in ten years?

"Try to visualize yourself," Mr. Phibbs says, like he's spotted me back here in the corner and knows that I'm floundering. I always liked Mr. Phibbs; he's kind of our own personal Gandalf or Dumbledore or somebody cool like that, complete with round, wire glasses and long white ponytail sticking out of the back of his collar. But right now he's killing me.

Visualize myself, he says. I close my eyes. Slowly, a picture starts to materialize in my mind. A forest beneath an orange sky. A ridge. Christian, waiting.

I open my eyes. Suddenly I'm furious.

No, I think at no one in particular. That is not my future. That's past. My future is with Tucker.

It's not hard to imagine it. I close my eyes again, and with a bit of effort I can see the outline of the big red barn at the Lazy Dog, the sky overhead empty and blue. There's a man walking a horse in a pasture. It looks like Midas, a beautiful glossy chestnut. And there's—this is the part where the breath suddenly hitches in my throat—a small boy riding the horse, a tiny dark-haired boy giggling as Tucker—the man is definitely Tucker; I'd know that butt anywhere—leads him around the pasture. The boy sees me, waves. I wave back. Tucker walks the horse over to the fence.

"Look at me, look at me," says the boy.

"I see you! Hi there, handsome," I say to Tucker. He leans over the fence to kiss me, taking my face between his hands, and that's when I see the glint of the plain gold band on his finger.

We're married.

It's the best daydream of all time. I know somewhere deep down that it's only a daydream, the combination of my active imagination and wishful thinking. Not a vision. Not the future that's been set for me. But it's the one I want.

I open my eyes, tighten my fingers around my pen, and write: "In ten years, I will be married. I will have a child. I will be happy."

I click the pen closed and stare at the words. They surprise me. I've never been one of those girls, either, who dreamed of getting married, never forced a boy to say vows with me on the playground or dressed up in bedsheets and pretended to walk down the aisle. When I was a kid I fashioned swords out of tree branches, and Jeffrey and I chased each other around the backyard yelling, "Surrender or die!" Not that I was a tomboy. I liked the color purple and nail polish and sleepovers and writing my crush's name in the margins of my notebooks at school as much as any other girl. But I never honestly considered being married. Being Mrs. Somebody. I guess I assumed that I'd get married eventually. It just seemed like it was too far away to worry about.

But maybe I am one of those girls.

I look at the page again. I've got three sentences. Wendy is obviously writing an entire book on how awesome her life is going to turn out, and I've got three sentences. I have a feeling they're not the kind of sentences that Mr. Phibbs is going to appreciate.

"Okay, five more minutes," says Mr. Phibbs. "Then we'll share."

Panic sets in. I'm going to have to make something up. What should I want to be? Angela's going to be a poet, Wendy's a vet, Kay Patterson over there is head of a sorority house and marries a senator, Shawn is an Olympic-gold snowboarder, Jason's one of those computer programmers who makes a gazillion dollars coming up with some new way to Google, and I'm—I'm—I'm a cruise ship director. I'm a famous ballerina for the New York City Ballet. I'm a heart surgeon.

I go with heart surgeon. My pen flies across the page.

"Time's up," says Mr. Phibbs. "Finish your sentence and then we'll share."

I read back over what I've written. It's good stuff. Completely bogus, but something. "There's nothing more inspiring than the complexity and beauty of the human heart," I write as my last sentence, and I can nearly make myself believe it. The daydream about Tucker has almost faded from my mind.

"Heart surgeon, huh?" says Angela as we walk together up the boardwalk on Broadway in Jackson.

I shrug. "You went with lawyer. You really think you're going to be a lawyer?"

"I'd make an excellent lawyer."

We step under the archway that says PINK GARTER, and Angela fishes out her keys to unlock the door. As usual for this time of day, the theater looks completely deserted.

"Come on." She puts her hand on my shoulder and pushes me through the empty lobby.

For a minute we stand there in the dark. Then Angela slips away, disappearing into the black, and a moment later a halo of light appears on the stage, which is still decked out with the set of *Oklahoma!*, a fake farmhouse and corn. I wander reluctantly down the aisle, past the rows of red velvet seats and up to the line of clean white tables in front of the orchestra pit, where all last year Angela and I sat with Angela's notebooks and stacks of dusty old books and talked angels, angels, angels until sometimes I thought my brain would melt.

Angela practically skips up to the front of the theater. She climbs the stairs at the edge of the stage and stands looking out, so she can get a clear view of anybody coming in. Under the lights her long black hair glows a shade of deep blue that isn't entirely natural. She sweeps her bangs behind her ear and looks down at me with this super-pleased-with-herself expression. I swallow.

"So what's this all about?" I ask, trying to sound like I don't care. "I'm dying to know."

"Patience is a virtue," she quips.

"I'm not that virtuous."

She smiles mysteriously. "You think I haven't guessed that already?"

A figure appears in the back of the theater, and I get that

panicky tightness in my chest. Then the figure comes into the light, and my breath catches for a different reason.

It isn't Christian. It's my brother.

I glance up at Angela. She shrugs. "He deserves to know everything we know, right?"

I turn back and look at Jeffrey. He shifts uncomfortably from one foot to the other.

Jeffrey's been hard to figure out lately. Something is definitely up with him. First, there was the night of the fire, when he came tearing out of the trees like the devil was chasing him, his wings the color of lead. I don't know if that means anything, the state of his spiritual well-being or whatnot, since my wings at that time were pretty dark too, on account of the soot. He said he was out there looking for me, which I don't buy. But one thing's for sure, he was out there. In the forest. During the fire. Then the next day he was glued to the television, watching every minute of the news. Like he was expecting something. And later we had this conversation:

Me (after spilling the beans about finding Christian in the forest and him being an angel-blood): "So it was kind of a good thing that I saved Tucker instead."

Jeffrey: "Well, what were you supposed to do, if your purpose wasn't about saving Christian?"

The million-dollar question.

Me (miserably): "I don't know."

Then Jeffrey did the oddest thing. He laughed, a bitter laugh, false, which instantly rubbed me the wrong way. I'd just confessed that I'd messed up the most important thing I was ever supposed to do in my life, my reason for being on this earth, and he laughed at me.

"What?" I barked at him. "What's so funny?"

"Man," he said. "This is like a freaking Greek tragedy." He shook his head in disbelief. "You saved Tucker instead."

I may have called him a jerk-face or something. But he kept laughing, until I seriously wanted to smack him, and then Mom caught wind of the impending violence in that uncanny way she has and said, "Enough, both of you," and I'd stalked off to my room.

Just thinking about it now makes me want to slug him.

"So what do you think?" Angela asks. "Can he join us?"

Tough call. But mad or not, I'm pretty curious to find out what exactly he knows. Since we don't seem to be communicating well these days, this might be the best way. I turn to Angela with a shrug. "Sure. Why not?"

"We have to make this quick," Jeffrey says, slinging his backpack down onto one of the chairs. "I've got practice."

"No problem." Angela suppresses another smile. "We're just waiting for—"

"I'm here."

And there is Christian, striding down the aisle with his hands in his pockets. His eyes roam over the theater like he's considering making an offer on the place, inspecting the stage, the seats, the tables, the lights and riggings in the rafters. Then his gaze lands on me.

"So let's do this," he says. "Whatever it is."

Angela doesn't waste any time. "Come join me up here."

Slowly we all make our way onto the stage and stand in a circle with Angela.

"Welcome to Angel Club," she says melodramatically.

Christian does his laugh/exhale thing. "First rule of Angel Club, you do not talk about Angel Club."

"Second rule of Angel Club," chimes in Jeffrey. "Do not talk about Angel Club."

Oh boy. Here we go.

"Hilarious. You're bonding already." Angela is not amused. "Seriously, though. I do think we should have rules."

"Why?" Jeffrey wants to know. Always with the attitude, my sweet little brother. "Why do we need rules for a club?"

"Maybe if we knew what the point of the club was," adds Christian.

Angela's eyes flare in a way I'm familiar with—this is not going according to her carefully constructed plan. "The point," she says in a clipped tone, "is to find out all we can about this angel-blood stuff, so we don't like, you know, end up dead." Again with the melodrama. She claps her hands together. "Okay, let's make sure we're all on the same page. Last week our girl Clara here stumbled upon a Black Wing in the mountains."

"Crashed is more like it," I mutter.

Angela nods. "Right. Crashed. Because this guy puts out a kind of toxic sorrow, which, because of all Clara's touchy-feely skills, took away the lightness she needed to fly, so she fell, dropped out of the sky, right where he wanted her."

Jeffrey and Christian are looking at me.

"You fell?" asks Jeffrey. I must have left out this part of the story when I told it at home.

"Touchy-feely skills?" asks Christian.

"I have a theory that Black Wings are incapable of flight, by the way," Angela continues. Clearly this is not the question-and-answer part of this event. "Their sorrow weighs them down too much to get airborne. It's only a theory at this point, but I'm kind of liking it. It means, if you ever came across a Black Wing, you might be able to escape by flying off, because he couldn't chase you."

What she needs, I think, is a chalkboard. Then she could really go to town.

"So Clara was incapacitated simply by being in the presence of a Black Wing," she says. "We should learn if there's anything we can do about that, some way to block the sorrow out."

I'm definitely on board with that idea.

"And since Clara and her mom defeated the Black Wing using glory, I think that's our key."

"My uncle says glory takes years to be able to control,"

Christian says then.

Angela shrugs. "Clara did it, and she's only a Quartarius. What level are you?"

"Only a Quartarius," he replies with a hint of sarcasm.

Angela gets this glint in her eye. She's the only Dimidius in our group, then. She has the highest concentration of angel blood. I guess that makes her our natural leader.

"Okay, so where was I?" she says. She ticks it off on her fingers. "Objective one, find a way to block the sorrow. That's mostly a job for Clara since she seems to be extra sensitive to it. I was with her when we saw the Black Wing at the mall last year, and I didn't get anything from him but a mild case of the creeps."

"Hold up," interrupts Jeffrey. "You two saw a Black Wing at the mall last year? When?"

"We were shopping for prom dresses." Angela heaves a meaningful look at Christian, as if the whole incident was his fault somehow because he was my date.

"And why did I not hear about this?" Jeffrey asks, turning to me.

"Your mom said it would put you in danger, knowing about them. According to her, when you're aware of Black Wings, they become more aware of you," Angela answers for me.

He looks skeptical.

"So she must think you're all grown-up, since she told you

about them now, right?" Angela offers helpfully.

I think about the stony look on Mom's face the morning after the fire, when she told Jeffrey about Samjeeza. "That, or she thought it might be necessary for Jeffrey to have a clue about Black Wings in case one of them shows up at the house wanting revenge," I add.

"Which brings us to objective two," Angela segues smoothly. She glances at me. "Did you finish the book I gave you?"

"Ange, you just gave it to me at lunch."

She sighs and gives me a look that conveys what an amateur she thinks I am. "Can you get it, please?"

I hop down to fetch the book out of my backpack. Angela decides that maybe a table would be more comfortable to get down and dirty with the research, which she evidently means to jump right into. We reconvene around a table, and Angela takes *The Book of Enoch* from me.

She flips through the pages. "Listen to this." She clears her throat. *"It happened after the sons of men had multiplied in those days, that daughters were born to them, elegant and beautiful. And when the Watchers, the sons of heaven, beheld them, they became enamored of them, saying to each other, 'Come, let us select for ourselves wives from the progeny of men, and let us beget children.'"*

"Okay. Enter angel-bloods," I comment.

"Just wait for it. I'm getting to the good part. . . . *Then their leader, Samyaza, said to them, 'I fear that you perhaps may be indisposed to the performance of this enterprise; and that I alone shall suffer for so grievous a crime.'* Does that name sound familiar?"

A shiver zings its way down my spine.

"That's him, then, Samjeeza? The angel who attacked Mom and Clara?" Jeffrey asks.

Angela sits back. "I think so. It goes on to talk about how they married the human women and taught mankind how to make weapons and mirrors, and showed them sorcery and all kinds of taboo stuff. They had tons of kids, which the book describes as evil giants—the Nephilim—who were abominations in the sight of God, until there were so many of them and the earth became so evil that God sent the flood to wipe them all out."

"So we're evil giants," repeats Jeffrey. "Dude, we're not that tall."

"People back then were shorter," Angela says. "Poor nutrition."

"But that doesn't make sense," I say. "How could we be abominations? How is it our fault if we're born with angel blood in our veins? I thought the Bible describes the Nephilim as heroes."

"It does," Angela answers. "*The Book of Enoch* isn't in the Bible. I have a theory that it might be some kind of anti-angel-blood propaganda. But it's interesting, right? Worth looking into. Because this Samjeeza fellow is right in the middle of it. He's the leader of this group of Black Wings called the

Watchers, which, according to some other research I've been doing, is a band of fallen angels whose basic job is to seduce human women and produce as many angel-bloods as possible."

Fabulous.

"Okay, so objective two is finding out more about Samjeeza," I say. "Roger that. Are there any more objectives?"

"One," Angela says lightly. "I thought one objective of Angel Club should be to help each other figure out our purposes. I mean, you two have had yours, but didn't fulfill them. So what does that mean?" she says, glancing at Christian and me. "And Jeffrey and I still have ours coming. Maybe if we all put our heads together, we can understand this whole purpose concept better."

"Great. Hey, look, I've got to go," Jeffrey says abruptly. "Practice started ten minutes ago. Coach is going to have me running laps until I drop."

"Wait, we haven't got to the rules part yet," Angela calls after him as he books it for the door.

"Clara can fill me in later," he calls back over his shoulder. "Or you could make, like, stone tablets or something. Angel Club ten commandments." Then he's gone.

So much for finding out exactly what he knows.

Angela looks at me. "He's funny."

"Yeah, he's a barrel of laughs."

"So. The rules."

I sigh. "Lay them on us."

"Well, first, and this one's a no-brainer, no one tells anybody about this. We're the only ones who know about Angel Club, okay?"

"Do not talk about Angel Club," says Christian with a smirk.

"I mean it. Don't tell your uncle." Angela turns to me. "Don't tell your mom. Don't tell your boyfriend. Got it? Second rule: Angel Club is a secret from everybody else, but we don't keep secrets from each other. This is a no-secrets zone. We tell each other everything."

"Okay . . . ," I agree. "What are the other rules?"

"That's it," she says.

"Oh. One per stone tablet," I joke.

"Ha. Ha." She turns back to Christian. "What about you? You've been awfully quiet this whole time. You've got to swear too."

"No, thank you," he says politely.

She leans back in her chair in surprise. "No, thank you?"

"To the rules. I won't go blabbing about this thing to my buddies on the ski team. But I tell my uncle everything, and I'm going to tell him about this." His eyes seek mine, pin me. "It's stupid not to communicate what you know to the adults. They're only trying to protect us. And as far as the no-secrets zone, I can't agree to that. I don't even really know you guys, so why would I tell you my secrets? No way."

Angela's speechless. I find this kind of funny.

"You're right," I say. "We ditch the rules. There are no rules."

"I think it's great, though," he says as a way of soothing Angela. "Meeting and finding out what we can do, trying to figure things out. Count me in. I'll be here, whenever, until it snows and then I have ski team, but maybe then we can move this to Sunday afternoons, which would work for me."

Angela recovers. She even whips up a smile. "Sure, that's doable. Probably better for Jeffrey's schedule, too. Sundays. Let's do Sundays."

There's a moment of uncomfortable silence.

"Okay then," Angela says finally. "I think this meeting is adjourned."

It's almost dark when I leave the theater. Storm clouds are brewing overhead, churning like a grumbling stomach. I guess I should be grateful for the rain, since the storm put out the fires, which in the end probably saved people's lives and homes. It's only weather, I remind myself, but sometimes I wonder if this particular weather's been sent to bother me personally, a punishment, maybe, for not doing my job, for failing at my purpose, or some other sort of ominous sign.

I try for a quick, casual good-bye to Christian at the corner, but he puts his hand on my arm.

"I still want to talk to you," he says in a low voice.

"I have to go," I manage. "My mom will be wondering where I am. Call me, okay? Or I'll call you. One of us should definitely call the other."

"Right." His hand drops away. "I'll call you."

"I gotta run. I'm late."

And then I'm off in the opposite direction.

Coward, says the nagging voice inside my head. *You should talk to him. Find out what he has to say.*

What if he says we belong together?

Well, then you'll have to deal with that. But at least you won't be running away.

I think it's more of a brisk walk.

Whatever.

I'm having an argument with myself. And I'm losing.

So not a good sign.

3

OTHER PEOPLE'S SECRETS

Mom comes out of her office the moment she hears me step through the front door.

"Hey," she says. "How was school?"

"Everybody talked about my hair, but it was fine."

"We could try to dye it again," she suggests.

I shrug. "It must mean something, right? God wants me to be blond this year."

"Right," she says. "You want a cookie, blondie?"

"Do birds fly?" I scamper after her into the kitchen, where, sure enough, I smell something wonderful baking in the oven. "Chocolate chip?"

"Of course." The buzzer goes off, and she puts on an

oven mitt, takes the sheet of cookies out of the oven, and sets it on the counter. I pull up a stool on the other side of her and sit. It feels so normal it's weird, after what's happened, all the drama and fight-for-your-life stuff and serious soul-searching, and now . . . cookies.

The night of the fire I came home assuming we'd have this big tell-all, and everything would be out in the open now that the stuff from my vision had happened. But when I got home, Mom was asleep, *asleep* on the most important night of my life, and I didn't wake her, didn't blame her because we were both, at the time, so literally fried, and she'd been attacked, almost died and all. But still. It wasn't exactly how I thought my purpose would go.

It's not like we haven't talked. We have, although mostly it was a debriefing of what's already happened. No new information. No revelations. No explanations. At one point I asked, "So what happens now?" and she said, "I don't know, honey," and that was it. I would have pressed her about it, but she kept getting this look on her face, this bleak expression, her eyes so full of pain and sadness, like she's so incredibly disappointed in me and how my purpose turned out. Of course she would never come right out and say that, never tell me that I've screwed up everything, that she thought I would be better than that, that she thought I'd make the right choices when my time came, that I'd prove myself worthy to be called an angel-blood. But the look says it all.

"So," she says as we wait for the cookies to cool. "I thought you'd be home a while ago. Did you go to see Tucker?"

And already I need to make a big decision: to tell her about Angel Club, or not tell her.

Okay. So I think about how the first thing out of Angela's mouth when it came to rules was not to tell anybody, especially the adults, and then I think about the way Christian refused, just like that, said that he tells his uncle everything.

Mom and I used to have that. Used to. Now I have no desire to share this stuff with her, not about Angel Club, not about the weird recurring dream I've been having, not about how I feel about what happened the day of the fire or what my true purpose might have been. I don't want to get into it right now.

So I don't.

"I was at the Pink Garter," I say. "With Angela."

Not technically a lie.

I brace myself for her to tell me that Angela, while full of good intentions, is going to get us all in deep trouble someday. She knows that any time spent with Angela is time spent talking about angel-bloods and Angela's many theories.

Instead she says, "Oh, that's nice," and uses a spatula to slide the cookies onto a wire rack on the counter. I steal one.

"That's nice?" I repeat incredulously.

"Get a plate, please," she tells me, and I do. Then, as I'm sitting there with a mouthful of chocolatey goodness, she says, "It was never my intention to shelter you from other angel-bloods forever. I only wanted you to live normal lives for as long as possible, to know what it's like to be human. But now you're old enough, you've been through your visions, you've had a glimpse of the evil in this world, and I don't think it's a bad thing to start learning what it truly means to be an angel-blood. Which means hanging out with others like you."

I wonder if she still means Angela, or if now she's talking about Christian. If she assumes being with him is my purpose. Not very women's lib of her, I think, if she believes my entire purpose on this earth is to hook up with some guy.

"Milk?" she asks, then goes to the fridge and pours me a glass.

And this is the point where I finally get the guts to ask her. "Mom, am I going to be punished?"

"Why?" She reaches for a cookie. "Did you do something today I should know about?"

I shake my head. "No. My purpose. Am I going to be punished because I didn't, you know, fulfill it? Am I going to hell or something?"

She halfway chokes on the cookie, then takes a quick sip of my milk.

"That's not really how it works," she says.

"How does it work, then? Will I get a second chance? Is there anything else that I'm going to be expected to do?"

She's quiet for a minute. I can practically see the wheels turning in her head, deciding how much she's going to tell me. This aggravates the crap out of me, of course, but there's not a lot I can do about it. So I wait.

"Every angel-blood is given a purpose," she says after what feels like an eternity. "For some that purpose manifests itself in a single event, a singular moment in time where we are led to be at a specific place at a specific time, to do a specific thing. For others . . ." She glances down at her hands, choosing her words carefully. "Their purpose can involve more."

"More?" I ask.

"More than a single event."

I stare at her. This has got to be the strangest conversation any mother and daughter has ever had over milk and cookies. "How much more?"

She shrugs. "I don't know. We're all different. Our purposes are all different."

"Which was it for you?"

"For me . . ." She clears her throat delicately. "It was more than one event," she admits.

Not good enough.

"Mom, come on," I demand. "Don't leave me in the dark."

Inexplicably, she smiles this tiny smile, like she finds me funny. "It's going to be okay, Clara," she says. "You'll figure it out when you're supposed to figure it out. I know that's frustrating to hear. Believe me, I know."

I swallow the rising craziness that's churning in my stomach. "How? How do you know?"

She sighs. "Because my purpose lasted more than one hundred years."

My mouth drops open.

One hundred years.

"So . . . so you're saying that it might not be over?"

"I'm saying that your purpose is more complicated than simply completing a task."

I jump to my feet. I can't keep sitting down for this. "You couldn't have told me this, oh, I don't know—*before* the fire?"

"I can't give you the answers, Clara, even if I know them," she says. "If I did it might change the outcome. You just have to trust me when I say that you'll get the answers when you need them."

And there's the look again, the sadness. Like I'm disappointing her right this minute. But I also see something else in her luminous blue eyes: faith. She still has faith. That there's some kind of plan for our lives, some kind of meaning, or direction, behind all of this. I sigh. I've never had her kind of faith, and I'm afraid I never will. But I find that even though I obviously have some issues with her, I do trust her. With my life. Not only because she's my mother, but because when it really counted, she saved it.

"Okay," I say. "Fine. But I don't have to like it."

She nods, smiles again, but the sadness doesn't quite leave

her face. "I don't expect you to like it. You wouldn't be my daughter if you did."

I should tell her, I think, about the dream. See if she thinks it's important, if it's more than a dream. If it's a vision. Of my possibly continuing purpose.

But right then Jeffrey comes through the door, and of course he hollers, "What's for dinner?" since food is always the first thing on his mind. Mom calls back to him, starts bustling around preparing a meal for us, and I'm amazed at her ability to switch off like that, to make it feel like we're any other kids coming home from our first day of school, no heavenly purposes set for us, no fallen angels hunting us, no bad dreams, and Mom is just like any other mother.

After dinner I fly over to the Lazy Dog to see Tucker.

He's surprised when I tap on his window.

"Hi there, handsome," I tell him. "Can I come in?"

"Absolutely," he says, and kisses me, then quickly rolls across the bed to close the door. I crawl through the window and stand, looking around. I love his room. It's warm and cozy, neat but not too neat, a plaid bedspread pulled haphazardly up over his sheets, piles of schoolbooks, comics, and rodeo magazines strewn about his desk, a pair of gym socks and a balled-up hoodie in the corner of the slightly dusty oak floor, his collection of cowboy hats set in a line across the top of his dresser along with some old green army men and a couple fishing lures. There's a rusty horseshoe nailed over his closet door. It's so *boy*.

He turns to look at me, scratches at the back of his neck.

"This isn't going to become one of those creepy situations where you show up at all hours of the night to watch me sleep, is it?" he asks playfully.

"Every moment I'm away from you, I die a little," I say in return.

"So that's a yes, then."

"Are you complaining?" I ask, quirking an eyebrow at him.

He grins. "Nope. Definitely not complaining. I just wanted to know so I can start wearing more than my boxers to bed."

That gets a blush out of me. "Well, don't—uh, change anything on my account," I stammer, and he laughs and crosses the room to kiss me again.

We spend a very nice few minutes hanging out on his bed. Nothing heavy, since Tucker still has this notion that since I have angel blood in my veins he should try to keep my honor intact. For a long time we simply lie there, catching our breath. I lay my head on his chest, feeling his heart thumping beneath my ear, and I think for the thousandth time that he is without question the best guy on the planet.

Tucker takes one of my hands and curls and uncurls my fingers around his. I love the texture of his hands, the calluses along his palms, evidence of all the hard work he's done in his life, the type of person he is. Such rough hands, but he's always so gentle with them.

"So," he says out of the blue, "are you ever going to tell me what happened the night of the fire?"

Moment over.

I guess I knew this question was coming. I was maybe hoping he wouldn't ask it. It puts me in this terrible position, knowing other people's secrets, especially when those secrets are all tangled up with mine.

"I—" I sit up, pull away from him. I seriously don't know what to say. The words catch in my throat. This must be what it's like for Mom, I think, keeping things hidden from the people she loves.

"Hey, it's okay," he says, sitting up next to me. "I get it. It's top-secret angel stuff. You can't tell."

I shake my head. I decide that I am not my mother.

"Angela's forming a club, for angel-bloods," I say as a start, even though I know this isn't what he asked me.

This is so not what Tucker thought I was going to say. "Angela Zerbino's an angel-blood."

"Yes."

He snorts. "Well, I guess that makes sense. There's always been something off about that girl."

"Hey. I'm an angel-blood. Are you saying there's something off about me, too?"

"Yep," he answers. "But I like it."

"Oh, okay, then." I lean in to kiss him. Then I pull away.

"Christian is an angel-blood too," I say, trying to be brave and look him in the face and say it. "I didn't know until the night of the fire, but he is. A Quartarius. Like me."

Tucker's eyes widen. "Oh," he says in this emotionless voice, and looks away. "Like you."

For a long time neither of us speaks. Then he says, "Big coincidence, huh, all these angel-bloods popping up in Jackson?"

"It was a pretty big surprise, that's for sure," I admit. "I don't know about coincidence."

He swallows, and there's this little click in his throat. I can see how hard he's trying to play it cool, pretend that the angel stuff doesn't scare him or make him feel like he's standing in the way of something more important than him. He'd still step aside, I realize, if he thought he was distracting me from my purpose. He's already putting on the breakup face. Like he did before.

"I don't know what was supposed to happen that night," I say quickly. "But the fire's over. I'm moving on with my life." I hope he doesn't detect the touch of desperation in my voice, how much I want to make the words true just by saying them. I don't want to think about the possibility that my purpose could last another hundred years. "So I'm all yours now," I say, and the words ring false, so terribly false, in my ears. And here I started out determined to tell him the truth.

Only I don't know the truth. Or maybe I don't want to know.

"All right," he says then, although I can tell he's not sure if he believes me. "Good. Because I want you all to myself."

"You've got me," I whisper.

He kisses me again. And I kiss him back.

But the image of Christian Prescott, standing with his back to me at Fox Creek Road, waiting for me, always waiting, suddenly flashes through my mind.

When I get home Jeffrey's out in the yard, chopping wood in the rain. He sees me and nods his head, lifts his arm and wipes sweat from above his top lip with his sleeve. Then he grabs a log, lifts the ax again, and splits it easily. He splits another. And another. The pile of chopped wood at his feet is already pretty big, and he doesn't look like he's stopping anytime soon.

"You deciding to stock up for the whole winter? Can't wait for the snow?" I ask. "You do know it's only September."

"Mom's cold," he says. "She's in there in her flannel pj's, wrapped up in blankets drinking tea, and she's shivering. I thought I'd build her a fire."

"Oh," I say. "That's nice of you."

"Something happened to her that day. With the Black Wing," he says, trying out the words. He looks up, meets my eyes. Sometimes he looks so young, like a vulnerable little boy. Other times, like now, he looks like a man. A man who's seen so much sadness in this life. How is that possible? I wonder. He's fifteen.

"Yeah," I say, because I've concluded the same thing. "I mean, he tried to kill her. It was a pretty rough fight."

"Is she going to be okay?"

"I think so." The glory healed her. I watched it wash over her like warm water, taking away the burns, the bruises from Samjeeza's hands. But thinking about it brings back the image of her dangling from his arm, flailing, gasping for breath as his hand tightened around her throat, her kicks growing weaker and weaker until she went still. Until I thought she was dead. My eyes burn at the memory and I quickly turn away to look at the house so Jeffrey won't see my tears.

Jeffrey chops some more wood, and I pull myself together. It's been a long day. I want to crawl into bed, pull the covers up over my head, and sleep it all away.

"Hey, where were you that day?" I ask suddenly.

He goes with playing dumb. "When?"

"The day of the fire."

He grabs another block of wood and places it on the stand. "I told you. I was in the woods, looking for you. I thought maybe I could help."

"Why don't I believe that?"

He falters and the ax strikes the log unevenly and sticks. He makes a noise like a growl and jerks it out.

"Why wouldn't you believe me?" he asks.

"Um, maybe because I know you, and you're acting all weird. So where were you? Cut the crap."

"Maybe you don't know me as well as you think." He throws the ax in the dirt, then gathers an armload of the chopped wood and pushes past me toward the house.

"Jeffrey . . ."

"It was nothing," he says. "I got lost." Suddenly he looks like he's the one about to cry. He goes into the house, and I can hear him offering to make a fire for Mom. I stand in the yard until the first curls of smoke drift out of the top of our chimney. I remember his face when he flew out of the trees that night, tight with fear and something like pain. I remember the hollow way he laughed at me when I told him that I saved Tucker, and suddenly I'm all twisted up with worry for him, because whatever he was doing out there that day, my gut tells me that it wasn't good.

My brother has his secrets, too.

4

FREAKING OUT

This time in the dream, there are stairs. A set of ten or twelve concrete steps, complete with a black handrail, leading up between two aspen trees. Why would there be stairs in the middle of the forest? And where do they lead to? I grab the rail. It's rough, the paint flaking off to expose patches of rust. The steps are edged with moss. As I climb I notice I'm wearing nice shoes, Mom's sensible black pumps, the ones she always loans me for formal occasions.

I see Jeffrey ahead of me in the trees. Others wait there too, shadowy figures at the top of the hillside, people I recognize: Angela, Mr. Phibbs, Wendy. It feels like they're all staring at me, and I don't know why. I glance back, and the heel on my nice shoe catches. I lose my balance on the stairs, almost falling, but Christian's there again, his hand at my waist, steadying me. For a moment we stare at each other. His body radiates a kind of heat that makes me want to step closer to him.

"Thanks," I whisper, and I open my eyes to my bedroom ceiling, a strong cold wind still rattling the trees outside.

"You're freaking out," Angela observes with a mouthful of green bean salad. We're sitting at a booth in the Rendezvous Bistro in Jackson on a Saturday night, post–action movie, eating salad because that's all we can afford at this place.

"I'm fine," I say.

"You are so not fine. You should see yourself."

"Well, it sucks, okay? I just wish I knew if it's a dream or another vision, or what."

Angela nods thoughtfully. "Your mom said that some angel-bloods have their visions as dreams, right, while they're sleeping?"

"Yeah, she said that, before I started having mine, way back when she was okay with telling me useful information. But I've always had my visions while I was awake."

"Me too," Angela says.

"So it makes me wonder, is this dream thing for real, or is it, you know, the result of bad chow mein at dinner? Is this a divine message, or my subconscious talking here? And either way, what's it telling me?"

"See, there you go freaking out," she says. "It's messed up, C. You won't even look at Christian during Angel Club. It's like you two take turns avoiding each other. I'd find it hilarious if I didn't find it so totally sad."

"I know," I say. "I'm working on it."

She cocks her head at me sympathetically. "I like Tucker, Clara. Really I do. He's a stellar guy, no one would argue with that. But have you considered the possibility that you're not supposed to be with him? That you're supposed to be with Christian, that he's your destiny, that you're supposed to fly off into the sunset together?"

"Of course I have." I put my fork down, not hungry anymore. Destiny can really put a damper on the appetite. "I don't know why he even cares," I say.

"Why who cares? Tucker? Or Christian?"

"God."

She laughs. "Well, that's the big mystery, isn't it?"

"I mean, I'm seventeen years old. Why does He care who I . . ."

"Love," she supplies when I don't finish the sentence. "Who you love."

We're quiet while the waiter refills our drinks.

"Anyway, you should write this dream stuff down," she says. "Because it could be important. Check for variations, like you did with your vision. You should ask Christian about it too, because who knows, maybe he's having the same dream, and if he is, then you can figure it out together."

It's not a terrible idea. Except that I'm not exactly crazy about spilling to Christian that I've been dreaming about him.

"What does your mom say?" Angela asks, gnawing on a bread stick.

"I haven't told her about it."

She looks at me as if I just told her I'd been thinking of dabbling in heroin.

"Why should I? She never tells me anything. Even if I did tell her, I'm sure she'd only bury me in platitudes about trusting my feelings and listening to my heart or some crap like that. Besides, we don't know that it means anything," I say. "It's probably just a dream. People have recurring dreams all the time."

"If you say so," she says.

"Can we talk about something else now?"

So we do. We talk about the rain, which Angela agrees is excessive. We talk about Spirit Week at school and whether or not it would be fair for us to use our special gifts to win the Powderpuff game on Wednesday. She tells me about this old book she found in Italy this summer that seems to be some kind of angel-blood roster during the seventeenth century.

"It's like a group of them," she tells me. "*Congregarium celestial*, literally like a herd of angel-bloods. A flock. It's actually where I got the idea to form the Angel Club."

"Anything else interesting happen in Italy?" I ask her. "With, say, a hot Italian boyfriend you're now going to tell me all about?"

Her cheeks go instantly pink. She shakes her head, suddenly super interested in her salad. "I don't have a boyfriend. Italian or otherwise."

"Uh-huh."

"It was silly," she says, "and I don't want to talk about it. I won't hound you about Christian, you don't talk about my nonexistent Italian boyfriend, okay?"

"You already hounded me about Christian. That's hardly fair," I say, but there's genuine pain in her eyes, which surprises me, so I let it drop.

My mind wanders back to the dream, to Christian, the way he's always looking out for me, catching me, keeping me on my feet. He's become my guardian, maybe. Someone who is there to keep me on the path.

If only I knew where that path was headed.

We're in the parking lot when the sorrow hits me. At least, I think it's sorrow. It's not as overwhelming as it was that day in the forest. It doesn't paralyze me in the same way. Instead it's like suddenly, in the space of a few minutes, I go from fine, laughing even, to wanting to cry.

"Hey, are you okay?" Angela asks as we walk to the car.

"No," I whisper. "I feel . . . sad."

She stops. Her eyes go saucer wide. She glances around.

"Where?" she says much too loudly. "Where is he?"

"I don't know," I say. "I can't tell."

She grabs my hand and pulls me through the parking lot toward the car, walking fast but trying to stay composed, like nothing's wrong. She doesn't ask me if she can drive my car; she goes straight to the driver's seat, and I don't argue. "Put on your seat belt," she orders me once we're both inside. Then she floors it out of the parking lot and onto the street. "I don't know where to go," she says in a half-terrified, half-excited rush. "I think we should stay somewhere well-populated, because he'd have to be crazy to obliterate us in front of a bunch of tourists, you know, but I don't want to go too close to home." She does a quick check of the mirrors. "Call your mom. Now."

I fumble in my purse for my phone, then call. Mom picks up on the first ring.

"What's wrong?" she asks immediately.

"I think . . . maybe . . . there's a Black Wing."

"Where are you?"

"In the car, on 191, driving south."

"Go to the school," she says. "I'll meet you there."

It's the longest five minutes of my life before Mom lands in the parking lot at Jackson Hole High School. She gets in the back.

"So," she says, reaching up and feeling my cheek like sorrow is some kind of fever, "how do you feel?"

"Better now. I guess."

"Did you see him?"

"No."

She turns to Angela. "How about you? Did you feel anything?"

Angela shrugs. "Nothing." There's an edge of disappointment in her voice.

"So what do we do now?" I ask.

"We wait," Mom says.

So we wait, and wait, and wait some more, but nothing happens. We sit in the car in silence, watching the windshield wipers push the rain off the glass. Occasionally Mom asks me how I'm doing, which is hard to answer in any clear way. At first, what I feel most is terrified that any second now Samjeeza's going to show up and murder us all. Then I downgrade to just plain scared—that we're going to have to run now, pack up and leave Jackson, and I'll never see Tucker again. Finally I arrive at mildly freaked out. Then embarrassed.

"Maybe it wasn't sorrow," I admit. "It wasn't as strong as before."

"It would surprise me if he came after us so soon," Mom says.

"Why?" Angela asks.

"Because Samjeeza's vain," Mom says matter-of-factly. "Clara mangled his ear, burned his arm and his head, and I don't think he'll want to show his face until he's healed, which is a long process for Black Wings."

"I would have thought they could heal quickly," Angela says. "You know, like vampires or something."

Mom scoffs. "Vampires. Please. Black Wings take a long time to heal because they've chosen to cut themselves off from the healing forces in this world." She touches my cheek again. "You did the right thing, getting out of there, calling me. Even if it wasn't a Black Wing. It's better to be safe than sorry."

Angela sighs and looks out the window.

"Sorry," I say. I turn to Mom. "I guess I'm kind of on edge."

"Don't be," she says. "You've had a lot to deal with."

She and Angela switch places. Then she pulls out of the school parking lot and onto the road, heading back toward town.

"What do you feel?" she asks as we pass the restaurant.

"Nothing," I say with a shrug. "Except I have a feeling I might be losing my mind."

"It doesn't matter whether this is a false alarm or not. Samjeeza will come after us, Clara, eventually. You'll need to be ready."

Right.

"How does one get ready to be attacked by a Black Wing, exactly?" I ask sarcastically.

"Glory," she says, which immediately gets the told-you-so look on Angela's face. "You learn to use glory."

"Hey, I think I see a flicker," Christian says, startling me. "You're doing it."

My eyes snap open. Christian wasn't here earlier, when I got up onstage and started trying this bring-the-glory thing, but here he is now, sitting at one of the tables down in the audience at the Pink Garter, staring up at me with amusement like he's watching a show. For a split second our eyes meet and then I glance down at my hand, which is definitely not glowing. No glory.

Clearly I suck at bringing glory if it's not a do-it-or-die situation.

"What flicker?" I ask.

One side of his mouth hitches up. "Must have been my imagination."

Uh-huh. Insert another one of the classic Christian-Clara awkward silences. Then he coughs and says, "Sorry I interrupted your glory practice. Carry on."

I should close my eyes and try again, but I know it's no use. There's no way I'm going to achieve glory with him watching me.

"God, this is frustrating!" Angela exclaims. She slams her

laptop closed and pushes it across the table, blowing out a long, aggravated breath. She's been scouring college websites, trying to figure out what college she's supposed to go to, which to most people is a pretty big deal, but for Angela, it's a huge deal, the hugest, since she thinks it's a college campus she's seeing in her visions. Talk about pressure.

"Didn't get that ancient text you wanted on eBay?" asks Christian.

She glares at him. "Funny."

"Sorry, Ange," I say. "Can I help?"

"The vision doesn't give me very much to go on. There's a set of wide steps, a bunch of stone archways, and people drinking coffee. That describes practically any college in the country."

"Look for trees," I tell her. "I have a good book if you're trying to identify what area certain trees grow in."

"Well, I hope I get something decent to go on soon," mutters Angela. "I have to apply, you know? Like, now."

"Don't sweat it," Christian says nonchalantly. He glances down at his notebook, where I think he's working on calculus homework. "You'll figure it out when you're supposed to figure it out." Then he looks up, and his eyes catch mine again.

"Did you?" I can't help but ask, even though I know the answer. "Did you figure it out when you were supposed to?"

"No," he admits with a short, almost bitter laugh. "I don't

know why I said that. Drilled into me, I guess. That's what my uncle always tells me."

He hasn't talked much about his uncle. Or his purpose, outside of the initial "I was having visions of you in the forest fire, I thought I was supposed to save you, and now I'm confused" conversation. Once, he showed us that he could fly without flapping his wings, Superman style, hovering over the stage like David Blaine while Angela, Jeffrey, and I gaped up at him like idiots. Occasionally he gives Angela some random angel fact, so she'll be satisfied with what he's contributing to the group. He seems to know more than we do, but mostly he's been pretty tight lipped.

"So," Angela says, and the expression on her face makes me nervous. She gets up and crosses to stand next to Christian's table. "What happens now?"

"What do you mean?" he asks.

"You haven't fulfilled your purpose, right?"

He stares at her.

"All right," she says when he doesn't say anything. "At least answer this: when you had your vision before, did it come during the day, or at night?"

He looks off at the shadows in the back of the stage area for a minute, deciding, then glances back at her. "At night."

"You dreamed it?"

"Usually. Except one time I was awake."

Prom. When we danced, and then we had the vision,

together.

"Well, Clara's having a new dream," Angela says. I give her what I hope is my most angry glare, but she ignores it, of course. "Like maybe it could be a vision. We need to figure out what it is."

Christian looks at me, immediately interested. I'm literally standing in the spotlight, so I jump down from the stage and walk over to them, feeling his gaze following me.

"What vision?" he asks.

"It might only be a dream," Angela answers for me. "But you've had it what, Clara, ten times now?"

"Seven. I'm walking up a hill," I explain, "through a forest, but not like the hill in my—in our vision. It's a sunny day, no fire. Jeffrey's there, and he's wearing a suit for some reason. Angela's there—at least she was last time I had it. And some other people too . . ." I hesitate. "And you're there," I say to Christian.

I can't tell him about how he takes my hand, how he whispers straight into my mind without saying anything out loud.

"It's probably only a dream, you know?" I manage. "Like my subconscious working something out, my fears, maybe, or like those dreams where you show up to school naked."

"What does the forest look like?" he asks.

"That's the weird thing about it. It's like a normal forest, but there are these stairs—a set of concrete stairs in the middle of the trees. And a fence."

"What about you, have you been having any strange dreams?" asks Angela. "Some clue to add to all this craziness?"

Christian finally drags his gaze away from mine to look at her.

"No dreams."

"Well, personally I think it's more than a dream," she says. "Because it's not over."

"What?"

"Your purpose. There's no way you go through all that, the visions and the fires and everything, and then that's it. No way. There has to be more."

My empathy chooses this moment to kick in, and I get a jolt of what Christian's feeling: Resolve. Determination. A yearning underneath everything that makes me catch my breath. And certainty. Pure, absolute certainty. That Angela is right. That it's not over. That there is more to come.

That night when I come into my room there's someone standing on the eaves outside my window. In a split second all my mom's baloney about Samjeeza being injured and vain and biding his time to come after us seems like exactly that—baloney—and I think, it's him, it *was* his sorrow I felt the other day, I knew it, and my heart goes into crazy-panicked mode and my blood starts pumping and I glance wildly around my room for a weapon. Which is a joke because, a) I don't have weapons so much as average teenage girl stuff in my room, and b) even if I were to procure something other than a nail file to defend myself with, what weapon works on a Black Wing? Glory, I think, got to call glory, but then I also think, wait. Why is he just standing there? Why hasn't he started in on the cheesy evil I-will-kill-you-little-bird lines yet?

It's not Samjeeza, I realize then. It's Christian. I can feel his presence plain as day, now that I've calmed down enough to think straight. He's come to tell me something. Something important.

I sigh, put on a sweatshirt, and open the window.

"Hey," I call out.

He looks over from his spot on the edge of the roof, a place that perfectly overlooks the mountains, which are still glowing a faint snow-dusted white in the dark. I climb out the window and sit down next to him. It's freezing outside, raining a chilly, miserable drizzle. I immediately hug my arms around myself and try not to shiver.

"Cold?" he asks.

I nod. "Aren't you?" He's wearing a black T-shirt and his usual Seven jeans, gray this time. I hate that I recognize his clothes.

He shrugs. "A little."

"Angela says that angel-bloods are supposed to be immune to cold. It helps with the flying at high altitudes, I guess." I shiver again. "I must not have gotten the memo."

He smiles. "Maybe that power only applies to mature angel-bloods."

"Hey, are you calling me immature?"

"Oh no," he says, his smile blossoming into a full-blown grin. "I wouldn't dare."

"Good. Because I'm not the one peeping into someone else's window."

"I wasn't peeping," he protests.

Right. Something important.

"You know, there's this new amazing invention," I tease. "It's called a cell phone."

"Yeah, because you and I have such amazing heart-to-heart conversations over the phone," he shoots back.

It's quiet for a second, then we both start laughing. He's right. I don't know why it's easier here, but it is. Out here we can finally talk. It's a bona fide miracle.

He turns toward me, his knee brushing mine. In the dim light from my window, his eyes are a deep, dark green.

He says, "In your dream, the fence you mentioned, it's a chain-link fence, on the right as you climb the hill."

"Yes, how did you—"

"And the stairs you see, they have moss growing on the edges, and a railing to hold on to, metal, with black paint?"

I stare at him. "Right."

"On the left side, back behind the trees, there's a stone bench," he continues. "And a rosebush, planted beside it. But the roses never bloom—it's too cold up there for roses."

He looks away for a minute. A sudden puff of wind stirs his hair, and he brushes it out of his eyes.

"You're having the dream, too?" I whisper.

"Not like yours. I mean, I dream about that place all the time, but—" He sighs, shifts uncomfortably, then looks at me.

"I'm not used to talking about this," he says. "I've sort of become a professional at not talking about this."

"It's okay. . . ."

"No, I want to tell you. You should know this. But I didn't want to tell you in front of Angela."

I draw my sweatshirt up to my chin and cross my arms against my chest.

"My mom died," he says finally. "When I was ten years old. I don't even know how it happened. My uncle doesn't like to talk about it, but I think . . . I think she was killed by a Black Wing. One day she was there, doing long-division flash cards with me at breakfast, driving me to school, kissing me good-bye in front of the boys at school and embarrassing me. . . ." His voice wavers. He stops, looks away, clears his throat lightly. "Then the next minute, they're pulling me out of class. They say there's been an accident. And she's gone. I mean, they let me see her body, eventually. But she wasn't inside of it. It was just . . . a body."

He looks at me then, eyes gleaming. "Her gravestone is a bench. A white stone bench, under the aspen trees."

Suddenly my head feels all cloudy. "What?"

"It's Aspen Hill Cemetery," he says. "It's not a real cemetery—well, it is a real cemetery, with graves and flowers and stuff like that, but it's also like part of the forest, this beautiful place in the trees where it's quiet and you can see the Tetons in the distance. It's probably the most peaceful place I know. I go there sometimes to think, and . . ."

And talk to his mom. He goes there to talk to his mom.

"So when you said that thing about the stairs, and the hillside and the fence, I knew," he says quietly.

"You knew I was dreaming about the cemetery," I say.

"I'm sorry," he whispers.

I look up at him, choking back a cry, putting it all together, the people wearing suits and me in a black dress, everybody walking in the same direction, the grief I feel, the way everybody looks at me so solemnly, the comfort Christian tries to offer. It all makes perfect sense.

It's not a Black Wing's sorrow I'm feeling, in the dream. It's mine.

Someone I love is going to die.

5

FIND ME A DREAM

"Clara? You still with us?"

Mom nudges me in the shoulder. I blink for a second, then smile up at Ms. Baxter, the guidance counselor. She smiles back.

"So what do you think?" she asks. "Do you have any ideas about the direction you want to go in, any visions of your future?"

My eyes flick over to Mom. Oh, I have visions, all right. "You mean, like college?" I direct at Ms. Baxter.

"Well, yes, education is a big part of that, and we want to encourage all our students to attend college, of course, especially a bright, clearly gifted girl like yourself. But every person has their own special path, whether that leads to college or not."

I look down at my hands. "I don't really know what I want to do, career-wise."

She gives an exaggerated, encouraging nod. "Perfectly okay. Lots of students don't at this point. Have you done any looking around, college visits or surfing the university websites?"

"Not much." Or at all.

"I think maybe that would be a good place to start," Ms. Baxter says. "Why don't you check out some of the brochures I have posted outside and make a list of five colleges that appeal to you and why. Then I can help you get started on applications."

"Thank you so much." Mom stands up and shakes Ms. Baxter's hand.

"You've got a special young lady here," says Ms. Baxter. I try not to roll my eyes. "I know she's going to do something remarkable with her life."

I nod awkwardly, and we get out of there.

"She's right though, you know, in spite of the cheesy lines," Mom says as we walk out to the parking lot. "You're going to do remarkable things."

"Sure," I answer. I want to believe her, but I don't. All I see when I examine my life these days is a messed-up purpose and a not-so-distant future where somebody important to me is going to die.

"You want to drive?" I ask her as a change of topic.

"No, you go ahead." She digs around in her purse for her big Audrey Hepburn–style sunglasses, which, paired with the scarf she's wrapped around her head and her long, sleek trench coat, make her look like a movie star.

"So, what's going on?" she asks. "I feel like something's bothering you, something more than the college stuff. Which will all work itself out, Clara, not to worry."

I hate it when she tells me not to worry. It's usually when I have a pretty darn good reason to worry. It seems like that's all I can do right now: worry about whose grave I'm going to in this new vision, worry that whoever it is died because of something I did or am supposed to do, worry that the sorrow attacks I've been having lately mean that Samjeeza is hanging around just waiting for the perfect moment to kill somebody I love.

"It's nothing major," I say.

We get into the car. I slide the key into the ignition. But then I stop.

"Mom, what happened between you and Samjeeza?"

She doesn't even look rattled by my question, which surprises me. Then she answers it, which floors me even more. "It was a long time ago," she says. "He and I were . . . friends."

"You were friends with a Black Wing."

"I didn't know he was a Black Wing at first. I thought he was a regular angel."

I can't imagine mistaking Samjeeza for a regular angel. Not that I've met any regular angels.

"Right. Are you friends with lots of angels?" I ask sarcastically.

"A few."

"A few," I repeat. How can she keep blowing my mind like this? I mean, really—she knows *a few* angels?

"Not many."

"Angela thinks Samjeeza's some kind of leader," I tell her.

"Ah," Mom says, nodding. *"The Book of Enoch?"*

"Yeah."

"That much is true. He was the leader of the Watchers, a long time ago."

Wow. She is actually telling me this.

"And what do the Watchers do, exactly?" I ask. "Other than, I assume, watch stuff."

"The Watchers gave up heaven so they could be with human women," she says.

"I take it God doesn't dig the idea of angels hooking up with humans."

"It's not that God doesn't like it," she explains. "It's that angels don't live in linear time like you and I do, which makes having a relationship with a human woman nearly impossible, since that would require the angel to stay grounded in the same time for a sustained period."

Oh. The time stuff again.

"It's difficult for us to fully understand how they live, moving between the different planes of existence, through space and time. Angels don't simply sit around on clouds looking down at us. They are constantly at work."

"Married to the job, huh?" I quip.

A flicker of a smile passes over her face. "Exactly."

"And the Watchers did what? Quit?"

"Yes. And Samjeeza was the first to put in his two-week notice, so to speak."

"And then what happened?"

"The Watchers married human women, had children, and for a while, everything was fine. I imagine they felt some sorrow, being away from heaven, but it was manageable. They were happy. But they never truly belonged on earth, and their children lived a long time and kept multiplying, until there were more Nephilim than humans on the earth. Which became a problem."

I think about Angela's story from *The Book of Enoch*. "So God sent the flood," I deduce.

"Yes," she says. "And Samjeeza . . ." She stops. Thinks about how much she should tell me. "Samjeeza couldn't save his family. His children and grandchildren and great-grandchildren, every single one of them drowned."

No wonder the guy's pissed.

"That's when the Watchers joined the other Black Wings and declared war against heaven," she says.

"The other Black Wings?"

"Satan and his crew."

I laugh at the idea of Satan having an entourage, even though I know it's not funny.

"They fight the sovereignty of God and try to ruin heaven's plans whenever possible," she explains. "But their desire doesn't stem from grief, it's just pure evil, being contrary for their own sakes."

"Uh-huh. How do you know all this?" I ask her.

"Sam told me."

"Because you were friends."

"Yes," she says. "Once upon a time."

Still can't get my head around that one.

"He's in love with you, you know," I add, just to see her reaction.

She smoothes her scarf down against her hair. "How do you know?"

"When he touched me I could feel him thinking about you. Well, first he was thinking about me. But after you showed up, he was completely distracted by you. I saw you, in his mind. You looked different. You had short brown hair and"—I stop myself from mentioning the cigarette—"a lot of lipstick. He's definitely obsessed with you and your lipstick."

Her hand rises like she wants to touch her neck where, if

she was a normal person, there might still be bruises from Samjeeza choking her. "Lucky me," she says.

I shudder, remembering the feeling of his cold hands moving underneath my shirt.

"If you hadn't shown up when you did, he would have . . ." I can't finish the sentence.

She frowns. "Rape is not a Black Wing's style. They prefer seduction. They want to win you over to their side."

"What about Angela's mom?" I point out. "She was raped."

"Yes, so she says."

"You think that's not true?"

"I don't know. I wasn't there."

"Well, I think Samjeeza was planning on it with me," I tell her. "He didn't exactly try to charm me."

"He was behaving strangely that day," she says. "The way he talked, all melodrama and clichés, like he was playing a part. It wasn't like him. It was as if he was trying to prove something."

"But nobody was watching him but us."

"Somebody was," she says cryptically. "Somebody always is."

Oh. I guess she means God. Always watching. Gulp.

Her mouth twists into a pained line. "I'm sorry you had to go through that."

"Me too."

"Anyway," she says like she's relieved to be changing the subject, "I thought we could go into town for some ice cream, maybe do some shopping."

"Can't," I tell her. "I'm supposed to go fishing with Tucker this afternoon."

She tries to hide her disappointment. "Oh."

"I've hardly had a chance to see him lately, because he got a job at Flat Creek Saddle Shop and he's been working all these hours. . . ."

"No, I understand," she says. "You should go be with him."

I wonder if she cares about Tucker at all now. If she still disapproves.

"Maybe we can do something this weekend?"

"Sure," she agrees. "I would love that."

"Okay."

Then there's nothing to do but turn the key in the ignition, put the car in gear, and drive home.

There's something magical about the way my head fits into the crook of Tucker's neck. I lie there, breathe in his scent, which is a delightful mix of earth and hay and his own brand of man smell and aftershave, a touch of bug spray thrown in there, and for a minute all my worries evaporate. It's just him and me, the lull of the water gently rocking the boat, particles of dust floating around in the warm air. I don't know what heaven's like, aside from the sense of brightness that Mom described for me once, but if I got to choose my heaven, this would be it. On the lake with Tucker. I'll take the mosquitoes and everything.

"I so needed this," I say, which comes out almost as a yawn.

I feel him smile against my hair. "Me too. Your hair smells like wind, did you know that?"

Yep, me and Tucker, smelling each other.

I tip my head up to kiss him. It starts out as something sweet, slow and lazy as the afternoon sun, but it heats up fast. We pull apart for a second and our breath mingles, and I twist around so I am practically lying on top of him, our legs tangling. He reaches up to take my head in his hand and kisses me again, then does this half groan, half laugh that drives me crazy and drops his hand down to my hip and tugs me closer. I slide my fingers under the collar of his shirt, along the solid breadth of his chest, where I can feel the hammering of his heart. I love him, I think. In that moment I know, if I tried, I would be capable of glory.

He breaks away.

"Okay," he gasps.

"You still think you'll get struck by lightning if we . . . you know?" I tease, arching an eyebrow at him and pinning him with my most seductive (I think) look.

He gives me a kind of tortured, bemused smile. "When I was a kid my mom used to tell me that if I had sex before I was married, my . . . junk would turn black and fall off."

That gets a startled laugh out of me. "Seriously?"

"Yeah, and I believed her, too."

"So you're not going to have sex before you're married? What if you don't get married until you're thirty?"

He sighs. "I don't know. I just love you. I don't want to mess anything up."

This doesn't make sense to me, but I nod. "So we'll be good."

"Right."

"Because you're scared."

"Hey!"

"Okay," I say with a sigh. "Even though that's not much fun."

He startles me by flipping me over, pressing me gently back into the blanket at the bottom of the boat. "You don't think this is fun?" he challenges, and then he kisses me until my insides turn to mush and my head goes all fuzzy.

Much, *much* later, we actually attempt to fish. I find that I still suck at it. And I still like that I suck at it. And Tucker is still some kind of fish whisperer.

"There now," he says softly as he carefully removes the hook from the lip of a gleaming cutthroat trout. "You be smarter next time."

He lowers it back into the water, where it darts away in a flash of green and silver. He looks up at me and grins wickedly. "Want to make out with me now?" he asks, holding up his fish-slimed hands.

"Um, tempting, but no," I answer quickly. "I think we

better be good, don't you think?"

"That's really funny," he says, then starts re-tying his fishing line, ". . . so-ho-ho-ho funny." A cloud moves over the sun, and suddenly it's colder. Quieter. Even the birds stop singing. A shiver passes through me.

"Want my shirt?" Tucker asks, always the gentleman.

"I'm okay. I'm working on becoming immune to cold."

He laughs. "Good luck with that. We probably won't get any more days like this, warm enough to fish out here." He threads some bait onto his line and casts again. Almost immediately he has a bite. The same fish.

"You deserve to be on a dinner plate," he tells the cutthroat, but releases him again anyway. "Go! Find your destiny. Stay away from the shiny hook-type things."

This reminds me, for some crazy reason, of my talk with the school counselor.

"So, all this work you're doing lately—" I start.

"Don't remind me."

"It's to buy a new horse?"

"And a new truck, eventually, and by new I mean used, and by used I mean probably on its last legs, since that's all I'll be able to swing."

"You're not saving for college?" I ask.

Bad question. His eyes stay focused on his fishing pole, which he quickly unties and disassembles. "Nope," he says with forced lightness. "After I graduate, I'll stay on the ranch.

Dad hurt his knee this spring, and we can't afford to hire more help, so I thought I'd stick around."

"Oh," is all I can think to say to that. "Did you have to go visit Ms. Baxter?"

"Yeah," he says with a scoff. "She got me set up for some talks with Northern Arizona University next week. I guess I'll probably go off to school in a year or two, because that's what's expected of me."

"What would you study? In college, if you go?"

"Agriculture, probably. Maybe forestry," he says, rubbing the back of his neck.

"Forestry?"

"To be a ranger."

I picture him in the green ranger uniform, wearing one of those hats like Smokey the Bear. Which is totally hot.

"Hey, it's getting late. Ready to go in?" he asks.

"Sure." I reel in my line and stick my pole with Tucker's at the bottom of the boat. He starts the motor, and in a few minutes we're gliding over the water toward the dock. Neither of us says anything, but he suddenly sighs. He slows the boat to a crawl, then stops us. We're right in the middle of the lake, the motor idling, the sun sinking behind the mountains.

"I don't want to leave," he says after a minute.

I look up at him, startled. "You don't want to leave?"

He gestures around, at the towering blue mountains

behind us, the gray heron skimming the water, the glimmers of the sinking sun on the lake. "This is it for me. This is what I want."

I realize that he's not talking about today, the lake, this moment. He's talking about his future.

"I might go to college, but I'm going to end up back here," he says. "I'll live and die here."

He looks at me like he's daring me to challenge him. Instead I scoot across the boat to him and circle my arms around his neck. "I get it," I whisper.

He relaxes. "What about you? What do you want to do?"

"I don't want to leave, either. I want to stay here. With you."

That night as I'm drifting off to sleep, my cell phone rings. At first I ignore it, let it go to voice mail, because I want to get into my dream and figure out who's dead. But then it rings again. And again. Whoever it is won't take no for an answer. Which makes me think it's—

"Okay, Ange, this better be good, because it's late and—"

"It's Stanford!" She laughs, a wild happy laugh that I've never heard from her before. "I'm going to Stanford, C. It was the trees—you were so brilliant to suggest I look at the trees."

"Wow. Big league. That's great, Ange."

"I know, right? I mean, I was prepared for it to be anything, even if it was this dinky school that nobody's ever heard of, because it's my purpose and that's more important, but Stanford's like a school I'd kill to go to even without my purpose. So it's perfect."

"I'm happy for you." At least I'm trying to be. I grew up near Stanford. It still feels like home.

"And there's something else," she says.

I brace myself for even more jolting news, like she already has a full-ride scholarship, or that a real-live angel, an Intangere, dropped off with a note for her, carefully detailing her purpose and everything she's supposed to do at Stanford, a memo from heaven.

"Okay. What?" I ask when she doesn't come out and tell me.

"I want you to go too."

"Huh? When?"

"For college, silly. I'm going to Stanford, and I want you to be there with me."

Three a.m. No possibility of sleep. I've been thrashing in my blankets all night, unable to quiet all the crazy thoughts bouncing around my head. My mother being friends with a fallen angel. College plans. Christian. Purposes that last a hundred years. A flood that kills all the angel-bloods on earth. Angela wanting me to go to Stanford with her. Tucker staying here, always and forever. Ms. Baxter all hopeful and sweet and completely annoying. And somebody dying, let's not forget. Somebody. And I still have no clue who.

Finally I get up and go downstairs. I'm surprised to find Mom sitting at the kitchen counter with a shawl wrapped around her shoulders, her hands circling a cup of tea like she's using it for warmth. She glances up and smiles.

"Insomniacs of the world unite," she says. "Want some tea?"

"Sure."

I find the pot on the counter and pour myself a cup, locate cream and sugar, then stand there absently stirring it for way too long, until Mom asks, "What's up?"

"Nothing," I answer. "The usual. Oh—and Angela's going to Stanford."

Her eyebrows lift. "Stanford. Impressive."

"Well, she hasn't even applied yet, but she thinks her purpose is going to happen there."

"I see."

"She wants me to go with her." I laugh. "Like I could ever get into Stanford, right?"

"I don't see why not," she says with a frown. "You're an excellent student."

"Come on. It takes more than that, Mom. I know I have good grades, but for a school like that it takes . . . being president of the debate team or building houses for the homeless in Guatemala or acing my SATs. I hardly paid attention to my SATs. I haven't done anything since I came to Wyoming." I meet her eyes. "I was so obsessed with my purpose I hardly noticed anything else."

She drinks her tea. Then she says, "Pity party over?"

"Yeah, I think so."

"Good. Not good to wallow for too long. It's bad for the complexion."

I make a face at her.

"You do have one big advantage when it comes to Stanford," she says.

"Oh yeah? What?"

"Your grandmother went there, and she happens to donate a large sum of money to the university every year."

I stare at her. My grandmother. I don't have a grandmother. Mom's mother died in childbirth back in like 1890.

"You mean Dad's mom?" I've never heard anything about Dad's mom. Neither of my parents have ever said much about their families.

"No," Mom says with a small, knowing smile. "I mean *me*. In 1967 I graduated from Stanford with a degree in history. My name back then was Margot Whitfield. That, according to the official records, anyway, is your grandmother."

"Margot Whitfield," I repeat.

"That's me."

I shake my head incredulously. "You know, sometimes I feel like I don't know you at all."

"You don't," she admits easily, which catches me off guard. "When you've been around as long as I have, you've lived several different lives, and each one of them is, in some ways, like a different person. A different version of yourself. Margot Whitfield is a stranger to you."

My thoughts shoot straight to Samjeeza and the way he calls my mom Meg, the image of her he carries around in his head, this smirking girl with cropped brown hair. Definitely a stranger.

"So what was she like, this Margot Whitfield?" I ask. "Nice name, by the way. Margot."

"She was a free spirit," Mom says. "A bit of a hippie, I'm afraid."

My brain instantly conjures an image of my mom in one of those flowy polyester dresses with the tiny sunglasses and daisies in her hair, swaying to the music at Woodstock, protesting the war.

"So did you do a lot of drugs?"

"No," she says a bit defensively. "I had my rebellious stage, Clara. But it definitely wasn't the sixties. More like the twenties."

"Then why were you a hippie, if you weren't rebelling?"

She hesitates. "I had a hard time with the conformity of the fifties."

"What was your name in the fifties?"

"Marge," she says with a laugh. "But I was never the fifties-housewife type."

"Because you weren't married."

"Right." She'd told me this. Early on I'd been nervous that

maybe, given her age, she'd already been married a few times and had lots of kids out there, but she assured me this wasn't the case.

"Did you ever almost get married?" Now this, I've never asked her. But she's been pretty forthcoming recently, so I try my luck.

She closes her eyes for a minute, takes a deep breath. "Yes."

"When?"

She looks at me. "In the fifties. Now back to Margot Whitfield, please."

I nod. "So you're a Stanford alum. How many times have you been to college, anyway?"

"Let's see," she says, obviously relieved to be off the fifties and back to a time she's comfortable with. "Four. I studied nursing, history, international relations, and computer programming."

I let that sink in for a minute. "International relations?"

"I'd tell you, but then I'd have to kill you."

"Don't tell me you were a spy?"

She smiles blandly.

"So that's why you keep telling me to relax about the college thing. I don't have to pick a single career. When you're going to live hundreds of years, you have time to be everything that interests you."

"When you live a long life," she says, "you can do a lot of things. You have time. But if you want to go to Stanford with

Angela, I think that might be great fun."

"I'll think about it," I say. But if I go with Angela, Tucker and I are going to be separated. We're going to have to do the long-distance thing, and that does not sound like great fun to me.

* * *

I crawl back to bed around four, completely exhausted by this point, hoping to grab a couple hours of sleep before tomorrow begins. But I'm instantly sucked into the cemetery dream, which is not at all restful. For a few seconds I fight it, completely disoriented, stumbling as I make my way up the hill. I try to slow my breathing, remind myself that I actually want to be here, try to calm the immediate desperation and panic I feel to figure out who is going to die. *Look around,* I tell myself. *See who's not here. Who should be here, and isn't.*

I spot Jeffrey, same as usual. I say his name. He doesn't look at me, says, *Let's get this over with,* like he does every time. I want to ask him, *Who is it?* But my lips won't form the words. I am locked into what future-Clara is doing at this moment, which is walking, focusing on putting one foot in front of the other, and wishing she could cry. *If I could just flipping cry,* she thinks—I think—*then maybe the ache wouldn't be so bad.*

All I can do is stay along for the ride and observe. Now that I know this is a cemetery, that this is a funeral procession, it seems so obvious. Everybody's wearing dark clothes. I notice gravestones scattered around under the trees. I try to pay attention to more than the grief raging in my head.

It's spring, I quickly figure out. The leaves on the trees, the grass, are new green. The air has that fresh-washed smell that comes after a spring rain, where you can still detect a hint of snow. There are the beginnings of wildflowers on the hillside.

It's going to happen in the spring.

I can clearly make out Angela walking way off to the side, wearing a long violet dress. There's Mr. Phibbs, my English teacher. Come to think of it, I recognize several people from school, maybe because school is the only place in Jackson where I know anybody. I see Mrs. Lowell, the school secretary, and her redheaded daughter, Allison. Kimber Lane, Jeffrey's girlfriend. Ava Peters. Wendy, walking next to her parents, clutching a white rose to her chest. I see a flash of her face, which is paler than usual, her blue eyes all red and puffy. She doesn't have a problem crying.

Who's missing?

Warm fingers enclose mine. I look up at Christian. He squeezes my hand. I shouldn't be letting him hold my hand, I think. I belong to Tucker.

You can do this, Christian says in my head. There's no doubt in him. No hesitation. He's not worried that Tucker's going to show up and have a problem with him holding my hand.

The bottom of my stomach drops out.

Tucker.

6

SOONER OR LATER

"Five more minutes, people."

Government class. I'm watching Tucker take a test on the U.S. Constitution. I finished it fifteen minutes ago, so I'm sitting watching him as he leans over his paper, frowning, pausing to tap his pencil in a crazy rhythm on his desk like that might jog his memory. Things are clearly not going well.

At any other time I'd find him adorable like this, all frustrated and pursed in concentration. But all I can think is, Who cares about a stupid government test? You're going to die. And it's my fault, somehow.

Stop it. Stop thinking that. You don't know for sure.

But it feels like I do know. The conclusion I've come to

is that Tucker was supposed to die in the fire. If I hadn't abandoned my purpose, if I hadn't flown off to save him, he would have died up there in the woods above Palisades. That was his destiny. I was supposed to choose Christian. Tucker was supposed to die. Now, with this new dream, it feels like the same thing playing out again. Christian and me, walking in the woods again. Tucker dead.

Only this time, it's not some split decision that I have to make. This time I'll have months to agonize over it.

And here's the other realization I've come to: it doesn't matter how much time I'm given to think it over. I'll still choose Tucker. I don't care if it screws up my purpose.

I'm not going to let him die.

The problem is, I don't know how it's going to happen, so I don't know how to stop it. It's like that movie *Final Destination*, where these people were supposed to die in a plane crash, but they got off the plane and so Death comes hunting them down, one by one, because they were *supposed to die*. I've been over the craziest scenarios, like: a) Tucker gets in a car wreck, b) he chokes on a piece of meat at dinner, c) he gets struck by lightning because it never ever stops raining, d) he slips and falls in the shower and drowns, or e) his house gets hit by a meteor. But what can I do about that? It's not like I can be with him all the time. I did get so wigged out that I sneaked out to his house a couple times in the middle of the night to watch over him while he slept, just in case,

I don't know, his comic book collection decided to spontaneously combust. This was dumb and admittedly creepy in an Edward Cullen kind of way, but it was the only thing I could think to do. Thank God he's not in rodeo anymore, since I don't think I could bear to watch him try to ride a bull right now.

So I've appointed myself his guardian. I've also picked him up for school every day this week and driven us there so slowly that he's started teasing me about driving like a granny. He's noticed, of course, that something's wrong. Nothing ever slips by Tucker. Plus I am not being very subtle in my spazzing out about this boyfriend-destined-to-die thing.

This morning, for example. We were sitting in the commons during breakfast break and there was this loud, sudden pop from the other side of the lunchroom, and I couldn't help it. I moved fast, too fast, so fast that Mom would have freaked if she'd seen, putting myself between that noise and Tucker. Then I stood there, waiting, hands clenched at my sides, until I heard a few boys laughing at the doofus who had crushed a soda can under his foot—a soda can!—and now everybody in his group was congratulating him on his spectacular noise-making ability.

And Tucker was looking at me. Wendy too, her bagel lifted halfway to her mouth. Everybody at my table, staring.

"Wow," I said breathlessly, trying to cover. "That scared me. People shouldn't do that."

"Shouldn't crush pop cans?" asked Wendy. "You're pretty jumpy, don't you think?"

"Hey, I'm from California," I tried to explain. "We had to go through metal detectors to get into the school."

Tucker was still looking at me, his eyebrows drawn together.

Now as I watch him struggle through his test, I think about telling him. I could tell him and then there would be no secrets between us, no lies. It would be the honest thing. But it would also be a terrible thing. A selfish thing.

Because what if I'm wrong? After all, I thought my last vision was telling me I was supposed to save Christian and wrong-o. It's not the kind of news you want to deliver unless you are pretty freaking sure.

But what if I'm right? Would I want to know if I was going to die?

My eyes wander past Tucker, two rows over, to Christian. He too is already done with his test. He looks up, like he can feel my gaze on him. He gives me a faint smile that only lasts a few seconds. Then he glances at Tucker, who's still frowning obliviously at his paper.

Nice move in the cafeteria this morning, Christian says suddenly in my mind.

He's talking in my head! For a minute I'm too shocked to form a response. Can he tell what I'm thinking right now? Has he been reading my mind this entire time? I'm torn between the desire to answer him or to attempt to block him completely.

Oh, you saw that? I answer finally, trying to push my words out to meet him the way I did when I talked with Mom that day in the forest, when we had an entire conversation in our heads.

I can't tell if he hears me. His eyes lock on mine.

Are you okay?

I look away. *I'm fine.*

"Okay, pencils down," says Mr. Anderson. "Bring your test to the front. Then you're free to go."

Tucker scowls, sighs, then makes his way up to Mr. Anderson's desk with his test. When he turns back, I give him my most sympathetic smile.

"Didn't go well, huh?"

"I didn't study," he says as we gather up our stuff and head for the hallway, me carefully avoiding Christian. "It's my own fault. Burning the candle at both ends, as my dad says. I have a Spanish test tomorrow that I'm probably not going to do much better on."

"I could help you," I offer. *"Yo hablo español muy bien."*

"Cheater," he says, but smiles.

"After school? I'll tutor you?"

"I have work this afternoon."

"I could come after." I know I'm being persistent, but I want to spend every possible minute by his side. I want to help him, even if it's only with his Spanish. That I can do.

"You could come over for dinner, and then we could hit the books. But we might have to stay up pretty late. I'm seriously that bad at Spanish," he says.

"Good thing for you, I'm kind of a night owl."

He grins. "Right. So tonight then?"

"I'll be there."

"*Hasta la vista,* baby," he tells me, and I shake my head and smile at how adorably dorky he can be. His Spanish only comes from Arnold Schwarzenegger.

That night I find myself sitting in the warm, lighted kitchen at the Lazy Dog Ranch. It's like a scene from *Little House on the Prairie*. Wendy sets the table while Mrs. Avery finishes up with the mashed potatoes. Tucker and Mr. Avery come in from the barn and both give Mrs. Avery a quick kiss on the cheek, then roll up the sleeves of their flannel shirts and scrub their hands in the kitchen sink like surgeons prepping for the OR. Tucker slips into the chair next to mine. He squeezes my knee under the table.

Mrs. Avery beams over at me from the stove.

"Well, Clara," she says. "I must say it's nice to see you again."

"Yes, Mrs. Avery. Thanks for having me."

"Oh, sugar, call me Rachel. I think we're past the formalities." She slaps her husband's hand away from the basket of dinner rolls. "I hope you're hungry."

Dinner turns out to be pot roast and gravy, potatoes, carrots, celery, and homemade buttermilk rolls, washed down with large glasses of iced tea.

We eat quietly for a while. I can't stop thinking about how devastated this whole family is going to be if they lose Tucker, can't stop remembering the way their faces look in my dream. Sad. Resigned. Determined to get through it.

"I tell ya, Ma," Tucker says. "This is really a fine meal. I don't think I've told you enough what an amazing cook you are."

"Why thank you, son," she replies, sounding pleasantly surprised. "You haven't."

Wendy and Mr. Avery laugh.

"He's seen the light," Mr. Avery says.

This seems to ignite something, and suddenly everybody's talking about the fires.

"I'll tell you what," says Mr. Avery, spearing a piece of meat with his fork and waving it around. "They ever catch the bastard who started those fires, I'm going to give him what for."

My head whips up. "Someone started the fires?" I ask, my heart suddenly thundering.

"Well, they think one was started by natural causes, like a lightning strike," says Wendy. "But the other was arson. The police are offering a twenty-thousand-dollar reward for anybody who gives them information leading to an arrest."

This is what happens when I stop watching the news. They call it arson. I wonder what the police would do if they found out who really did it. Uh, yes, officer, I believe the one who started the fire was about six foot three. Black hair. Amber eyes. Big, black wings. Residence: hell. Occupation: leader of the Watchers. Birth date: the dawn of time.

In other words, that's twenty thousand dollars that no one's ever going to see.

"Well, I for one hope they catch him," says Mr. Avery. "I want a chance to look him in the eye."

"Dad," says Tucker wearily. "Give it a rest."

"No." Mr. Avery clears his throat. "That was your land, your grandfather's legacy to you, that was everything you ever worked for, your truck, your trailer, your horse, all those odd jobs, scrimping and saving to be able to afford the rodeo fees, the gear, the gas for the truck. Years of backbreaking work, sweat and more sweat, hours of practice, and I will not give it a rest."

"Wait," I say, still catching up. "It was the Palisades fire where they suspect arson?"

Mr. Avery nods.

So, not the fire Samjeeza started trying to flush out my mom and me out at Static Peak. The other fire. Someone deliberately started the other fire?

"It doesn't matter," Tucker says offhandedly. "It's over and done with. I'm grateful just to be alive."

So am I. And what I'm thinking in this moment is, How can I keep you that way?

Later Tucker and I go out to the porch. We sit in the swing and rock. It's cold, freezing actually, but neither of us seems to mind it. It's too cloudy to see the stars. After we've been sitting there for a while, it starts to snow. We don't go in. We lie there in the swing, swaying back and forth, our breath mingling as it rises in foggy puffs above our heads.

"The sky is falling," I whisper, watching the flakes drift with the wind.

"Yeah," he says. "It kind of looks that way." He sits up in the swing to look into my face, and my heart starts pounding a mile a minute for no good reason.

"Are you okay?" he asks. "You've been tense all week. What's going on?"

I stare up at him and think about losing him and my eyes suddenly brim with tears. And tears—any girl's tears, but mine especially—really get to Tucker.

"Hey," he whispers, and instantly gathers me up in his arms. I sniffle against his shoulder for a few minutes, then get myself together and look up and try to smile.

"I'm fine," I say. "I'm just stressed."

He frowns. "Angel stuff," he says, not even as a question.

He assumes, every time something's weighing on me, it must be angel stuff.

I wish I could tell him. But I can't. Not without knowing for sure.

I shake my head. "College stuff. I'm applying to Stanford, you know." This is true. Even though I think it's pretty farfetched, even though I can't drum up much enthusiasm for college, even Stanford, I've been applying.

Tucker's expression clears, like he suddenly understands everything perfectly. I'm upset because I am going to college and he's staying here.

"It'll be okay," he said. "We'll make it work, wherever you end up, okay?"

"Okay."

He hugs me again, his playful shoulder-squeeze hug. "Everything's going to be all right, Carrots. You'll see."

"How do you know so much?" I ask, only half playfully.

He shrugs. Suddenly he frowns, cocks his head slightly to one side.

"What is it?" I ask.

He holds up a hand to quiet me. Listens for a minute. Then he lets out a breath. "I thought I heard something, that's all."

"What?" I ask.

"A horse. I thought I heard a horse."

"Oh, Tuck," I say, hugging him tighter. "I'm sorry."

But then I think I hear something too. A rumbling kind

of noise. Maybe hoofbeats.

I listen for a few moments and still hear it, the steady rhythmic strike of something against the earth. Then the huff of air from a large moving animal, running, breathing heavy.

My eyes meet Tucker's. "I hear it too," I tell him.

We pop out of the swing, dash onto the front yard. I turn a slow circle in the yard, listening, as the sound gets closer.

"That way," I breathe, pointing toward the Tetons. Tucker starts running in that direction, leaps over a low fence. That's when Midas breaks the tree line, running hard, sweat gleaming along his flanks. Tucker sees him and gives this great, joyous whoop. Midas neighs. I stand there and watch as Tucker and Midas meet each other in the field near the house. Tucker throws his arms around Midas's shoulders, buries his face in the glossy neck. They stay that way for a long time, and then Tucker pulls away and starts moving his hands all over Midas's body, looking for injury.

"He's burned, real skinny, but nothing bad," he calls out. "Nothing we can't deal with." Then he says to the horse fondly, "I knew you'd make it. I knew that fire couldn't get you."

His parents and Wendy come out onto the porch, see Midas, and run down into the field with us to marvel over this crazy miracle. Wendy holds my hand tight as we all bring the horse back into the barn, back where he belongs.

"What once was lost, now is found," Mrs. Avery says.

"See, Carrots," Tucker says, stroking Midas's nose. "Things have a way of working out the way they're supposed to."

That's what I'm afraid of.

Sorrow descends on me again the next day. I'd almost forgotten how awful it feels, the way my throat closes up and my chest constricts and my eyes burn. This time I'm in the grocery store with Jeffrey, and the minute I tell him he goes all angel-blood ninja, paranoid and crouching down right there in the middle of the aisle between the yogurt and the cottage cheese while I call Mom again on my cell. I would have thought Jeffrey was funny if I hadn't been so freaked out by the prospect of getting killed by a Black Wing, only this time I assume I can't get killed. If I die here on aisle nine, I'll never make it to spring and the day at the cemetery.

So Samjeeza's not here to kill me, I think. But it's not really me I'm worried about. In spite of all my loony ideas about possible ways that Tucker might die, the one that strikes me as the most likely is that a Black Wing shows up and kills him. To get to me. To punish me, maybe, for turning my back on my purpose. To balance the scales. Or maybe simply because Black Wings are bad and they like to do bad things, such as do away with those the good people care about.

The idea terrifies me. But again the sorrow feeling is gone even before Mom gets there. Like it never happened. Like it's all in my head.

A few days later, at Angel Club, Jeffrey's showing us this trick he can do where he bends a quarter in half using only his fingers. Then of course we all have to try it, first me, and Jeffrey's none too pleased when I can bend the quarter too, then Angela, who tries so hard that her face turns purple and I think she's going to pass out, then Christian, who can't do it, either.

"Apparently not my thing," he says. "Pretty neat, though."

"It could be genetic," Angela theorizes. "Something that runs in the family with you and Jeff."

Jeffrey snorts. "Oh, yes. A quarter-bending gene."

I think, what good is it that I can bend quarters? What kind of useful skill is that? And suddenly I feel like I want to cry. For no good reason. Bam—tears.

"What's the matter?" Christian asks immediately.

"Sorrow," I croak.

We call my mom. Angela is super spazzing out this time because this is her home and it sucks for your home to not feel safe. My mom shows up ten minutes later, all out of breath. This time she doesn't look that worried. Just tired.

"Still feeling it?" she asks me.

"No." Which means I am feeling very stupid at this point.

"Maybe it's your empathy thing," Angela says to me as she walks me to the door of the theater. "Maybe you're picking up on people around you who are sad."

I guess that would make sense.

Mom, it turns out, has a different theory. I find this out later that night, when she comes into my room to say good night. It's still snowing, has been since the night of Midas's return, coming down in big flakes at a slant outside my window. It's going to be a cold night.

"Sorry I keep, you know, crying wolf," I say to Mom.

"It's all right," she says, but her expression is pinched, like I'm giving her new wrinkles.

"You don't really seem that alarmed," I point out. "Why is that?"

"I told you," she says. "I don't expect Sam to come after us so soon."

"I really feel sorrow, though. At least I think I do, when it happens. Doesn't that mean something?"

"It means something." She sighs. "But it might not be a Black Wing's sorrow you're feeling."

"You think it's somebody else's?"

"It could be yours," she says, looking at me with that quasi-disappointed look again.

For a second it feels like all the air is gone from the room. "Mine?"

"Black Wings feel sorrow because they are going against their design. The same thing happens to us."

I'm stunned. Seriously, I have no words.

"What Black Wings feel is much, much more intense," she

continues. "They have chosen to separate themselves from God, and that causes them an almost unbearable pain."

I can never go back. That's what Samjeeza kept thinking that day. *I can never go back.*

"With us it's a little more subtle, more sporadic," she says. "But it happens."

"So," I choke out after a minute, "you think I'm feeling flashes of sorrow because I didn't . . . fulfill my purpose?"

"What are you thinking about, when it happens?" she asks.

I should tell her about the dream. The cemetery. All of it. But the words stick in my throat.

"I don't know." That's true. I don't remember exactly what I was thinking about all those times, but I would hazard a guess that it involved Tucker and my dream and how I'm not going to let it happen.

Fighting my purpose.

Which means I'm going against my design.

The sorrow is mine.

7

GO TAKE A HIKE

The next morning there's two feet of snow on the ground. Our yard's a winter wonderland, covered neatly in a downy white blanket that makes everything seem muffled. That's the way it is in Wyoming, I've learned. One day it's autumn, red leaves spiraling down from the trees, squirrels running around frantically burying acorns, a tinge of smoke in the air from people's fireplaces. Then, like overnight, it's winter. White and soundless. Really freaking cold.

Mom's downstairs frying up bacon. She smiles when she sees me.

"Have a seat," she says. "I've just about got your breakfast whipped up."

"You're perky this morning," I observe, which I find odd considering our conversation last night.

"Why shouldn't I be? It's a beautiful day."

I step into the kitchen and discover Jeffrey sitting at the counter looking as half awake as I feel.

"She's gone crazy," he tells me matter-of-factly as I slide in next to him.

"I can see that."

"She says we're going camping today."

I swivel around to look at Mom, who's flipping pancakes, whistling, for crying out loud.

"Mom?" I venture. "Did you happen to notice the snow outside?"

"What's a little snow?" she replies, an extra twinkle in her twinkly blue eyes.

"Told you," Jeffrey says. "Crazy."

As soon as we're finished with breakfast, Mom turns to us like she's the director of a cruise ship, ready to get us started on our day.

"Clara, how about you tackle the dishes? Jeffrey, you load the car. I have some final things to do before we go. Pack for the weekend, both of you. Dress warm, but with layers, in case it warms up. I want to leave at about ten. We're going to be hiking for several hours."

"But Mom," I sputter. "I can't go camping this weekend."

She fixes me with a steady, no-nonsense look. "Why,

because you want to stay home and sneak over to Tucker's?"

"Busted," laughs Jeffrey.

I guess I wasn't being as quiet as I thought sneaking out of the house.

"I call shotgun," Jeffrey says, and that's that.

So by ten o'clock we're all showered and dressed and packed and bundled into the car, the heater on full blast. Mom passes me back a thermos of hot chocolate. She's still in this supernaturally good mood. She puts the car in four-wheel drive and turns the windshield wipers on to clear away the dusting of snow that's coming down, humming along with the radio as she drives into Jackson. Then she pulls up in front of the Pink Garter.

"Okay, Clara," she says with a mischievous smile. "You're up."

I'm confused.

"Go get Angela. Tell her to pack a bag for the weekend."

"Is she expecting me?" I ask. "Does she know that she's going on some loony camping trip in the snow?"

Mom's smile widens. "For once, Angela doesn't know anything about it. But she'll want to come, I have a feeling."

I go to the door of the theater and knock. Angela's mom answers. Her dark eyes go immediately past me to my mom, who's now out of the car and coming toward us. For a second, Anna Zerbino looks like she's going to pass out. Her face gets this strange, part-terrified, part-reverent expression, her hand involuntarily coming up to touch the gold cross dangling around her neck. Apparently Angela's enlightened her about my family being made up of angel-bloods, and in Anna Zerbino's experience, we're something to be feared and worshipped.

"Hi, Anna," my mom says in her nicest, sweetest, trust-me voice. "I wonder if I might borrow your daughter for a couple of days."

"This is about the angels," Anna whispers.

"Yes," answers my mom. "It's time."

Anna nods silently, clutching at the doorway like she suddenly needs it for support. I dart up the stairs to find Angela.

"I think my mom might be hypnotizing your mother, or something," I say as I push open the door to Angela's room. She's sprawled out on her stomach on her bed, writing in her black-and-white composition book. She's wearing a red Stanford hoodie and only a blind person wouldn't notice the huge Stanford banner she's tacked on the wall over her bed.

"Wow, go Cardinals," I comment.

"Oh hey, C," she says, surprised. She flips her notebook closed and tucks it under her pillow. "Were we supposed to hang out today?"

"Yep, it's written in the stars."

"Huh?"

"I've come to steal you away for a magical two days and

one night in the freezing-cold snowy wilderness. Courtesy of my mom."

Angela sits up. For a minute she looks like an exact replica of her mother, except for the golden eyes. "Your mom? What?"

"Like I said, she's taking us camping, and you're invited. We've got tents and sleeping bags and even those metal poles you roast hot dogs on."

"I don't understand," Angela says. Her gaze flits to the window. "It's snowing."

"So true. I don't understand either, believe me," I say. "So are you coming camping with us or not?"

In less than ten minutes she's packed a duffel and is seatbelted into the back of our SUV, looking like she's had a few too many cups of coffee, she's that jittery. To some extent, Angela is always this way around my mom. It has something to do with her never knowing any other angel-bloods before she met us. Certainly she's never had an adult angel-blood to look up to, just her quiet, broody, fully human mom with all her religious beliefs, who right now is standing on the boardwalk waving good-bye with tears in her eyes, like she's afraid she'll never see Angela again.

Mom rolls down the window. "It's all right, Anna. I'll bring her back to you safe and sound."

"Yeah, it's fine, Mom," Angela mutters, embarrassed. "I'll

be home Sunday night."

"Yes, okay," Anna says in a low voice. "You have a good time."

It's quiet on the drive into the mountains. Jeffrey turns the radio on, but Mom lowers the volume so we can barely hear it. Then we wind our way up a series of hairpin turns, the road narrowing to a single lane, one side cut against the sheer rocky face of the mountain, the other dropping to a ravine below. I wonder what would happen if we came upon somebody on the way down. Finally, after more than an hour, the road levels into a small turnout. Mom pulls over and parks.

"This is as far up as we go in the car. We'll have to hike from here." She gets out. We're met by a blast of absolutely freezing air as we open our doors to grab our packs from the back. We stand for a minute staring at the trailhead and the distant ridges of the mountain over the treetops.

"At least it stopped snowing," Jeffrey says.

Mom leads us into the fresh powder, followed by Jeffrey, then Angela and me walking side by side. The snow on the trail is halfway up our boots. We walk for a long time. The air seems to get thinner. The whole trip reminds me of the time Mom brought me to Buzzards Roost when I was fourteen, where she told me about the angel-bloods and flew out across the valley to prove that she was serious. I wonder what she's going to reveal to us this time.

After a couple of hours of monotonous trudging, Mom turns off the trail and toward a deeply wooded part of the forest. It's colder here, darker, in the shade of the towering pines. The snow is much deeper off the trail, sometimes almost to the knees. Within minutes I am chilled to the bone, shivering so violently that my hair pops loose from its ponytail. Beside me, Angela suddenly slips and falls, getting herself completely covered with snow. I reach down to help her up.

"Bet you're wishing you'd given this whole camping trip thing a bit more thought," I say through chattering teeth. Her nose and cheeks are bright pink, almost clownlike against her shock of black hair.

"We're supposed to have an immunity to cold," she says with her eyebrows drawn together, like she just can't figure out why it's not working.

From ahead of us, Mom barks with laughter.

"Sometimes, Angela," she says, not without affection, "you really are full of crap."

Angela's mouth opens in shock for a second, but then Mom keeps laughing, and it quickly spreads to the rest of us, even Angela.

"I read it in a book," she protests. "Seriously."

"It's when you use glory," Mom explains. "Glory keeps you warm. Otherwise, I'm reasonably certain you could freeze to death."

"Like now, for example," I chime in.

"Okay," says Angela sheepishly. "I'll have to write that down. Just as soon as I can make my hands work again."

"It's not much farther," Mom promises. "Hang in there."

Sure enough, after another ten minutes of miserable progress in the snow through the deep woods, Mom stops us. She lifts her head and smells the air, smiles in a kind of serene way, then tells Jeffrey to make a sharp right turn.

"There," she says, pointing to a narrow gulley a bit farther down the mountain. "We need to go through there."

Jeffrey leads the way, taking us down the slippery trail until he stops so suddenly that Mom almost crashes into him. His pack slips from his shoulder. Mom grins, a tired but triumphant gloaty expression, and steps aside to let Angela and me pass through so we can see what they're looking at. Then we stop too, our mouths dropping open, our own packs dropping to the ground.

"Holy . . . ," breathes Jeffrey.

Yep. That's the right word.

It's some sort of meadow, a vast, flat stretch of land surrounded on two sides by mountains, the third edge a beautiful shining lake that's clear enough that you can see the landscape reflected back perfectly. A few feet from where we're standing the snow disappears, becoming instead a long, soft grass, so green it almost hurts the eyes to look at it after so many hours of white on white. It's not snowing here. The sun is sinking behind the far mountain, and the sky is a riot of oranges and blues. Birds are winging their way back and forth across the meadow, like they too can't believe that they've stumbled into this paradise out here in the middle of nowhere.

But the meadow's not what we're looking at. What has the three of us (not Mom, of course, since she obviously knows all about this) gaping stupidly out into the sunshine is the fact that the meadow is crowded with tents. About two dozen people are bustling around, some building campfires, some fishing on the lake, some simply standing or sitting or lying down in the grass talking.

My eyes are drawn to one particular woman, mahogany-skinned with long, lustrous dark hair, a face like the Sacagawea golden dollar. And a pair of dazzling wings folded like a magnificent white robe against her back.

"This," Mom says, gesturing around the meadow, "is what's called a congregation. A gathering of angel-bloods."

"Congregarium celestial," breathes Angela.

The lady with the wings sees us and waves. Mom waves back.

"That's Billy," she says. "Come on." She removes her coat and the rest of her winter gear until she's only wearing a flannel shirt and jeans. Then she strides off barefoot into the grass. "Come on," she calls back to us again. "They'll be eager to meet you."

We leave our packs at the edge of the grass and move hesitantly into the meadow. Several people stop what they're doing to watch us.

"What is this?" Jeffrey asks beside me, still confused.

Mom's already reached Billy, who throws her arms around my mother like the two are old friends. Then they turn and start back toward us, and when she gets close enough this Billy woman hugs me too, a giant bear hug with surprising strength.

"Clara!" she exclaims. "I can't believe it. I haven't seen you since you were knee high to a grasshopper."

"Uh, hi," I reply stiffly against her hair, which smells like wildflowers and leather. "I don't remember. . . ."

"Oh, of course not," she says with a laugh. "You were tiny." She peers over my shoulder. "And this is Jeffrey. Good God above. Already a man."

Jeffrey doesn't say anything, but I can tell he's pleased by this announcement.

"Meet Wilma Fairweather," announces my mom as a formal introduction.

Wilma smirks at us. "Billy," she corrects.

"And this is Angela Zerbino," says my mom, not to overlook any of us.

Billy nods, looking at Angela so intently that Angela actually blushes. "The Pink Garter, am I right?"

"Yeah," says Angela.

"Welcome! Are you hungry?"

We glance around at each other. Food is the last thing on our minds.

"Of course you are," Billy says. "Why don't you go over there and get some grub?" She gestures off to one side of the meadow, where there's a plume of smoke coming up over what looks like a big stone barbecue grill. "Corbett makes the best burgers, I swear, enough to get me to eat meat a few times a year, anyway." She laughs again. "Go eat and then you can start setting up your tents. I want you all right by me." She links her arm with Mom's. "You finally got the guts to bring them, Mags. I'm proud of you. Although I guess this means—"

"Bill," Mom says with a warning in her voice, looking at me. Then she shakes it off and smiles at Billy. "We've got a million things to talk about, you and I." And with that, they walk away, leaving us staring after them.

We make our way over to the barbecue. When we get there we can see that it's being manned by a white-haired guy with a long ponytail wearing a Hawaiian-style flowered shirt, khaki shorts, and flip-flops. He's flipping meat on the grill like a professional.

"What'll it be, young'uns?" he calls back without bothering to turn around. "Cheeseburger or regular?"

"Cheese," answers Jeffrey, who can always be counted on

to think with his stomach. "I'll take two."

"Right-o," says the guy, and then he turns and squints at us. "What about you, Clara?"

It's Mr. Phibbs. My English teacher. Mr. Phibbs in flip-flops. My head is going to explode.

"A bit of a shock?" he says good-naturedly, taking in our expressions, as if it has only now occurred to him that we might be surprised to see him. "We decided that it was for the best if you didn't know."

"Who decided?" I can't help but ask.

"Your mother, mostly," he says. "But it was something we all agreed upon."

"You've known about us all this time?" Angela manages.

He snorts, which is the strangest sound ever coming from him. "But of course. That's why I'm there. You kids need someone to keep an eye on you."

He turns back to the grill, whistling. He serves us up two hamburgers each, which we balance on paper plates with potato chips and fruit salad like this is a Fourth of July picnic. We wander off dazedly to sit in the grass and eat. I discover that I'm ravenous. And the food is wonderful.

"Oh my God," Angela says, when she finally stops eating long enough to talk. "This is so cool. I would never have guessed there's a *group*. The congregation." She says the word like she's trying it out on her tongue, like it's a word with magic powers. "I want to talk to Billy again. She seemed fabulous. Holy geez," she exclaims, pointing across the meadow. "That's Jay Hooper, you know, who manages the rodeo arena in Jackson."

"Are all these people from Jackson?"

"Don't think so," she says. "A few, though. I can't believe that I've lived here for my *entire* life and I didn't know about this. I wonder if it's like this in every city, or if it's just Jackson. I have that theory that angel-bloods are attracted to the mountains, did I ever tell you? Whoa, that's Mary Thorton. Wow, I wouldn't have pinned her as the angelic type."

I stare at her blankly.

"I guess you never know," Angela says, still looking around. "Oh, and there's Walter Prescott. He owns the bank."

"Walter Prescott?" I whip around to see where she's looking. "Where?"

"The blond one, in front of that big green tent."

I locate him, a tall light-haired man building a fire. I wouldn't have guessed he was Christian's uncle, looking at him, mostly because his hair is that towheaded blond that almost looks white, nothing resembling Christian's dark messy waves.

"I wonder if we'll see Christian," says Angela.

In that moment I know he's here. I can feel him.

"There he is." Angela points to a group of people who are helping to guide a motorboat trailer into the lake. "Christian!"

she yells suddenly. She cups her hands around her mouth and belts it out. "Paging Christian Prescott!"

Mortifying, but effective. Christian turns at the sound of his name. Sees us. Then he's striding toward us through the grass, wearing rolled-up jeans and a T-shirt, no shoes, which seems to be the style here in the meadow. He seems relaxed, hands in his pocket, not in a particular hurry to get to us.

"Christian," someone yells from by the lake. "I thought we were going to water-ski?"

"Maybe later," he calls back, waving. He stops in front of us. "Hey, Clara. Angela." His gaze swings to Angela briefly before coming back to me. "Jeffrey here, too?"

I look around but can't see Jeffrey.

"Yep, we're all accounted for," says Angela. "The Angel Club has arrived. Isn't this crazy?"

"Right. Crazy. I guess." He shrugs.

"Don't tell me, this is old news for you. You knew about all of this before, didn't you?" Angela asks.

He grabs a potato chip off her plate and tosses it in his mouth, crunching it loudly.

Angela glares at him, then sniffs and stalks off across the grass toward Billy and Mom.

Christian raises an eyebrow at me. "What'd I do?"

"Dude," I say with a smile. "You are in so much trouble."

Later, after we watch the most spectacular sunset I've ever

witnessed that wasn't in a movie, Christian helps me set up the tent that Angela and I are supposed to share tonight. Angela, predictably, is nowhere to be found. She didn't even bother to retrieve her pack from the edge of the meadow. Christian and I lug both packs over to the campsite, pick out a space, and start pitching like crazy. We have to hurry because soon it will be too dark to set everything up, but it's no problem, really. Christian seems to have done this tent thing a hundred times before.

"So," I ask him as he's pounding in the tent pegs, the final step in the process. "How long have you known about this place?"

He shifts to work on another peg. "My uncle brought me up here last May. I was pretty surprised by the whole thing, too, believe me. Before that I had no idea."

"So you really were camping with your uncle," I muse, finally putting two and two together. "And here I thought . . ." I stop myself.

He stops hammering to look at me. "You thought what?"

"Oh, nothing. I thought it was an excuse so you could skip. Because of—"

"Kay," he finishes for me. "You thought I skipped school to dodge Kay."

"I guess so."

He starts hammering again. "Nope. But it was because of her, in a way. When I broke up with Kay, my uncle saw that as a sign that I was getting serious about my purpose. So he said it was time. He brought me up here, and we spent the week flying, training, meditating, all that, and then on the weekend the congregation showed up."

What made my mom decide it was time to bring us here? I wonder. "Did you see my mom?" I ask, because even though she hasn't been up front with the angel info, part of me still can't believe that she was involved with all of this and never told me.

"No. I heard some people mention a Maggie," he answers, "but I didn't know who she was."

"Oh." Suddenly I realize that I've pretty much been peppering him with questions for the past half hour, and he's done most of the work putting up the tent.

"You must think I'm an idiot," he says then.

I look up, startled. There are a lot of words I'd use to describe Christian Prescott: mystery, enigma, conundrum, destiny, terrifying, and, well, just plain hot, if I'm being honest, but the word *idiot* has never crossed my mind. Except maybe that one time at prom. "Idiot?"

"Because all the signs were there, pointing to you being the girl from my vision, you being an angel-blood, and I never figured it out. If I'd only figured it out sooner, maybe . . . ," he trails off.

I swallow. "What signs?"

"I always felt like there was something different about you, even the first time I saw you," he says.

"You mean when I passed out in the hall? I guess I must have seemed different, all right."

"I hadn't had my vision yet," he says. He sits back in the grass. "I thought I did something bad to you, and that's why you passed out."

"Something *bad* to me?"

"With my mind."

"Like your talking-in-my-head thing."

He starts picking at the grass, pulling on tufts and smoothing it between his fingers. "I didn't know how to control it yet," he says.

"Have you always been able to do that? Talk in people's heads?"

"It started last year, right before you showed up, actually. I still can't do it with everybody. I can pick up what people are thinking, and sometimes I can send thoughts back, but I think the person has to be able to receive them, too."

"So that day in the hall, you talked to me?"

"I tried to."

"What did you say?" I ask.

"I said . . . hello."

"And then I . . ."

"Then you dropped to the floor like I'd hit you over the head with a baseball bat."

I groan at what a graceful picture that must have been.

"Sorry," he says. "I didn't mean to."

"You didn't do anything, Christian. I passed out because, when I saw you, I had the vision. It was the first time I ever saw your face, and then the fire came, and everything was so intense, I blacked out."

"Oh," he says a bit sheepishly.

"I didn't figure things out, either, you know. So if you're an idiot, I guess that makes two of us."

He seems relieved to hear me say that. I guess idiots love company.

Then we both hammer the stakes, an awkward silence between us, until I blurt out, "What about the other signs?"

He smacks the last stake, sinking it into the ground, before resting back on his heels.

"Nothing much. The way you danced at prom," he says. "The way you talked about your future that night out on your porch, when I came to apologize about prom." He glances at me, then down at his bare feet, smiling. "Once I knew it was you, I sensed that I was supposed to do more than save you."

I try to react casually, but my heart starts to pound anyway. Because, deep down, I knew it too. And it may be the thing that confuses me most out of this whole situation.

What do you see in a guy like Christian Prescott? Tucker had asked me when he brought me home from prom, and I'd said I didn't know, because I couldn't explain it to him. I still can't explain it.

Tucker. I didn't even tell him I was coming here. Some

guardian I'm turning out to be. Some girlfriend.

"Okay," I say too loudly. "Uh, thank you, Christian, for setting up my tent." I start collecting the tools we used, acting busy, brushing grass from my pants that isn't really there. "I'm sure Angela would thank you, too, but I think you're going to be in her doghouse for a while. There are no secrets in Angel Club, remember?"

"I never agreed to that," he protests. "Besides, it's not like Angela's such an open book herself."

I wonder what he knows. But before I get a chance to ask him, someone calls his name, a man's voice floating over to us from the center of the meadow. We both turn.

"We should go over there," Christian says. "The fire's started." He jumps up, then holds out his hand to me.

"Come on," he says. "You'll like it."

I only hesitate for a moment before I put my hand in his, let him haul me to my feet, then quickly pull away and start walking toward where I can see the smoke billowing up from a large campfire people are building in the center of the meadow.

"Okay, bring on the fire," I say.

Christian jogs along next to me, grinning his slightly lopsided grin.

Don't you dare admire his smile, I tell myself.

I can't deny it, though. His hand in mine felt as familiar as my own.

8

SUMMER WITHOUT CRICKETS

I'm crammed shoulder to shoulder between Mom and Angela in the circle by the fire, looking around at the faces lit by its glow. Billy is spinning this tale about one time back in the thirties when she and my mom literally bumped into a Black Wing at the Santa Anita racetrack.

"It was Asael," Billy says. "In a three-piece dove-gray linen suit, if you can believe that."

"What did you do?" someone asks in a hushed voice, like this big baddie might be able to hear us.

"We couldn't exactly fly away, now could we?" Billy says with a wry smile. "There were so many people around. But then he couldn't confront us, either, not the way he would have wanted to. So we went back to our seats with our lemonade, and he went back to his, and after the race he was gone."

"We were lucky," Mom says.

"Yes, we were," agrees Billy. "Although I'll never for the life of me figure out what he was doing there."

"Betting on Seabiscuit, like everybody else," Mom says.

A few people laugh.

Billy sighs. "What a race that was. You can't find sport like that anymore. Things aren't the same now."

"You sound like little old ladies," says Jeffrey good-naturedly, though not about to let anybody knock his beloved sports. Then he does his old lady impression: "Back before the war . . ."

Billy laughs and reaches to ruffle his hair. He blushes. "We are old ladies, kid. Don't let our appearance fool you." She slings an arm around my mom and squeezes. "We're crones."

"If you could have flown—I mean, if there hadn't been so many other people around to see you—would it have made any difference?" pipes up Angela. "Can Black Wings fly?"

Everybody gets quiet, sobering fast, the only noise the crackling of the fire.

"What?" asks Angela, looking around. "It was only a question."

"No," answers my mom finally. "Black Wings don't fly."

"Unless they turn into birds," corrects Billy. "I've seen them do that."

"Black Wings don't have anywhere to go but down," says a man with red hair and a short, neatly trimmed beard. Stephen, I think I heard my mom call him. He has a deep voice, like one of those movie-trailer voices. The voice of doom.

I officially have goose bumps.

"But not literally down, right?" says Angela. "Because hell is a dimension underneath our own, so it's not some sort of bottomless fiery pit."

"Right," Mom says, which blows my mind. Why is she suddenly so free with information? I remind myself that this is a good thing, although my brain is already starting to overload with so much new stuff to take in.

"Plus hell is typically chilly. Nothing fiery about it. Lots of cold days in hell," says Billy.

"And how would you know that, Bill?" someone from across the fire teases.

"Mind your own business," Billy retorts with a grin.

"In all seriousness, though," says Stephen, since he's a serious kind of guy. "None of us has ever been to hell, so it's pure speculation about the temperature."

I dare a glance at Mom, who doesn't meet my eyes. So she hasn't told them about our fantastic trip to the underworld with Samjeeza, and if she hasn't told them, I'm certainly not going to.

"Why?" Angela never did know when to shut up. "Why haven't you been to hell?"

You'd think the answer to that would be, *Because we're not evil, thank you very much*, but instead Stephen says, "Because we can't pass between dimensions on our own. We need the Intangere to help us, and no angel-blood who's been taken to hell by a Black Wing has ever returned to tell us what it's like there."

Again I look at Mom. Again she looks away.

The campfire gives a sudden loud pop, which makes us all jump.

"Steve, you're scaring the children," Mom scolds.

"We're not children," Jeffrey says. "We want to know."

Billy nods. "Understandable," she says, casting a significant glance at Mom. "That's why you're here. To get answers."

I get a glimmer of what Mom's feeling. Resignation. But she's accepted that this is going to happen, even if it's so very dangerous for us. It makes her heart beat fast, but she sits there and tries to keep her breathing even.

I guess we really are going to get some answers.

"So you fight the Black Wings?" I ask. "Is that the point of the congregation?"

"No." Billy shakes her head. "We don't fight them, not physically speaking, at least not if we can help it. We'd lose, nine times out of ten, maybe ten times out of ten. Our best defense against Black Wings is to stay undetected. Which we've largely managed to do. Most of the people here have never even seen a Black Wing, let alone fought one."

"So what do you do, then?" Jeffrey asks, a tad belligerently, like he's disappointed not to be battling the fallen angels one-on-one. "If you don't fight them?"

"We track down angel-bloods," answers Mr. Phibbs. "Get to them before the other side does. Tell them about who and what they are. Help them."

"And we follow our purpose," Mom adds, finally looking at me. "That's how we do our part. We figure out what we're supposed to do and we do it."

Interesting.

I'm still not going to accept my purpose if it means that Tucker has to die.

Walter Prescott suddenly stands up on the other side of the fire. "Enough talk," he says. "I think it's time for s'mores. Who wants s'mores?"

I look across at Christian. He's holding a bag of marshmallows in one hand and a bag of chocolate bars in the other like some sort of peace offering. He smiles.

"I do," Jeffrey says.

Once again, ladies and gentlemen, my brother and his stomach.

Everyone settles into eating. Angela looks downtrodden that the Black Wing conversation is done, but in a few minutes she's over it, leaning forward again, listening to more stories with a glow in her golden eyes, big smile on her face. She's on cloud nine, basking in this sense of community she's never had before. Even Jeffrey likes it here. Earlier he played a game of soccer with some of the other angel-bloods, a real game where he didn't have to hold anything back. He's got this air about him of deep satisfaction, like that's all he ever wanted, just to play some serious sports and eat some good food and not have to be anything but what he is.

I should feel like that too, I guess, enjoying this thing. So why don't I?

Let's see, chimes the voice in my head, *well, you failed at your purpose. How many of the people here did that? And it looks like your boyfriend is destined to die. And your mom clearly doesn't trust you as far as she can throw you. And you don't know these people, but they're all looking at you like they know you.*

"So, Mr. Prescott," says Mr. Phibbs when we're all tapped out on s'mores, sticky with marshmallow and smeared with chocolate. I wonder if angel-bloods can have sugar comas.

"Me?" asks Christian. He has chocolate on his chin.

"Yes, you," says Mr. Phibbs. "You're our newest member, I hear."

"Yes, sir," says Christian, his face getting red.

You're a member? I think at him incredulously.

He blinks in surprise that I am talking to him via brain. That it could be that easy, between us, when it's so hard with everyone else. *Yes. As of this morning.*

And how does one become a member, exactly?

You make a promise to serve the light. To fight for the side of good.

I thought they said they didn't fight.

He gives me the mental equivalent of a shrug.

And that's what you did this morning?

Yes, he says unwaveringly. *I took an oath.*

And so the revelations keep on coming.

"How is any of this possible?" I ask Angela later, when we're both in our pj's, snuggled up in our sleeping bags. We zipped the top off the tent so we can look up and see the spattering of stars over our heads. The air is cooler than it was earlier, but still completely comfortable. We don't even need tents, at least not for the weather, although they do afford us some sense of privacy out here in the open meadow, where separate fires are spread all around us. Every now and then I catch the scent of snow on the wind, and it reminds me that we're in this magic oasis in the middle of the forest, that everywhere else it's winter, but here it's summer.

"Toto, I don't think we're in Kansas anymore," I say to Angela.

"I know, right?" Angela says with a laugh. "It's Billy."

"What do you mean?" I turn over onto my side to look at her.

"Billy can do things with the weather. I guess it's an extremely rare gift for an angel-blood. I'd never even heard of it before. Billy comes out here about a week before the meeting and makes it all grow."

"So Billy told you all this?"

"She told me some," Angela says. "Not as much as I wanted her to. She was nice to me and all, but she really just wanted to gab with your mom. They seem like best friends."

"They do," I agree. "It's so weird."

My mom has a best friend, someone I don't remember, someone I didn't even know about until today. I think about the way they sat together at the fire, with the same blanket wrapped around them, and how Billy would sometimes lean to whisper something in Mom's ear that made her smile.

How could she not tell me about her best friend?

"This is so awesome," Angela says. She turns to me with bright eyes. "Want to hear more about what I did learn?"

I can't help but giggle at the excited puppy-dog expression on her face. "You're like a kid in a candy store here, aren't you?"

"Oh come on, can you blame me? This is an amazing research opportunity."

Leave it to Angela to see this as a "research opportunity."

"Okay, let's hear it," I say.

She fishes her notebook out of her bag and turns on a flashlight, flips through the pages to find her place.

"Okay," she says, clearing her throat, "here's the skinny: the northwest branch of the congregation has been meeting here since just after Wyoming officially became a state back in 1890. Right now there are about forty members."

"So it's not all Jackson people?"

She shakes her head. "They're from all over the northwestern United States. But I did find out that Jackson is a kind of angel-blood hot spot, with the highest concentration of us living here than anywhere else in the area. I couldn't get anybody to tell me why though. I have a theory that it's the mountains, but that's just a theory."

"Okay, Miss Wikipedia," I tease.

She grins, swats at me feebly, and then returns to the notebook. "Most of the angel-bloods here are Quartarius. There are only nine Dimidius, and they're the leaders of the group."

"Right. Because the Dimidius are so rare and special," I say with a hefty dose of sarcasm.

Angela scoffs, but there's an excited glitter in her eyes. Here, where most of the people are a mere quarter angel, Angela is a half. She *is* rare, and special, and all that.

"I've also noticed that everybody treats your mom differently than the others," she adds. "Like at the campfire, everyone always listened carefully to what she said, like she's a font of wisdom or something, even though she didn't talk very often."

It's true. When Mom got up and said she was going to go to bed, everybody moved carefully out of her way as she passed. There was something about the way they responded to her, a particular kind of reverence.

"Maybe she's their leader," Angela says. "I think it's a democracy here, but maybe she's like the president."

Man. How could she not tell me any of this?

"Are you okay?" Angela asks. "You look like you're freaking out again."

"Yeah, well. This isn't exactly a place I expected to be when I woke up this morning, you know?"

"I know. I can't believe Christian knew all about this, and he never told us," she says, still peeved.

"Oh, lay off Christian. It's not like you're such an open book yourself," I snap, using Christian's words. "Hypocritical much?"

Angela sucks in a breath. Her jaw tightens. Then she tosses her long pigtails over her shoulders, snaps her journal closed, and lies down, putting her back to me. Off goes the flashlight. We lie there in the dark, stars overhead, the whispering of trees. It's way too quiet. Angela doesn't say anything, but I can tell that she's not asleep. Her breaths are shaky, and I know she's mad.

"Ange . . . ," I say when the silence grows unbearable. "You're right, I'm sorry. I get so sick of it, too, all the secrets. Sometimes I feel like nobody in my life is completely straight with me, ever. It really ticks me off."

"No, you're right," she says after a minute, her voice muffled by the sleeping bag. "Christian never promised he'd tell us anything. This place is classified, I get that."

"Did you just say I'm right?" I say as solemnly as I can

manage.

"Yeah. So?"

"Nothing. I just wanted to write it down or something. In case I never hear you say that again."

She turns slightly and shoots a grin over her shoulder. "Yeah, you should do that, since you're unlikely to be right ever again."

Fight officially over. Which is a relief, because Angela can be a royal pain in the behind when she's angry.

"The secrecy is part of being an angel-blood," she says right as I'm starting to fall asleep. "You know that, right?"

"What?" I say groggily.

"We always have to hide ourselves. From the Black Wings, from the rest of the world. Take your mom, for instance. She's over a hundred, but she looks like she's forty, which means all her life she's had to keep moving so that people wouldn't notice that she didn't age naturally. She always has to have a secret identity. After that long, the secrecy would become second nature, don't you think?"

"But I'm her daughter. She can trust me. She should tell me about these things."

"Maybe she can't."

I think about this for a minute, remember the fear I sensed from her earlier at the campfire. Fear of what? I wonder. What's so scary about us talking about hell? Besides the obvious, that is. And why hasn't she told the congregation about what happened with Samjeeza?

"Do you really think she's the leader of the congregation?" I ask.

"I think it's highly possible," Angela says.

Then I realize something else: my mom knows Walter Prescott, Christian's uncle. Which means that she probably knew from the day I came home and said his name that Christian was more than just a boy I had to rescue from a forest fire. All that time, she knew that Christian was an angel-blood. She knew that my purpose was more than a simple search and rescue.

She knew.

"Why didn't she tell me?" I whisper. Suddenly I don't feel so bad that I never told her about Angel Club.

"Just catching up now, are we?" Angela whispers back.

"I guess."

"She could have a good reason," Angela says.

"She'd better have a good reason," I say.

It's a long time before I fall asleep.

I dream of roses, white roses, the edges already starting to brown. I'm standing in front of a mound of freshly turned earth, staring down at Mom's nice black pumps on my feet, and I'm holding roses. Their sweet scent fills my nose. I can sense the presence of other people around me, but I don't look up from the dirt. This time, I don't feel grief so much as I feel hollow inside. Numb. The wind stirs my hair, blows it across my face, but I don't brush it back. I stand there, holding the roses, staring at the grave.

Death is a transition, I try to tell myself, a passing from one plane of existence to another. It's not the end of the world.

That's what Mom has always told me. But I guess that depends on how you define the end of the world.

The roses are wilty. They need water, and suddenly I can't stand the thought of leaving them to dry up and die. So I crush them between my hands. I tear off their heads and then I let the petals sift through my fingers, falling oh so slowly, gently, onto the dark soil.

Christian is standing by the lake in the moonlight. I watch him bend to pick up a rock, turning the smooth stone in his hand a few times before he leans and skips it across the water.

Every time I see him I'm struck by the fact that I don't actually know him. In spite of all the conversations we've had, the time we've spent in Angel Club together, the way I memorized practically every detail about him last year like some obsessed little Mary Sue, he's still a mystery to me. He's still that stranger who I only get glimpses of.

He turns and looks at me.

"Hi," I say awkwardly, suddenly aware that I'm in my jammies and my hair must look like a bird's nest. "Sorry. I didn't know anybody would be out here."

"Can't sleep?" he asks.

The smell of roses lingers in my nose. My hands still feel pricked by the thorns, but when I inspect them, they're fine. It's all in my head. I am driving myself loony tunes.

"Angela snores," I say, instead of trying to explain myself. I bend down to look for my own skipping rock, find one—a small flat stone the color of charcoal. I stare out at the lake, where the moon is rippling. "So how do you do this?" I ask.

"The trick is in the wrist," he says. "Kind of like Frisbee."

I toss the rock and it goes straight into the water without even a splash.

"I meant to do that," I say.

He nods. "Sure. Perfect form, by the way."

"There's something off about this weather," I say.

"You think?"

"No, I mean, something missing. It feels like summer except—" I think back to all my late nights with Tucker last summer, gazing up at the stars from the back of his pickup, naming the constellations and making up the ones we didn't know. The thought of Tucker makes my throat get tight. I remind myself that my dream doesn't happen until spring. I don't even know if it's *this* spring. I have time. I'll figure this out. Stop it, somehow.

"Crickets," I say as it occurs to me. "In the summer, there are always crickets chirping. But here it's quiet."

We listen to the sound of the water lapping at the shore.

"Tell me about your vision, Clara. The new one, I mean," Christian says then. "If you don't mind, I'd like to know, officially. Because you're thinking about it pretty much nonstop, and I'm not doing a very good job at not noticing."

My breath catches. "I already told you most of it. It's Aspen Hill. Springtime. I'm walking up the hill with all these people, apparently headed for a grave. And you're there."

"What do I do?"

"You . . . uh . . . you try to comfort me. In my head you say, 'You can do this.' You hold my hand." I start searching around for another rock so I won't have to meet his eyes.

"You think it's Tucker who's going to die," he says.

I nod, still not daring to look over at him. "I can't let that happen."

He coughs, then does his laugh/exhale thing. "I guess I shouldn't be surprised that you've decided to fight your vision."

This should be the part where I feel sorrow, if Mom is right. I'm definitely fighting my purpose, pushing back against all that I think is expected of me. But all I feel in this moment is anger. Even though I suppose it's true; I can never accept things. I can never let them be what they are. I'm always trying to change them.

"Hey, you asked me, and I told you. You don't like it, tough beans." I start to storm off back toward my tent. He catches my hand.

I really wish he would stop touching me.

"Don't get mad, Clara. I want to help," he says.

"How about you mind your own business?"

He laughs, lets go of my hand. "Okay, too late to tell you not to get mad. But I mean it. Tell me why you think it's Tucker's funeral."

I stare at him. "You don't believe me? That's not exactly helpful."

"I didn't say that. It's just—" He's tongue-tied in a way I've never seen. "Well, I thought my vision was showing me one thing, and then it turned out totally different."

"Right, because I blew it for you," I say.

"You didn't blow it." He catches my eye. "I think you changed it. But what I'm saying is that I didn't really understand it before. I couldn't."

"And you understand it now?"

His gaze breaks away. "I didn't say *that*." He picks up a rock and skips it perfectly across the water. "I want to make sure you know that I don't think you ruined anything, Clara. It's not your fault."

"How do you figure that?"

"You followed your heart. That's nothing to be ashamed of."

"You actually mean it." I'm stunned. I'd always assumed he'd blame me.

"Yes," he says with a ghost of a smile. "I actually do."

9

PARADISE LOST

"Farewell, happy fields, / where joy for ever dwells! hail, horrors! Hail, / infernal world! and thou, profoundest hell / receive thy new possessor! one who brings / a mind not to be changed by place or time," reads Kay Patterson. She has a nice reading voice, I'll give her that, even though I suspect that underneath her polished exterior beats a heart of pure evil.

Okay, so not pure evil. Because Christian liked her, and Christian's not an idiot. Even Wendy says that Kay's not so bad when you get to know her. So there must be something I'm not seeing.

"The mind is its own place, and in itself / can make a heaven of hell, a hell of heaven," she continues.

"Good, Kay," Mr. Phibbs says. "So what do you think it means?"

Kay's immaculately tweezed eyebrows squeeze together. "Means?"

"What is Satan saying here? What's he talking about?"

She looks at him with clear annoyance. "I don't know. I don't speak old English, or whatever this is."

I'd mock, but I'm not doing much better. Or any better, truthfully, when it comes to this book. Which doesn't make sense. I'm supposed to be able to speak and understand any language ever spoken on earth, so why am I so lost on *Paradise Lost*?

"Anyone?" Mr. Phibbs looks around the room.

Wendy raises her hand. "I think maybe he's talking about how terrible hell is, but for him, it's better than heaven, because at least in hell he gets to be free. It's that 'better to reign in hell than serve in heaven' idea."

Creepy. I always get squirmy every time the topic of angels comes up in any regular-person conversation, and now that's happening in English class. I'm sure my mother would not approve this reading material.

But then again, she probably already knows all about it. Since she knows everything. And tells me nothing.

"Excellent, Wendy," praises Mr. Phibbs, "I can see you've read the CliffsNotes."

Wendy turns a lovely shade of crimson.

"No harm in reading the CliffsNotes, dear," Mr. Phibbs says jovially. "It's good to get someone else's interpretation. But it's more important that you wrestle with these texts on your own. Feel the words with your gut, not just hear them in your head. *But O, how fallen! how changed / from him, who, in the happy realms of light, / clothed with transcendent brightness, didst outshine / myriads though bright,*" he recites from memory. "Beautiful words. But what do they mean?"

"He's talking about the angel he used to be," says Angela from up front. She hasn't said a word during this entire conversation, neither of us have, but now it's obviously getting to be too much for her to sit here and be quiet when he's talking about angels. "He's lamenting how far he's fallen, because even though he'd rather make the rules in hell than obey God in heaven, like he said, he still feels sorrow, because now he's"—she glances down at her book to read—"*in utter darkness, . . . / as far removed from God and light of heaven, / as from the center thrice to the utmost pole*. I'm not sure how far that is, exactly, but it sounds like pretty far."

"Did you feel that in your gut?"

"Uh . . ." Angela's a brain person, not a gut person. "I'm not sure."

"Well, an insightful interpretation, anyway," he says. "Remember what Milton tells us at the beginning of the book. His goal here is to explore the idea of disobedience to God, both in the rebellion of the fallen angels and in the heart of man, which leads to the fall of Adam and Eve in the Garden of Eden. . . ."

I shift uncomfortably in my seat. I don't want to explore the idea of disobedience to God—not exactly a gut-friendly topic of conversation for me right now, since I've pretty much made up my mind to fight my purpose.

"Mr. Phibbs, I have a question," Angela says then.

"Wonderful," he says. "Judge a man by his questions rather than his answers."

"Right. How old are you?" she asks.

He laughs.

"No seriously. How old?" she presses.

"That's not at all related to the subject at hand," he says crisply, and I can tell that she's rattled him, although I'm not sure why. He smooths back his white hair, fiddles with the piece of chalk in his hand. "Now shall we get back to Satan and his plight?"

"I just wanted to know if you're as old as Milton," Angela says, acting playfully, nauseatingly dumb, like she's teasing him, like it's not a serious question, even though it is. "Like, did the two of you ever hang out together?"

Milton, if I remember what Mr. Phibbs told us last week, died in 1674. If Mr. Phibbs ever hung out with Milton that would put him well over three hundred and fifty years old.

Is it possible? I look at him, noting the way his skin sags in places, the host of deep wrinkles on his forehead, around his eyes, circling his mouth. His hands have that gnarly tree quality to them. He's clearly old. But how old?

"I only wish I could have had that pleasure," Mr. Phibbs says with a tragic sigh. "But alas, Milton was a bit before my time."

The bell rings.

"Ah," he says, his blue eyes sharp on Angela's face. "Saved by the bell."

That night I sneak out to fly to the Lazy Dog. I can't help it. Maybe it's my angelic nature. I sit outside Tucker's window with snow in my hair, and I watch him, first as he works on his homework, then getting ready for bed (and no, I turn away when he's changing, I'm not a total perv), and then as he falls asleep.

At least, right this minute, he's safe.

Again I consider telling him about my dream—I hate keeping this from him. It feels like something he deserves to know. I'm so angry with Mom, I realize, for all the secrets she keeps from me, but am I any different? I'm keeping this secret to avoid alarming him needlessly if by some stroke of luck I'm reading my vision wrong. I'm holding back because his knowing about it won't change it. I'm protecting him.

But it still sucks.

Around twelve thirty or so, his window suddenly jerks open. I'm so startled—I'd been half asleep—that I almost fall off the roof, but a strong arm grabs me and hauls me back over the edge.

"Hi there," Tucker says brightly, like we're bumping into each other on the street.

"Uh, hi."

"Nice night for stalking," he observes.

"No. I was—"

"Get your butt in here, Carrots."

I climb awkwardly into his room. He puts on a T-shirt and sits cross-legged on the bed, looking at me.

"It's not stalking if you're happy to see me?" I suggest tremulously.

"How long have you been out there?"

"How long have you known I was there?"

"About an hour," he says. He shakes his head in disbelief. "You're a crazy girl, you know that?"

"I'm starting to figure that out about myself."

"So why are you really here?" He pats the spot on the bed next to him, and I sit. He slings an arm around me.

"I wanted to see you," I say as I curl into his side. "It was a long and lonely weekend and I didn't get to see you much at school today."

"Oh, right. How was camping? I don't think I've ever been camping in the snow," he says, raising his eyebrows. "Sounds chilly."

"It wasn't exactly in the snow." Then I tell him about

the congregation. Not everything, exactly, not about hell or the Black Wings or Mr. Phibbs as an angel-blood, but I tell him most of it. I know my mom wouldn't approve. Christian wouldn't approve. Of course Angela wouldn't approve. The congregation is confidential, she said, like I should take this entire weekend and put a big old CONFIDENTIAL stamp across it.

I tell him anyway. Because I'm not ready to set up my own secret identity just yet, not from Tucker. Because the one thing I know for sure is that I love him. Because if I'm honest about one thing it makes me feel slightly better about not telling him about other things.

He takes the news of the congregation pretty well.

"Sounds like church camp," he says.

"More like a family reunion," I say.

He leans over and kisses me, a soft, featherlight kiss that only catches the side of my mouth, but still leaves me breathless.

"I missed you," he says.

"I missed you, too."

I curl my arms around his neck and kiss him, and everything goes away but this moment, his lips on mine, seeking, his hands in my hair, drawing me in, our bodies together on the bed, realigning to get closer, his fingers on the buttons of my shirt.

I can't let him die.

"You're so warm," he murmurs.

I feel warm. I feel like I could burst into flame, simultaneously light and heavy, and time is slowing down, like I am seeing everything frame by frame. Tucker's face hovering above my own, a tiny mole just below his ear that I never noticed before, the shadows we're making on the ceiling, the dimple appearing in his cheek as he smiles, the way his heartbeat is speeding up, his breath. And I can feel what he's feeling too, on the edges of my mind: love, the way he thrills to the feel of my skin under his hands, my smell filling his head—

"Clara," he says, breathing hard as he pulls away.

"It's okay," I say then, drawing his head down to mine again, pressing my cheek to his, our lips not quite touching, our breath on each other's faces. "I know you have your ideas about this, and I think that's sweet, but . . . what if this is all the happiness we get? What if this is our chance, before everything changes? What if this is it? Shouldn't we just . . . live?"

This time when we kiss, it's different. There's an urgency that wasn't there before. He pauses to pull his shirt over his head, revealing all that golden brown skin, his rodeo/farm/work hard-physical-labor-all-his-life muscles. He's beautiful, I think, so crazy beautiful it almost hurts to look at him, and I close my eyes and lift my arms over my head and let him take my shirt off too. The cool air hits my skin, and I shiver,

I quake, and Tucker runs his calloused fingertips gently along the top of my shoulder, strumming over my bra strap, across the line of my collarbone and up my neck, ending below my chin where he tips my head up to kiss me again.

This is really going to happen, I think. Me and Tucker. Right now.

My heart is beating so fast, skimming more than beating, like a hummingbird's wings in my chest, my breath coming in shudders like I'm cold, like I'm scared, but I'm neither. I love him. I love him, I love him—the words have a pulse of their own.

Suddenly he freezes.

"What?" I whisper.

"You're glowing." He sits up abruptly.

I am. It's very faint, not full glory by any stretch of the imagination, but as I spread my fingers and examine the back of my hand I see that my skin is very definitely glowing.

"No, your hair," he says.

My hair. I immediately grab at it with both hands. It's shining, all right, beaming. A sparkly shiny sunbeam in the dark of Tucker's room. I'm a human lamp.

Tucker isn't looking at me.

"It's nothing. Angela calls it *comae caelestis*. Sign of a heavenly being. It's why Mom made me dye my hair last year." I'm babbling now.

"Can you . . . turn it off?" he says. "I'm sorry, but when I look at it, I feel . . . dizzy, like I'm going to fall over or pass out or something." He takes a deep breath and closes his eyes. "Also a little nauseated."

Great to know I have that kind of effect on a guy.

"I can try," I say, and it turns out not to be too hard to shut it off. Just seeing the strained expression on Tucker's face does the trick.

I swear I hear Tucker breathe a sigh of relief.

"Sorry about that," I say again.

He looks at me, swallows hard, tries to regain his composure. "Don't be sorry. It's part of who you are. You shouldn't have to apologize for who you are. It's pretty, really. Awe inspiring. Fall down on your knees and worship, all that."

"But it makes you want to puke."

"Just a little."

I lean over to kiss his still adorably bare shoulder. "So. My light's out. Where were we?"

He shakes his head, scratches at the back of his neck the way he does when he's uncomfortable. Coughs.

I sit there awkwardly for a moment. "Okay," I say. "I guess I should . . ."

"Don't leave." He catches my hand before I can stand up. "Stay."

I let him draw me back down into the bed. He lies behind me, spoons me, rests his hand on my hip and breathes steadily onto the back of my neck. I try to relax. I listen to the ticking of the clock on his nightstand. What if I can never find a way to control the glow? What if every time I feel happy in that particular way, I light up? I'll light up, he'll get queasy, and then—*freakus interruptus*.

There's a bleak thought. It's like my own special form of birth control. The full body glow.

And then I think, He's going to die without ever having made love to a woman.

"It doesn't matter," Tucker whispers. He moves his hand up and takes mine, squeezes it.

Oh. My. God. Did I just say that aloud?

"What doesn't matter?" I ask.

"Whether or not we can . . . you know," he says. It's crazy that he can't read minds but still he knows almost exactly what I'm thinking. "I still love you."

"I still love you, too," I answer, then turn and snuggle my face into the side of his neck, wrap my arms around him, and that's where I stay until he falls asleep.

I wake up when somebody opens the curtains, and here's what I see: Mr. Avery, in overalls, with his back to me, looking out the window where the sun is just cresting the barn.

"Rise and shine, son," he says. "Cows won't milk themselves."

Then he turns. Sees me. His mouth falls open. My mouth

is already open, my breath lodged in the back of my throat, like if I don't breathe he somehow won't know I'm here. So we stare at each other like a couple of beached fish.

Outside a rooster crows.

Tucker mumbles something. Turns over, pulling the blanket off me.

I yank the blanket back up to cover my bra. Thank God I'm still wearing my jeans, otherwise it would look really bad.

It still looks really bad.

Really bad.

"Um," I say, but my brain is like a block of ice. I can't chip words out of it. I reach over and shake Tucker. Hard. Harder when he doesn't respond right away.

"It can't be six thirty already," he groans.

"Oh, I think it can," I manage.

Suddenly he jolts upright. Now all three of us are staring at each other like fish. Then Mr. Avery closes his mouth so quickly I hear the click of his teeth coming together, turns, and walks out of the room. He shuts the door firmly behind him. We listen to his footsteps march down the stairs, down the hall toward the kitchen. We hear Mrs. Avery say, "Oh good, here's your coffee, dear. . . ." Then nothing. He's not talking loudly enough for us to hear.

I grab my shirt and tug it over my head, hunt around for my shoes in a panic.

Tucker does something I've almost never heard him do. He swears.

"Do you want me to stay and try to explain?" I ask.

"No," he says. "Oh no, *no*, don't do that. You should just . . . go."

I open the window, turn back. "I'm sorry. I didn't mean to fall asleep."

"I'm not sorry." He swings his legs out of bed, stands up, and crosses over to me, gives me a quick but tender kiss on the mouth, holds my face in his hands, and looks into my eyes. "Okay? I'm not sorry. It was worth it. I'll take the heat."

"Okay."

"It's been nice knowing you, Clara," he says.

"Huh?" My brain is still a bit shell-shocked.

"Say a prayer for me, will you?" He gives me a shaky grin. "Because I'm pretty sure my parents are going to kill me."

When I get home it only gets worse. My bedroom window is locked.

Awesome.

I slip in the back door (thankfully not locked) and close the door gently behind me.

Mom works late nights. She sleeps in a lot, these days. There's a chance she didn't notice.

But my window's locked.

Jeffrey's drinking a glass of orange juice at the counter.

"Oh man," he says when he sees me. "You are so busted."

"What should I do?" I ask.

"You should have a really good excuse. And maybe you should cry—girls do that, right? And possibly be gravely injured. If she has to fix you, she might go easier on you."

"Thanks," I say. "You're so helpful."

"Oh, and Clara," he says as I'm tiptoeing upstairs, "you might want to turn your shirt so it's not on backward."

I'm amazed I make it all the way up to my room without being pulled over. I put on fresh clothes, wash my face, and comb out my hair, and I start thinking everything's going to be fine, no worries. But then I come out of the bathroom and see Mom sitting in my desk chair.

She looks like one pissed-off mama.

For a minute, a minute that feels like eternity, she doesn't say anything. She stares at me with her arms crossed over her chest.

"So," she says finally, her voice like drips of ice. "Tucker's mother called a few minutes ago. She asked me if I knew where my daughter was, because last time she checked you were in her son's bed."

"I'm so sorry," I stammer. "I went over to the Lazy Dog to see Tucker, and I fell asleep."

Her hands clench into fists. "Clara—" She stops herself, takes a deep breath. "I'm not going to do this," she says. "I can't."

"Nothing happened," I say.

She scoffs. Gives me a look that tells me not to insult her intelligence.

"Okay, something almost happened." Maybe if I go with the truth, she'll see it as a sign of good faith, I rationalize. "But nothing did. Happen, I mean. I fell asleep. That's it."

"Oh, that makes me feel so much better," she says sarcastically. "Something almost happened, but didn't. Great. Wonderful. I'm so relieved." She suddenly shakes her head. "I don't want to hear about last night. We're done with this, young lady. If I have to nail your window shut, you are staying here, in your own bed, in your own house, every night. Do you understand me?"

"Furthermore," she continues, when I don't answer, "you and Tucker are no longer to see each other on a one-on-one basis."

I whip around. "What?"

"You're not to be alone with him."

All my breath leaves me in a rush. "For how long?"

"I don't know. Until I figure out what to do with you. I think I'm being very generous with you, considering what you've done."

"What I've done? This isn't the year 1900, Mom."

"Believe me, I know," she says.

I try to meet her gaze. "Mom, I have to keep seeing Tucker."

She sighs. "Are you really going to make me say the my-house-my-rules thing?" she says in a weary voice, rubbing at her eyes like she doesn't have the time or the energy right now to deal with me.

My chin lifts. "Are you really going to make me move out just so I can do what I want with my own life? Because I will."

It's a bluff. I don't have anywhere to go, any money, any place to be but here.

"If that's what it takes," she says softly.

That does it. My eyes fill with humiliating tears. I know she has a right to be mad, but I don't care. I start screaming all the stuff I've been wanting to say for months: Why do you have to be this way? Why don't you care about Tucker? Can't you see how good we are together? Okay, so you don't care about Tucker, but don't you care about my happiness?

She lets me yell. I throw my tantrum while she looks down at the floor with an almost embarrassed expression and waits for me to finish. Then, after I'm done, she says, "I love you, Clara. And I do care about Tucker, as much as I know you won't believe that. I do care about your happiness. But I care about your safety first. That has always been my first priority."

"This isn't about my safety," I say bitterly. "This is about you getting to control my life. How am I not safe around Tucker? Seriously, how?"

"Because you're not the only thing out there in the night!"

she exclaims. "When I woke up and you weren't here. . . ." Her eyes close. Her jaw tightens. "You will stay in this house. And you will see Tucker, under supervision, when I think it's allowable for you to do so." She gets up to leave.

"But he's dying," I blurt out.

She stops, her hand on the doorknob. "What?"

"I've been having a dream—a vision, I think—of Aspen Hill Cemetery. It's a funeral. And Tucker's never there, Mom."

"Sweetie," Mom says. "Just because he's not there doesn't mean—"

"Nothing else makes sense," I say. "If it was someone else who died, Tucker would be there. He'd be there for me. Nothing could keep him away. That's who he is. He'd be there."

She makes a noise in the back of her throat and crosses over to me. I let her hug me, breathing in her perfume, trying to take comfort in her warmth, her solid, steady presence, but I can't. She doesn't seem that warm to me right now, or solid, or strong.

"I won't let it happen," I whisper. I pull away. "What I need to know is how I can stop it, only I don't know how it's going to happen so I don't know what to do. Tucker's going to die!"

"Yes, he is," she says matter-of-factly. "He's mortal, Clara. He will die. More than a hundred people on this earth die every minute, and someday he will be one of them."

"But it's Tucker, Mom."

I'm on the verge of tears again.

"You really love him," she muses.

"I really love him."

"And he loves you."

"He does. I know he does. I've felt it."

She takes my hand. "Then nothing can ever truly separate you, not even death. Love binds you," she says. "Clara . . . I need to tell you—"

But I can't let her talk me into placidly accepting Tucker's death. So I say, "Love didn't exactly bind you and Dad together, did it?"

She sighs.

I'm sorry I said it. I try to think of some way to make her understand. "What I mean is, sometimes people do get separated, Mom. For good. I don't want that to happen to me and Tucker."

"You stubborn, stubborn girl," she says under her breath. She gets up and goes to my door. Stops. Turns back toward me. "Have you told him?"

"What?"

"About the dream, or what you think it means," she says. "Because ultimately, you don't know what it means, Clara. It's not fair to put that on him unless you know for sure. It can be a terrible thing to know you're going to die."

"I thought you said that we're all going to die."

"Yes. Sooner or later," she says.

"No," I admit. "I haven't told him."

"Good. Don't." She tries to smile but doesn't quite manage it. "Have a good day at school. Be home before dinner. We have more to talk about. There's more I want to say."

"Fine."

After she goes I throw myself down on my bed, suddenly exhausted.

Sooner or later, she said. And she would know, I guess. At her age, most of the people she's known have grown old and died. Like the thing with the San Francisco earthquake. There was a news story she cut out of the paper a few months ago about how the last survivor of the earthquake had died. Which makes her the last true survivor.

She's right. Sooner or later Tucker is going to die.

Later, I think. I need to make sure it's later.

Angela catches me by the cafeteria door at lunchtime.

"Angel Club," she whispers. "Right after school, don't be late."

"Oh come on." I am so not in the mood for Angela's endless Q and A, her intensity, her wild theories. I'm tired. "I've got other stuff too, you know."

"We have a new development."

"How new? We just spent the weekend together."

"It's important, okay!" she screeches, which totally startles me. Angela's not a screecher. I look at her more closely. She looks worn out, dark and puffy around the eyes, frazzled.

"All right, I'll be there," I agree quickly. "I can't stay super late, but I'll definitely be there, okay?"

She nods. "Right after school," she says again, then walks quickly away.

"What's with her?" Christian materializes beside me and together we stare after her. "I told her I had a meeting for ski team, and she practically ripped my head off."

I shake my head, because I have no idea what's up with her.

"I guess it's important," he says. Then he's walking away too, joining his posse of popular people, heading out to lunch. I stand there for a minute feeling weird and lonely and finally move toward the lunch line. I get my lunch and flop down at my usual seat next to Wendy, who's sitting with Jason at the Invisibles table.

She gives me this piercing look. She knows about this morning.

Jason says he has to go check on something, and off he goes.

I'm in so much trouble. With everybody.

"Where's Tucker?" I ask immediately. "He's still, like, alive?"

"He had to go home and do some chores during lunch

hour. He wrote you a note." She holds out a single sheet of notebook paper. I snatch it out of her hand. "I didn't read it," she says quickly as I unfold it, but something in her voice makes me think she might have.

"Thanks," I say, my eyes scanning down the words. In his awkward script he's written, *Keep your chin up, Carrots. We'll get through this. We just have to follow the rules for a while,* and drawn an *X*—a kiss.

"Were your parents furious?" I ask, putting the note in the inside pocket of my jacket. I flash back to how Mr. Avery's eyes bulged when he saw us.

She shrugs. "Mostly they were shocked. I don't think they ever expected . . ." She coughs. "Okay. Heck yeah, they were mad. They kept saying the word *disappointed*, and Tucker looked like a dog getting kicked every time he heard it, and then when he seemed sufficiently whipped they sent him out to muck the barn so they could deliberate on a punishment."

"And what's the punishment?" I ask.

"I don't know," she says. "Let's just say my parents are not your biggest fans right now, and things were tense at the Averys' this morning."

"I'm sorry, Wen," I say, and I mean it. "I guess I made a mess of things."

She puts a hand on my shoulder, squeezes briefly. "It's okay. It's relationship drama. We all have relationship drama, right? You just happen to have a relationship with my brother.

I guess I should have seen that coming.

"I have to mention one thing, though," she adds good-naturedly, after a minute. "If you hurt my brother, you're going to have to deal with me. I will bury you in horse manure."

"Right," I say quickly, "I'll remember that."

"So, what's the big emergency?" Jeffrey says. He jogs down the aisle of the Pink Garter toward where Christian and I are sitting, waiting for Angela, who is uncharacteristically late. "I thought we weren't going to meet this week because we like, you know, spent all weekend together. I'm kind of sick of you people."

"Glad to see that you decided to grace us with your presence, anyway," Christian says.

"Well, I couldn't miss it," he says. "You do know this whole club rotates around me, right? I move that we change the name to the Jeffrey Club." He grins as he reaches the table. On pure sisterly instinct I stick out my foot like I'm going to trip him, and he scoffs, steps over my leg and shoves my shoulder.

"How about the doody-head club?" I suggest.

He snorts. "Doody-head." That was our highest form of insult when we were kids.

We tussle around for a second, trying to give each other noogies. "Ow," I say, when he accidentally bends my wrist backward. "When did you get so freaking strong?"

He steps back and grins. It feels weirdly good, roughhousing with Jeffrey. He's been almost his normal old self since we came back from the congregation, like he has finally given himself permission to move on from whatever it was weighing him down before.

Christian is staring at us. He's an only child and could never understand the delicate joys of sibling abuse. I give Jeffrey one last push for good measure and take my seat at the table. Jeffrey plunks down on the chair opposite me.

Angela comes in from the back. Sits down without a word. Opens her notebook.

"So. Emergency," I say.

She takes a deep breath. "I've been looking into the life span of angel-bloods," she says.

"Does this have anything to do with you asking Mr. Phibbs how old he is?" I venture.

"Yes. After seeing the congregation last weekend, I was curious. Mr. Phibbs is a Quartarius, I'm pretty sure, but he looks a lot older than your mom, who's a Dimidius. So you can see why I was confused."

I don't see.

"Either Mr. Phibbs must be a lot older than your mother," she goes on to explain, "or your mom must age at a different rate than Mr. Phibbs does. Which made me think, what if Quartarius, who are only a quarter-angel—seventy-five percent human—age at like seventy-five percent the rate that humans do? Humans don't live much past one hundred, typically, so a Quartarius angel-blood might live to be a hundred and twenty-five. Which would account for Mr. Phibbs looking old."

She stops. Drums her pen against her notebook. Looks worried.

"Go on," I say.

Another deep breath. She doesn't look at me, which is really starting to freak me out. "I thought Dimidius, who are only half human, might live at least twice as long, somewhere between two hundred and two hundred and fifty years. So your mom would be a middle-aged angel-blood. She'd look like she was forty. Which she does."

"Sounds like you have it all figured out," says Christian.

She swallows. "I thought I did," she says in an oddly flat voice. "But then I read this."

She flips a few pages in her notebook, then begins to read. *"When men began to increase in number on the earth and daughters were born to them, the sons of God*—that's angels; at least it's largely interpreted as angels—*saw that the daughters of men were beautiful, and they married any of them they chose."*

I know this passage. It's the Bible. Genesis 6. Enter the Nephilim: angel-bloods.

But Angela keeps reading: *"The Lord said, 'My Spirit will not remain in man forever, for he is mortal, his days will be a hundred and twenty years.* Then it goes back to talking about the Nephilim, when 'the sons of God went to the daughters of men and had children by them' and all the 'heroes of old' stuff, and it occurred to me that something's weird here. First we're talking about the Nephilim, then God sets a limit on the life span of man, then we go back to talking about the Nephilim. But then I realized. It's not a limit on the life span of man. That part in the middle isn't about man. It's about us. God wants us to be mortal."

"God wants us to be mortal," I repeat cluelessly.

"It doesn't matter whether or not we're capable of living for hundreds of years. We don't live more than a hundred and twenty years," concludes Angela. "I researched it all last night, and I can't find a record of a single angel-blood, Dimidius or Quartarius, who's lived longer. Every single one I've been able to find a paper trail on dies either before or during their hundred and twentieth year, but nobody ever makes it to one hundred and twenty-one."

Suddenly Jeffrey makes a choking sound in the back of his throat. He jumps up. "You're full of crap, Angela." His face contorts into an expression I've never seen on him before, wild and desperate, full of rage. It scares me.

"Jeffrey—" Angela begins.

"It's not true," he says, almost like he's threatening her. "How can it be? She's completely healthy."

"Okay," I say slowly. "Let's all calm down. So we get a

hundred and twenty years. No biggie, right?"

"Clara," whispers Christian, and I feel something like pity from him, and then it all hits home.

I'm so stupid. How could I be so stupid? Here I am thinking it's fine, a hundred and twenty years is fine, because at least we get to stay young and strong. Like Mom. Mom, who doesn't look a day over forty. Mom, who was born in 1890. Margaret and Meg and Marge and Margot and Megan and all those strangers, those past lives she got to live. And Maggie, my mother, who turned a hundred and twenty a few weeks ago.

I feel dizzy.

Jeffrey punches the wall. His fist goes right through like it's made of cardboard, spilling plaster everywhere, his blow strong enough that the whole building seems to shudder.

Mom.

"I have to go," I say, standing up so fast that I knock over my chair. I don't even stop to pick up my backpack. I just run for the exit.

"Clara!" Angela calls from behind me. "Jeffrey . . . wait!"

"Let them go," I hear Christian say as I reach the door. "They need to go home."

I don't remember the drive back to my house. I'm just here, suddenly parked in the driveway, hands clenched on the steering wheel so hard that my knuckles are white. In the rearview mirror I see Jeffrey's truck parked behind me. And now that I'm here, now that I've probably broken a dozen traffic laws to get here as fast as I possibly could, some part of me wants to drive away. I don't want to go inside. But I have to. I have to know the truth.

Angela's been wrong before, I think, although right now I can't remember when. She's been wrong. She's full of crap.

But she's not wrong.

It's not Tucker's funeral, in my dream of Aspen Hill Cemetery. It's Mom's.

I feel like I've been on the teacups at Disneyland, all vertigo, my head spinning even when the rest of me is holding still. My emotions are a jumbled cocktail of relief about Tucker, mixed with shock and crazy hurt, guilt and a whole different level of grief and confusion. I could throw up. I could fall down. I could cry.

I get out of the car and walk slowly up the steps to the house. Jeffrey falls in behind me as I open the front door and move through the entryway, past the living room and the kitchen and straight down the hall to Mom's office. The door's open a crack, and I see her reading something on her computer, her face the picture of concentration as she stares at the screen.

An odd calm comes over me. I knock, a gentle rap of knuckles on the wood. She turns and glances up.

"Hi, sweetie," she says. "I'm glad you're home. We really

do need to talk about—"

"Angel-bloods only live a hundred and twenty years?" I blurt out.

Her smile fades. She looks from me to Jeffrey standing behind me. Then she turns back to her computer and shuts it down.

"Angela?" she asks.

"Who cares how we know?" I say, and my voice sounds sharp in my ears, shrill. "Is it true?"

"Come in here," she says. "Sit down."

I sit on one of her comfy leather chairs. She turns to Jeffrey, who folds his arms over his broad chest and holds his ground in the doorway.

"So you're dying," he says in a total monotone.

"Yes."

His face goes slack with dismay, his arms dropping to his sides. I think he expected her to deny it. "What, you're going to die just because God decided that we shouldn't live too long?"

"It's more complicated than that," she says. "But essentially, that's the gist."

"But it's not fair. You're still young."

"Jeffrey," Mom says. "Please sit down."

He sits in the chair next to mine and now she can turn and address us both. I watch her face as she tries to collect her thoughts.

"How does it happen?" I ask.

"I'm not sure. It varies for all of us. But I've been getting progressively weaker since last winter. Markedly so these past few weeks."

The headaches she keeps having. The fatigue she blamed on work problems. The coldness in her hands and feet, the way her normal warmth seemed to leave her. The new wrinkles. The shadows under her eyes. The way she's always sitting down these days, always resting. I can't believe I didn't put it all together before.

"So you're getting weaker," I say. "And then what, you'll just fade away?"

"My spirit will leave this body."

"When?" Jeffrey asks.

She gives us that sad, thoughtful look I'm so familiar with by now. "I don't know."

"Spring," I say, because that's one thing I do know. My dream has shown me.

Something hot and heavy starts to rise up in my chest, so powerful it roars in my ears, squeezes the air out of my lungs. I gasp for breath. "When were you planning to tell us?"

Her midnight eyes flash with sympathy, which I find ironic, since she's the one who's dying. "You needed to focus on your purpose, not on me." She shakes her head. "And I suppose I was also being selfish. I didn't want to be dying yet. I was going to tell you today," she says with another weary sigh. "I tried to tell you this morning—"

"But there's something we can do," interrupts Jeffrey. "Some higher power we can appeal to, right?"

"No, honey," she answers gently.

"We can pray or something," he insists.

"We all die, even angel-bloods." She gets up and goes to kneel in front of Jeffrey's chair, putting her hands over his. "It's my turn now."

"But we need you," he chokes out. "What will happen to us?"

"I've given this a lot of thought," she says. "I think what's best for you might be to stay here, complete the school year. So I will transfer guardianship to Billy, who's agreed to take you. If that's all right with you."

"Not Dad?" Jeffrey asks with a quiver in his voice. "Does Dad even know?"

"Your father, he's not . . . He doesn't really have the resources to take care of you."

"He doesn't have the time, you mean," I add woodenly.

"You can't die, Mom," Jeffrey says. "You can't."

She hugs him. For a split second he resists, tries to pull away, but then he gives in, his shoulders shaking as she holds him, a terrible rough sob rumbling out of his chest. I hear that hurt-animal noise come out of my brother and part of me starts to split in half. But I don't cry. I want to be mad at her, accuse her of being a big fat liar my whole life, shout that she's abandoning us, maybe punch a hole in the wall myself, but I don't do that either. I remember what she told me this morning, about death. I thought she was talking about me and Tucker, but now I know she was talking about me and her.

I find myself sliding out of my chair, moving on my knees over to Jeffrey's chair. Mom pulls back and looks at me, her eyes shining with tears. She opens up the hug to let me in, and I snuggle against her, enveloped in a mix of her rose and vanilla perfume and Jeffrey's cologne. I can't feel anything—it's like I'm floating out of my body, somehow, disconnected. I still can't breathe.

"I love you both so much," she says against my hair. "You have made my life into something so extraordinary, you can't even know."

Jeffrey sobs. Big, macho Jeffrey, crying like his heart will break.

"We're going to make it through this together," Mom says fiercely, pulling back again to look into our faces. "We're going to be all right."

She's different at dinner. It's just her and me at the table, since Jeffrey has a wrestling match, and she insisted he go. She doesn't say much, but there's something lighter about her, something in the way she sits up so straight that makes me realize that lately she's been slumping, something in the way that she eats every last bite of her meal that makes me see that lately she's been picking at her food. She's acting so much stronger all of a sudden, like it hasn't been the sickness that's been weighing her down, but the secret. Now we know, and it's like that secret's been lifted off her, and momentarily she feels like herself again. It will not last. She knows it will not last. But she's determined to enjoy the moment of normalcy.

She puts her fork down with a sigh, then looks at me across the table and raises her eyebrows. It takes me a second to realize that I'm reading her emotions.

"Sorry," I mumble.

"Didn't feel like spaghetti?"

I glance down at my plate. I've hardly touched my food. "It's good. I'm just—"

You're dying, I think. How can I eat when I know you're dying and there's nothing we can do to stop it?

"Can I be excused?" I'm out of my chair before she has a chance to answer the question.

"Sure," she says with a bemused smile. "I'm going to go to Jeffrey's match in a bit. Do you want to come?"

I shake my head.

"We can talk later, if you want," she says.

"Can I say no? I mean, maybe sometime, but right now, I don't really want to talk. Is that okay?"

"Of course. This is going to take some time to get used to, for all of us."

I retreat to the quiet of my bedroom and lock the door. Will I ever get used to the idea that I'm going to lose my mother? It seems so ridiculous, such an impossible thing to happen, my mother, who's like Supermom, cheering at all Jeffrey's games, videotaping my dance recitals, whipping up cupcakes for the wrestling team bake sale, not to mention fending off Black Wings, able to literally leap (okay fly, but what's the diff?) over buildings in a single bound. And she's going to die. I know exactly what it will be like. We're going to put her body in a coffin. In the ground.

It's like a bad dream, and I can't wake up.

I reach for my phone. Dial Tucker's number automatically. Wendy answers.

"I need to talk to Tucker."

"Um, he's kind of lost his phone privileges."

"Wen, please," I say, and my voice breaks. "I need to talk to Tucker. Right now."

"Okay." She runs to get him. I hear her telling him that she thinks something's wrong with me.

"Hey, Carrots," he says when he picks up, "what's the matter?"

"It's my mom," I whisper. "It's my mom."

There's movement outside my window. Christian. I can feel his worry radiating like a heat lamp. He wants to tell me that he understands. He lost his mother too. I'm not alone.

But he's making up his mind not to say those things to me, because he knows that ultimately words are meaningless at times like these. He just wants to sit with me, for hours, if that's what I need. He would listen if I wanted to vent. He'd hug me.

It's something I didn't entirely expect from him. When I told Tucker he kept saying he was so sorry, over and over again, and I could tell he didn't know what else to say, how to react to news like this, so I told him I had to go and let him off the hook.

I get up and go to the window and stand for a minute looking at Christian, at his back, since he's turned away from me, perched in his usual spot on the eaves. He's wearing the black fleece jacket. I know this angle of him so well. He's here for me. It's like he's always been here, in some way or another.

A snowflake strikes the glass. Then another. Then it really starts to come down, big, heavy flakes, floating toward the house. Christian unzips the pocket of his jacket and pulls out a black knit hat and puts it on. He stuffs his hands into his pockets. And he waits.

I have the urge to call for him. In my mind I can see how it would play out. I'd open the window and say his name into the chilled air. I'd go to him. He'd turn. He'd try to say something but I'd stop him. I'd take his hand and lead him back through the window, back to my room, and then he'd take me in his arms. It'd be like my dream. He'd make it better. I could lean on him. It would be as easy, I think, as calling his name.

His back stiffens. Does he hear all these thoughts rattling around in my brain?

I back away from the window.

I tell myself that I don't want to feel better. There should be no happiness or comfort in all of this. I want to be devastated. So I turn away from Christian and slip into the bathroom to change into my pajamas. I ignore Christian's presence when I come out and he's still here. He must be freezing out there, but I push the thought out of my head. I lie down on my bed, my back to the window, and the tears finally arrive, running down my face, into my ears, onto my pillow. I lie there for a long time, for hours maybe, and right as I'm about to finally drift to sleep I think I hear the flutter of Christian's wings as he flies away.

10

THE ABSENCE OF CERTAINTY

I close my physics book, where I've tried unsuccessfully to solve the same problem about the Heisenberg principle three times this morning. So much for good grades, I think. Who cares about grades, anyway? At least I've already applied to my colleges, even caved to Angela and applied to Stanford, which I still think is a long shot, regardless of what Mom says.

Maybe I shouldn't even go to college. I mean, Jeffrey will turn sixteen about the time Mom dies, and even though he's agreed to this whole Billy-the-legal-guardian thing, he's going to need me here, too, right? I'm his only family.

I lie back on my bed and close my eyes. The days have

started to blur together. Weeks have passed since Mom confirmed her death sentence. I go to school like nothing has changed. I come home. I do my homework. I keep showering and I brush my teeth and I carry on. We've had a few Angel Club meetings, but it doesn't seem so important now. Jeffrey has stopped going altogether. I've stopped trying so hard to bring the glory, now that I understand that there's not a lot I can do. I can't save my mother. I can't do anything but trudge through my semblance of a life like a zombie. Tucker and I have gone on double dates with Wendy and Jason, and I try to pretend everything's fine, everything's normal. But it's like somebody has hit the pause button on my life.

My mom is dying. It's hard to think about anything else. Some part of me still doesn't believe it's true.

Something smacks my window. I open my eyes, startled. A clump of snow slides down the glass. It takes me a second to compute: somebody threw a snowball at my window.

I hurry over and open the window as a second snowball comes sailing through the air. I have to duck at the last second so I don't get beaned in the head.

"Hey!" I yell.

"Sorry." It's Christian, standing down in the yard. "I wasn't aiming for you."

"What are you doing?" I ask.

"Trying to get your attention."

I look past him toward the front of the house, where I see

his shiny black truck parked in the driveway. "What do you want?"

"I've come to get you out of the house."

"Why?"

"You've been holed up here all week, brooding," he says, squinting up at me. "You need to get out. You need to have some fun."

"And you've appointed yourself as the bringer of fun."

He smiles. "I have."

"So where are you taking me? Assuming, that is, that I'm crazy enough to go."

"The mountain, of course." The mountain. Like there's only one. But when he says that my heart automatically starts to beat faster.

Because I know exactly what he means.

"Dust off your gear," he says. "We're going skiing."

Okay, so I can't say no to skiing. It's my drug of choice. So that's how I find myself, about an hour later, perched on the chairlift next to Christian, sucking on a cherry Jolly Rancher, dangling over a snowy slope watching skiers weave lines down the hill. It's a rush being so high up, the cold air on my face and hearing the scrape of skis on snow. It's heavenly.

"There it is," says Christian, looking at me with something like admiration.

"There what is?"

"The smile. You always smile when you ski."

"How do you know?" I challenge, even though I know it's true.

"I watched you last year."

"Yeah, well, when you race you do this funny grimace thing with your mouth."

He makes a shocked face. "Do not."

"Do so. I watched you, too."

The wheels rattle when our chair crosses a tower, and a few skiers call to each other below. I turn away from his seeking green eyes. I remember last year, when it seemed like a magical turn of fate when I ended up on the chairlift with him, able to talk to him, really talk to him, for the very first time.

Now I don't want to talk.

He senses my withdrawal, or maybe he reads it.

"You can talk to me, Clara."

"Wouldn't it be easier for you to read my mind?"

His expression clouds. "I don't just scan your mind whenever I want, Clara."

"But you could."

He shrugs. "My power's unpredictable when it comes to you."

"It's amazing that anything in your life could be unpredictable," I say.

He looks away and knocks snow off his skis. We watch it

tumble down to the ground.

"Reading minds isn't all it's cracked up to be, you know. I mean, how would you like it, walking down the hall at school, knowing exactly what everyone thinks about you?"

"That would suck."

"But with you, it's different," he says. "It's like, sometimes you just talk to me, even if you don't know you're doing it. I don't know how to block that out. I don't really want to."

"Well, it's not fair. I don't ever get to know what you're thinking. You're Mr. Mysterious who knows more about everything than I do, but you don't tell me."

He watches my expression for a moment, then says, "Most of the time what you're thinking about, when it comes to me, is that you want me to go away."

I let out a breath. "Christian."

"If you want to know what's going on in my head, ask me," he says. "But I get the distinct impression that you don't want to know."

"Hey, I want to know everything," I protest, even though that's not completely true. Because I don't want to understand what our future would have been if I hadn't chosen Tucker. I don't want to feel what he always makes me feel: confused, scared, excited, guilty, yearning, aware of myself and everything I feel and he feels, like he has the power to magically switch on my empathy, even when it's true—I don't want to know. I don't want to need him.

"I want to know what my purpose was supposed to be, for crying out loud," I go on. "Why can't somebody just tell me: here's your purpose, so go do it? Would that be too much to ask? Or where my brother was that night in the woods? Or about Angela's secret boyfriend? I also want to know why a Black Wing is in love with my mother, and what her purpose was, and why she still, even when she's dying, won't tell me anything about it, and if you tell me it must be for my protection or my own good or something, I think I will push you off this chairlift. And is all this some kind of punishment for not fulfilling my purpose? Which brings me back to what, exactly, is my freaking purpose? Because I would really, *really* like to know."

Christian shakes his head. "Wow."

"I told you."

"So Angela has a secret boyfriend . . . ," he says.

"Oh crap, I shouldn't have told you that."

"No, you shouldn't have. Way to go," he adds with a laugh. "I won't tell. Although now I'm pretty curious."

I groan. "I'm so not good with secrets."

He glances over at me. "I don't think you're being punished."

"You don't?"

"Hey, I don't even know what *my* purpose is," he says, and then his voice softens. "But I do know that if you hadn't had your vision about the fire, you never would have come to

Wyoming. We wouldn't be sitting on this chairlift right now. If your mom had told you about the congregation earlier, you would have been at the last meeting, the one I went to, and we would have found out about each other before the fire. Everything would have been different. Right?"

Yes, it would have been different. We would have known that we weren't supposed to save each other. We would have known that our meeting in the forest was supposed to be something else. And where did that leave us? Would I have still flown off to save Tucker, knowing that?

"It feels like a test." I lean back in the chair and look up at the clouds. "Like it's all one long final examination, and now this vision with the cemetery, it's the next question. Although it doesn't seem like I'm supposed to do anything. At least, with my fire, I knew I was supposed to do something."

"What were you supposed to do?" he asks in an amused voice.

"Save you. Only I wasn't actually supposed to do that, was I?"

"That's the hardest part," he says. "The absence of certainty."

The phrase has a nice ring to it. It could be the motto of my life.

"So if it's a test, what do you think the answer is?" he asks.

You, I think, the answer is supposed to be you, but I don't say that. I guess I'm still fighting my purpose, even now that I know it's my mom dying and not Tucker. It still feels like I am being asked to choose between Christian and Tucker.

"No clue," I answer finally.

"Right. So," he says. "Is there something you want to ask me, specifically? I can't promise that I can give you a good answer, but I'll try."

I say the first thing that comes to mind. "Did you . . . love Kay?"

He looks away, toward the valley and the town below, knocks his skis together again, gently. Resents me for asking.

Sorry, I think at him.

"No, it's a fair question," he says. Sighs. "Yes. I loved her."

"Then why did you break up with her?"

"Because she was going to find out about me."

"You didn't tell her?"

He leans back in the chair too and exhales out his nose. "I've had it hammered into my head since Day One that we shouldn't tell humans. It's bad for both parties, my uncle says. And he's right—it's impossible to have a relationship with a human, a real relationship, anyway, without them noticing there's something off about you. Once they do, then what?"

Suddenly I think about my dad, how he moved to the other side of the country after he and Mom split, which in retrospect seems extreme, although it now occurs to me, maybe he found out she wasn't normal. Maybe that's why he abandoned us. Maybe Christian's uncle is right. Maybe any relationship with a human is doomed.

A corner of Christian's mouth turns up. "I guess we could pick really dumb people to be with."

"Kay's not dumb," I say. She might be a royal queen bee you-know-what, she might play dumb in class sometimes, but she's no dummy.

"No, Kay's not dumb," he agrees. "And eventually she would have made it impossible not to tell her. She was going to get hurt."

I think of the night Tucker found out, his hounding questions, the crazy assumptions he made. He wouldn't relent until I revealed myself.

"I get it," I say quietly, looking down at my gloves.

"So how much does Tucker know?" he asks. "Because he's not dumb, either."

It embarrasses me that Christian was such a good little angel-blood and did the right thing and kept the right secrets while I so obviously did not. Like a lovesick puppy, compulsively, selfishly, I told a human everything. I put everyone at risk, especially Tucker.

"That much, huh?" Christian says.

"I've told him . . . a lot."

"About me?"

"Yes."

His eyes when he looks at me now are about ten degrees colder than they were a minute ago.

"I told you. I'm not good with secrets," I say again.

"Well, you did keep one thing from him, and aren't you happy you did?"

He's talking about my dream, of course. How it turned out to be Mom's grave, and not Tucker's, that I was seeing.

"Yeah," I admit, "although I don't know if *happy* is the right word for it."

"I know." He puts his gloves back on, claps his hands together, which startles me into looking up. The chair is quickly approaching the top of the mountain.

"So serious talk is officially over. I brought you here to have fun." He adjusts his ski poles. I do the same. The chair comes up to the top of the hill. I put my ski tips up the way Christian taught me last year. The chair levels out, and I stand up and push off, brush shoulders playfully with Christian as I slip easily by him. I'm a blue square girl now, not a newbie to the skiing thing anymore.

"My little prodigy," he says with mock pride. He pulls his goggles down over his eyes. Smiles wickedly. "Let's do it!"

I hardly think about my mom the entire morning. Christian and I braid patterns down the face of the slope, weaving back and forth, occasionally invading each other's space, cutting each other off, playing around like kids. Sometimes we race, and Christian lets me get ahead a bit before he uses his super-racer powers to leave me in the snow, but he never goes carrying a tray.

"Sorry that took so long. I put everything on it," he says, nodding at my cheeseburger. "I didn't know what you liked."

Tucker turns, looks at Christian, looks at the food, looks at Christian again. "She doesn't like onions," he says. He turns back to me. "You came up here with him?"

"Uh, he asked me and I thought it sounded like a good idea. I kind of needed to get out of the house for a while."

Tucker nods absently, and I'm suddenly aware of how my hair is still wet from the snow melting into it, my cheeks flushed, my skin bright, and it's not just from the cold.

Get a grip, Clara, I tell myself. Nothing happened. You and Christian are friends, and Tucker gets that, and it's okay to go skiing with your friend. Nothing happened.

Sorry, Christian says in my head. *I'm getting you in trouble, aren't I?*

No. It's all good, I reply, mortified that he can hear me thinking right now, picking out the guilty thoughts from my brain.

"I was a bit afraid to ask her, frankly," Christian says to Tucker.

Tucker crosses his arms. "Is that right?"

"I went skiing with her last year, and she almost killed us both."

Hey, I protest silently. *I did not almost kill us. Don't tell him that.*

"Come on, don't bother denying it," Christian aims at me.

"It was my first time on a chairlift. Cut me some slack," I shoot back.

"Well, she was just telling me that she's getting so much better now," Tucker says.

"I took her up to Dog Face," Christian tells him. "You should have seen the wipeout she had. Killer."

"Oh yeah? I didn't know she ever fell," Tucker says.

It's like watching a train wreck, this conversation.

"Partial yard sale," Christian says. "Biffed it big-time."

"Hello? I'm standing right here." I punch him on the arm.

"It was pretty damn—"

"It was not funny," I cut him off. "It was cold."

"You're supposed to be immune to cold," he says. "It's good practice."

"Right. Uh-huh." I try not to smile. "Practice."

"Sounds hilarious," Tucker says. He glances at his watch. "Okay, so I have to go. Some of us have to work." He leans in and kisses my cheek, which is a bit awkward with the ski boots and the full winter gear and all, but we manage. "So, meet me at four at the bottom of the Moose Creek quad? I can take you home, if Chris here doesn't mind."

"No problem," Christian says like it doesn't bother him at all. "At four o'clock, she's all yours. That still leaves us what, three good hours of skiing?"

"Great," Tucker says. Then he says to me, "Try not to hurt yourself, okay?"

* * *

Tucker hardly talks on the drive home.

"You okay?" I ask him, which I know is the dumbest question ever, but I can't help myself. The silence is killing me.

Suddenly he pulls over to the side of the road and puts the old farm car in park.

"You finish each other's sentences." He turns and stares at me with quiet accusation in his eyes. "You and Christian. You finish each other's sentences."

"Tuck. It's no big—"

"Yes, it is big. It's more than that. It's like you can read each other's minds."

I put my hand on his arm, search for the right words.

"He was making you smile," he says softly, refusing to look into my eyes again.

"We're friends," I say.

His jaw tightens.

"We're connected," I admit. "We've always been kind of connected. It's because of the visions. But we're just friends."

"Do you hang out with him, as friends? Outside of that Angel Club thing of Angela's?"

"A few times."

"A few times," he repeats slowly. "Like how many? Three?

Four?"

I make a mental count of the times he's shown up on the roof of my house. "Maybe five. Six. I don't keep count, Tuck."

"Six," he says. "See now, that's more than a few. I'd say that counts as 'quite a few.'"

"Tucker—"

"And you didn't tell me because . . ."

I sigh. "I didn't tell you because I didn't want you to be—"

I can't say it.

"Jealous," he fills in. "I'm not."

He leans back against the seat, closes his eyes for a minute, then blows out a long breath. "Actually, you know what? I'm crazy jealous."

He opens his eyes and looks at me with a kind of puzzled amusement. "Wow. I hate being that guy. All afternoon I've been about a horse hair from going all Bruce Banner and Hulk-smashing a locker. I bet that's attractive, right?"

I can't tell if he's serious, so I act like he's joking. "Actually, it's kind of cute, in a caveman sort of way. Green is definitely your color."

He looks at me steadily. "You can't blame me, though. You had the hots for Prescott all last year."

"But that was because I thought he was my . . ." Again, I can't say it.

"Your destiny," Tucker says. "Why does that not make me feel any better?"

"See, now who's finishing my sentences? He and I are *friends*," I insist again. "I admit I was a bit obsessed by the idea of Christian last year. But it was an *idea*. I didn't even know him. You're the real deal."

He laughs. "I'm the real deal," he scoffs, but I can tell he likes it.

"Christian is my past. You're my future."

Now I'm talking in clichés.

"You're my right now," I say quickly, and that's not any better.

The side of his mouth lifts in an attempt at a smile. "Sheesh, Carrots, did you just say I'm your Mr. Right Now?"

"Sorry."

"Man, do you ever have a way with words. Be still my heart."

"I didn't mean it like that."

"So you and Prescott are friends. Friendly, friendly friends. That's fine. I can be cool with that. But tell me one thing: did anything happen between you and Christian, for real, not in your visions or what your people want from you or anything like that, but in real life, anything I should know about? Even before we started dating?"

Uh . . . I think we've established that I'm not the best liar. Most of the time, when confronted by the choice between fessing up and concocting a whopper, even if it's for a good reason, like protecting my family or keeping the world from finding out about the angel stuff, I freeze, my face gets all wooden, my mouth gets dry. In other words, I choke. Which is why I surprise myself right then by looking straight up into Tucker's vulnerable blue eyes, those eyes that say he loves me but he wants to know the truth, no matter how much it hurts, and I say in this perfectly calm and steady voice: "No. Nothing happened."

And he believes me.

I feel sorrow then. Just a flash, there and gone in the space of a few heartbeats, so fast that Tucker doesn't notice the single tear that slips down my face.

This time I don't even consider that it might be a Black Wing. It's me.

I brush it away.

11

STORM'S COMING

Last year when the snow melted, it was great to pack up our winter coats, breathe in that new earth smell, and feel that first hint of warmth return to the valley. But this year, the sight of the snowmelt dripping off the roof, tiny sprouts pushing up and out of the flower beds, green leaves uncurling on the aspens, it all fills me with dread.

It's spring. Between now and summer, my mother will leave us.

In the latest dream I'm in the cemetery, walking up the hillside among the graves on a sunny day. Looking at the people around me, I realize that this crowd is largely made up of the congregation. Walter holding a handkerchief. Billy, who doesn't look sad in the least, cheery even, and smiles at me when I catch her eye. Mr. Phibbs in a gray tweed sport coat. Then there are others who I don't recognize, angel-bloods from other parts of the world, people my mom lived and worked with during her one hundred and twenty years on earth.

It seems so obvious now that this was about my mom. Why couldn't I see that from the start?

The answer is simple: because Tucker never shows up. Never. Not in any of the visions. Not this time, either. I try to ignore my growing sense of betrayal, that there could be no possible reason that's good enough for him not to be there at my mother's funeral. He's not dying, which is a huge relief. But he's not there.

If only there was something that this vision's telling me to do, an action to take, some sense of—pardon the pun—*purpose* in all of this, a way to train and plan and prepare the way I did for the forest fire. But the dream doesn't seem to be telling me to do anything but to get ready for the biggest loss of my life. I feel like a bug waiting under God's enormous shoe, and all this dream is telling me, all it's leading me to, is to show up and stand there and wait to be crunched.

If I ever do get to meet God, the way Mom used to talk about, then He's going to have some serious explaining to do, is all I'm saying. Because this just feels mean.

In the dream, we reach a place near the top of the hill where everybody stops. I walk like I'm underwater, one slow foot in front of the other. As the crowd parts to let me pass, something starts to freeze up inside of me. I stop breathing as I take the final steps. I think, I don't want to see.

But I do see, and nothing could have prepared me for the sight of my mother's coffin, a rich and gleaming mahogany-colored coffin, topped with a mass of white roses.

I have the weirdest thought at this moment. I can't tell if it's me or future-Clara, but I think, Did Mom pick the coffin herself? It's so *her*. I imagine her coffin shopping, strolling around a showroom eyeballing coffins the way she does antique furniture, sizing them up, finally glancing over at the salesman and pointing to one and saying, "I'll take this one."

This one.

My vision blurs. I sway on my feet. Christian's hand abruptly leaves mine. He steps closer to me, encircling my waist with his arm, steadies me. Then his other hand, his right hand this time, returns to mine. He squeezes briefly.

Do you need to sit down? he asks gently in my mind.

No, I reply. My sight clears. I stare at Jeffrey, who's gazing at the coffin so intently I think it could burst into flames, fists clenched at his sides. At first I want to look everywhere but at the coffin, and then when I do, when I cast around it, all I get are people's faces, searching eyes, sympathetic expressions. I force myself to focus on a single white rose. The light is filtering through the trees at an angle, which strikes this one small rosebud, just beginning to open its petals, a perfect glowing white.

Then the sorrow comes, a wave of grief so fierce I struggle to suppress the choking sound in the back of my throat. I feel strangely detached, floating away. Someone moves to the other side of the coffin, clears his throat. It's a red-haired man with solemn hazel eyes. It takes me a second to place him. Stephen. A priest or something. He meets my eyes.

He wants to know if you're ready, says Christian in my mind.

Ready?

For him to start.

Please. Yes.

Stephen nods solemnly.

"Dearly beloved," he says.

That's when I check out. I don't hear what he says as he goes on in his slight Irish brogue. I'm sure he's saying good things about my mother. About her wit. Her kindness. Her strength. Words that couldn't even begin to describe her.

I focus on the rose.

The sorrow grows, expanding like a frozen lake inside me. Soon they will lower the coffin into the ground. They will cover it with earth. My beautiful, spirited, sweet Meg will be gone forever. . . .

My heart leaps. This isn't like the sorrow attacks I had before. These are words, and they're not my words. Not my sorrow, or my feelings.

There is a Black Wing here, after all.

Samjeeza.

I'm suddenly über-aware of everything. I feel the breeze against my bare arms. Birds sing distantly in the trees. I smell pine, roses, wildflowers. I search all the faces around me, some of which are gazing back mournfully, but I don't see Samjeeza. His feelings are coming through loud and clear now. It's him. I'm sure of it. He is watching us from a distance and can't stand how we can gather so near her grave to say good-bye in her last moments above earth. He loved her, he thinks. He loved her and he's furious that he lost her, after all these years of waiting for her. He hates us. If his hate were the sun, it would burn us all to ash.

"Okay, everybody, let's calm down," says Billy, looking around the circle of angel-bloods who are gathered in the meadow around the campfire. "This is really no big deal."

"No big deal?" exclaims a woman from across the circle. "She told us that a Black Wing will be at Maggie's graveside."

"Maybe she's wrong. Black Wings can't enter cemeteries. They're hallowed ground," says someone else.

"Is Aspen Hill hallowed, though? It's not a traditional cemetery. There's no churchyard."

"It is hallowed. Others of our kind are buried there," Walter Prescott says.

Christian meets my eyes across the flickering flames.

I'm not making this up, I send to him as practically the entire congregation starts arguing again. *He was there.*

I believe you.

"People, please." Billy raises her hand, and amazingly everybody begins to quiet down. She smiles with the confidence of a warrior princess. "This is *one* Black Wing we're talking about, and it's Samjeeza, who's probably there to grieve for Maggie, not to fight. We're all going to be there. We can handle this."

"I have children to think about," says a woman stiffly. "I won't put them in unnecessary danger."

Billy sighs. I know she's this close to rolling her eyes. "So don't bring them, Julia."

"And there could be more of them," someone else announces loudly. "It's dangerous."

"It's always dangerous," rings out an authoritative voice. Walter Prescott, again. "Black Wings could come for any one of us at any time. Let's not pretend otherwise."

Mom casts a knowing look at Walter.

"How long has it been?" asks Julia, the woman with the kids. "Since you've had contact with Samjeeza?"

"We've been over this. I hadn't seen him in fifty years, until this past summer," Mom says.

"When he happened upon your daughter at Static Peak," someone else supplies. "And you defended yourself using glory."

"That's correct."

So they all know about it. It's like there's an angel tabloid, and I've been on the front page. It makes me feel guilty, somehow, like if it hadn't been for my purpose and my flying over the mountains that day, scouting for the fire, we wouldn't all be caught up in this unpleasant conversation about fallen angels and where it's safe for us to be.

"You told us that you didn't think he'd be back anytime soon," Julia accuses. "You said he was injured."

So much for them all treating my mom with reverence, I think. But it makes sense now. It wasn't reverence, before. It was pity. They all knew that she was going to die, and they treated her like she was delicate, breakable. They weren't treating her like their leader. They were treating her like an elderly woman. Which now, since her death might turn out to be dangerous or inconvenient for them, is apparently yesterday's news.

"He was," Mom answers smoothly. "I was able to grab hold of him while I was in glory, and I took off his ear. I thought he was too vain to show himself until he was fully healed."

Again with her not wanting them to know the full story of what happened that day. It's a bald-faced lie. I look at her sharply, but she doesn't even glance in my direction.

"So he's healed, then," Julia says.

"I don't know," she admits. "What I do know is that Clara feels his presence in the cemetery."

All eyes turn back to me.

"You're sure," Walter says, not really as a question. "You're sure it was this Black Wing's sorrow you felt and not simply grief over your . . ."

"My mother's death?" I finish for him, surprising myself with how calm I sound. "No. It was him."

For a minute or two nobody says anything else.

"So tell us, Clara." Walter again, his eyes that are so like Christian's, deep pools of emerald, trained on me like he wants to pluck this information right out of my head. "What did you feel, in your dream, at the cemetery? What did he feel, exactly?"

"Sorrow," I answer slowly. I don't want to get Mom into trouble or embarrass her further, by telling them that Samjeeza is in love with her.

"Just tell them," Mom says. "Don't worry about me."

Okay, then. I close my eyes, cast myself back to that moment in the dream, trying to recapture his feeling.

"I feel sorrow. Separation. Pain. And you're right, I thought it was me at first. But then I started feeling his despair. He knows he's never going to see my mom again. He can't go where she has gone. He's lost her, forever. He never got a chance to plead his case. To make amends."

"He should have tried to make amends last summer, then," Billy says hotly, "instead of trying to choke the life out of her."

Mom looks at her with a mournful, pleading expression, and Billy quiets.

"The point is," I continue, "he's angry. At some of us, specifically."

"Who?" Julia asks.

"Well, me, for starters. He thinks I'm an insolent child. I humiliated him. I said things that hurt him." I shiver. "He wants to destroy me. I remind him of . . ."

"Who else?" Mom prompts then. "Tell them who else."

"Mr. Phibbs—I mean Corbett. For some reason he really hates you."

"Glad to hear it," says Mr. Phibbs gruffly.

"He's not too fond of Billy either. Or you, Walter."

Billy snorts. "Tell us something we don't know."

"That's why I thought it'd be appropriate for you to know. So you can decide whether it's worth the risk to attend my funeral," Mom says.

"Oh, we're all going to be there," Billy insists. "Like I said, we can handle Samjeeza. He wouldn't take on forty of us."

The rest of the group doesn't look so sure.

"We're all going to be there," Billy says again, like she's daring someone to cross her. "We stand by each other."

Mom sighs in exasperation. "Bill, I'm not going to be standing anywhere. I won't be there. It's very nice for you to pay your respects, but it's really unnecessary. Not worth the risk, if you want my opinion."

Billy doesn't bat an eye. She turns to my mom, my serene and dying mother, who wouldn't have had the strength to hike out here to the meadow without us helping her, who can hardly keep herself sitting up straight now, and Billy looks at her like she's a total moron.

"Mags, sweetie," she says. "I know that. It's not for you, dear. We're going to be there for Clara. For Jeffrey. For everyone else who loves you. And if there's a Black Wing, it's all the more reason for everyone to be there. To protect them."

Mom closes her eyes. "It's only a funeral."

"It's *your* funeral," says Billy, slinging an arm around her affectionately. "We love you. We're going to take care of your kids."

There's another wave of whispering from the crowd, this time in agreement.

"I don't think the funeral is really the issue here," Mr. Phibbs says suddenly.

"So what is?" Billy asks.

"Clara says Samjeeza is at the graveside. And that he's hurting, sure, as Black Wings are like to do. But she also says he's mad at us. I'd say the larger question here is, what are we going to do between then and now to piss him off?"

Okay, so that ruffles more than a few feathers. People start arguing again.

"The last time one of us fought a Black Wing, she ended up dead," that Julia lady says. "And she sacrificed her life so that the Black Wings wouldn't find out about the rest of us, in case you forgot."

This time Christian does not meet my eyes. He's looking down into the crackling fire.

"We didn't forget," Walter says in a low voice.

"It's understandable that you're afraid," says Mr. Phibbs. "But that was seven years ago. We've become sleepy since then. Sleepy and safe."

"You're careless, Corbett, but you can afford to be," Julia replies. "You don't have anything to lose, since your time is almost up, yourself."

Mr. Phibbs regards her like a troublesome student. "Maybe that's true," he fires back. "But we're at war, in case you've forgotten. You can ignore that and go on with your human lives in your human houses and your special camping trips in the woods a few times a year, but the reality is, we're angel-bloods. This is a war. We've been chosen to fight."

His words ring out in the cool night air, which has gone suddenly still.

"Stop," Mom protests. "I'm responsible for this mess with Samjeeza, and no one else."

"Mags, dear, be quiet," Billy says.

I look around the campfire. Mr. Phibbs is right. Everyone knows he's right.

"I'll be there, at the cemetery," says Christian suddenly, fiercely. "It doesn't matter who else shows up."

"As will I," says Walter, clapping a hand on Christian's

shoulder.

"And me," pipes up someone else. "To the end."

They go around the circle, each angel-blood vowing to be there in Aspen Hill Cemetery that day. Even Julia begrudgingly agrees. When it gets to Jeffrey, who hasn't said anything this entire weekend, he shrugs and says, "Kind of a given, right?" and then Angela says, "Bring it on," and then it's me and I just nod, because I'm suddenly too choked up to get the words out. Then our impromptu meeting is adjourned, everyone going back to normal, except that there's a new energy in the air, because we are angel-bloods, and we aren't cowards, and we've been given a call to battle. Mom looks exhausted and Billy escorts her back to our tent, then returns to the fire to where the other members of the inner circle are gathered to discuss, I assume, what they're going to do about this situation. I glance over at Mr. Phibbs, who's still sitting in the circle, leaning back with a pleased expression on his face.

"You're a troublemaker, you know that?" I tell him.

He raises his scraggly white eyebrows. "Takes one to know one."

I laugh, but later, when everyone else is asleep, I keep going over what he said. That we're meant to fight. That this is a war. And that would put me, and Jeffrey, and Christian, and Angela and all the people I care about, right smack in the middle of it.

In the morning there's this crazy-loud angelic trumpeting, and everyone gets up for the sunrise. This time they haven't planned an official meeting. We had enough talk last night, Stephen says. He waves us all, even those of us who are not official members, into a circle in the middle of the meadow.

"We want to take this moment to honor Margaret Gardner, as this is the last meeting that she'll be able to attend," he says when we're all assembled. I look for Jeffrey, but I don't see him. He's probably sneaking in some extra fishing or something, which makes me mad. He should be here for this.

Mom bows her head and steps into the center of the circle. Everybody summons their wings. Stephen puts his hand on the snowy feathers at Mom's shoulder.

"You have been a faithful servant and an inspiration to us all," he says. "We give our love to you, Maggie."

"Love to you," murmurs the rest of the congregation, and we all close in, the other members of the inner circle each laying one hand on her wings and one hand on the person next to them, the rest doing the same to the person in front of them, back and back until we make a great web of angel-bloods with my mother at the center. The sun breaches the mountain, casting her in a pool of radiance, a combination of sun and glory that almost hurts my eyes to behold. The meadow fills with an angelic hum, and then the hum becomes a word in Angelic, the word *love*, I think, coming across in that multitoned music of the language of angels, or maybe it's a combination of words, everyone saying a different word that ends up all meaning the same thing, something that transcends translation.

I realize I'm crying, tears sliding down my face and off my chin and falling down into the grass at my feet. And I'm smiling. I have a sense that no matter what, no matter what darkness lies ahead, there is nothing that can overcome this power.

All it takes to punch a big old hole in that joy is seeing Mom struggle as we hike back to the car, Jeffrey, Billy, and I flanking her so we can catch her if she starts to fall. It'd be easier to fly, but we all have gear to carry, which is cumbersome, and Mom's not safe to fly alone. She keeps saying she's fine. She's not. She's sweating, and twice we have to stop to rest.

"What's the point?" Jeffrey spits out when we're stopped the second time.

"The point?"

"The point of the whole congregation. It's not like they really do anything. It's not like they could heal her."

"Of course not," I say, although the thought did cross my mind, what with all the light and power spilling everywhere and the fact that glory heals people, maybe somewhere deep down I'd hoped that Mom would be miraculously saved, at least strengthened for a few days or something. But eventually that spectacular light faded into regular sunshine, and the congregation dropped their hands, and Mom went back to dying. "Don't be a jerk, Jeffrey. The congregation cares about us, or weren't you there when they all said they were coming to Mom's funeral?"

"We'll see," he replies like he couldn't care less. "We'll see who actually shows up."

"They do come."

"Why, because you saw them in your dream?"

"Yes. I saw them."

"And what if your dream doesn't mean anything?" he asks with sudden bitterness. "What if it's only a dream?"

"It's a dream, yes, but it's also a vision," I say irritably. "Of course it means something."

"You think it's part of your purpose?"

I stare at him. I wish I knew the answer to that question.

"It's the future," I say.

Jeffrey's eyes are a blaze of silver fire. "What if it's not? What if it's a practical joke somebody's playing on you? Maybe we don't even have a purpose, Clara. Just because someone told you that you were put on this earth to do something, to be something, doesn't make it true."

I don't know what's gotten under his skin, but I do know that he's questioning everything we've ever been taught, and it bothers me. "You don't believe Mom?"

"Right, because she's been so upfront with us so far."

"Hey, what are you two arguing about over here?" Billy interrupts, jogging over to us from where she left Mom sitting at a picnic table at a campground under the trees. "Do I need to break this up?"

"Nothing," says Jeffrey, turning away from her. "Are we ready to go yet? I have homework I have to do before tomorrow."

"Yeah, we can go. I think she'll make it the rest of the way," Billy says, looking at me. I study the laces of my hiking boots. I wonder if Mom heard any of that. I wonder if what Jeffrey said hurt her, each bad thought, each doubt like a dart striking her. I swallow painfully.

"Everything okay?" Billy asks.

I lift my head and try to smile and nod. "Yeah. I'm good. I just want to go home."

"Okay then, let's go," she says, but as Jeffrey moves away from us, she grabs my arm. "Keep your chin up, okay?"

"I know."

"Storm's coming, kid," she says, smiling in a way that reminds me of how she looks at my mother's graveside. "I can feel it. Things are going to be rough. But we'll make it."

"Okay."

"You believe me, right?"

"Right," I answer, nodding.

Even though the truth is, not all of us are going to make it, and I don't know what to believe.

12

DON'T DRINK AND FLY

It all starts happening pretty fast, then. Mom quits her job. She spends a lot of time in front of the television wrapped up in quilts, or out on the back porch with Billy, talking for hours and hours. She takes long naps. She stops cooking. This may not seem like a big thing, but Mom loves to cook. Nothing fills her with more domestic joy than putting something wonderful on the table, even if it's something simple like her signature coffeecake or five-cheese macaroni. Now it's too much for her, and we fall into a predictable pattern: cereal for breakfast, sandwiches for lunch, frozen dinners. Jeffrey and I don't complain. We don't say anything, but I think that's when it really hits us, when Mom stops cooking. That's the beginning of the end.

Then one day she says to Billy and me, out of the blue, "I think it's time we talk about what we're going to tell people."

"Okay," I say slowly. "About what?"

"About me. I think we should say that it's cancer."

I suck in a shocked breath. Before that moment I hadn't given any thought to what we would tell people, how we would explain Mom's "illness," as she likes to call it. Cancer would definitely explain it. People are starting to notice, I think. How she stays seated now at Jeffrey's wrestling matches. How quiet and pale she's become, how this one strand in the front of her hair has turned silver and she always wears hats now to cover it. How she's gone from slender to just plain thin.

It seems so sudden, but then I think, I wasn't paying attention before. I was so consumed with my own life, my dream, with the idea that it was Tucker who was going to die. She's been getting weaker all this time, and I didn't really notice until now.

Some stellar daughter I am.

"What kind of cancer?" Billy asks thoughtfully, like this is not at all a morbid topic.

"Something terminal, of course," Mom says.

"Okay, so can we not talk about this?" I can't take this anymore. "You don't have cancer. Why do we have to tell them anything at all? I don't want to have another lie I'm going to be forced to tell."

Billy and Mom share this amused look I don't understand.

"She's honest," remarks Billy.

"To a fault," Mom replies. "Gets it from her father."

Billy snorts. "Oh come on, Mags, she's like a carbon copy of you at that age."

Mom rolls her eyes. Then she turns her attention back to me. "A rational explanation will help everybody. It will keep them from asking too many questions. The last thing we want is for my death to appear mysterious in any way."

I still find it crazy that she can say the words *my death* so calmly, like she's saying *my car* or *my plans for dinner*.

"Okay, fine," I concede. "Tell them whatever you want. But I'm not going to be involved. I'm not going to call it cancer or lie about it or anything. This is your thing."

Billy opens her mouth to say something smart-alecky or maybe chew me out for how insensitive I'm being, but Mom holds up her hand.

"You don't have to say anything at all," she says. "I'll take care of it."

So, cancer it is. But Mom was wrong about me not having to deal. Maybe it would have worked before I got slammed by the power of empathy, but now it's impossible not to know how everyone is feeling about me. The news that my mother has terminal cancer is like an atom bomb going off at Jackson Hole High School. It doesn't even take a whole day before everybody, and I mean everybody, knows. First it's people looking away, some of the nicer girls shooting me sympathetic looks. Then whispers. I quickly know the script by heart. It starts with, "Did you hear about Clara Gardner's mom?" and it ends with something like, "That is *so* sad."

I keep my head down and do my work and try to act normal, but by the second day I'm suffering through overwhelming waves of sympathy, and this from people who didn't even bother to learn my name last year. Even my teachers are solemn, with the exception of Mr. Phibbs, who just looks at me like he was quite disappointed in the half-assed paper I wrote on *Paradise Lost*, for which he gives me a D minus and demands that I rewrite. It's like I'm a tiny boat adrift in an ocean of pity.

For instance: I'm in a stall in the ladies' room, minding my own business, when a bunch of freshman girls come in. They chatter like squirrels, even while they pee, and then one of them says, "Have you heard about Jeffrey Gardner's mom? She has lung cancer."

"I heard it was brain cancer. Stage four, or something. She's only got something like three months to live."

"That is *so* sad. I don't even know what I'd do if my mom died."

"What's Jeffrey going to do?" asks one. "I mean, when she dies. Their dad doesn't live with them, does he?"

Amazing, I think, what they know about us, this group of

total strangers.

"Well, I think it's tragical."

They murmur their agreement. The most tragical thing ever.

"And Jeffrey's so broken up about it, too. You can totally tell."

Then they move on to discussing their favorite flavor of lip gloss. Either watermelon or blackberry cream. From my dying mom to lip gloss.

Tragical.

"*O goodness infinite, goodness immense! / That all this good of evil shall produce, / and evil turn to good; more wonderful / than that which by creation first brought forth / light out of darkness!* Wait," I say, laying my book on the floor next to my feet. "I don't even know who's talking here. Michael, or Adam?"

"Adam," supplies Wendy, homework buddy extraordinaire, looking down at me from her perch on my bed. "See where it says, *So spake the Arch-Angel Michael, then paused, / as at the world's great period; and our sire, / replete with joy and wonder, thus replied*. So now it's Adam speaking. He's our sire, get it? I love that line, 'as at the world's great period.'"

"Ugh! What does that even mean?"

"Well, Michael was telling him about redemption, about how good is going to triumph over evil in the end, all that stuff."

"So now he's okay with it? He's going to get thrown out of Eden but everything's great because someday, thousands of years after he dies, the side of good is going to win out?"

"Clara, I think you're taking this a tad too seriously. It's only a poem. It's art. It's supposed to make you think, is all."

"Well, right now it's making me think that my physics homework looks really super fun and I should get to it." I close the offending book and slide it away from me.

"But Mr. Phibbs said you had to turn in that rewrite tomorrow. No more dragging your feet, he said."

"Yep, and I'm probably going to get a D on that paper too, whether I study or not. I swear, he's trying to torture me."

Wendy looks concerned. "It will probably be on the AP test."

I sigh. "I don't want to think about the AP test. Or college. Or my stupendously bright future. I want to live in the now, I've decided."

She closes her book and looks at me with this ultra let's-be-serious expression.

"You should be excited, Clara. You applied to all these awesome schools. You have a great chance at getting in to at least one of them. Not everybody has that."

She's nervous. Our acceptance letters should be coming this week. She's already gone to the post office like three times since Monday.

"Okay, okay, color me excited," I say to placate her.

"Woo-hoo! So. Excited."

She gets out her chemistry book, apparently done talking. I open up my physics book. We study. Suddenly she sighs.

"It's just . . . Tucker's the same way," she says. "My parents kept trying to talk him into college, but he wasn't even a little bit interested. He didn't apply to a single school. Not even University of Wyoming, as a backup."

"He wants to stay here," I say.

"Do you?" Wendy asks.

"Do I what?"

"Do you want to stay here? Because Tucker does? Because I think that's romantic and everything, Clara, but don't—" She stops, tugs at the end of her braid in an agitated way, trying to decide if she's going to go ahead and say this to me. "Don't give up your life for a guy," she says then firmly. "Not even a great guy. Not even Tucker."

I don't know what to say. "Wendy—"

"I'm going to break up with Jason," she adds. "And I like him. A lot. But when it's time to leave for school, I'll have to cut him loose."

"He's not a fish, Wen," I point out. "What if Jason doesn't want to be cut loose? What if he wants to try the long-distance thing?"

She shakes her head. "He'll be in Boston, or New York, or one of those fancy schools he applied to. I'll be in Washington, hopefully. It wouldn't work. But that's being a grown-up. You have to think about the future."

I want to remind her that we're not grown-ups yet, we're only seventeen. We shouldn't have to think about the future. Besides, my future, the one I see almost every night when I close my eyes, is a cemetery. An incredible, staggering loss. What happens after that, my life after that day, is like a videotape that's been deleted: gray and static. Yes, I will probably go to college. I might make new friends, go to parties, and end up thinking that life is okay. But right now I'm trapped inside a single sunny day on a hillside.

"Are you okay?" Wendy asks. "I'm sorry. I don't have the right to lecture you. I know you're having a hard time, what with your mom and everything."

"It's okay," I try to reassure her, shake the bad feelings off, ignore the pity I'm starting to feel from her.

"Hey, I have an idea," I say to change the subject. "Let's go check the post office."

"It's different than what I thought it would be," Wendy says as we walk along the boardwalk in downtown Jackson.

I hold the door open for her as we duck into the post office. "What is?"

"You and Tucker. I thought you were so perfect for each other, you'd balance each other out, your yin to his yang, something like that, and I thought he'd be so happy all the time, but—" She chews on her bottom lip for a minute. "Sometimes you're so intense, so focused on each other that you don't even seem to notice anything else. Like, um, me."

"Sorry, Wendy," I say. "You're still my bestie, you know that, right?"

"Darn straight," she says. "But boyfriend trumps best friend, is all I'm saying. Although I guess I'm guilty of that too."

She's right. I haven't seen nearly as much of Wendy this year, partially because, when I have free time, I tend to spend it with Tucker or at Angel Club and partially because Wendy is with Jason a lot. That's to be expected, like she said; when a girl gets a boyfriend she doesn't spend as much time with her girlfriends. I always thought that was dumb, but that didn't stop us from doing it when it happened. I also hang out less with Wendy because there's a lot that she doesn't know now, that she can't know, and I'd rather stay away than constantly lie to her. Last year I could pretend, at least most of the time, that I was normal. This year I can't.

We separate to check our mailboxes. In ours is the usual junk, bills, grocery store ads, but then, at the bottom, a fat envelope. I swallow hard. Stanford University.

Wendy appears by my side, her face white under her tan, blue eyes wide. She holds up an envelope. WSU. This is it. Her dream school. Her future. Her life. She tries to smile but it comes out as more of a wince. Her eyes drop to the envelope in my hand, and she gasps.

"Should we . . . wait until we get home?" she asks, her voice almost a squeak.

"No. Definitely not. Let's open them. Get it over with."

She doesn't have to be told twice. She tears right into her envelope, takes one look at the top page, then presses her hand over her mouth. "Oh," she says.

"What? *What?* You got in, right?"

There's a shimmer of tears in her eyes. "There is a God," she says. "I got in!"

We hug and jump around and squeal like little girls for a few minutes, then settle down.

"Now you," she says.

I open it carefully. Pull the papers out. A brochure for the on-campus housing drops out, floats down to the floor. Wendy and I stare at it.

"Clara," she breathes. "You got in too."

I read the first line of the first page—*Dear Clara, we are pleased to inform you*—then try to work up a smile that matches Wendy's, although what's moving through my head in this moment is something different than excitement, something different from elation or happiness, like a combination of incredulity and dread. But this is a good thing, I tell myself. I could go home to California. I could actually attend Stanford University, and study anything I want, and build a new life for myself.

"I got in," I whisper in disbelief.

Wendy's arm comes around my shoulders. "This is amazing," she says. "And trust me. Tucker's going to be so happy for you."

"So that's it," Angela says matter-of-factly later when I show up for Angel Club. "You're going."

"Not necessarily." I'm back to my usual position on the stage at the Pink Garter, back to glory practice, because that's all I can think to do in the dreamy sort of daze I've been in since this afternoon.

Angela puts down her pen and gives me her best you-absolute-moron stare. "Clara Gardner. You got accepted to Stanford. You got a scholarship, even. Don't tell me you're not going."

The money thing is the new bone of contention with her. Here I am, Miss Moneybags, Mom's been loaded since the Second World War, investing in things like, say computers back when one computer took up an entire room, and I get a scholarship. Not a huge one, granted, and one that's alumni-related, because of my "grandmother," but more than I need, all the same. And Angela (of course she was accepted) is going to have to scrimp and save and stretch and take loans to make tuition. She got scholarships too, because she's like, Super Student, but not a full ride.

I should feel guilty about my indecision, but I don't. I don't have room for fresh guilt in the massive clutter of conflicting emotions in my head. What I'm turning over, what's been on my mind ever since earlier in the post office when I saw the Stanford logo on the envelope, is that I don't *have* to go. I'm formulating a different plan. A new and improved plan. A great one.

"Maybe I won't go to college this year," I say as casually as I can manage. "I might take a year or two off."

"To do what?" she sputters.

"I'd stay here. Then I'd get to stick around while Jeffrey finishes high school. I'd get a job."

"What, like working in a gift shop? Selling fudge on the boardwalk? Waitressing?"

"Sure, why not?"

"You're an angel-blood, that's why not. You're supposed to be doing something special with your life."

I shrug. There are other angel-bloods in Jackson, and they work regular jobs. Besides, I like this plan. It feels right. I can stay here in Jackson. I can make sure Jeffrey's okay. It's a good plan, one where I don't have to leave my house or my family (or at least, what will be left of it, after Mom goes), and I can build myself a nice, normal life.

Angela shakes her head, gold eyes narrowing. "This is about Tucker."

"No." I glare at her. But I confess that part did cross my mind.

"Oh my God, you're going to throw Stanford away so you can stay with Tucker," Angela says in disgust.

"Lay off, Angela," Christian says suddenly. He's been in his usual spot at one of the far tables, doing his homework while this whole conversation was going on. "It's Clara's life. She can do what she wants."

"Yeah, what he said." I shoot Christian a grateful smile. "Anyway," I say to Angela, "you only want me to go to Stanford so you won't have to be out there by yourself and face your purpose alone."

She looks down, smoothes the tablecloth like she's taking a momentary rest before she's going to jump up and punch me in the nose. I brace myself.

"Okay, so maybe that's true," she admits then, which surprises me. "You're my best friend, Clara, and you're right. I don't want to go alone."

"Ange, I'm sure you'll be fine. You're the most advanced, most knowledgeable, most capable angel-blood the world has seen in a thousand years. If anyone is going to totally kick butt at fulfilling her purpose, it's you."

"I know," she says, with a pleased smile. "It's not that. It's . . ." She pauses, looks up at me with serious catlike eyes. "I know you go to Stanford, C. Because I've seen you there."

"What?"

"In my vision. I've seen you."

I spend the next fifteen minutes standing on the stage, trying to concentrate on bringing the glory, trying to ground myself, but all I can think about is how unfair it is that my future keeps getting plotted out for me. First by my own visions. Now by Angela's.

"Okay, I can't take it anymore," Christian says (again suddenly, since he's never much of a talker at Angel Club), slamming his textbook closed. I open my eyes.

"Huh?"

"I can't stand to watch you, like, fake meditate like that." He jogs up the steps onto the stage and crosses swiftly toward me. "Let me help you."

My heartbeat picks up. "What, you know how to call the glory?"

"See, that's exactly what you've got wrong. You think it's like calling something, like glory is out here"—he gestures into the empty black space around us—"instead of in here." He lays a hand on his chest, takes a deep breath. "It's inside you, Clara. It's part of you, and it will come out naturally if you stop standing in your own way."

I'm embarrassed but intrigued. "You can do it?"

He shrugs. "I've been learning."

He holds out his hand. I stare at it, his fingers extended, beckoning, and I instantly flash back to my vision, the moment when we take hands under the trees as the fire roars down the mountain. Then I remember my dream, where holding his hand is what brings me back to myself when I think I'm going to float away on a cloud of misery. I put my hand in his.

Heat zings through me. He holds my hand carefully but casually, not squeezing or stroking his thumb over my knuckles the way he did in my forest-fire vision, that move that used to drive me crazy thinking about what it might mean.

"What are you thinking about?" he asks.

Blood rushes to my face. "What?"

"When you try for glory, what do you think about?"

"Oh. Well . . ." Most of the time I try to think about Tucker, about how I love him, which only really worked for me that one time in the forest, but it worked then, when it really counted. "I . . . I think about times when I was happy."

"Okay, forget that." He grabs my other hand, turns me so we're standing facing each other in the middle of the stage, palm to palm. I see Angela lean forward to watch us, her head resting in one hand, the other poised to write in her notebook.

"Don't look at her," Christian says. "Don't think about her, or the past, or anything else."

"All right . . ."

"Just be here," he says softly. His eyes are gorgeous under the stage lights, amber flecks shooting out sparks. "Be in the present."

Let go of everything else, he urges in my mind. *Just be here.*

With me.

I stare at him, allow myself to focus on his face in a way I typically avoid, tracing the angles of his cheekbones, the lines of his mouth, the sweep of his dark eyelashes and the curve of his brow, the shape of the shoulders that I memorized so long ago. I don't think. I let myself look at him. Then the heat from our joined hands moves up my body, settles into my chest as I let myself fall into his eyes.

I feel what he feels. Certainty, always so much certainty with Christian, no matter what he said about the absence-of-certainty thing before. He knows himself. He knows what he wants. I see myself from his point of view, understand my beauty through his eyes, my hair a messy golden halo around my face, the contrast of pale skin and pink lips and cheeks so striking, the stormy luminous eyes that right now seem blue, like a deep pool of blue you could slip into. It's like he's laughing inside, so pleased with himself, because I am glowing, the light in me pushing through, we're glowing together, light breaking at where our hands come together, his own hair starting to shine now, a radiance rising around us.

He wants to tell me something. He wants to open himself up completely, let me see everything, let me know everything about him, rules be damned. . . . Suddenly we're walking together in the cemetery, the sun warm on our backs, and he's holding my hand, leading me. I feel so strong in this moment, strong and alive and full of energy.

"Holy Mary, Mother of God!" screams a voice.

Christian and I spring back from each other. The light around us dissipates. For a moment I'm completely blinded in the sudden transition from light to dark, but as my eyes adjust, I see Angela's mom standing in the aisle staring at us. She brings a hand up to her mouth, her face ashen. Angela jumps up and goes to her, barely getting to her in time to catch her as she falls to her knees.

"Mom, it's okay," Angela says, tugging her back to her feet. "They were just trying something."

"None of that in here," Anna whispers, her dark eyes boring into me with such intensity it makes me avoid looking at her. "None of that in here, I told you."

"We won't. I promise. You need to go upstairs and lie down," Angela says.

Anna nods, and Angela puts an arm around her shoulders and practically drags her out of the theater. We listen to their footsteps on the stairs leading to their apartment, Anna still talking, Angela trying to soothe her. The creak of the door. Then silence.

Christian and I glance at each other, then away.

"Well, it worked," I say, just to say something. "We did it."

"Yes, we did," Christian says. He wipes at the sheen of sweat on his forehead.

"You were going to tell me something," I say.

He frowns. "Now who's reading minds?"

"It was my empathy. I could feel what you felt. You wanted to tell me something."

This totally freaks him out, for some reason. He jumps down to the floor, goes to the table where he left his homework, and starts to gather it up. I follow him and put my hand on his shoulder. He stiffens. I feel like I should apologize for something, for reading him the way I did, or for bringing it up when Angela is so close and might hear.

"Christian, I . . ."

Angela bursts back into the room, her face wild with excitement.

"Holy awesome! I can't believe how bright it was, I mean, wow. Did you see my mom? She, like, dropped. Her face was all pasty. I've never seen her like that. She's okay now, though. I gave her some water, and she just, like, shook it off. She's fine."

"Glory terrifies humans," I remind her, trying to remain serious, but it's hard not to get swept up by her enthusiasm. It *was* awesome. And it's like the magic's still in the air, floating around with the motes of dust and absorbed by the velvet curtains. I don't want to let it go.

"Yeah, I think we've learned that's true, haven't we? Let's do it again. Try it with me, this time," Angela insists to Christian.

"I don't think I could."

"Come on, I want to learn. Pretty please!" she begs.

He drops his head, sighs, giving in. "All right. We can try."

This ought to be good. I sit in Angela's chair as the two of them march back up to the stage, take hands, concentrate.

"Be in the present," Christian says again. "That's the key. Not the present, like what you're thinking about now, but apart from your thoughts. This is going to be hard for you, because you overthink everything. Just remember that you are not your thoughts."

"Okay, Sensei, let's go," she cracks.

They both close their eyes. I lean forward, watching, waiting for the glow to start, trying to contain my envy that it's Angela up there and not me. But nothing happens. They just stand there like they're suspended in time.

"None of that in here!" comes a voice from the lobby. Anna must be afraid to come in.

Angela and Christian drop hands, open their eyes. For a minute Angela looks disappointed, but then a mischievous smile spreads across her face.

"That was so hot," she says. She turns to look at me with one eyebrow arched. "Right, Clara?"

"Uh—"

"I think you wanted to tell me something, too," she purrs to Christian, totally faking and he knows it. I remember how she told me once that she and Christian played spin the bottle in ninth grade and she thought kissing him was like kissing a brother.

"Oh yes," he replies without inflection, "that was pretty hot, Ange. You're like my dream girl. I always wanted to tell you that."

"None of that in here!" Anna Zerbino calls again.

We all bust up laughing.

A loud noise wakes me in the middle of the night. For a minute I lie in bed, listening, not sure what's happening. I feel like I've just woken up from a bad dream. I glance at the alarm clock. It's four in the morning. The house is absolutely quiet. I close my eyes.

Something crashes. I sit up in bed. The best weapon I can come up with this time is a can of hair spray, like that will do any good if Samjeeza's here.

Note to self: buy some nunchucks or something.

Another crash reverberates through the house, then a loud curse, the sound of breaking glass.

The noise is coming from Jeffrey's room.

I throw on my robe and hurry down the hall. There's another loud bang. He's going to wake Mom up if he hasn't already. I open his door.

"What are you doing?" I call into the dark, irritated.

I flip on the light.

Jeffrey is standing in the middle of the room with his wings out, dressed in just his jeans. He yells in surprise as the light goes on, then swings around with his hand in front of his eyes like I've blinded him. His wings catch a stack of books on his desk, which crash to the floor. He's soaking wet, his hair clinging to his face, a pool forming under him on the hardwood. And he's laughing.

"I can't remember how to retract my wings," he says, which he obviously finds hilarious.

I look beyond him to the open window, where the blinds are all twisted up and dangling from one side.

"Did you just get home?" I ask.

"No," he says, grinning. "I went to bed early. I've been here all night."

He takes a step toward me and stumbles. I catch him by the arm to steady him. That's when he laughs into my face and I get the full, nasty brunt of his breath.

"You're drunk," I whisper in amazement.

"At least I didn't drive," he says.

This is bad.

I stand there for a minute, hanging on to him, trying to get my brain to function at four in the morning. I could go get Mom, assuming she isn't already on her way up the stairs to find out what the racket is about. If she still has the strength to make it up the stairs. I don't even know what she'll do or, worse, what this might do to her. This is way beyond any kind of punishment she's ever had to dole out. This is like grounded-for-a-year kind of behavior.

He's still laughing like he finds this whole situation

incredibly funny. I grab him by the ear. He yelps, but he can't really fight me off. I drag him over to his bed and push him down on it, face-first. Then I tackle his wings, trying to fold them, press them down to rest against his back. I wish there was some magic word in Angelic that would instantly retract them—*fold yourself!* comes to mind—but at least if I can get them to fold up he won't do any more damage.

Jeffrey says something into the pillow.

"I can't hear you, moron," I reply.

He turns his head. "Leave me alone."

"Whatever," I mutter, still trying to get his wings lined up. "Where's your shirt? And how did you get all wet?"

That's when I notice his gray feathers. The wings are lighter than when I saw them the night of the fire. Then they were a dark gray, I hoped from soot. My wings were covered that night too, but it washed off, mostly. Jeffrey's wings are still gray. Dove gray, I would call it. And there are a couple of feathers on the back of one wing that are the color of tar.

"Your feathers . . ." I lean in closer to look at them.

He chooses that moment to remember how to retract his wings. I fall on him clumsily, then scramble off. He laughs.

"You are in such deep trouble," I say furiously.

He rolls over on his back and looks at me with an expression that's so mean it literally sends shivers down my spine. It's like he hates me.

"What, you're going to tell Mom?"

"I should," I stammer.

"Go ahead," he snarls. "It's not like you never sneak out. Tell Mom. I dare you. See what happens."

He sits up. He's still glaring like any minute he's going to lunge at me. I take a few steps back.

"All you ever do is think about yourself," he says. "Your vision. Your dumb dreams. Your stupid boyfriend."

"That's not true," I say shakily.

"You're not the only one who's important here, you know. You're not the only one with a purpose."

"I know—"

"Just leave me alone." He smiles, a hard, ironic baring of his teeth. "Leave me the hell alone."

I get out of his room. I fight the urge to scream. I want to run downstairs and wake up Mom and get her to fix it. Fix him. Instead I go to the linen closet. I get a towel. Then I go back to Jeffrey's room and throw the towel at him. It hits him in the chest. He looks up at me, startled.

"I know your life is crap," I tell him. "It's not exactly a picnic being me either." My heart is pounding, but I try to look cool and collected. "I won't tell Mom this time. But I swear, Jeffrey, if you don't pull yourself together, you'll be sorry. You pull anything like this again, Mom will be the last thing you have to worry about."

Then I march out of his room before he can see me cry.

13

GO OUT WITH A BANG

"You look lovely, Clara," Billy says when I come into Mom's bedroom in my prom dress. Just for her sake I do a twirl, the layers of my red silk ball gown ballooning around my legs. The dress is a little extreme. Plus it cost a small fortune, but when Angela, Billy, and I saw it in the mall in Idaho Falls last week, it kind of called to me. *Wear me,* it said. Then Billy said something like what the heck, it's your last formal dance of high school, go out with a bang. The theme of prom this year is Paradise Found—yep, organized by seniors who were forced to read *Paradise Lost* with Mr. Phibbs this year. My favorite book of all time.

It's either this or a fig leaf.

I tried not to fixate on that spot in front of the GNC where I first felt Samjeeza's gaze on me. I used to find it mildly funny that I saw a Black Wing at the mall. I tried to picture him shopping, drifting through the bookshelves of Barnes & Noble with the latest Dan Brown novel, in Macy's fingering the ties, perusing the underwear, because even angels need underwear if they're going to walk among us, right? I remember laughing about it with Angela, and when I think about that now, how we could joke about it, I think, man, we were dumb. We knew Black Wings were terrifying and powerful, we knew Mom's face went sheet white that day in the mall, we were scared too, but we had no idea. So I tried not to look at where he stood and I tried not to remember the way his voice rasped into my ear telling me not to be afraid. The way he thought of me as something he could take. And almost did.

The other off thing about this mall trip was that this time, Mom wasn't there. She sent Billy. It feels like Billy is already stepping in for Mom, always in the house these days, cracking Mom-style jokes, taking me shopping, and now it's Billy and not Mom who helps me fix my hair for prom. It's Billy who tells me how lovely I am, while Mom lays back against the pillows, watching with tired eyes.

"Doesn't she look amazing, Mags?" Billy prompts when Mom doesn't say anything. "Red's your color, Clara."

"Yes," Mom agrees faintly. "You're beautiful."

"Trust me, Tucker's jaw is going to drop when he sees

you," Billy says, ushering me out of the room so Mom can rest. "He's going to feel like a millionaire with you on his arm."

"I'm arm candy, is that what you're saying?"

"Tonight, yes," Billy says. "Own it."

I have to go pick Tucker up, since this year he's rideless—the old ranch car finally kicked the bucket. Wendy's riding with us too, since Jason Lovett's car broke down two days ago, so she agreed to meet him there. Not the most romantic arrangement for any of us, but I'm sure we'll make it work.

Billy stops me on my way out the door to spritz some amazing, yummy perfume in the air and has me walk through it.

"Home by twelve thirty or I'll come looking," she says, and I can't tell if she's serious.

"Yes, *Mom*," I mutter.

She smiles sympathetically. "Have a good time at the dance."

I plan to. Spring is passing too quickly, marching relentlessly toward the cemetery and summer and college and all the other things I don't want to think about. This night might be the only good time I get for a while. I'm going to live it up.

The dance this year is at the Snow King ski lodge. The prom committee has done up the place like a jungle, fake trees, big fake flowers, even a giant apple tree in the corner with a plastic snake coiled in the branches.

Last year was classier.

But it doesn't matter. This year, I'm with Tucker. Normally, in his cowboy clothes, his boots and T-shirts and tightish jeans, his flannels and Stetson, he's unbelievably attractive. There's a ruggedness about him that's crazy sexy. But then there are times like these, when he shaves and puts on a rented tuxedo, wears a tie and everything, combs his hair just so, when he's like a movie star.

"They're looking at you," I whisper as we pass through the lobby, and a group of girls turns around to stare.

"Nah," he says. "They're looking at you. That is one amazing dress."

We dance. Tucker's not a great dancer, but what he lacks in skill he makes up for in jokes. He has me laughing the entire time. He tries to teach me to two-step at one point, then to western swing. Then a slow song starts and I lay my head on his shoulder and try to savor the moment, like it's just him and me here, no worries, no work schedules, no impending calamities, no future plans at all.

I feel Christian watching me before I see him. He's dancing with Ava Peters on the other side of the dance floor. I lift my head and peek over Tucker's shoulder at him expertly maneuvering Ava through the crowd. Ava laughs up at him, says something coy while looking at him through her false eyelashes.

I press my cheek back into Tucker's shoulder, close my eyes. But when I open them again I still automatically look for Christian, and when I find him, he looks right at me, meets my gaze and holds it.

Will you dance with me, Clara? he asks. *Just one time tonight?*

Before I can answer, Tucker pulls away. He lifts my hand to his mouth and kisses it, thanks me for the dance. I smile at him.

"Let's get something to drink," he says. "It's hot in here."

I let him lead me over to the punch bowl and get me a glass. We stand for a few minutes by the door, the cool air washing over us.

"You having a good time?" he asks.

"Super." I grin. "But I was wondering, where are your other dates?"

"My other dates?"

"If I remember correctly, last year you brought three different women to prom. Where's the elusive Miss Allison Lowell?"

"This year I only have eyes for you."

"Good answer." I loop my arms around his neck and sneak in a kiss.

"Ah, ah, ah, people," says Mr. Phibbs, clearing his throat. Chaperone. I give him my best go-away look.

"Chastity is a virtue," he quips.

"Yes, sir," says Tucker with a respectful nod. Mr. Phibbs nods back and moves off to find some other couple's bliss to break up.

I slip into the bathroom to powder my nose and happen to bump into Kay Patterson. She's examining herself with approval, reapplying her lipstick. She looks ravishing, wearing a long black mermaid-style dress, sparkling with what I hope are fake jewels.

"I'm sorry to hear about your mom," she says.

I meet her big brown eyes in the mirror. I don't think she's uttered a single word to me since last year, back when she and Christian had just broken up.

"Uh, thanks."

"My dad died of colon cancer," she says flatly. "I was three. I don't remember it."

"Oh, I'm sorry. I didn't know."

I can't think of anything to say, so I start washing my hands at the next sink. She finishes perfecting her already perfect face and returns her lipstick to her bag. But then she stands there staring at me. I brace myself for an insult.

"Most people don't know. I have a stepdad, and everybody assumes that he's my father."

I nod, unsure why she's telling me this, and glance at the door.

"Anyway," continues Kay, "I want to offer my condolences. Whatever that's worth."

I murmur thanks again and start waving my hand in front of the paper towel dispenser to get the infrared mechanism to spit out the paper. Nothing happens. Kay hands me a paper towel from a stack on the counter.

"Christian's worried about you," she says. "I can tell. He lost his mom when he was young, too. That's one of the first things that we understood about each other."

"I know," I say to Kay smugly. Meaning: he told me too.

She nods. "You should go easy on him. He deserves to be happy."

"He's not my boyfr—"

"You're looking at him," she says. "You might be all snuggly-wuggly with your boyfriend, but you're looking at him."

"I am not."

She rolls her eyes. After a moment, she says, "He dumped me for you, you know."

I stare at her, a deer caught in the headlights.

Her mouth purses up for a minute like she's suppressing a smile. "He didn't say that to me, of course. He gave me a bunch of phony lines about being fair to me and what I needed and acted like he was doing me a favor. Not that I didn't see it coming. He'd been acting weird for a while. Not himself. And I saw how you looked at him and how he looked at you."

"He didn't look at me," I protest.

She scoffs. "Whatever."

"Christian and I are friends," I try to explain. "I have a

boyfriend."

"Maybe you do," Kay says with a shrug of her bare shoulder. "But you still look at him."

My face must be the color of beets.

Then she looks me up and down, taking in my dress. "You're going to have to step it up if you want to be with him."

"Mind your own business, Kay," I say then, pissed, and storm out.

And plow straight into Christian. Just as another slow song begins to play.

I'm starting to think that prom is forever cursed for me.

"Hi," he says. "Dance with me, Clara?"

We belong together, springs to my mind. I can't tell if it's him or me who thinks it.

Insert fluttery panicky feeling in my chest.

"What . . . I . . . God," I stammer, then sigh in exasperation. "Where's Ava?"

"Ava's not my date. I came stag."

"Stag. You. Why?"

"So my date wouldn't get offended when I wanted to dance with you," he says.

That's when I notice Tucker about five feet away, listening. "You're forgetting one thing," he says, moving to my side and slipping his arm around my waist. "Clara has a date. Me. So your tough luck."

Christian doesn't look fazed.

"It's one dance," he says. "Clara and I are friends. What's the big deal?"

"You had your chance," Tucker replies coolly. "You blew it. So go step on someone else's toes."

Christian hesitates. Looks at me.

Tucker shakes his head. "Dude, don't make me knock you around in here. I don't want to mess up my tux."

A muscle ticks in Christian's cheek. I get an I-could-kick-your-sorry-butt-if-I-wanted-to vibe from him, clear as day.

God. Men.

I step between them.

"No offense, Tuck," I say, turning to him, "but I am not a piece of meat, okay? Stop growling over me. I can handle this myself."

I turn to Christian. "No," I say simply. "Thank you for the offer, but I have a date."

I decide where I belong, I tell him silently.

He nods, takes a step back. *I know.*

Then I take Tucker's hand and lead him away to the dance floor, leaving Christian standing there alone.

The dance isn't much fun after that. I expend a huge amount of energy trying to block Christian out, while at the same time trying not to think about him at all, which turns out to be impossible. Tucker and I are both tensed up for the rest of the night, quiet, pressing close as we dance, holding on like we're afraid we might slip away from each other.

We don't talk on the way home.

Before I moved here, I never got the whole love-triangle thing. You know, in movies or romance novels or whatnot, where there's one chick that all the guys are drooling over, even though you can't see anything particularly special about her. But oh, no, they both must have her. And she's like, oh dear, however will I choose? William is so sensitive, he understands me, he swept me off my feet, oh misery, blubber, blubber, but how can I go on living without Rafe and his devil-may-care ways and his dark and only-a-little-abusive love? Upchuck. So unrealistic, I always thought.

Joke's on me, I guess.

But Christian and I were kind of assigned to each other. He's not interested in me because of my devastating good looks or my winning personality. He wants me because he's been told to want me. I feel things for him because he's like this big mystery to me, and because I've been told to want him, and not by just my mother but by the higher powers, the people upstairs, the Big Guy. Plus Christian's hot, and he always seems to know the right thing to say and he gets me.

Joke's really on me.

And why—this is what I can't understand—do the people upstairs care about who I love when I'm seventeen years old?

Tucker is my choice. My heart, making its own decisions.

I suddenly feel the urge to cry, the biggest surge of sorrow I've felt in a long time, and I think, God, will you just leave me alone?

"Everybody okay?" Wendy says, nervously, from the backseat.

"Peachy," I say.

And then Tucker says, "What's that?"

I stomp on the brakes and we screech to a stop.

Someone's standing in the middle of the road. Waiting for us, it seems. A tall man wearing a long leather coat. A man with coal-black hair. Even from fifty yards away, I know who is it. I can feel it.

Not my sorrow, then.

Samjeeza's.

We're toast.

"Clara, who is that?" Tucker asks.

"Bad news," I mutter. "Everybody buckled in?"

I don't wait for an answer. I don't know what to do, so I go with my gut. I slowly take my foot off the brake, and move it to the gas. Then I floor it.

We pick up speed fast, but at the same time we are in slow motion, creeping along in some alternate time as I clutch the steering wheel and focus on Samjeeza. This car, I figure, is my only weapon. Maybe if I knock him into next week with it, we'll be able to get away, somehow. It's our only chance.

Tucker starts to yell and clutch at the seat. My head gets cloudy with sorrow, but I push through. The beam from the headlights falls on the angel in the road, his eyes glowing like an animal's catching the light, and in that last crazy moment, as the car bears down on him, I think I see him smile.

For a second everything is black. There's white dust floating around my head, from the air bags, I think. Beside me, Tucker suddenly comes to, inhales deeply. I can't see him too well in the dark, but there's a bright silver web of cracked glass on the passenger window. He groans.

"Tucker?" I whisper.

He lifts a shaky hand to his head, touches it gingerly, then looks at his fingers. His blood looks like spilled ink against the sudden whiteness of his skin. He moves his jaw back and forth, like someone punched him.

"Tucker?" I hear the note of panic in my voice, almost like a sob.

"What the heck were you thinking?"

"I'm sorry, Tuck. I—"

"Man, those air bags really hit you, don't they?" he says. "How about you? You hurt?"

"I don't think so."

"Wendy?" he calls.

I crane my head around so I can look toward the backseat,

but all I can see from this angle is a bit of her long hair in front of her face. Tucker starts wrenching on the door, trying to get out, to go to her, but it's partly crushed and refuses to open. I try my door—same problem. I close my eyes, try to clear my head of the fuzzy cobwebs that are collected there.

Do this, I tell myself.

I grasp the door handle firmly and pull it, then press my shoulder into the door and push as hard as I can. There's a pop, then metal shrieking, giving way, and suddenly the door comes completely off its hinges. It falls to the ground. I unbuckle my seat belt and slide out, hurry to the other side of the car, pull the door smoothly off for Tucker, throw it into the weeds at the side of the road. He stares up at me for a second, his mouth slightly open. He's never seen me do anything like that before.

I've never seen me do anything like that before either.

I hold out my hand. He grabs it, and I pull him out of the car. He moves straight back to Wendy's door, which opens easily. He tries to pull her out, but something's keeping her there.

"Her seat belt," I say.

He curses, still dazed, and fumbles around for the latch, then lifts her out. She doesn't make a sound as he carries her to the side of the road, lays her gently on the gravel at the shoulder. He takes off his tuxedo jacket and slips it beneath her head and back.

"Wake up, Wendy," he orders her, but nothing happens. I kneel down next to him and watch the rise and fall of her chest. I listen for the beating of her heart, slow and steady, the most welcome sound in the world.

"She's breathing," I tell Tucker. "Her pulse is strong."

He bows his head in relief. "We have to call 9-1-1. Right now. Where's your phone?"

Back to the car I go. It's totaled, the whole front end completely mangled like I hit a telephone pole at eighty. No sign of the angel. Maybe he poofed himself back to hell. I go back to the driver's side and start digging around in the mess for the small black clutch with my phone in it. I can't find it anywhere. This feels so surreal, like it's not even really happening, a bad dream.

"I don't know where it is," I cry. "I know I had it when we left."

"Clara," Tucker says slowly.

"Just give me a minute. I know it's here."

"Clara," he says again.

Something in his voice stops me. It sounds like it did that day in the mountains when we hiked to see the sunrise, when the grizzly bear came out of the brush. *Don't run,* Tucker had said, exactly that way. I move like molasses back out of the car, straighten up, look toward his voice, and freeze.

Samjeeza is standing next to Tucker. There's not a scratch

on him. My car looks like it's been through a compactor, but here he is, smiling slightly, his posture all casual, like he and Tucker are merely hanging out at the side of the road. He's holding my cell phone.

"Hello, little bird," he says. "Good to see you again."

That name sends a jolt of fear and revulsion straight to the pit of my stomach. My entire body starts to tremble.

"You hit me with your car," he observes. "Is this your boyfriend?"

He turns to Tucker as if he wants to shake his hand, but Tucker looks away, at the ground, at the car, anywhere but into the angel's burning amber eyes. His hands clench into fists.

Samjeeza gives a short laugh. "He's considering whether or not he should hit me. After you struck me with your car, he still thinks that maybe he should fight me." He shakes his head. The motion has that strange blur to it, like there are really two of him, one laid on top of the other, a human body, and some other creature. I'd almost forgotten about that. "Humans," he says with cheerful amusement.

I swallow so hard it hurts my throat. I refuse to look at Wendy lying there. I can't look at Tucker, either; I can't be afraid for him right now. I have to be strong. Find a way to get us all out of this. "What do you want?" I ask, fighting to keep my voice steady.

"An excellent question, one I've asked myself for a very

long time. I was angry with you, little Quartarius, since you . . ." He turns his head and lifts his hair to show me his ear, which even in the dark looks misshapen. It's growing back, I realize. I pulled it off last summer, when I had the glory in my hands, and all this time he's been growing it back.

"I didn't try to . . . ," I say. "I didn't mean . . ."

He waves his hand at me dismissively, turns back. "Of course you did. But it's not worth getting upset over."

"Why are you here?" I ask. "Let's just skip to that part, okay? If you're going to destroy me, do it already."

"Oh no," he says, like the idea offends him, like the last time I saw him he didn't try to do exactly that. "I want to talk to you. I've been watching you, and you seem unhappy, my dear. Conflicted. I wondered if I could help."

"You don't want to help me."

"Oh, but I do," he says. "I've found you very interesting, fascinating even, ever since I first came upon you. There's something your mother's hiding about you, I think."

"She told me all about you," I say.

His eyebrows lift. "All about me? Really. Well, that's a good story, but not so relevant to you. What interests me more is what you're expected to do. Your purpose. Your visions. Your dreams."

"My purpose doesn't have anything to do with you."

He shakes his head. "Or is it something else?" I feel him prodding around in my brain. "She hasn't told you," he says, disappointed. "I would feel it on you if you knew."

The dumb thing is, I'm curious. I want to know what he's talking about, and of course he knows that, which is why he's smiling, and now I'm playing right into his hands because I'm thinking about what he's saying instead of how to get us away from him.

I can't help it. "She hasn't told me what?" I ask.

He holds out my phone. "Let's ask her."

Do something! I need to come up with a strategy, bring the glory, which feels impossible with the heavy cloak of his sorrow around me. The cobwebs in my head won't go away, his sorrow clouding everything.

Think.

"Is this some kind of plan to take me hostage? Because I'm sure Mom will think that's super romantic."

His expression darkens. "Don't make me do something I'll regret," he says, and steps closer to Tucker.

I meet Tucker's eyes. He swallows, a jerk of his Adam's apple. He's scared. Samjeeza's going to kill him, I think. This is why he's not in the cemetery. It would be so easy for Samjeeza—it would only take a moment, a flick of his wrist. Why am I so stupid? Why didn't I see this? All those months I spent trying to think of how to protect him, then dismissing it all when I found out about my mom, and now it comes to this.

I wish I could tell him I'm sorry to have drawn him into

my insane life.

"Go on, call her," Samjeeza says.

I nod, then walk toward him to take the phone, one step and then another. I try to block the sorrow as I suddenly reach that invisible radius around him, this bubble made of pain. Tears burn my eyes. I blink them back. Keep walking. Stand right in front of him and look him in the eye.

Samjeeza puts the phone in my hand.

I press the number two. It rings for a long time, so long I think it's going to go to voice mail, but then I hear Mom's voice.

"Clara?" I know by the sound of her voice that she knows something's wrong.

"Mom . . ." For a moment I can't make my throat work to form the words, the words that will bring her here to Samjeeza and who knows what kind of fate. "Samjeeza's here."

"Are you sure?" she asks.

I feel Samjeeza's eyes on me, his presence in my head poking around, not pushing me, exactly, but trying to read me or listen in or something. "He's standing right here."

Silence on the other end. Then she asks, "Where are you?"

"I don't know." I glance around, disoriented. I can't remember where we are, and all I see are dark fields, telephone poles stretching out into the distance.

"Coltman Road," Tucker says under his breath.

I tell her. "I crashed the car," I say, because some stupid

part of my brain needs to confess just how much I've screwed up.

"Clara, listen to me now," she whispers. She takes a deep, shuddering breath. "You know I can't come to you."

I did know that. Still, shock reverberates through me. I know she's too weak to fly, too weak to even walk upstairs without getting winded, but in my heart, some tiny part of me believed she would come anyway, in spite of everything.

"What does she say?" asks Samjeeza, stepping close to me, his mouth almost against my ear. He's excited. He thinks she's going to rescue me, like last time. The idea pleases him so much, seeing my mother again, looking at her face, hearing her voice. He is practically dancing around with anticipation. He has a plan now, something that will redeem him with the others, a plan that will keep my mother with him forever. In hell.

Only she's not coming.

I think now is the part where we're officially screwed.

"What does she say?" Samjeeza asks again, his mind pressing down on mine, trying to find the information himself. I push back against him and find it surprisingly easy this time to keep him out of my thoughts. I'm stronger, mentally, than last time. I can force him out. Which is good, considering that now I have to lie.

"She's on her way."

"Be brave, my darling," Mom says to me then. "Remember

what I said about fighting him with your heart and your mind. You're stronger than you think. I love you."

"Okay." I hang up the phone. Samjeeza holds out his hand, and I try to contain my trembling as I put the phone back into it.

"Now we wait," he says. He nods like a nervous schoolboy, smiles. "I've never been very good at waiting."

Panic rises like a fluttering bird in my chest, but I squash it back down.

Stall for time, I think. Figure out a way to get him away from Tucker and Wendy so you can bring the glory.

"We need to call an ambulance for my friend." I gesture to Wendy, laid out at Tucker's feet like a rag doll in a black velvet dress. My dress. My responsibility.

Samjeeza glances down at my phone, closes his fingers around it possessively. "I don't think so."

I swallow. "She's hurt. She needs help. It won't matter to you, anyway. We—or you and me and Mom, I mean—could be gone long before the paramedics arrive."

"Please," Tucker asks, and there's no mistaking the genuine plea in his voice. "She's my sister. She could be dying. Please, sir."

Maybe it's the "sir" that gets him. The sorrow around me pulses, and in it I feel a glimmer of something human, compassion maybe. Something conflicted. He glances down at my phone again, opens it. His eyes scan over the buttons, but he doesn't seem to know which one to push. He doesn't know how to use a cell phone, I realize.

"I'll do it," I tell him. "You can watch me. I'll only dial 9-1-1. If I do anything else, you can crush me or whatever it is that you do."

He smiles. "But if I crush you I won't get what I came here for, will I? How about this? You call, and if you try any funny business, I'll crush him."

He cocks his head to indicate Tucker. A cold ripple of fear washes over me. "Okay," I whisper.

"Make it quick," he says.

He hands me the phone. I dial, hold it to my ear with a shaky hand.

"9-1-1, what is your emergency?" a woman answers.

"There's been—" I clear my throat and start again. "There's been a car accident on Coltman Road. Please send an ambulance."

She asks for my name. I can't tell her that, because then, when the paramedics arrive, they'll expect to find me here, and I won't be here. But maybe it doesn't matter. Maybe I'll be too dead to care by then. "I, uh— I'm—" I stammer.

Samjeeza holds out his hand. I've done what I said I would do. I called. I give the phone back to him. The operator's still talking, asking questions, wanting to know the extent of the injuries.

"Hello," Samjeeza says, his voice solemn, but there's

something else in his eyes.

"Hello?" I hear the lady say faintly. "Who is this?"

"I've just come upon the scene. Terrible, terrible accident. I'm afraid the girl's unconscious now. And a young man. They look like they're dressed for a dance. Please hurry. They're both badly injured."

He closes the phone.

Both badly injured.

"But my mom—"

"She isn't coming," he says, his eyes so knowing. He sounds truly disappointed. "I'll just have to be satisfied with you."

He starts to turn toward Tucker.

I look into Tucker's face, his stormy blue eyes comprehending what Samjeeza means to do. Accepting it. Bracing for it.

Time grinds to a halt.

I have to bring the glory. This is the moment I've been practicing all year for. Now.

I look at Tucker but I don't feel anything but my heart beating, so slowly it's like a low thump every five seconds, and I can feel the blood it's pumping through my body, to my lungs, in and out, filling me with strength, with life, and then with a sense of myself and something more than just my body. Something more than human. My spirit. My soul.

Light explodes around me. I turn toward Samjeeza and at the same moment, slowed down twenty times, it seems, he looks at my face and knows what I'm up to. He flares with rage, but doesn't have time to act on it. He moves with unearthly speed away, out of reach of the glory.

I take a deep breath, let it out slow, feeling the light tingling at my fingertips, shining out of my body, my hair gleaming with it, my chest filling with warmth. A feeling of calm settles over me. I turn again to Tucker. He lifts a hand to shield his eyes from my light. I take his other hand in mine. It feels cool, clammy, against my almost feverish skin. He flinches at my touch, then forces himself to relax, lowers his hand, squints at me like he's trying really hard to look at the sun. Unshed tears in his eyes. And fear.

I reach up and put my finger against the cut on his head, watch as the light caresses him, the skin knitting itself back together, until there's no trace of the wound.

"It's okay," I whisper.

A laugh pierces my tranquility. Samjeeza, a safe distance away, laughing.

"I keep underestimating you," he says almost admiringly. "You are a tough little bird."

"Go away."

He laughs again. "I want to find out what happens next, don't you?"

"Go. Away."

"You can't hold that forever, you know."

He said something like that to my mom, that day in the

woods. She brought the glory and he said, *You can't hold that forever,* and she said, *I can hold it long enough.*

What is long enough? Even now, after only a few minutes, I feel myself starting to tire. It's like holding the door to my soul wide open while the wind pushes steadily against it. Sooner or later, that door will close.

Samjeeza closes his eyes. "I can almost hear the sirens. Racing this way. Things will be interesting when they get here."

I squeeze Tucker's hand. He tries to smile at me. I try to smile back.

A plan would be nice. Sitting here waiting for my lightbulb to burn out, so not a plan. Waiting for the ambulance to come, adding more people to the mix, also not a plan.

"Why don't you just drop this nonsense?" Samjeeza says. "Not that I'm not impressed. For someone your age, your dilution of blood, to exhibit glory on your own, it's rather unheard of. But you should stop this now."

He's speaking calmly, but I can feel that he's getting mad.

I've seen him mad before. It's not pretty. He tends to do things like launch fireballs at your head.

Headlights turn onto the road. My breath freezes in my lungs. I nearly lose the glory. It flickers, dims, but I hold on.

"Come now, enough foolishness," Samjeeza says impatiently. "You and I must go."

It's too late. The vehicle approaches us slowly. Stops, a

squeak of brakes. But it isn't an ambulance. It's a beat-up silver Honda with a rusty green fender. I strain to look past my own radiance to see the figure inside. A man with white hair and a beard.

Mr. Phibbs.

I've never seen a more welcome sight than Mr. Phibbs in his tacky brown polyester suit, strolling toward us with a smile like he's taking a leisurely walk in the middle of the night. I feel stronger as he nears, like I can do this, whatever I'm asked, whatever it takes. I feel hope.

"Evening," Mr. Phibbs says, nodding to me. "How's everybody?"

"She's hurt." I point down to Wendy. Still breathing, thank God. "The paramedics are on their way. They should be here soon."

Samjeeza eyes him.

"I see," Mr. Phibbs says. He turns his attention to the brooding Black Wing. "What seems to be the problem here?"

"Who are you?" Samjeeza asks.

"I'm a teacher." Mr. Phibbs readjusts his glasses. "These are my students."

"I have business with the girl," Samjeeza says almost politely. "We'll be on our way, and then you can tend to the others."

"Afraid I can't allow that," says Mr. Phibbs. "Yes, you could probably squash me like a bug if you took a mind to.

If you could get to me," he adds. "But I come against you in the name of the Lord Almighty, whom you have defiled. So slither back into the dark, Watcher."

I hope, for our sake, that he's not bluffing.

Samjeeza doesn't move.

"Are you having trouble hearing me?" Mr. Phibbs asks like this fallen angel is a tardy student. "I see you have some damage to your ear. That your doing, Clara?"

"Um, yeah."

"Well, good for you." He turns back to Samjeeza.

"Be careful, old man," growls the angel. Around him the air starts to crackle with energy. I begin to get very worried that he's going to zap us into hell.

"Corbett," I say nervously.

Faster than a blink, Mr. Phibbs holds up one of his hands and the light surrounding us brightens into it, swirling itself into a long, thin shape with a point of fiercely shining light at the end. An arrow, is my first thought, an arrow made from glory, and before I even have time to analyze what that could mean, Mr. Phibbs makes a sweeping motion with his arm and fires the thing straight at Samjeeza.

I watch in slow motion as the arrow arcs through the air like a falling star, then strikes the angel in the shoulder. It makes a noise like a knife sinking into a watermelon. He looks at it, startled, then back at Mr. Phibbs incredulously. The light from the arrow seeps from his shoulder like blood, and wherever it touches it hisses, eating away that second layer that he wears over his true self. He reaches up and closes his hand around the shaft. His brows knit together, then he wrenches the arrow out. He howls in pain as it comes free. He drops it, and it bursts into tiny sparkles when it strikes the ground. Breathing hard, he looks right at me, not at Mr. Phibbs or Tucker but at me, and his eyes are sad. His body suddenly has a transparent quality to it, muted and gray, even his skin, like he's becoming a ghost.

And then he's gone.

Beside me Mr. Phibbs exhales slowly, the only indication that any of this was mind-blowingly scary. I finally let go of the glory, and it fades.

"Well, now we know why he's mad at me, don't we?" he says cheerfully.

"How did you do that?" I gasp. "That was *so* cool."

"David and Goliath, my dear," he answers. "All it takes is one smooth little pebble to drop a giant. Although, to be honest, I was aiming for his heart. I've never been the best shot."

Tucker stumbles off a few steps into the weeds to throw up. Mr. Phibbs wrinkles up his nose as we listen to him losing his dinner.

"Humans and glory don't mix well, I'm afraid," Mr. Phibbs says.

"You okay?" I call to Tucker.

He straightens up and comes back out to the road, wiping his mouth on his tux sleeve.

"Will he be back?" he asks.

I look to Mr. Phibbs, who sighs.

"I'd assume so."

"But you wounded him," I say, my voice straining. "Doesn't it take time for them to heal? I mean, I tore his ear off months ago, and that wasn't fixed yet."

Mr. Phibbs nods grimly. "I should have struck at the heart."

"Would that have killed him?"

"Lord, no. You can't kill an angel," he says.

"Look." Tucker points off in the distance, where we see a police car, followed by an ambulance and a fire truck, tearing along the highway toward us.

"Took them long enough," I say.

Mr. Phibbs kneels to examine Wendy, his fingers touching lightly at her neck. Her eyes flutter, but she doesn't wake. She moans. It's kind of a beautiful sound.

"Will she be okay?" Tucker asks, his face still a bit green.

"Oh yes, right as rain, I think," Mr. Phibbs answers.

Then we're all quiet as the sirens get closer, the pitch changing as it draws near, until we're bathed in the red and blue flashing lights of the clueless people coming to help.

14

SING A SONG OF SORROW

It's almost morning when I walk through the front door, still wearing my stained-and-rumpled prom dress, missing my shoes. Jeffrey and Mom are waiting in the living room. She makes this strangled cry when she sees me, gets up so fast that it alarms Billy, and practically falls into my arms to hug me.

"I'm so sorry," she says against my hair. "Are you all right?"

Dumb question.

"Mom . . . ," I say awkwardly, holding her. "I'm okay."

Behind me, Mr. Phibbs clears his throat. He stayed with me the whole time at the emergency room, even after Billy showed up, through all the unnecessary exams they put me through, waiting in the lobby with the Averys for news about

Wendy, who was okay, just as Mr. Phibbs said she would be, and the barrage of questions from the police I didn't know how to answer.

Mom pulls away from me, looks at Mr. Phibbs with shining eyes. "Thank you, Corbett."

"Welcome," he says gruffly.

"What did you tell them happened?" Jeffrey asks, and by "them" he means everybody fully human.

"The official story is that she hit a moose." Corbett chuckles.

A moose. Maybe someday I'll find that funny. But not today.

"I shouldn't have tried to hit him with the car," I say, rubbing my temples. "That was stupid."

"Are you kidding? That was gutsy as all get-out," Billy says.

"You were amazing tonight, Clara," Mom adds. "You faced him. You kept everyone safe. You summoned glory all by yourself, under an incredible amount of pressure, and you held it until help came. I have never been so proud of you."

There's wet stuff on my cheeks. I wipe at it.

"Oh, honey," Mom says, taking me by the arm, drawing me into the living room, where I think she means to plop me down in front of the fire and try to make everything better with words.

I pull my arm away. "How about you tell me now, Mom?"

"What?"

"Samjeeza said there's something you're not telling me, about my purpose or my visions or something strange about me. Is there?"

She flinches like I slapped her. She and Billy exchange a look that's a silent argument.

So there is something.

"Samjeeza had some sort of plan," I say. "He wanted to make you stay with him this time."

Mom frowns and goes quiet. Then Billy says, out of the blue, "Mags, don't even think about it."

"I wasn't," Mom says.

"You were. I know you. That man, if you want to call him a man, can't be redeemed. He's made his bed. You can't talk him out of being a Black Wing."

"He thought if he took you to hell with him, it would make things right with the other Black Wings. What does that mean?" I ask.

"He was supposed to kill me, once," Mom says like it's no big deal. "He didn't do it. For that he was punished."

"He hasn't been quite right since then," fills in Billy. "He's fractured. Which is why there's no way on God's green earth I'm going to let you anywhere near that crazy-ass angel. He'll kill you."

Mom sighs. "Bill, I'm already dying. I don't have anything to lose."

Mr. Phibbs coughs. "I'm with Billy. I think it best that you stay away from him. You have everything to lose. He could grab on to your soul and not let you go, keep you down there with him for who knows how long."

"He couldn't keep me," Mom argues. Her gaze flickers over to Billy. "Not forever. No matter what he thinks."

Mr. Phibbs shrugs. "It's not the kind of place I'd want to spend even ten minutes."

"All right." Mom's mouth twists in frustration. "I won't get near him. I'll stay right here and fade away."

It's the first time she's ever come off as anything but graciously accepting of what's happening to her. The first time I've ever seen her act truly beaten.

"You should go to bed," she says to me. "We can talk more about this later, but you're exhausted. You need to sleep."

"I guess I'd better go pack," I say as I turn toward the stairs.

Mom gives me a blank look.

"Don't we have to get out of here? I mean, Samjeeza said he'd been watching me. He must know where we live. We're not safe here. He'll come back. You know he will."

She nods. "I'd say that's a given. It's only a matter of when. But he knows you now, Clara. If he truly wants to find you, he will. It won't do us any good to run away."

Somehow I don't find that comforting.

She closes her eyes like she needs a nap, right now. "We have to stay here, Clara. This is where I'm supposed to be."

She means that this is where she's supposed to die. I swallow.

"The house is safe," she says.

"And the school grounds," adds Mr. Phibbs. "I saw to that years ago."

"Wait," I interrupt. "How is it safe?"

"Hallowed," he answers. "The ground's been consecrated. A Black Wing can't set foot on holy ground, it's too painful for them."

"So our house is on hallowed ground?" I ask. The word is familiar. The congregation was talking about whether or not the cemetery was hallowed.

"Yes," Mr. Phibbs answers.

I think back to the day I first saw our house, the sense of warmth and security and well-being that filled me as soon as I got out of the car. I wonder if that was its hallowed-ness, or whatever you'd call it.

And school. That's why Mom had Angela and me go to the school, that time I had the sorrow attack. Because it was safe.

Mr. Phibbs turns back to Mom. "Billy and I can shuttle the children to and from school every day."

"All right," Mom says. "We'll work out a schedule. I'm sorry, Clara, but I'm afraid it will feel a bit like being grounded."

"What about me?" Jeffrey asks.

I'd totally forgotten he was there, standing in the corner with his arms crossed over his chest.

Mom's midnight eyes flash with sadness. "You'll have to stay home, too. I'm sorry."

"Fantastic," he mutters. "Just what I needed, another heavenly dictate. For how long?"

"Until I'm gone," Mom says.

He turns and glares at me like this is my fault, his jaw flexing like he's clenching his teeth, then off he goes to his room to brood about it. We listen to the door slam.

"And as for you," Billy says, "absolutely no more middle-of-the-night trips to the Lazy Dog. I will be the one nailing your windows shut, I swear. This is no time to be gallivanting off to see your boyfriend."

Tucker. I keep flashing back to the look on his face when Samjeeza was going to hurt him. The way I felt in that moment, unable to stop it.

But you were able to stop it, says my inner voice.

Yeah, but what about next time? What about Wendy, her arm broken in two places, moderate concussion, her confused expression at the hospital when she woke up and they explained what had happened. *A moose?* she kept saying. *I don't remember. . . .*

All my fault. They would never have been in danger if not for me.

"How is Tucker?" Mom asks. "Is he okay?"

"He's shaken up. But he's fine. They say Wendy's going to be okay, too." I don't want to think anymore about what might have happened. I'm too thrashed. "I think I have to go to bed now. Good night. Or should I say, good morning?"

Mom nods. "Good night." Then as I'm climbing the stairs, she says, "You really did make me proud tonight. I love you, don't forget that."

I know she loves me. But she's keeping something from me. Still.

The secrets never end.

The sun is coming up by the time I get out of the shower. I put on a clean cami and pajama pants, then gather my ruined ball gown from where I left it by the bathroom door, take it and dump it in a corner, where it lays like a deflated balloon.

No more dances for me. No more formal wear. No more stupid guys doing stupid things like fighting over who gets to dance with me, who I belong with.

No more car.

But Tucker is alive.

I detect movement outside, and jump back, heart beating fast even though now I know Samjeeza can't come here. Then Christian moves into the window, stands there looking in like he has every right to be here. I wait for his voice in my head or a flicker of what he's feeling now, but I get nothing. My head is completely quiet, locked up tight.

Christian frowns. Then he reaches up and taps softly on the window.

I'm so freaking tired. It's like every muscle registers the night I've had at the same time. I want to ignore him, stumble over to my bed and hide under the covers.

Instead I go to the window and force it open.

"It's not a good time," I say.

"Are you okay? I came by earlier, to apologize for being such an idiot at the dance, and your mom said you got in a car accident."

I don't have the energy to tell him the story. So I reach out the window, lay my hand on his shoulder, and unlock my mind for him, let him see every terrifying moment of the entire ordeal. When I'm done his face is pale. An involuntary shiver passes through him. He coughs.

"Are *you* okay?" I ask.

He leans against the windowsill. "I've never done that before," he says. "Had something like that . . . dumped directly into my head. It's a lot."

"Try living it."

"And your mom is sure you're safe here? She doesn't think it would be safer to—"

"Flee? Run screaming for the hills? Go into the witness protection program? Nope. Mom says it won't do us any good. Plus the house is on hallowed ground."

He nods like that nugget of information is no surprise. Of course my house is on hallowed ground. Aren't all the good houses?

"I wish I could have been there for you," he says. "Helped you."

He means it. And it's nice. But I'm crabby. I'm tired. I'm not in the mood for nice.

"I should go," he says.

"You really should."

"I am sorry about what happened at the dance," he says. "I don't want you to think that I'm that kind of guy."

He thinks I'm mad at him about that. Like I'm still thinking about that.

"What kind of guy?"

"Who'd move in on another guy's girlfriend."

"I don't. Think you're that kind of guy. So it's okay, really."

"I do want us to be friends, Clara. I like you. I'd like you even if it weren't for all the duty stuff. I wanted you to know that."

Seriously, I am way too tired to be having this conversation. "We are friends. And right now I have to tell you, as your friend, go home, Christian. Because I really need this day to be over now."

He summons his wings and goes. I shut the window. And even though I'm exhausted, and the last thing I want to think about is the dance and my purpose and how all arrows still seem to be pointing at him being at the center of it, now that he's gone I feel lonely, as lonely as I've ever felt.

I hate these freaking stairs in the woods. I hate how well I know them, how I've got every inch of them memorized, the cracks, the grooves in the cement, the dark green moss like velvet pushing its way out. I hate the rough scrape they make under my feet. I hate the rail I cling to. If I had a choice right now, I'd take a jackhammer to these stairs, shatter them to pieces, take the pieces one by one and drop them at the bottom of Jackson Lake.

I'd bulldoze this entire cemetery.

I'd burn this black dress I'm wearing. I'd chuck Mom's nice shoes in the garbage.

But I can't. I'm in the dream, and in the dream the one in control is future-Clara, who hardly feels her feet moving. She wears her numbness like a cloak around her, hiding, weighing her down so each step forward is an effort. She thinks that she should cry. But she can't. She wants to let go of Christian's hand, but she doesn't. It's like we're both paralyzed, incapable, in this moment, of any kind of action other than walking, always with the freaking walking, always up, to the spot where the people are gathering.

To the hole in the ground.

To death. My mother's death. And there's a Black Wing on the fringes of my mind, grieving, out-of-his-mind grieving, a gaping hole in his heart.

Mom wasn't joking about it like being grounded, that next

week. Every morning Billy drives us to school. She always acts casual, like it's no biggie, but she's hyperalert.

I made a case for quitting school altogether, spending the time with Mom, but she wouldn't hear of it. "What would Stanford say?" she jokes.

"You have cancer. I'm pretty sure they'd understand," I reply. A solid argument.

No go. Mom has this thing about normalcy. Acting like everything's fine for as long as you can. It's annoying, because since when have we ever been normal? It feels pointless to pretend otherwise. But she's adamant. Normal kids go to school. So to school we will go.

I want my life back. I want to go to the Garter and hang out with Angela. I want to have dinner at the Averys on Sunday nights, smooch Tucker on the back porch. That's what normal people do, right? See their friends? Their boyfriends? Plus I want to fly. Sometimes I feel the presence of my wings like they're itching to stretch themselves out in the wide-open sky, aching to feel the wind carry me.

"That sucks," Angela says at lunch on Thursday, four days post-crash. She takes a huge bite of a green apple and chews it noisily. "But you did get attacked by a Black Wing, Clara. Better safe than sorry."

"I feel safe *and* sorry."

She gives me her no-nonsense, snap-out-of-it look. "Okay, better safe than dead."

"Good point."

"God, I wish I could have been there," she exclaims, so loudly that two people passing by pause like, what's gotten into Angela Zerbino? She glares at them and they move on.

"You have all the fun without me," she whines more quietly.

"It wasn't fun. Trust me."

"I bet it was a rush. All that adrenaline pumping. Nerves firing."

"Since when are you an adrenaline junkie?" I ask. "And no, it was not a rush. Just terrifying. I-hope-I-don't-soil-myself, I-hope-I-don't-die kind of terrifying."

"The Black Wing was magnificent though, wasn't he? Was he something spectacular to look at? Did you see his wings?"

"He's not an animal in the wild, Ange."

"Definitely not a moose, that's for sure," she says with a sniff.

"Did I mention the terrifying? The whole time I was thinking, that's it, that's why Tucker's not at the cemetery. Samjeeza's going to kill him."

She stops mid-bite with her apple. "What cemetery?"

Crapzol.

Angela looks at me intently. "Clara, what cemetery?"

I might as well tell her.

"My recurring dream is a vision. That strange forest with the stairs, it's Aspen Hill Cemetery. It's a graveside. At first I thought it was Tucker who was going to die, because he's not there, in my vision, but then it turned out to be my mom."

She puts her hands to her head like I am blowing her mind. "How'd you figure it out?"

"Christian. His mom is buried there. Although I probably would have figured it out on my own, eventually. It's pretty obvious now."

"So you told Christian." She looks truly hurt. "You told Christian and not me."

I try to come up with a good excuse, like that I didn't want to distract her from her purpose, I didn't want to say anything until I knew for sure what it was about, point out that I didn't even tell my mom until I had to, but all I can say is, "Hey, you're the one who made me tell Christian about the dream in the first place."

"Don't you trust me?" she asks.

She's about to say something else, but suddenly there's an upset in the cafeteria. A public breakup, that much is obvious right away, in the middle of the lunchroom. A girl starts crying, not a hysterical kind of cry, nothing so dramatic as, like, Kay last year, but the crowd still moves away from her. Then I recognize this pathetic creature as Kimber, my brother's girlfriend. And Jeffrey, like an impassive stone statue beside her.

"Jeffrey," Kimber says, between gasps of air. She has hold of his letterman's jacket. "You don't mean it."

"It's not working, Kimber," he says, and without another word, he twists, pulls her hands away from him, and heads for the door.

I catch up with him before he gets there. "Jeffrey, you can't dump her in front of everybody," I whisper, trying not to attract any more attention. "Come on."

"Don't tell me what to do," is all he says. Then he's gone.

Kimber's friends have all gathered around her by this point, making sympathetic cooing noises, shooting glares in the direction that Jeffrey slunk off to, loudly declaring that he's a jerk, he didn't deserve her, his loss. She doesn't say anything. She sits at a table, shoulders slumped, the very picture of dejection.

I wander back to my table. "What's going on with him?" Angela asks. "Or can you not tell me that, either?"

Ouch. "He's not taking this thing with my mom very well."

"Makes sense," she says with a flash of sympathy in her eyes. "Too bad, though. Kimber's a sweet girl. That was kind of . . . cold."

I remember this one time when we were kids, when a bird flew into our window. We were watching Saturday morning cartoons, and then, *thump*. Jeffrey ran out to see what it was. He picked the bird up, held it gently in his hands, asked me if we couldn't fix it, somehow. It was a starling with its neck broken. It was already dead.

"Where did it go?" he asked when I tried to explain it to him.

"Heaven, maybe. I don't know."

He'd wanted to bury it in the backyard, said things like a miniature pastor about the life the bird must have lived, flying free, how its brother birds would miss him. And when we covered it with dirt, he'd cried.

What happened to that kid? I wonder now, struggling to push down the lump that's risen in my throat. Where did he go? And I suddenly want to cry. I feel like everything is falling apart in our lives.

"So," Angela says. "We should talk."

"Um——" This could be a problem, being that we're under lock and key all the time. "The thing is, I'm grounded——" I say. But then I stop, because something else catches my attention. A feeling, lingering on the edges of my mind. Something that shouldn't be here, not this way, this heaviness pushing in.

Sorrow.

I go to the window and look out. Storm clouds, blue-black and threatening, cover the mountains. There's a charge in the air, like lightning.

And sorrow. A very definite flavor of sorrow.

Samjeeza is here.

"Clara?" Angela says. "Earth to Clara."

It's not possible, though. The school is on hallowed ground. Samjeeza can't come here.

I scan the distance, past the parking lot, past the fence where the school grounds end and a field begins, an empty grove of cottonwood trees. I don't see Samjeeza, but he's there. There's a pull to his sorrow this time, a loneliness that calls to me. I lay my hand on the cool glass and let it tug at me. I strain my eyes to see into that field. There's something black in the tall grass.

"What is it?" Angela asks, coming up beside me. Her voice breaks the spell the sorrow was casting on me. I back away from the window.

Christian is suddenly by my side, and he puts his hand on my shoulder, making me jump again. His green eyes are wide with alarm.

"Do you feel it?" I gasp.

"I feel *you*. What's wrong?"

"Samjeeza is here." Somehow I have the presence of mind to keep my voice low, so I'm not shouting this thing to the entire school.

"Here?" Angela repeats in a stunned voice from behind him. "Seriously? Where?"

"In the field behind the school. I think he's in a different form, but I can feel him."

"I feel him, too," Christian says. "Although I can't tell if it's coming on its own or through you."

Angela's eyebrows come together. She concentrates for a few seconds, then exhales.

"I don't feel anything." She glances down the hall toward the side door, in the direction of the field. She wants to go out there. She wants to see this angel.

I squeeze her arm, hard. "No." I reach into my pocket for my cell, then realize Samjeeza still has it. "Do you have your phone?"

She nods and drops her backpack on the floor to pull her phone out of an outer pocket.

"Call my house. Not my cell," I say quickly, before she dials. "Billy will probably answer. Tell her what's going on."

I turn to Christian. "Go get Mr. Phibbs. He usually eats lunch in his office. Go find him."

He nods once, then sprints back toward the exit. Angela starts talking excitedly into the phone.

"Where's Tucker?" I ask, ice forming in my chest at the image that flashes through my brain of Tucker heading out to the parking lot, off to rodeo practice. Samjeeza knows him now. He knows that I love him.

Tucker's not at the cemetery, I think again.

"He's right over there," Angela answers quickly, seeing the terror in my face.

I whip around, spot Tucker immediately, and everything inside me goes limp with relief. He stands up when he sees me coming, crosses toward me, and puts his arms around me without me even having to ask.

"What's up?" he asks. "You look like—"

"The angel's here, out in the field behind the school." I shiver.

"Right now?"

Oh yes. It's still there. The sorrow weaving its way to me, wrapping tendrils around my heart, Samjeeza's sad loneliness like the aching notes of a siren's song.

"Yes," I say. "Right now."

"What do we do?" he asks grimly.

"Stay inside. He can't enter school grounds. It's holy ground."

In spite of the dire situation, a side of Tucker's mouth twists in a wry smile. "School is holy ground. You've got to be kidding me."

Angela, still on the phone, holds her hand up.

"Billy wants to know if we're all accounted for," she says.

No, I realize. We're not. One of us isn't here. Jeffrey. He stormed out.

Toward the parking lot.

"Clara, wait!" Tucker calls after me, as I run. "You're running *toward* him?"

"Stay there!" I yell over my shoulder.

I don't take any more time to explain. I don't think about how it might look to the other students. I just run. I barrel out of the cafeteria and down the hall, burst out of the side door, run straight toward the parking lot, following the sorrow. Then I see Jeffrey, walking between the cars, head lifted like he's listening to something. Curious. Following the call.

"Jeffrey!" I cry.

He stops, glances over his shoulder at me. Scowls. Turns back toward the field. He's so close to the end of the parking lot. I run, as fast as I've ever run, not caring if people see. I focus on closing the distance between my brother and me. I focus everything I have on saving him. And right at the edge of the low wooden fence that marks the beginning of the field, I reach him. I grab him by the shoulders and tug him backward so hard we both lose our balance and fall. He tries to push me away from him.

"Jeffrey," I gasp. "Stop."

"God, Clara. Calm down. It's just a dog," he says, still trying to shake me off.

I scramble to my feet, still hanging on to him. I look out into the field. He's right. It's a dog, a large black dog, about the size and shape of a lab, but with thicker fur. Something wolfish in the way it's sitting there so completely still, looking at us, one ear erect, the other slightly bent. Something definitely human in its yellow eyes.

"It's a dog, see?" Jeffrey says again. "It's hurt." He steps toward the fence. "Here, boy."

I yank him back, put my arms around him, and cling. "It's not a dog. Look at its ear. See how the right one's mangled? That's because I pulled it off last summer. He had to grow it back. See on its shoulder, where it's bleeding? That's where

Mr. Phibbs got him with the glory arrow."

"What?" Jeffrey shakes his head like he's trying to clear it.

"It's a Black Wing."

The dog stands up. Approaches the fence. Whines. A low, plaintive sound that stirs the sorrow up to an even higher intensity. *Come. Come.*

"That's Samjeeza," I insist, pulling back on Jeffrey's shoulder, but he's stronger than me. I'm not moving him.

"I think you've officially gone off the deep end," Jeffrey says.

"No, she hasn't, son," comes a voice. Mr. Phibbs, walking up briskly behind us. "Come away from there now, children," he says.

Jeffrey stops pushing against me. We turn and walk slowly to Mr. Phibbs. He keeps his eyes trained on the dog. It growls.

"What, do you want another one?" Mr. Phibbs asks. "I can put one right between the eyes this time."

It growls again, a sound full of so much hate it makes the hairs stand up on the back of my neck. Then it vanishes. No poof or magic words or anything. A chill in the air, a hint of ozone, and he's gone.

We all take a minute to catch our breath.

"Crazy," Jeffrey says finally. "I would have taken him home if you hadn't stopped me."

15

ANGEL ON MY DOORSTEP

From then on I can feel Samjeeza in that field almost every day. He doesn't always call to me, that sad seductive music that I can't keep out of my head. But he shows up even if it's just for five minutes. He wants me to know he's there.

He doesn't cause any trouble, doesn't harm any of the students, doesn't show himself. He doesn't attack us coming and going to school, but he knows where we live now. He follows us home. I can't usually feel him while I'm in the house, since our land is all hallowed and there's so much of it, from the main road to the woods to the stream behind the house. He can't come close enough to bother me. Still, if I try, if I listen for him, I can sometimes hear him. Waiting.

I wonder if Mom can feel him, too.

"You have to learn to block him," she says when I ask her. "It would be a good idea to learn how to block your empathy completely, because there are times you're going to need to."

"How?"

"It's like closing a door," she answers. "You erect a spiritual barrier between you."

"A spiritual barrier?"

"You close yourself off from the force that connects us to each other. It's not good for you, in the long run. It will make you numb if you do it all the time, but it might be the best solution for now. Just so you can get through school without so many distractions. Try it."

"What, you mean right now? With you?"

"Yes," she says. She reaches out and takes my hand. "Use your empathy on me."

For some reason this scares me a little.

"I don't know," I say. "I can't control it. The only times my empathy really works when I ask it to is when I'm with Christian. And sometimes . . . it's not just feelings I get from people. It's thoughts, too. Why is that?"

"Our thoughts and feelings are entwined," she tells me. "Memories, images, desires, feelings. You seem to have a knack with feelings. It will be stronger when you touch the person, skin to skin. And sometimes you might get an image or a specific sentence that they're thinking at the moment.

But mostly it will be feelings, I think."

"Can you do it?"

"No." She lowers her gaze for a minute. "I don't often pick up feelings. But I am telepathic. I can read thoughts."

Hello, news flash! No wonder she always seems two steps ahead of me. When I was a kid I seriously thought she had eyes in the back of her head.

Yes, it's been a particularly effective parenting tool, she says in my mind. She smiles. "Don't look at me like that, Clara. I haven't been reading your every waking thought. Most of the time I choose to stay out of people's heads, especially the heads of my children, because you deserve some privacy."

Now let's practice, she says. *Open yourself up. Try to feel what I feel.*

I close my eyes, hold my breath, and listen, like what she's feeling is something I could hear. Suddenly I see a flash of pale pink behind my eyelids. I gasp.

"Pink," I whisper.

"Concentrate on it."

I try. I try to look into the pink until my head starts to ache, and just when I'm about to give up I see that it's curtains, pink eyelet curtains hanging in a window.

Pink eyelet curtains is not a feeling.

But there's more—laughing, a baby laughing, that kind of laugh they get where you think they're going to pee, they're laughing so hard. And a man laughing, a sweet, delighted kind of laugh. I recognize it. Dad. My throat closes up a bit, thinking of Dad.

"Don't let your own feelings interfere," Mom says.

Pink. Laughter. Warmth. I can feel what it is to her. "Joy," I say finally. I open my eyes.

She smiles. "Yes," she says. "That was joy."

"Mom—"

"Now try to block it out."

I close my eyes again, but this time I visualize building an invisible wall in the space between us, brick by brick, thought by thought, until there's nothing left behind my eyelids, no color, no feeling, nothing but a gray and empty void.

"Okay, I don't feel anything." I open my eyes again and she has a strange expression on her face: relief.

"Well done," she says, and pulls her hand from mine. "Now you'll just have to practice it until you can shut out who you want to, when you want to."

That would certainly be handy.

So all that next week, whenever I feel Samjeeza at school, I work on erecting a spiritual barrier between us. At first, absolutely nothing happens. Samjeeza's sorrow continues to flow into me, making it hard to think about anything at all. But slowly but surely I begin to feel the ways in which I am connected with the life around me, with that energy inside me where the glory is, and when I recognize it in myself I can then work on shutting it down. It's like the opposite of using glory, in some ways. To bring glory, you have to still the inner voices. To shut it off, you have to keep yourself completely occupied by your thoughts. It's hard work.

What makes it even worse is that on Friday, Mom lies down and never really gets back up. She stays in bed in her pajamas, laid back on the pillows like a porcelain doll. Sometimes she reads but mostly she sleeps, for hours, day and night. It becomes a rare thing to catch her awake.

In the middle of the next week a nurse shows up, Carolyn. I'd seen her before at the congregational meetings. Her specialty seems to be end-of-life care for angel-bloods.

"I don't want you to worry about any of the details," Mom says one day when Jeffrey and I are both keeping her company. "Billy is going to take care of everything, okay? Just be there for each other. That's what I want. Hold fast to each other. Help each other through. Can you do that?"

"Okay," I say. I turn and look at Jeffrey.

"Fine," he mutters, and then leaves the room.

He's been pacing around our house all week like a caged animal. Sometimes I feel his rage like a blast of heat, at how unfair this all is, our mom dying because of a stupid rule, our lives dictated by some force that doesn't seem to care that it's ruining everything. He hates his own powerlessness. And he especially hates all this isolation, having to stay inside, hiding out. I think he'd rather just go out there and face Samjeeza and have it over with.

Mom sighs. "I wish he wasn't so angry. It's only going to make things harder for him."

But truth be told, the isolation is starting to get to me too. All I have now is school, where the presence of Samjeeza keeps me on constant alert, and then home, where the thought that Mom's about to die is always with me. I talk to Angela on the phone, but we decided it was best for her to lie low since Samjeeza showed up, since he doesn't know about her. Plus she's been quiet in an offended way since I told her about Aspen Hill Cemetery.

"I have a theory," she says to me one night over the phone. "About your dream."

"Okay."

"You keep thinking that the reason Tucker's not there is because he's hurt or something."

"Or something," I say. "What's your point?"

"What if he's not there because the two of you break up?"

It's funny that somehow that thought scares me even more than the idea that he'll be hurt. "Why would we break up?" I ask.

"Because you're supposed to be with Christian," she says. "Maybe that's what the dream is telling you."

It hurts me, that thought. I know I could make it better by going to see Tucker in person, by kissing him and assuring him that I love him and letting him hold me, but I don't dare.

It doesn't matter what Angela thinks. I can't risk putting him in danger. Again.

I'm upstairs doing the laundry, sorting the whites from the darks, and all I can think about is what Angela said. Maybe we break up. And not because I'm "supposed to be with Christian," I think then, but because I want him to be safe. I want him to be happy. I want him to have a normal life, and I'd have to be tripping to think that kind of thing is possible with me. I toss the whites in the washer and put in some bleach and I feel such a heaviness and a sense of dread that I want to scream, fill this silent house with my noise. This is not another person's sorrow, not a Black Wing's, but my own. I'm bringing it on myself.

I go to my room to take a crack at my homework, and I'm sad.

I talk on the phone with Wendy, and I'm sad. She's all excited about college, going on about what the dorms are like at WSU and how awesome it's going to be, and I'm sad. I try to play along, act like I'm excited too, but all I feel is sad.

Sad, sad, sad.

Later, the washing machine beeps. I go to transfer the clothes to the dryer. I'm elbow deep in damp clothes when suddenly the sadness lifts. Instead I feel this incredible, permeating joy, warmth flooding me, a sense of well-being, a whirl of true happiness so overwhelming it makes me want to laugh out loud. I put my hand over my mouth and close my eyes as the feelings wash over me. I don't understand why. Something strange is happening.

Maybe I'm finally cracking under the pressure.

The doorbell rings.

I drop a pair of Jeffrey's underwear on the laundry room floor and run downstairs for the door. I get up on tiptoes to peer out the small window at the top of the door. My breath catches.

There's an angel standing on my doorstep. I can feel him. An *angel*. A White Wing, to be exact. A tall golden-haired man with such love pouring off him that it brings a whole different kind of tears to my eyes.

I fling open the door.

"Dad?"

He turns to me and smiles, a goofy lopsided grin that I had totally forgotten about until right this minute. I stare at him wordlessly, take in the way the sun glints off his hair with this definite unearthly kind of light. I examine his face, which hasn't aged a day, not since I saw him four years ago, not ever, in all my memory of him. He hasn't changed. Why did I never notice that before?

He's an angel.

"Don't I get a hug?" he asks.

I move zombielike into his arms.

Here's what I would expect to feel in this moment: Um, surprised. Amazed. Astounded. Knocked over flat by the sheer impossibility of the idea. But all I feel right now is his joy. Like pink curtains, Dad's hands on my waist, holding me up high. That kind of joy. He hugs me tight, lifts me off my feet, laughs, then sets me down.

"I've missed you," he says.

He's stunningly handsome. Just like Samjeeza, like he was molded from the perfect male form, sculpted as a statue, but where Samjeeza has this dark beauty to him, Dad's all golden. Golden hair. Golden skin. Silver eyes that seem cool and warm at the same time, something ancient about them, so much knowledge in their depths. And like Samjeeza, he's ageless, like he could pass for twenty, thirty, or forty, depending on how closely you look at him.

How is this guy the awkward, absent father of all those tortured phone calls over the years?

"Dad . . . ," I say. "How?"

"There will be time for explanations. But right now, can you please take me to see your mother?"

"Sure." I step back into the entryway, watch as this glowy, broad-shouldered man comes into our house, his movements fluid and graceful, so clearly not human. There's something else about him, too, something that makes me see him in two layers, like that human suit Samjeeza wears, a blurring around him when he moves. With Dad both layers seem more solid, shifting over him. I can't tell which is the real him and which is the suit.

He smiles again. "I know this must come as quite the surprise now that you're able to perceive these kinds of things."

Understatement of the year. My mouth feels dry, like it's been hanging open for a while.

"Your mother?" he prompts.

Right. Here I was just staring at him. I start down the hall.

"Can I get you anything? Like a glass of water or juice or coffee or whatever?" I babble as we pass the kitchen. I realize that I don't know him at all. I don't know my father well enough to know what kind of beverage he prefers.

"No, thank you," he says politely. "Just your mother."

We reach Mom's door. I knock. Carolyn answers it. Her eyes go straight to my dad, and her face instantly goes slack with astonishment, eyes so wide it almost looks cartoonish.

"He—uh—he wanted to see Mom."

She recovers quickly, nods, then steps out of the way so we can pass into the room.

Mom is sleeping, propped up on pillows, her long auburn hair spread out around her face, her face pale but peaceful. Dad sits in the chair next to her bed and touches a strand of hair, that one at the front that's gone silver. He reaches down and gently takes her hand in both of his.

She stirs, sighs.

"All days are nights to see till I see thee, / And nights bright days when dreams do show thee me," Dad whispers.

Her eyes open. "Michael."

"Hello, beautiful." He lifts her hand to his mouth and kisses it, places it against his cheek.

I don't know what I expected if my parents ever happened to bump into each other again. Not this. It's like there was never any leaving us standing in the driveway while he drove away. Never any divorce. Never any separation at all.

"How long can you stay?" she asks.

"A while," he answers. "Long enough."

She closes her eyes. Smiles this beautiful smile. When she opens her eyes again there are tears in them. Happy tears. My dad is making my mom cry happy tears.

Carolyn, who's been standing at the back of the room, coughs delicately. "I'm going to be on my way. I don't think you'll need me."

Mom nods. "Thank you, Carolyn. And if you could do me an enormous favor, please don't mention this to anyone. Not even the congregation. Please."

"Of course," Carolyn says, and then she closes the door.

Mom finally seems to notice I'm here. "Hi, sweetie."

"Hi," I answer dazedly, unable to look away from my parents' hands, still joined.

"How's your day going?" she asks, the hint of mischief in her voice I haven't heard for weeks now.

"Oh, fine. I just found out that my dad's an angel," I say offhandedly. "It's kind of blowing my mind."

"I thought it would."

"This is the thing, right? The thing you're not telling me?"

Her eyes sparkle. I'm floored by how happy she looks. It's impossible to be mad at her when she looks like that.

"I've been waiting to tell you for so long. You have no idea." She laughs, a weak but delighted sounded. "But first I'm going to need two things. A cup of tea. And your brother."

Dad volunteers to make the tea. "I think I can still remember how," he says, and strides off to the kitchen.

That means I'm in charge of fetching Jeffrey.

He's in his room, as usual. Music blaring. As usual. He must not have even heard the doorbell, or maybe he didn't care. He's lying in his bed reading a *Sports Illustrated*, still in his pj's and it's getting close to noon. Slacker. Where was he when I was neck deep in laundry? He glares at me when I come in. As usual.

"Don't you knock?"

"I did. You might want to have your hearing checked."

He reaches and turns down his stereo. "What do you want?"

I can't decide how much to tell him here, or how to break it to him. So I go for the direct approach. "Dad's here."

He goes still, then turns to me like he really does need to have his hearing checked. "Did you say *Dad* was here?"

"He showed up about ten minutes ago."

How long has it been for him, I wonder, since he last saw Dad? How old was he then? Eleven? Jeffrey wasn't even two years old yet when Dad left, not old enough to remember anything but those few times we visited him, the birthday cards with cash in them, the gifts, which were typically extravagant (like Jeffrey's truck, which was his birthday gift from Dad this year), the handful of phone calls, which were generally brief.

"Just come downstairs," I tell him.

We arrive in time to see Dad burn himself on the teakettle. He doesn't curse or jump back or anything. He examines his finger like he's curious about what just occurred. There's no damage to his skin, not even a red mark, but he must have felt it. He goes back to pouring Mom's tea, setting her teacup on a delicate china saucer with some vanilla cookies he must have found in the pantry. Two lumps of sugar. A dollop of cream. Just how she likes.

"Oh, there you are," he says when he sees us. "Hello, son."

"What are you doing here?" Jeffrey's voice is sharp, almost cracking. "Who are you?"

Dad's expression sobers. "I'm your father." It's impossible to deny that, seeing the two of them standing so close together. Jeffrey is like a shorter, bulkier carbon copy of Dad. They have the same hair, the exact same eyes.

"Let's go see your mother," Dad says. "She can explain."

* * *

It takes her all day to tell the story, because she doesn't have the strength to tell it all at once. That and we keep getting interrupted, first by Billy, who bursts in and gives Dad a giant bear hug, calls him Mikey, actually gets all teary-eyed for a minute, she's so happy for Mom. She knew, of course. All this time, she knew. But I guess I stopped being surprised by that kind of thing a while ago.

Then there's the fact that Jeffrey keeps freaking and walking out of the room. It's like he can only stand to hear so much before he thinks his head will explode. Mom'll say something about the way she always knew, deep down, that she and Michael (my dad's name, which we have almost never heard her utter, these last fourteen or so years) were meant to be together, and Jeffrey will get up, tug at his hair, nod or mumble something incoherent, then leave. We have to wait for him to come back before she can finish the story.

But what a story it is.

It starts with the day of the great San Francisco earthquake. That's when she and Dad officially met. By the time she gets to this part of the lurid tale, I'd already figured out that Dad is the angel who saved her that day, the one who broke the news to her, told her she was special, an angel-blood. She was sixteen then.

And when she was ninety-nine years old, she married him.

"How?" I ask her.

She laughs. "What do you mean, how? We showed up at the church, said the words, exchanged rings, you may now kiss the bride, all of it."

"He was allowed to do that? An angel can marry anybody he wants?"

"It's complicated," she answers. "And rare. But, yes, an angel can choose to marry."

"But then why did you divorce? Why did he leave?" Jeffrey asks with an edge of sullenness.

Mom sighs. "An angel can't stop being an angel. They have duties, tasks that require their constant attention. Your father was given a vacation, so to speak, a seven-year period where he could stay with me in linear time and live a human life. Marry me. See the two of you born, spend some time with you. Then he had to go back."

For some reason this makes me want to cry. "So you're not divorced?"

She smiles. "No. We're not divorced."

"But you couldn't see him, all this time?"

"He visited on occasion. Once a year, sometimes twice, if we were lucky. We had to make do with that."

"He couldn't visit *us*?" Again, Jeffrey with the anger. He's not taking this whole your-dad's-an-angel-and-he's-back surprise very well. I guess he doesn't feel the incredible-joy thing. "His kids?"

"I wish I could have," Dad says from the doorway to Mom's

room. He does that. Appears, out of thin air. It's weird.

He comes in and sits next to Mom on the bed, takes her hand. They're always touching each other, I've noticed. Always in contact.

"We decided that it would be best if I stopped seeing you. For your own good," Dad says.

"Why?"

"Because, when you were little, it was easy for me to hide what I am. You didn't notice anything unusual about me, or if you did, you didn't know enough to understand it was unusual. But when you got older, it became more difficult. The last time I saw you, you could definitely feel my presence."

I remember. It was at the airport. I saw him and I felt his joy. And here I thought it was because I was hopelessly screwed up.

"But I have watched you from a distance," he says. "I've been with you your entire lives, in one way or another."

Okay, so this is the fantasy of every child of divorced parents, come true. Turns out, my parents love each other. They want to be together. My dad, all this time, wanted to be with me.

But it's also like watching someone take an eraser to my life story, and then rewrite it as something completely different. Everything I thought I knew about myself has changed in the past few hours.

Jeffrey's not buying it.

"Who cares if we knew what you are?" he says. "You said it was for our sake, but that's bull. So our dad's an angel? So what?"

"Jeffrey . . . ," Mom warns.

Dad holds up his hand. "No, it's all right. It's a good question." He looks at Jeffrey solemnly. There's something regal about him, something that commands respect even if you don't want to give it to him. Jeffrey swallows and lowers his eyes.

"This isn't about me. This is about you," Dad says.

"Michael," Mom whispers. "Are you sure?"

"It's time, Maggie. You knew this would come," he says, caressing her hand. He turns back to us. "I am an Intangere. Your mother is a Dimidius, a half blood. That makes you and your sister a very rare, very powerful breed of angel-blood. We call them the Triplare."

"Triplare?" Jeffrey repeats. "Like three-quarters?"

"This is a dangerous world for a Triplare," Dad continues. "They're rare enough that their powers are largely unknown, but there has been speculation that the Triplare, who are, after all, more angel than human, have nearly the same abilities as full-blooded angels, but with one crucial difference."

"What difference?" prompts Jeffrey.

"Free will," Dad says. "You'll feel the repercussions too,

your subtle sorrows or joys, whatever your actions lead you to, but in the end you are utterly free to choose your own path."

"And this is dangerous because . . ." I say.

"It makes you very, very attractive to the darkness. The few Triplare who have walked this earth have been greatly sought after by the enemy. They are relentlessly hunted, and if they cannot be converted to the cause, destroyed. That's why your mother and I have taken great pains to make sure that no one knew about you. It was crucial to keep your identities hidden, even from yourselves. We only wanted to keep you safe."

"So why tell us now?" Jeffrey asks.

He smiles faintly. "It seems you've already caught the enemy's attention. That was inevitable, I think. Therefore your safety has become a relative concept. We always knew we couldn't hide you forever. We just wanted you to have as human a life as possible, for as long as possible. Now that time is over."

It gets quiet while Jeffrey and I try to absorb this news. Triplare. Three-quarter angel. Not Quartarius, after all. And there's something Dad said that burns like a live coal in my mind.

More angel than human.

So Dad's an angel. Which makes us freaks, even among angel-bloods. Suddenly it makes sense that Mom never took us to the congregation before this year. She was hiding us, even from the other angel-bloods. Even, as Dad said, from ourselves.

Mom is quieter now, sleeping a lot. It took a lot out of her to tell the story, which she's worked so hard and for so long to keep buried inside. She's tired, but noticeably happy during those times when she's awake. Unburdened, is the word. Like telling us the truth has set her free.

I spend all that evening Dad-watching. I can't help it. Sometimes he seems like a normal man, joking around with Billy, eating the dinner she whips up for us, which he digs into with gusto. This makes me wonder if angels need sustenance the way we do. And then there are other times where he seems like, quite frankly, an alien. Trying to use the remote, for instance. He gazes at it for a while like it's some newfangled magic wand. He understands how to use it quickly, though, and then he gets all amped up about the wonder of cable.

"So many channels," he muses. "Last time I watched television there were only four. How do you decide what to watch?"

I shrug. I don't watch a lot of TV. I'm pretty sure Dad's not going to be into *The Bachelor*. "Jeffrey always watches ESPN." Dad gives me a blank look. "The sports channel."

"There's a channel entirely devoted to sports?" he says with a kind of awe.

Turns out Dad's a huge baseball fan. Too bad that Jeffrey won't hang around to watch it with him. I can't stop looking at Dad, can't help but scrutinize every move he makes, but Jeffrey can't stand to be around him. The minute he was "excused" from our family powwow, he bolted for his room. There hasn't been a peep out of him for hours, not even the regular music.

I try to feel him out, which isn't too hard. I've been getting better at turning my empathy on and off since my lesson with Mom. Sitting here, feeling Dad's barely contained glory pulsing out from him, it's ridiculously easy to cast my awareness upstairs to Jeffrey's room.

He's mad. He doesn't care why they did it. He wants to, but he can't stop being mad. They betrayed us, both of them. It doesn't matter why. They lied.

He doesn't want to play by their rules anymore. He's sick of it. He's sick of feeling like a pawn on some cosmic chessboard.

I get it. Part of me feels exactly the same way. It's just hard to be mad when Dad, with his sheer joyous presence, sweeps everything dark and hurtful out of my mind. Which in and of itself feels kind of unfair, like I'm not even allowed to feel what I feel. Maybe I'd resent him for it if I could.

"I think we could have handled it," I tell Mom later. I am helping her walk back from the bathroom. There's something so undignified about it, I think, this tiny shuffling walk she has now, the way she has to have help even to pee. She doesn't like it, either. Every time we do this she gets this grim expression, like she would do anything for me not to see her this way.

"Handled what?" she asks.

"The truth. That Dad was an angel. That we're Triplare. All that. We could have kept the secret."

"Uh-huh," she says. "Because you're so good at that."

"If it was life or death, if I knew that, I could be," I protest. "I'm not an idiot."

I pull back the covers and carefully steady her while she slides into the bed. Then I pull the covers up to her waist, smooth them.

"I couldn't risk it," she says.

"Why not?"

She gestures for me to sit down, and I do. She closes her eyes, opens them again. Frowns.

"Where's your dad?"

"Gone. Where does he go, anyway?"

"He probably has work to do."

"Yeah, gotta go burn a bush for Moses," I quip.

She smiles. "Marge Whittaker, 1949."

It takes me a second to understand what she's referring to. "You mean the one before Margot Whitfield?"

"Yes."

"Marge. Nice. Did you always go by some form of Margaret?" I ask.

"Almost always. Unless I was running from something very bad. Anyway, Marge Whittaker fell in love."

I get the feeling that she's not talking about Dad. She's talking about the time she mentioned before, the time she almost got married. In the fifties, she said.

"Who was he?" I ask softly, not sure I want to know.

"Robert Turner. He was twenty-three."

"And you were . . ." I quickly do the math. "Almost sixty. Mom. You cougar, you."

"He was a Triplare," she says. "I'd never known too many angel-bloods before, Bonnie and Walter, who I met when I was thirteen, before I even knew what an angel-blood was, and Billy, who I met during the Great War, but never anybody like Robert. He could do anything, it seemed. He was capable of anything. One day he walked into the office where I was working as a secretary, and he asked me to dinner. Naturally I was surprised; I'd never seen him before. I asked him why he thought I'd agree to go to dinner with a complete stranger. And he said we weren't strangers. He'd been dreaming of me, he said. He knew that I liked Chinese food, and he knew exactly the restaurant he was going to take me to, he knew I'd order sweet-and-sour pork, and he knew what my fortune would say. So you see, I had to go, to find out if he was right."

"And he was right," I say.

"He was right."

"What was it? Your fortune, I mean."

"Oh." She laughs. "'A thrilling time is in your immediate future.' And his said, 'He who laughs at himself never runs out of things to laugh at.' And both of those were right, too."

"You were a part of his purpose?"

"Yes. I think he was meant to find me."

"And what happened to him?" I say after a minute, because I sense it's bad.

"The Black Wings found out about him. When he would not join them, they killed him. Samjeeza was there. I asked him to help us, but . . . he wouldn't. He stood by and watched."

"Oh, Mom . . ."

She shakes her head. "That's what happens," she says. "You need to understand. That's what happens when they know. You have to fight for your life."

The next morning Billy drives us to school, as usual. Everybody but Jeffrey seems way more relaxed about the Samjeeza problem since Dad showed up. If Samjeeza is powerful, I figure that Dad must be twice as macho, with no sorrow to impede him, the righteousness of the Lord and all that. We don't talk most of the way, each of us lost in our own world, until Billy suddenly says, "So, how you holding up?"

Jeffrey stares out the window and acts like he didn't hear her. She looks over at me.

"No idea," I tell her.

"Not the kind of news you get every day."

"Nope."

"It's good news, though," she says. "Your dad being an Intangere. You know that, right?"

It seems like it should be a good thing. Except for the part where it means Jeffrey and I were pretty much born with a target on us. "Right now it just feels weird."

She glances at Jeffrey in the rearview mirror. "You alive back there?"

Affirmative grunt. Usually Billy can charm Jeffrey, coax the occasional smile out of him, no matter what mood he's in. Probably because she's so pretty. But today, Jeffrey's not cooperating.

"I bet it feels weird," she says to me. "Everything's been turned upside down on you."

"Have you ever met a Triplare?" I ask after a minute.

She scratches the back of her head, considers. "Yes. Two of them, besides you and Long Face back there. Two, in all of my hundred and twelve years on this earth."

"Could you tell they were different? From other angel-bloods, I mean?"

"Honestly, I didn't get to know either of them. But on the outside I'd say they looked and acted like everyone else."

"You're a hundred and twelve?" Jeffrey suddenly pipes up from the back.

Her pleasant smile stretches into a mischievous grin. "Didn't your mother ever teach you never to question a woman about her age?"

"You just said it."

"Then why'd you have to ask?" she shoots back playfully.

"So you only have eight years left." He looks down into his lap as he says this.

I feel a pang of something like loneliness then, knowing that Billy only has eight years left. I won't get to have her in my life very long. In some ways I was taking a lot of comfort in the idea that Billy was going to hang around after Mom died. She was like a tiny piece of Mom I got to keep. She has all these memories of her, all this time they spent together. "Eight years isn't very much," I say.

"Eight years is plenty of time for what I have planned."

"Which is?"

"I want to get to know you two, for one thing. That's one part of your parents' master plan I never agreed with. You know, when you were babies, I used to change your diapers."

She winks at Jeffrey. He blushes.

"Don't get me wrong. They had their reasons for keeping you isolated. Good reasons. But now, I get to spend time with you. See you graduate. Help you pack up for college. I hear it's Stanford, right, Clara?"

"Right. Stanford." I did accept their offer. I'm destined to go there, according to Angela.

Billy nods. "Mags always did have a thing for Stanford."

"Did you go with her?"

She snorts. "Gracious, no. I never had any tolerance for school. My teachers were the wind, the trees, the creeks and rivers."

We pull up to the school.

"And on that note," Billy says cheerfully, "off you go. Try to learn something."

I want to tell Tucker about my dad, but every time I open my mouth to say something about it, try to frame the words, it sounds so dumb. *Guess what? My dad just dropped into town yesterday. And you know what else? He's an angel. Which makes me this super-special-über angel-blood. What do you think of that?*

I glance over at him. He appears to be actually paying attention to the lecture in government class. He's cute when he's concentrating.

Mr. A's about to call on you.

Christian. I tune in just in time to hear Mr. Anderson say, "So, who knows the rights included in the First Amendment? Clara, why don't you take a crack at it?"

"Okay." I glance down at my blank notebook.

Congress shall make no law respecting an establishment of religion, or prohibiting the free exercise thereof; or abridging the freedom of speech, or of the press; or the right of the people peaceably to assemble, and to petition the Government for a redress of grievances, Christian reads off in my mind.

I repeat what Christian said.

"Good." Mr. Anderson looks impressed that I had the whole thing memorized. He moves on, and I relax. I smile at Tucker, who's looking at me like he can't believe he landed such a genius for a girlfriend.

Thanks, I say to Christian silently. I look over at him. He nods slightly.

My empathy blinks on like one of those fluorescent bulbs that takes a minute to charge up. Sorrow descends on me like a cloud moving over the sun. Loneliness. Separation, always this sense of separation from everything good in this life. The field where Samjeeza stands is full of sunshine, but he can't absorb its warmth. He can't smell the new grass at his feet, the fresh rain from this morning's spring shower. He can't feel the breeze. All of that is beauty, and it belongs to the light. Not to him.

I should be used to it by now, the way he pops up and plays with my head.

He's here again, isn't he? Christian again. Now worried.

I give him the mental equivalent of a nod.

What should we do?

Nothing. Ignore him. There's nothing we can do.

But it suddenly occurs to me that maybe that's not true

anymore. I sit up. I raise my hand and ask Mr. Anderson for a hall pass, suggest in a vague way that I need to use the restroom, possibly for female reasons.

Where are you going? Christian asks, alarmed, as I gather up my stuff. *What are you doing?*

Don't worry. I'm going to call my dad.

I call my house from the phone in the office. Billy picks up.

"Trouble?" she asks immediately.

"Can I talk to my dad?"

"Sure thing." Silence as she sets the phone down. Muffled voices. Footsteps.

"Clara," Dad says. "What do you need?"

"Samjeeza's here. I thought maybe you could do something."

He's quiet for a moment. "I'll be there in a minute," he says finally.

It literally takes him a minute to get here. I barely have time to sit down on one of the hall benches to wait for him before he comes striding through the front door. I stare at him.

"Did you fly here?"

"In a manner of speaking."

"Wow."

"Show me." There's a fierceness in his eyes that strikes me as familiar, like I've seen this look on his face before. But when? I lead him outside, across the parking lot, to the field. I hold my breath as he steps without hesitation over the fence and onto unprotected ground.

"Stay here," he orders. I do.

Samjeeza is standing, in human form, on the far edge of the field. He's afraid. It's his fear that I'm remembering, I realize, from the day of the fire. Mom suggested that someone was going to come looking for her, and Samjeeza pictured two white-winged angels, one with red hair, the other blond, glowing and fierce, holding a flaming sword.

My dad.

Samjeeza doesn't move or speak. He stands perfectly still, his fear radiating out of him along with the sorrow now, and humiliation, that he would be so afraid.

Dad takes a few steps toward him, then stops. "Samyaza."

The man suit Samjeeza wears seems transparent, false, next to Dad's solid radiance. Dad's hair glitters in the sunlight. His skin glows. Samjeeza wilts before him but tries to sneer. "Why are you here, Prince of Light? Why do you care about this weak-blooded girl?"

He's going to be playing the part of super-villain in today's performance.

"I care about her mother," Dad answers. "I warned you about that, before."

"Yes, and what is your relationship with Margaret, I wonder?"

Dad's joy wavers. "I promised her father I would look after her," he says.

Her father? Good grief. So there's more stuff I don't know. "Is that all?"

"You're a fool," Dad says, shaking his head. "Leave this place, and don't bother the child, or her mother, again."

"Don't you mean the children? There's a boy too, isn't that right?"

"Leave them be," Dad says.

Samjeeza hesitates, although I know he has no intention of fighting Dad. He's not that crazy. Still, he lifts his chin, meets the quicksilver of Dad's eyes for a few seconds, and smiles. "It's hard not to fall in love with them, isn't it? There's a Watcher somewhere in you too, Michael."

The glow around Dad brightens. He whispers a word that feels like wind in my ears, and suddenly I see his wings. They are enormous and white, a pure sweet white that reflects the sun so it's hard to look directly at them. I have never seen anything so magnificent as my father—my throat closes on the word—this creature of goodness and light, standing there protecting me. He is my father. I am part of him.

"I will crush you under my heel," he says in a low voice. "Go. And do not come back."

"No need to get excited," Samjeeza says, taking a step back. "I'm a lover, not a fighter, after all."

Then he simply closes his eyes and disappears.

Dad's wings vanish. He walks back across the grass to me. "Thanks," I say.

He looks sad. "Don't thank me. I've just put you in more danger than you know. Now," he says in a completely different tone of voice. "I would like it very much if I could meet your boyfriend."

We wait around until the bell rings. People flood the halls. They part around us, giving Dad a wide berth, staring at him.

Dad looks a bit strained.

"Are you okay?" I ask. I wonder if that bit that Samjeeza said, about Dad being like a Watcher, got to him.

"Fine," he says. "It's just that around so many people I have to work harder to hold back the glory. Otherwise they might all fall down on their knees and worship."

He sounds like he might be joking, but I know he's not. He's completely serious.

"We don't have to stay here. We can go."

"No, I want to meet this Tucker kid."

"Dad. He's not a kid."

"Don't you want me to meet him?" he asks with the hint of a smile. "Are you afraid I'll scare him off?"

Yes.

"No," I say. "But don't try to scare him off, okay? He's been pretty cool with all the crazy stuff so far. I don't want to push it."

"Got it. No threatening his life if he doesn't treat my daughter right."

"Dad. Seriously."

Jeffrey appears at the end of the hall. He's talking with a buddy of his, smiling. He sees us. The smile fades from his face. He spins around and walks the other way.

Dad stares after him.

"He'll come around," I say to Dad.

He nods absentmindedly, then says, "So, lead the way. I promise I'll behave."

"Come on, then. His locker's this way."

Down the hall we go to Tucker's locker. He's there, as I thought he would be, fumbling around with his notes. Last-minute studying for a makeup test in Spanish.

"Hola," I say, leaning up against the locker next to his. I'm suddenly a bundle of nerves. I'm about to introduce my dad to my boyfriend. This is huge.

"Hi," he says, not looking up. "What happened in government? You just left."

"I had something I had to take care of."

"What's the Spanish word for slacker?" he says wryly. *"Mi novia, la chica hermosa que huye."* Translation: My girlfriend, the beautiful girl who runs away.

"Tuck."

"Sorry," he says, still not looking up from his notebook. "I am panicking over this test. I swear, my palms are sweating and my heart's going and I'm this close to an anxiety attack. I think. Never had an anxiety attack before. But I have under three minutes to fill my brain with useful information."

"Tuck, can you just stop for two seconds? There's someone I want you to meet."

He glances up, sees my dad standing behind me. Freezes.

"Tucker, this is my dad, Michael. Dad, this is Tucker Avery."

Dad smiles, holds out his hand. Tucker swallows hard, staring, then shakes it.

"Sir," he manages. He looks at me. "Your dad?"

"He showed up yesterday, to help us, since Mom . . ."

"It's a pleasure to meet you," Dad says warmly. I think Dad says pretty much everything warmly. He's a warm guy. "I've heard so much about you. Sorry to take you from your studies, but I wanted to meet this young man who stole my daughter's heart away from her."

Stole being the operative word. I give Dad a sharp look.

"Pleased to meet you, too, sir," Tucker says. "You're a physics professor at NYU, right?"

I swing around to look at Dad. I haven't asked him about that particular falsehood yet.

"I'm on sabbatical," Dad says.

Smooth. Very smooth.

"Well, um, geez, nice of you to show up to help," Tucker says haltingly. He doesn't know what to say. "I, uh, really admire your daughter."

This is not going well. Tucker's face is beyond pale now.

It's actually getting green. There's a sheen of sweat on his forehead. I worry that Dad's barely suppressed glory is going to make him throw up. Time to bail.

"So, I wanted to introduce the two of you, and now I have, and Tucker's got a big test in a minute, so we should go." I loop my arm in Dad's and pull him away, shoot Tucker a look that I hope he understands as an apology for springing all this on him. "Call me later, okay?"

"Okay," he says. He doesn't go back to his Spanish. He leans against his locker, long after the bell rings, catching his breath.

16

SQUARE ICE-CREAM CONES

Angela is practicing her violin when we come in. She likes to do it on the stage at the Pink Garter, under the lights, letting the music fill the empty theater. It's not a song I recognize, but a beautiful, haunting kind of tune that winnows its way up to my dad and me as we stand at the entrance. When the last note fades away, we clap. Angela lowers the violin and shades her eyes to peer out at us, unable to see beyond the stage lights.

"Awesome song, Ange," I call to her.

"Oh, C, it's you. God, you scared me. I thought you were under house arrest. Not that I'm not glad to see you. I've been studying some wild theories this week—this historian who analyzed *The Book of Enoch* back at the turn of the century. Fascinating stuff."

"I have some news myself. Can you come down?"

She starts down the stairs. Nothing motivates Angela like news. As soon as her eyes adjust to the dimmer light in the audience section, she sees Dad.

"Holy crap!"

"Not exactly." I have to admit, I enjoy surprising Angela.

"You're an Intangere," she blurts out.

"Hello," Dad says. "I'm Michael. Clara's father."

Cat's really out of the bag now. It seems odd, since he and Mom worked so hard to keep this all a secret, and now he's going around introducing himself as my dad like it's the most natural thing in the world. But that's who he is, I realize. He is simply incapable of hiding what he is.

"Clara's father . . ." Angela's eyes are like saucers. "Clara's . . ."

"Yes."

"But that would mean . . ."

"We're putting a great deal of trust in you, Angela," he says. "You must guard this information from everyone."

She nods solemnly. "Right. Of course I will." Smiles. "Wow. Didn't see that one coming." She looks at me. "Don't tell me you've known about this the whole time."

"I found out yesterday. When he showed up."

"Wow."

"You're telling me."

She turns to Dad all businesslike. "So. What do you think of *Enoch*?"

He thinks for a minute. "He was a good man. I liked him. Although he allowed himself to be used in terrible ways."

She obviously meant the book.

He meant the man.

"So you're not a Quartarius," she says then. Something about the tone of her voice makes me look at her. Her face is blank, like she's trying really hard to hide what she feels.

Jealousy. Wow, jealousy. I feel it without even trying. All this time she thought she was the powerful one of the two of us. She was Dimidius, I was Quartarius, and she liked it that way. Now . . . she doesn't even have a name for what I am. And my dad is here, handsome and powerful and good, and he cares about me, and he's a link to more information than all the dusty old books in the world. Because my dad is older than all the dusty old books in the world.

Her jealousy is like something slimy in my mind.

"Okay, let's not get all melodramatic or anything," I say. "It's not such a big deal."

"It's a huge deal!" she exclaims, then sucks in a quick breath. "You were reading me. You were using your empathy."

"Sorry. But you're feeling some pretty stupid crap about me, right?"

"You can't do that," she says, then remembers that my dad

is right there and shuts up. Her face is alabaster pale, then suddenly a flare of blue light sparks from her hair just once, like a lone firework against the black backdrop of the theater.

"I couldn't help it," I say.

Yeah, she's pissed.

"It was really nice to meet you, Mr. Gardner," she says, "but I should get back to practicing." She looks at me. "You know the way out."

"Fine." I head for the door. "Come on. We're done here."

"Nice to meet you as well, Angela," Dad says. "You're just as Maggie described—very impressive for having been alone in this for so long."

"Thanks," she says with a bit of a squeak, unable to hang on to her sucky attitude with him around.

Yep, my dad's a charmer.

He teaches me to become invisible. Well, maybe *teach* is a strong word. It's a complicated thing, something that involves the bending of light. He tells me all about it like it's a formula a genius is going to scribble in marker on a window someday. I only half understand, but then he does it. He makes us both invisible, which proves handy for flying around wherever you want, without someone pointing up into the sky and saying, *Look, an angel!* It's even better than Jeffrey's white bird theory.

I'm still in a bad mood, after Angela, but it's hard to stay mad when my dad radiates joy, and then I'm flying with him, the wind carrying me like notes of a song. I haven't flown in so long I was afraid I forgot how, but it turns out to be as easy as breathing, with Dad. We spiral down, swooping the edges of the trees. We shoot upward, breaking the cloud banks, up and up until the air grows thin around us. We soar.

We end up at a car dealership in Idaho Falls. We come down behind a building, Dad in the lead, and he makes us reappear.

Angela would have peed herself to see this, I think. Serves her right.

But I used to be jealous, too. All that time, thinking she was the strong one, the one who always had it all together. She knew everything before I did, even about my mom dying. She mastered flight first. She could change the form of her wings. She'd met a real angel, and spent her summers in Italy.

"Don't dwell on it," Dad says. "Her reaction was natural. As was yours, before."

"You read minds?"

"I can. I'm better with feelings. Like you."

Like me. I can't help but shake my head at the craziness of that idea, that he and I resemble each other, even in that small way.

"So, we're in Idaho Falls," I glance at my watch. Four p.m. It took us twenty minutes to get here, what would be more than a two-hour drive by car. We flew *fast*.

"What are we doing here?" I ask.

"I want to buy you a new car."

What sane girl would say no to that?

Dad turns out to be quite the haggler. I'm pretty sure we get the base bottom price for the new white Subaru Forester we end up driving off with.

I drive us home, since driving is another thing he hasn't had to do in a while. I wonder if this is going to become a regular thing, spending time with him. Or if, the moment Mom is gone, he will be too.

"I will be here as long as you want me," he says. "Not every minute, by your way of seeing things, but in a sense I will always be with you."

"It's a time thing, right? Yeah, Mom tried to explain."

"For you, time is like a line drawn across a piece of paper, a succession of events. A to B to C, one moment following another. Where I come from, there are no lines. We *are* the paper."

"Okay, totally confused now." I pull over into the Rainy Creek Country Store, a gas station.

"You'll understand, someday."

"Looking forward to it."

"Where are we?" he asks.

"Swan Valley. You've got to taste their square ice-cream cones."

"*Square* ice-cream cones?" he repeats, blank-faced again, like this must be another newfangled thing he hasn't learned about yet.

"See, you don't know everything. I get to teach you something, too."

We get our ice-cream cones, made with special scoopers that shape the ice cream into perfect squares. Dad chooses chocolate mint. I go for strawberry.

"When you were small, you were my strawberry girl," he says as we're leaving the store. "Your mom planted a patch in the backyard in Mountain View and if we couldn't find you, that's often where you'd be, eating strawberries, smeared with juice. Your mother had quite the time getting the stains out of all your tiny outfits."

"I don't remember." I walk around to behind the building where there's a bench to sit on. I sit. He stands behind me for a minute, then sits next to me. We look out in the fading light at the mountains, listening to the voice of a small stream gurgling not too far away, the sounds of cars passing on the highway, which sets a kind of rhythm. "I don't remember much," I admit.

"I know. You were very small."

"I remember you shaving."

He smiles. "Yes. You were fascinated with that. You wanted to do it yourself. Your mother came up with the ingenious idea of cutting up old credit cards into the shape of razors, so then you sat up on the bathroom counter and shaved along with me."

"Weird that an angel would have to shave."

He rubs a hand over his smooth chin. "I don't. Although sometimes, in my profession, I'm required to wear a beard."

His *profession*. I turn the word over in my mind.

"In those days, with your mother, things were different for me, physically speaking. I had to shave, wash my body, eat, and drink."

"And you don't now?"

"I can. But I don't have to." He takes a big bite of his ice cream, crunching the cone. It dribbles down his chin, and he tries to wipe at it. I hand him a napkin.

"Because you have a different body."

"There are two parts, to all of us," he says. "Body and spirit."

"So the body is real. And the spirit is . . . ghostly," I say.

"In humans. The body is solid, and the spirit, translucent. Until the two separate, and the body returns to dust, and the spirit passes to another plane. Then the spirit becomes solid."

"What about me?" I ask. "What's my spirit like? Can you see it?"

"Beautiful." He smiles. "You have a gorgeous spirit. Like your mother's."

It's fully dark now. A few feet away a lone cricket starts to chirp. We should go, I think. It's still more than an hour's drive to home. But I don't get up.

"Will Mom . . . go to heaven?"

He nods, and something in his face brightens. He's happy, I realize, about her dying. Because in heaven he'll probably get to see her all the time. He's happy, but for my sake he tries to dampen it down, understand it from my point of view.

"Her body is fading now," he says. "Soon she will give it up entirely."

"Can I go and visit her?" Hope blooms in my chest. We can cross, I know we can, back and forth from heaven and earth. Mom's already been to heaven at least once. I could go there. It wouldn't feel so terrible if I could see Mom every now and then, talk to her. Fill up on her advice and her jokes and her witty remarks. I could still have my mom.

"You can travel to heaven," Dad says. "As a Triplare, you have the ability to cross between worlds. Dimidius must have help, but historically the Triplare can learn to travel there alone."

I almost laugh, this is such good news.

"But you are unlikely to see your mother," he says then. "She has her own journey to undertake when she arrives, and you cannot accompany her."

"But why?" I know I must sound like a three-year-old, crying for my mama, but I can't help it. I wipe at sudden, infuriating tears. I jump to my feet, hurl the rest of my ice-cream cone into the trash can behind us.

He doesn't respond, which only makes me feel more embarrassed.

"We should go," I tell him. "Everyone will be wondering where we went."

He finishes off the last of his cone and follows me back to the car. We drive in silence for the next half hour, past the glowing farmhouses tucked back from the roads, the silhouettes of horses in the fields, then up into the forest of lodgepole pines, past the YONDER IS JACKSON HOLE sign at Teton Pass. Dad doesn't seem angry, but like he's respecting my need for space. I appreciate that, and resent it, at the same time. I resent that he can make me appreciate that, even though he thinks it's perfectly okay to waltz back into my life and start dropping bombs on me. And then I feel guilty that I resent him, because he's an angel, and he's the epitome of good.

"I'm sorry," I say finally as we start to descend the hairpin turns into Jackson.

"I love you, Clara," he says after a long moment. "I want you to feel that. Can you?"

"Yes."

"And I promise, you will see your mother again."

I remind myself that he's the kind of guy who never breaks a promise.

It's quiet at dinner, me and Dad and Jeffrey at the table.

Jeffrey practically inhales his food to get away from us, which makes Dad sad, or as close to feeling sad as Dad is capable of.

"Nice talk, today," he tells me as we're loading dishes into the dishwasher. "I've wanted that with you."

"You used to call me," I remind him. "How come you never seemed to want to talk to me then?"

"I was uncomfortable with the pretense," he says, looking down.

"You mean lying to me?"

"Yes. It does not come naturally. It causes me pain."

I nod. It makes sense. Finally, it's starting to make sense. Not that it makes up for it. But it helps.

I smile at Dad and excuse myself and go up to my room to knock out my homework. I'm not in there ten minutes before Christian alights on the roof. He comes right up to the window and stands there, staring at me, then raps on the glass.

I open the window. "You're not supposed to show up here. It's not safe. There's a Black Wing hanging around, remember?"

His green eyes are sharp, assessing me. "That's funny, because I thought I saw an angel banish Samjeeza from the field today. I figured it was safe now."

"You saw that?"

"I went to the window at the end of the second-floor hallway. Pretty impressive, I thought. Those wings, wow."

I don't know what to say. So I say something dumb. "You want to come in?"

He hesitates. He's never been inside my room before. "Okay."

I'm embarrassed by the girliness of my bedroom, the sheer amount of pink stuff I have lying around. I kick a pink teddy bear under my bed, snatch a bra from where it's draped over my bedpost and try to discreetly dump it into my hamper. Then I tuck a strand of runaway hair behind my ear and try to look anywhere but straight at Christian.

He seems embarrassed, too, unsure of what to do in this situation. Imagine our mortification when at exactly that moment there's a gentle knock on my door and Dad comes in.

"Oh, hello," he says, looking at Christian.

"Dad! Don't you . . . this is . . ."

"Christian Prescott," Dad supplies. "I'd recognize those eyes anywhere."

Christian and I look at each other, him all confused about Dad knowing anything about him, me freaking out because I don't want Christian to think I've been waxing poetically about his eyes to my dad.

"I'm Michael. Clara's father," Dad says, extending his hand.

Funny how he says that exactly the same way, every time.

Christian doesn't hesitate. He takes Dad's hand and shakes it firmly.

Dad smiles. "It's remarkable, really, how much you resemble your mother."

"You knew my mother?" Christian's voice is almost painfully neutral.

"Quite well. She was a charming woman. A good woman."

Christian glances down for a minute, then up to meet my father's gaze. "Thank you." His eyes flicker over to me, linger on my face like he's seeing it in an entirely new way. Then he says, "Well, I should go. I just wanted to make sure Clara was okay after she left in the middle of class today."

Dad couldn't look more approving of the idea of Christian looking out for me. "Don't go on my account. I'll leave you to talk."

And he does. And he closes the door on the way out. What kind of Dad leaves his teenage daughter alone in her room at night with a boy and the door closed? He's got a lot of catching up to do, parent-wise, I think. Or maybe he doesn't really see parenting as his role. Or maybe he's just that confident that Christian would have to be crazy to do anything inappropriate with an angel on the other side of the door.

"So," Christian says after a minute. "Your dad's an angel."

"So it would seem."

"He seems cool."

"He is. Cooler than I ever would have given him credit for."

"I'm glad for you," he says.

He is. I can feel it. He's sincerely pleased to find out that I get to have a dad who cares about me, who is powerful enough to protect me, who can be here for me now during this rough time. He also has something he wants to tell me. It's right there, like the words are hovering on the forefront of his mind, something he thinks will connect us now more than ever. But he holds it back.

"Come on, what is it?"

He gives me this mysterious, closed-lipped smile.

"I want to take you somewhere, after school tomorrow. Will you go with me?"

I find my voice. "Sure."

"Okay. Good night, Clara." He goes to the window and steps out.

"Good night," I murmur after him, and then I watch him summon his wings, those gorgeous speckled wings, and lift off.

17

THE PART WHERE I KISS YOU

I drive myself crazy wondering where Christian means to take me, but when he shows up at my locker after school the next day, part of me hesitates. I'm not sure why. Maybe because of the steady way he's looking at me now, warm gold flecks in his eyes.

"You ready?" he asks.

I nod. We walk out into the sunshine. There's not even a whisper of Samjeeza here. Dad must have scared him off for good, because suddenly Mom is totally okay with Jeffrey and me leaving the safety of hallowed ground.

Christian unlocks his truck and I climb in. I try not to scan the vicinity for Tucker as we make our way out of the parking lot. He called me last night and we tried to talk about my dad, but neither of us had much to say. I couldn't come right out and tell him that my dad's an angel, even though he's probably already guessed. It would be too dangerous for him, knowing that, a tidbit that Samjeeza would just love to pluck out of his head. The less he knows, the safer he is, I've realized, and anyway, he shouldn't be here—he has a rodeo competition tomorrow and left school earlier than usual today to get in some extra hours of practice. He was preoccupied. He didn't ask me what I was up to and I didn't share.

Christian turns up a dirt road that curls up the mountainside behind town. I spot a sign, crane my neck to read what it says.

ASPEN HILL CEMETERY.

All at once it feels like everything inside me turns to stone. "Christian . . ."

"It's okay, Clara." He pulls off to the side of the road, puts the truck in park. He opens his door, swings down, and turns to look at me. "Trust me." He holds out his hand.

I feel like I'm moving in slow motion as I put my hand in his, let him draw me out of the truck on his side.

It's beautiful here. Green trees, aspens whispering, a view of the distant mountains.

I hadn't expected it to be so beautiful.

Christian leads me off the road into the forest. We step

around graves, most of them standard pieces of marble, nothing fancy, simple inscriptions with names and dates. Then we're to a set of concrete stairs, stairs in the middle of the forest, with a long, painted black metal bar on one side. My heart jumps to my throat when I see them, a field of gray pressing in on the edges of my sight, something I used to feel last year right before I'd have the vision. I bite my lip so hard I taste a hint of blood. But I don't go, don't rocket away to the day of Mom's funeral. I stay here. With Christian.

"This way," he says, tugging gently on my hand. We walk, not up the hill this time, not toward the place where a hole will be dug in the ground, my mother lowered into it, but across the hillside to a small white marble bench, framed by aspens, a rosebush planted beside it, which bears a single, perfect white rose.

Christian sees that rose and laughs in this kind of choked-up way. He lets go of my hand.

"I thought you said this rosebush never blooms," I say, staring at the inscription on the bench. LOVING MOTHER, DEVOTED SISTER, TRUEST FRIEND. There's a plaque in the ground, too, a plain white rectangle bearing the words BONNIE ELIZABETH PRESCOTT. An etching of a rose. No birth or death dates, which strikes me as odd, but if Bonnie were even middle-aged as an angel-blood when she passed, her birth date would have definitely raised some eyebrows.

"It doesn't bloom," Christian answers. "Today's the first time."

He takes a deep breath, reaches to touch the rose gently. Then he looks at me. There is so much emotion in him at the moment that I instinctively try to close the door between us; it's too much, but I can still see it in his face. He has something he wants, no, he *needs*, to say to me.

"My mother had beautiful hair," he says.

Okay, not exactly what I was expecting.

"It was this pale blond, like corn silk. I used to watch her brush it. She'd sit at her vanity in her bedroom and brush it until it shone. She had green eyes. And she liked to sing. She sang all the time. She couldn't seem to help herself."

He sits down on the bench. I stand there for a minute, watching him get lost in the memory of his mother.

"I think about her every day," he says. "And I miss her. Every. Single. Day."

"I know."

He looks up at me earnestly. "I want you to know, I'm going to be there. When it happens to you. I will be by your side the whole time, if you'll let me. I promise you that."

People are making a lot of promises to me lately. I nod. I sit down on the bench next to Christian and gaze at the mountains, where I can barely make out the white point of the Grand Teton. A breeze lifts my hair, blows it onto Christian's shoulder.

This is the most beautiful place for a cemetery. It's peaceful here, removed from life and all its worries, but also still connected to it. Overlooking the town. Watching over us. This is the perfect place for Mom's body to rest, I think, and in this moment, when I imagine her here as something other than a recurring nightmare, it's the first time I picture what will happen after she dies. Not the funeral or the graveside, or the stuff in my vision. After. We're going to leave her here, and it's all right. When it happens we will put her body to rest here, in this beautiful place, by Christian's mother. I'll come up here once in a while like he does, and lay flowers on her grave.

Christian slips his hand into mine again. "You're crying."

I lift my free hand up to my cheek; he's right. I'm crying. But it's a good kind of crying, I think. Maybe it means I'm letting go.

"Thank you for bringing me here," I say.

That's when he says, "Clara, there's something I need to tell you."

He stands up. He keeps hold of my hand and moves in front of me. The afternoon sun strikes his hair and makes a golden lining around him. I squint up at him, into his eyes.

"Your dad's an angel, and your mom's a Dimidius," he says, "which makes you a Triplare."

"How do you even know what that is?" I gasp. I thought it was some kind of super secret.

"My uncle. When I was ten years old he sat me down and told me all about the Triplare, how rare they are—he believes only seven Triplare ever walk the earth at the same time—how powerful they are. How they must be protected, at all costs."

Is that what he wants, I wonder, to protect me? Is that what the I'll-always-be-here-for-you stuff is really about? Is his purpose to be a kind of guardian for me?

"I've been wanting to tell you for months," he says. "I thought it was just going to burst out of me at times, like in *Alien*."

"Wait," I say. "You've been wanting to tell me what? That I'm a Triplare?"

"I've known since that Angel Club with the glory." He runs a hand through his hair, blows out a long breath. "But I suspected it since the fire."

I stare at him. How could he have known that I'm a Triplare even before I did?

"I've never told this to anybody," he says. "My uncle has pounded it into my brain again and again: no one must know. No one. Not even the other angel-bloods. Especially the other angel-bloods, as a matter of fact. He says there isn't anybody, not anybody, you understand, who we can trust."

His hand tightens in mine.

"But he's wrong," he says fiercely. "Even though you say you're bad with secrets. You didn't tell Tucker, when you thought he was going to die. That took strength. You're so strong, Clara, you don't even know. You're amazing. You're beautiful and brave and sarcastic and hilarious and I think . . ." He takes a breath. "My visions keep telling me, over and over and over again, that I can trust you. I can trust you."

Something shifts in his face. He's going to tell me. He's going to throw caution to the wind and put it all out there.

"My mother was a Dimidius. She was beautiful, so unbelievably beautiful it almost hurt to look at her sometimes. Like you. And almost twenty years ago, she was seduced by a Watcher, who thought he could collect the most beautiful angel-bloods in the world. And that's how she ended up with me."

I've had a lot of bombs dropped on me this year, enough mind-shattering revelations to last a lifetime, in my opinion. But nothing quite like this, like Christian staring me down with gleaming green-gold eyes, eyes like his beautiful mother's, telling me that his father was a Black Wing.

"You're a Triplare, too," I whisper.

"Yes." There's relief in his voice. "Don't you see what that means?"

He doesn't say it, but I know. We belong together. We're two of a very rare kind. Meant to watch out for each other, meant to join hands and walk side by side, through fire, through death, meant to guard and protect and . . .

I feel like I'm falling from far up, plummeting to earth, and at the same time, drowning in a deep pool, struggling upward toward the surface, my lungs bursting for air.

He pulls me to my feet. "I didn't know at first, how I felt about it. I didn't want to be forced, you know? I wanted it to be my choice. But every time I'm around you, it feels right," he says. "I feel stronger. Braver, even. I feel the glory inside me, this power moving through me. I feel like I could do anything, face anything. With you."

I wish he would stop talking. I wish the forest would stop spinning around me, wish I could step outside of my body right now and ask myself, So, Clara, what do you think?

But I don't know.

I love Tucker, I think.

His eyes grow sober. "I know."

"You do?"

"I loved Kay. Whatever that says about me, I did love her. Part of me still does. My uncle says it's because she was my first love. He says we never really get over our firsts."

Right. But Tucker's not just my first love. He's my present.

"I had to choose," Christian says. "Last year, when I started to understand that my vision was more than a search and rescue for some mystery girl." The side of his mouth hitches up briefly. Me. His mystery girl. "When the vision showed me how it was supposed to be, the way we took hands, and . . . touched, and how I felt in that moment, I knew then that I had to choose. It wouldn't have been fair to Kay. So I broke up with her."

He closes his eyes for a second, and I catch a hint of the turmoil he still feels when he thinks of Kay.

There must be something I'm not seeing in that girl. There must be.

"I had to choose," he says again. "And it wasn't like I had to choose between you and Kay; I hardly knew you then. I had to choose who I was going to be. But now . . . Clara, I think . . ."

"I have to go," I say, pulling away from him abruptly. "I can't think. I can't choose."

To my bewilderment, he smiles, this completely sweet, sinful smile that sends a flock of butterflies straight to the pit of my stomach.

"What?" I demand to know. "What is it now?"

"You're not going to go," he says.

"Watch me."

"I've been having a vision of this place, too." This stops me from my wild, cowardly (how can he think I'm brave?) retreat back to the road. I turn. He's still standing there by his mother's grave, hands in the pockets of his jeans, looking at me with such heat behind his eyes that a tremble works its way through me from my head to my toes.

"You're having a new vision, too?" I ask.

"It's right here." He walks toward me, his strides long and

purposeful across the grass. "Right now. I've been seeing it for weeks, and it's happening right now."

He stops in front of me.

"This is the part where I kiss you," he says.

And that's when, there under the swaying pines, the trembling aspens on Aspen Hill, in the waning sunlight of that late spring day, with birds singing over our heads, traces of earlier tears still drying on my face, and the faint smell of roses in the air, Christian Prescott kisses me for the first time. He pulls me in.

I'll never, if I live to be my full hundred and twenty years, forget the way he tastes. It's not anything I can describe, it's just Christian, a little sweet and a whole lot of spice, and it feels, in that moment, absolutely right. His fire and mine combine, and it's greater than any forest fire, hotter than the hottest part of flame. Any walls I've tried to build between us crumble down. His heart pounds beneath my palm. He wasn't lying to me just now. This is his vision, his dream literally coming true, and it is everything he thought it would be. More. I am more than he ever could have hoped for, ever could have dreamed. His mystery girl. The girl he was meant to find. And now I belong to him like he has always belonged to me.

It's this thought that brings me back to myself. I reel backward, breaking the contact between us with an agonizing force of sheer will.

"I'm not yours," I gasp up at him, and then I run. Because if I stay one more second I will kiss him back. I will choose him.

So I push away, tear off through Aspen Hill Cemetery like the devil is chasing me, and then I fly, not caring if anybody sees me, shooting like a falling star across the sky, toward home.

18

THE ALTERNATIVE TO ME

I stay home from school the next day, and no one gives me grief about it.

After school Angela calls me.

"I'm sorry," is the first thing out of her mouth. "I'm really, really, ridiculously sorry, okay? It was stupid to get jealous. I'm so over it."

She thinks I cut school to avoid her.

"It's okay. I shouldn't have read you. You kind of deserve what you get, when you read what somebody else feels about you."

"Still, it wasn't cool. I shouldn't have felt that way."

"We can't always control what we feel," I tell her. Boy, is

yesterday the perfect example of that. "Hey, I've been jealous of you, too, occasionally. And this thing with my dad was a big surprise. You're only half human."

This last bit was meant to be a joke. Only she doesn't laugh.

"So you . . . forgive me?" she asks. It's strange whenever Angela sounds vulnerable, when she's usually so strong. It lets me see through a tiny window into her world, where I'm her only real friend. If she screws it up with me, she's totally alone.

"Sure. Water under the bridge," I tell her.

She sighs. Relief. "Want to come over?"

"I can't. I have something I have to do today."

I'm going to see Tucker.

The regional high school rodeo competition this year is being held in the Jackson Hole Rodeo Arena, one of the few times this year the team is competing at home. At the entrance the owner, Jay Hooper, waves me by when I try to pay admission. I'd almost forgotten he's an angel-blood.

"Because you're Maggie's kid," he tells me.

I don't argue.

I pick a seat way in the back of the bleachers. I shouldn't be here, I know, shouldn't be away from home right now, when no one else knows where I am. But I want to see Tucker. Part of me thinks that if I can just lay eyes on him,

I'll find myself again. I'll know.

I watch the rodeo as they start up with the calf-roping section, but I can't concentrate. Ever since yesterday I've felt lost in a sea of my own guilt, and it truly feels like I'm underwater. The voices of the announcers sound muffled. I can't see clearly. I try to breathe and I get a mouthful of guilt.

I let Christian kiss me. I can still feel it tingling on my lips, still taste him.

The thought makes me feel physically ill. This is not me, I think. I can't be that girl who makes out with another guy when her boyfriend is this strong, amazing, wonderful, loving, honest and totally funny, hot and tumble, you'd-have-to-be-freaking-crazy-to-cheat-on-this-total-catch kind of a guy.

I groan and close my eyes. Tucker is all of those things, and so much more. Right now I feel like I'm that empty beer can under the bleachers.

I hear Tucker's name called. There are hoots and hollers from people in the stands. Then he and Midas are out of the gate chasing down a black-and-white calf. Tucker has a long loop of rope in his hand, swinging it almost gently around his head, one, two, three times, then lets it fly. It catches the calf perfectly around the neck. Tucker slides down from Midas's back, runs to the calf's side, holding another piece of rope between his teeth, flips the calf expertly into the dirt, and ties his legs. The whole thing takes all of two minutes, maybe less. And he's done. He waves at the crowd.

My eyes fill. It seems like I'm crying all the time these days, but I can't help it. He's so beautiful, even dusty and dirty and sweating with effort, he's the most beautiful boy in the world.

Christian might be right. We belong together. That's hard to deny. He's my purpose, at least a big part of it.

But Tucker is my choice. I love him. That isn't going to go away.

I wanted an answer, and that's as close to one as I'm going to get. Now I should slip out of here before he spots me and sees the guilt that has to be plain as day all over my face.

The crowd around me cheers again as the time is announced. He's done well. Even with all the other emotional garbage piling up on top of me, I'm proud of him.

I stand and edge my way over to the aisle, then move quickly down the stairs. Almost out. But then someone whoops loudly at Tucker from the front row of the stands. A female someone. And something about the whole thing makes me pause.

It only takes me a second to locate her: a girl wearing formal western wear, a white button-up shirt with stars on the shoulders, white jeans with fringe, white boots. A cascade of long red hair flows in perfect curls down her back. She's looking at Tucker with this kind of light in her eyes that instantly twists me up inside.

I feel like I should know her. There's something

familiar—she must go to our school, of course—and then it hits me. This is Allison Lowell. She's one of the girls Tucker took to prom last year. She was sitting right next to me when he drove us all home that night, a petite redhead in a deep navy dress.

Don't do it, Clara, I tell myself. *Don't read her.*

But I do. I lower the walls, just a smidge, and I reach for her with my mind. I feel what she feels. And I don't like it.

Because she thinks he's beautiful, too. He makes her palms get sweaty and her voice get squeaky in this mortifying way. But he's always nice to her. He's really nice, which is so rare in a guy so gorgeous, she knows. He doesn't even seem to know how hot he is. She remembers dancing with him, his rough and calloused palm as he held one of her hands while they danced a two-step, the other on her waist. She thought she would burst. His eyes blue as cornflowers. Writing his name in the margins of her notes in Spanish class. She has a million things she wants to say to him.

Me gustas. I like you.

Still, she knows it's fantasy. He's never looked at her. He doesn't even really see her standing here now. If only he could see her, and the longing that shoots through her in this moment causes me physical pain. If he would only open his eyes.

"You showed them, Tuck!" she cries, cheering for him.

I back away from her, reeling, dizzy. There were all these

jokes between him and me, about little Miss Allison Lowell. And all this time she's been totally crushing on him.

I take a good long look at her. The first thing that strikes me is the red hair, a natural, shiny copper, not like the orange nightmare mine was last year, but the color of a new penny. She's willow thin, but I get a sense of muscle about her, too, regular exercise, fresh air. She's stronger than she looks. Pale, milky skin smattered with freckles, but it suits her. Coral lips. Expressive brown eyes.

She's pretty.

And she does rodeo. And she's from around here, maybe wants to stay. She's a regular girl. A redhead. He likes redheads. And she likes him.

If I had never shown up at school last winter, maybe he would have seen her in her prom dress that night. They might have talked. He might have even ended up calling her Carrots.

She's like the healthy alternative to me.

I can't breathe. I head for the exit. Now more confused than ever.

But as I push through the crowd, I turn one last time to look for Tucker, who's back on Midas now, and I can barely make out his head, his hat, his serious eyes as he pivots the horse back toward the gate, before I turn to go.

That night I curl up next to Mom in her bed and we watch

home videos together. Dad comes in every now and then, watches with us with this half-sad expression, seeing the evidence of all he missed. Then he goes out. I never know where he goes when he's not in the house. He's just gone.

This one we're watching now is of the beach. I'm around fourteen. It must have been right before Mom took me out to Buzzards Roost, told me about the angels. I am your typical girl here, walking along the sand, checking out the hot surfers. It's kind of embarrassing how obvious I am, when the cute guys come along. I try to act all poised, toss my head to show off my hair, move with a dancer's grace along the shore. I want them to notice me. But when it's just us, just Mom and Jeffrey and me, I'm a total kid. I splash in the water, run around in the sand with Jeffrey, build sand castles and destroy them. At one point I grab the camera away from Mom to film her. She's wearing a flowy white cover-up over her bathing suit, a large straw hat, big sunglasses. She looks so vital, so healthy. She joins in with our play, laughs, darts along the shore being chased by the waves. It's funny how when people change, you forget the way they used to be. I'd forgotten how beautiful she was, even though she's still beautiful. It's not the same. There was an energy about her then, an unconquerable spirit, a light in her that never went out.

Right now she's quiet. I think she might be asleep, but then she says, "That was my happiest time, right then."

"Even without Dad?" I ask.

"Yes. You two made me so happy."

I offer her my bag of popcorn, but she shakes her head. She's completely stopped eating now. Carolyn can only get her to take sips of water, maybe a bite or two of chocolate pudding on good days. It bothers me, because living people have to eat. It means she's not really living anymore.

"I think maybe that was my happiest time, too," I say, watching myself smile up into the camera.

Before visions. Before purpose. Before fires. Before all these choices I'm not ready to make.

"No," Mom says. "Your happiest times are still to come."

"How do you know that?"

"I've seen it."

I sit up to look at her. "What do you mean?"

"All my life, I've seen glimpses of what's to come, mostly for myself, like the visions, but sometimes for others as well. I've seen your future, or variations of it, anyway."

"And what do you see?" I ask eagerly.

She smiles. "You go to Stanford."

"Tell me something I don't know."

"You like it there."

"So Stanford equals happiness? Great then, I guess I'm all set. Can you tell me the color scheme for my dorm room, because I'm trying to decide between a lavender theme or royal blue." Yes, I'm being sarcastic, and maybe I shouldn't, when it seems like she's trying to tell me something important. But the truth is, I can't imagine real happiness. Not without her.

"Oh, sweetie." She sighs. "Do me a favor," she says. "Look in the top dresser drawer. In the back."

I find a dusty red velvet box hidden behind her socks. I open it. Nestled inside is a silver charm bracelet, old and a little tarnished. I hold it up.

"What is this?" I've never seen her wear it before.

"It's for you to wear to the cemetery."

I look at the charms, which seem ordinary enough. A heart. A horse. A couple of what I think must be fake gems. A fish.

"It was mine, a long time ago," she says. "And now it's yours."

I swallow. "Aren't you going to tell me that you'll always be with me? Isn't that what people say? You'll be in my heart, something like that?"

"You are part of me," she replies. "And I am part of you. So yes, I will be with you."

"But not a real, conversational part, right?"

She lays her hand on mine. It feels so light, lighter than a hand should be, her skin like the softest white paper. Like she could blow away on the wind.

"You and I have a connection that nothing, not on heaven or earth, or even hell, could ever break. If you want to talk to me, talk to me. I'll hear you. I might not be able to answer, at least not in a timely manner. . . ."

"Because a day is a thousand years . . ."

She smirks. "Of course. But I will hear you. I will be sending my love to you every moment."

"How?" I'm unable to push back the tears in my voice.

"In the glory," she answers. "That's where we'll find each other. In the light."

I'm crying again and she wraps her arm around me, kisses the top of my head. "My dear sweet girl. You take on so much. You feel things so deeply. But you will be happy, my darling. You will shine."

I nod, wiping at my eyes. I believe her. Then I go ahead and say the next thing that pops into my head.

"Mom, are you ever going to tell me about your purpose?"

She pulls back, looks at me thoughtfully. "My purpose is you."

That night she tells me another story, a different version of the one she told Jeffrey and me earlier, about the day of the earthquake. What she didn't mention before.

That when she saw Dad, when he lifted her out of the rubble that had been her bedroom, when he carried her off to heaven, she recognized him.

"I'd been dreaming about him," she says.

"What was the dream about?" I'm sitting cross-legged at the foot of the bed so I can face her as she talks.

"A kiss," she confesses.

"A kiss?" I get a twinge of guilt, just hearing the word. Remembering Christian's lips on mine.

"Yes. In the dream, I kissed him. He was standing on a beach." Her eyes flick up to the television, the glittering, rolling water. "And I walked up, took his face in my hands, and kissed him. Not a word passed between us. Only a kiss."

"Whoa," I breathe. So romantic. "So when you saw him after the earthquake, you recognized him as the guy you kissed."

"Yes."

"So what did you do?"

She laughs lightly, almost a giggle. "I immediately developed a huge crush on him. I was sixteen, after all, and he was . . ."

"Hotness personified," I finish for her, a bit sheepishly, since this is my dad we're talking about here.

"He was one gorgeous specimen, yes he was."

"And what happened?"

"He stayed with us for three days, after the earthquake, in Golden Gate Park, and on the last night, I tried to seduce him."

"And . . ."

"He wouldn't have it. He rejected me, rather rudely, I thought. And the next morning he was gone. I didn't see him again for three years."

"Oh, Mom . . ."

"Don't feel too sorry for me," she reminds me with a small smile. "It worked out, in the end. I landed him."

"But what happened when you saw him again? I bet it was awkward."

"Oh, by then I'd decided I didn't want him."

My mouth drops open. "You didn't want him? Why not?"

"For a lot of reasons. By then I knew what he was. I knew that he would want to marry me, and even if I didn't know all that would entail, I knew it would never be a traditional marriage. I didn't think I wanted to be married. I didn't want my life to be decided for me. That's probably the biggest reason of all. So when I saw him again, I let him know in very clear terms that I wasn't interested."

"How'd he take that?" I can't imagine anyone refusing Dad anything.

"He laughed at me. Which didn't help matters much. But he would not go away. I would feel his presence near me often, although sometimes years would pass where he never showed himself."

"But what about your vision?"

"I kept having it."

"And you just ignored your purpose?"

"Oh no," she says gravely. "I did more than ignore it. I fought it. I resisted with every bit of strength I had in me. I wasn't about to let anyone control my life."

"For how long?" I ask breathlessly.

"Oh, sixty years, give or take."

"Sixty years." There I go, Clara the parrot. I belong on a pirate's shoulder. "So that's why you didn't tell me. Aside from the fact that you were trying to hide that Dad's an Intangere. If you'd told me that you fought your purpose, instead of the way I'd always assumed it went down, maybe I would have fought mine too."

"Exactly," she says. "Except you ended up fighting yours anyway. I guess the apple doesn't fall far from the tree."

"And they let you do that? Heaven, I mean."

"They let me do that. I had free will, you see, and, boy, did I ever use it."

"What did you do?"

She sighs. Something clouds her eyes. I feel a hint of regret. Obviously this part of her life was not her favorite time.

"I made mistakes," she confesses. "One after another after another. I brought a whole world of hurt down on myself. I fumbled through my life. Hurt people, even people I loved. Became an expert at lying to myself. I suffered, sometimes in unimaginable ways. And I learned."

I stare at her. "Did you think you were being punished? For not fulfilling your purpose?"

She meets my eyes. "You're not being punished, Clara. But yes, it was terrible at times, and it felt like punishment. I wouldn't want that for you. But you're forgetting that in the end it was all as it should be. That kiss on the shore happened, after all."

"What changed your mind?" I ask, but looking at the quiet certainty on her face, I think I can guess.

"I started seeing beyond the kiss," she answers. "And I saw you. And Jeffrey. And I got a glimpse of that happiest time."

She looks again at the TV. The scene has shifted. Now we're on the boardwalk at Santa Cruz. I am eating cotton candy, complaining about how sticky it is, licking my fingers. Mom demands a taste and the camera lunges in at the cotton candy. I catch a part of her face, her nose, chin, lips, as she bites off a piece.

"Yum," I hear her say, smacking her lips for the sake of the camera.

Fourteen-year-old Clara rolls her eyes at her mother. But she smiles. Up the boardwalk, Jeffrey calls, "Look at me. Mom, look at me!" I can't believe his voice was ever that high pitched.

The camera finds Jeffrey standing near the strong man game on the boardwalk. He's twelve years old, scrawny as all get-out, like a stork wearing a Giant's cap. His silver eyes are all lit up with excitement. He grins at us, then lifts the rubber mallet and brings it down hard. A ball shoots up from the base of the platform and rings a bell at the top. Lights flash. Music sounds.

My little brother just won the strong man prize.

The guy running the booth looks flabbergasted, suspicious, like Jeffrey must have cheated somehow. But he hands over the giant stuffed panda Jeffrey picks out.

"Here, Clara," Jeffrey squeaks, running up to us with his chest all puffed out. "I won this for you."

"Way to go, little man!" Mom says from behind the camera. "I'm so proud of you!"

"I'm little but I'm strong," Jeffrey boasts. He never was one for being modest. "I'm Mr. Amazing!"

"How'd you do that?" Younger Clara seems as puzzled as the carny as she accepts the giant black-and-white bear. I still have that bear. It's on the top shelf of my closet. I named him Mr. Amazing. Until now I'd forgotten why.

"Want to see me do it again?" Jeffrey asks.

"That's okay, buddy," Mom says gently. "We should give the other people a chance. Besides, we don't want to show off."

The camera tilts as she hugs him, up into the blue, cloudless sky. For a moment the noise of the boardwalk lulls, and you can hear the crash of the surf, the cries of the seagulls. Then the screen goes blank. Happy time over.

I turn to look at Mom. Her eyes are closed and her breath is deep and even. Fast asleep.

I pull the blankets up over her. I kiss her, lightly, on the cheek, breathe in her smell of rose and vanilla. *I was her happiest time,* I think. And it seems, after all that she's lived, all that she's experienced in a hundred and twenty years on earth, being her happiest time is a huge honor.

"I love you, Mom," I whisper, and even in sleep she hears me.

I know, she answers in my head. *I love you too.*

Later Dad carries her out to the back porch to see the stars. It's a warm night, crickets chirping their hearts out, light breeze blowing. Spring is about to give way into summer. Watching my parents together, the way they seem to speak to each other without words, the way his touch seems to strengthen her, it is undeniable that their love is a powerful, transcendent thing. This love will survive her death. But was it worth it? I can't help but wonder. Was it worth all the hardship she mentioned, the suffering of their separation, the pain of having him for such a short time and then having to let him go?

Watching them, I think it must be. When he kisses her lightly on the lips, brushes a tendril of hair out of her face, adjusts the shawl around her shoulders, she gazes up at him with nothing but pure love in her midnight eyes. She's happy.

You will be happy, she told me.

You will shine.

Mom asks to speak with Jeffrey. He comes out on the porch with her and they have a long talk. I watch them from the living room. Jeffrey is slumped in the Adirondack chair next to Mom's, his hands folded in his lap, looking down. I can't hear what they're saying, and anyway it's none of my business, but I think maybe it's the same thing she told me earlier. My purpose, she said, is you.

Jeffrey keeps nodding, and then he kneels in front of her, leans in stiffly to hug her, and I turn away from the window. I'm startled to see Dad standing by the fireplace, a glass of red wine in his hand. His eyes are filled with knowledge.

"Now's the time for you to be brave, Clara," he says. "Very soon."

I nod silently. Then I go to Dad and step into the circle of his joy, and try to let it fill me, push aside the sudden ache that's growing in my chest.

19

THE D-WORD

I wake up before dawn with this strange feeling, something like déjà vu. I sit up with a gasp, then tear out of bed and down the stairs and burst into Mom's room as Carolyn is coming out. She nods at me. "Today," she says.

Now we're all assembled in there: Jeffrey, whose anger has deserted him for the moment, sitting in a kitchen chair by her bed, leaning forward onto his knees. His eyes never leaving her face. Billy stands in the corner and doesn't say a word, but whenever Mom looks at her, she smiles. Carolyn flits in and out to take her pulse and try in vain to get her to drink something. Dad sits at the foot of the bed, passing the time cracking angel jokes.

"Do you know why angels can fly?" he asks us. We all kind of shake our heads. "Because we take ourselves so lightly."

Killer, I know. But it's comforting, him being there. He's only been hanging around with us for a little more than a week, but already I feel used to him, his silent joy, his steadiness, his weird sense of humor that fits just perfectly with Mom's.

And then there's me. I'm holding her hand. Waiting. All of us waiting, like we are a wheel and Mom is the center of it, the hub. We rotate around her.

"Such serious faces," she whispers. "Geez, is someone dying?"

But then she stops talking altogether. It takes too much effort. She sleeps, and we watch the rise and fall of her chest. I have to pee in the worst way, but I'm afraid to leave the room. What if she goes while I'm not there? What if I miss it?

I cross my legs and I wait. I examine her hand in mine. She's wearing her wedding ring again, a simple slender silver band. She and I have the same hands, I realize. I've never noticed that before. Hers are frail now, light as the hollow bones of a bird's, but the resemblance to mine is there. We have the same long nail beds. The same spacing of our knuckles, lengths of our fingers, the same vein that crosses the back of our left hand.

All I have to do to find my mother is to look at my hands.

Then she takes a deep, shuddering breath and opens her

eyes, and I forget about having to pee.

She looks at Dad. He reaches for her free hand, the one I'm not squeezing on to for dear life, and he kisses her wrist.

She looks around without moving her head, just her wide blue eyes, but I can't tell if she really sees any of us anymore. Her lips move.

"Beautiful," I think she says.

Then I'm distracted for a minute because Dad disappears. Right in front of our eyes, he simply vanishes. One second he's sitting on the bed, holding Mom's hand, and the next, gone.

It takes me a moment to realize that Mom's gone too. It's so quiet, I should have known. We're all holding our breath. Mom's lying back on the pillows with her eyes closed again. But she's not there. Her chest isn't moving. Her heart has stopped beating. Her body is here, but she's gone.

"Amen," Billy says.

Jeffrey jumps up. The noise of his chair clattering back against the wall seems unbearably loud. His face looks like a mask to me, stretched at the lips, eyebrows drawn low over his red-rimmed eyes. A single tear makes its way down his cheek, hovers on his chin. Furiously he dashes it away and flees the room.

I hear the front door bang as he goes. His truck roars to life, then peels on down the driveway, scattering gravel.

Something floats its way up from my chest, not a sound

but a terrible choking ache that makes me think my heart will explode.

"Billy . . . ," I call desperately.

She's here. Her hand comes down on my shoulder.

"Just breathe, Clara. Breathe."

I focus on getting the air to move in and out of my lungs. I don't know how long we stay in this position, Billy with her fingers dug into the flesh of my shoulder, hurting me but a hurt that feels good, reminds me that I, unlike my mother, still inhabit my body.

Seconds tick by. Minutes. Possibly hours. It occurs to me that Mom's hand is being warmed by mine. If I take it away, it will get cold. Then I'll never hold her hand again.

Outside the sky goes gray. A light drizzle of rain falls against the house. It feels appropriate for it to rain at a time like this. It feels right.

I glance up at Billy.

"Is this you?" I tip my head toward the window.

She smiles this odd, hurt twist of her lips. "Yep. I know it's a silly human perspective, but I can't help it."

"I don't want to let her go." It's one of those sentences I know I will hear echoing around in my head forever, along with the sound of my own ragged, broken voice.

"I know, kid," Billy says with her own bit of a rasp. "But you're not really holding her now. You know that's not her anymore."

***

After the initial quiet the phone starts ringing every few minutes, and then the doorbell, and people start pouring in. At first I feel compelled to greet them, like it's my duty as the only member of my family who actually stuck around for this, as Mom's child, to let them in and thank them personally for their abundance of sympathy and food. They should warn you about the food. When this kind of thing happens, when someone you love dies, people bring food. So here's the contents of the Gardner refrigerator: one giant lasagna, three separate and equally disgusting macaroni salads, two fruit salads, one cherry pie, two apple pies and an apple crisp, one bucket of cold fried chicken, one mystery casserole, one spinach-cranberry-and-walnut salad that comes with an unopened bottle of blue cheese dressing, and a meat loaf. The shelves of our poor refrigerator sag under the weight of it all.

Here's another thing they don't tell you beforehand: people will bring enough food to feed an orphanage in China, but you won't be hungry.

It starts to feel like every person who shows up is chipping away a piece of me when they say, "I'm so sorry, Clara. If there's anything you need, don't hesitate to call."

"She's suddenly very supportive, isn't she?" mutters Billy after Julia—yep, that angel-blood who kept asking all the biting questions at the last congregational meeting—leaves one of those macaroni salads and her deepest condolences.

"Yeah, I was tempted to tell her that Samjeeza's hiding out there in the woods."

Billy's dark eyes widen. "Is he?"

I shake my head. "No. When Dad banishes someone, I think they stay banished. I just wanted to freak her out a bit."

"Right. Well, you should have told her. Then we could have seen just how fast she can fly."

We smile together. It's the closest we can come at the moment to joking around. The ache is still here inside me, like an open, raging hole in the middle of my chest. I catch myself touching that spot, right in the center of my sternum, like one of these times I'll actually be able to put my fist in there.

Billy looks at me. "Why don't you go upstairs? You don't have to be here for these people. I'll take care of it."

"Okay." Except that I can't think what I'm going to do with myself upstairs.

When I get to my room I find Christian sitting on the eaves. This might appear strange to visitors, it occurs to me, but I decide I don't care. The ache is becoming an ugly hollowness that is in some ways worse than the original ache. But at least I can't feel Christian's emotions on the other side of the window. Or his memory of our kiss.

When did you get here? I send to him.

Earlier. Around nine.

I don't feel my own surprise. My mother died at a few minutes to ten.

I told you I'd be here, he says. *You can ignore me, though. Whatever you want.*

I want to take a nap.

Okay. I'll be here.

I lie down on top of the covers, not bothering to slip under the sheets. I turn my face to the wall. Christian's not looking at me now, but still.

I should cry, I think. I haven't cried yet. Why haven't I cried yet? I've been crying for months now at every little thing, boo-hoo-hoo, poor me, but today, on the day that my mother actually dies, nothing. Not one tear.

Jeffrey cried. Billy wept using the entire sky. But not me. With me there's just the ache.

I close my eyes. When I open them again I see that two hours have passed, although I don't feel like I've slept. The sun is lower in the sky.

Christian's still on the roof.

I get the sudden urge to call him, to ask him to come in and lay down with me. Just like before, the night I found out about the hundred-and-twenty-years rule. Except this time, I wouldn't want him to touch me or anything. Or talk. But maybe if he got close to me I could feel something. Maybe I could cry and the ache would go away.

He turns his head, meets my eyes. He can hear me.

But I don't ask him in.

***

It's late afternoon when suddenly Christian stands up without a word, and flies away.

Then there's a light knock at my door, and Tucker sticks his head in.

"Hey."

I shoot out of bed, hurl myself into his arms. He hugs me close, presses my head into his chest, says something I don't hear into my hair.

Why can't I cry?

He pulls back. "I came as soon as I found out."

I would have called Tucker right after it happened, of course, but he was at school, and I didn't have the energy to have him pulled out, find him a ride, all that. "Does everyone at school know?"

"Pretty much. Are you all right?"

I don't know how to answer this. "I was sleeping."

I disentangle myself from his arms and go over to the bed and sit down. It's hard to look at him while he's staring so intently right into my face, trying to meet my eyes. I pick at the stitching on the quilt.

Tucker seems to be at a loss for something to say. He glances around my room. "I've never been in here before," he says. "It's nice. It fits you." He clears his throat. "Wendy's downstairs. We brought you a chocolate cream pie my mom wanted to send over. And a roast chicken and some green-bean thing."

"Thanks," I say.

"It's a good pie. Do you want me to get Wendy?"

"Not yet." I dare to look at him. "Could you just . . . hold me, for a while?"

He looks relieved. Finally, something he can do. He drops onto the bed behind me and I stretch out and we spoon, his hand resting on my hip.

I don't feel anything. I don't think anything. I just breathe. In and out. In and out.

Tucker strokes my hair. There's something so tender about the gesture. It might as well have been him whispering *I love you*.

I love you too, I send to him, even though he won't hear it.

But I don't feel love. I say it because I know it to be true, but I don't feel it. I'm too numb for that. I don't deserve his love, I think. Even now, that moment with Christian in the cemetery is like a dark cloud in my mind.

Three days pass. That's something you don't expect, either. You think, death, then funeral, then graveside and all that, then done. But between the death and the funeral there's a million small events nobody ever thinks about. Writing obituaries. Choosing flowers. Picking out what my mom will wear as she lies in the casket, and what clothes I will wear to her funeral, which for me is a no-brainer: black dress, Mom's sensible pumps, her silver charm bracelet. I even tell Jeffrey which tie he should wear, the striped silver one, but when I say that he gives me this cold look, and tells me he's going to wear a black tie.

I don't know what this means. It's like my purple corduroy jacket the day of the fire. Could the balance of the universe be affected by the color of a tie?

Tucker skips school the first day to stay with me. Mostly this entails him sitting in the chair next to mine while I sit and do nothing, trying to talk to me, occasionally asking me if I need anything, and I almost always say no, until later that night, when I say, "Can you go home? No offense, but I want to be alone right now." It's true. I want to be alone. But I also specifically don't want to be around Tucker right now, because there are things I'm not telling him, big things, and I don't want to think about those things.

He says yes, of course, sure, he understands, but he's offended. I don't need my empathy to see the hurt on his face.

Every day I sense Christian somewhere nearby. Not trying to talk to me. Not pushing anything on me, any kind of response. Just near. He lets me be alone, but he's also there, on the edges, in case I don't want to be.

How does he understand to do that? He was only a kid when his mom died, but still, he gets it. Is it the same for everybody, I wonder, or is Christian so in tune with me that he understands what I need on some other level?

On the third day, Tucker confronts me, not in a mean

sort of way, but in a please-let-me-help-you-why-won't-you-let-me-help-you sort of way. I'm lying in bed, not sleeping, not doing anything, and he suddenly comes into my room.

"I want to be here for you," he says, no hello or anything. "It's that simple."

My eyes dart to the window. No Christian.

"Okay."

"But you won't let me. You won't let me in, Clara. You're pushing me away. You won't tell me what you're feeling."

"I'm not feeling anything," I tell him. "I don't mean to push you away."

But the truth is, I do mean to push him away.

He doesn't accept this. "You've been pushing me away for months. You don't tell me things, like you didn't tell me about that bad angel. I'm still waiting, you know, for you to tell me about what happened with that guy, but you don't say anything. You think I can't handle it."

"Tucker."

"Why do I get the feeling lately that you're just biding your time with me? That you're going to break this off."

"My mom died," I snap, sitting up. "I'm not really thinking about anything else."

He shakes his head. "What aren't you telling me? Why don't you think I can handle it? Haven't I handled everything you've ever thrown at me?"

"Okay, fine." I know I must sound angry, but I'm not. I'm

tired. I'm tired of hiding things, tired of being what people want me to be in this moment, tired of being that girl whose mom has died and we better tiptoe around her. In some ways, Tucker talking to me this way is a relief. At least he's not walking on eggshells anymore.

Tucker waits.

"What do you want to know?"

"Everything," he answers simply.

"All right. Let's start here. I thought you were dying, for a while. I've been having visions of Aspen Hill Cemetery, everybody there because someone was dead, and you weren't there. So I thought it was you. I didn't want to tell you because, what if I was wrong, how would you feel about that, and it turned out I was wrong, so I'm glad I didn't tell you."

"But you told Christian," he says.

"Yeah. He can see into my mind, so he knew."

"Huh," he says, but I can tell he's very unhappy at the idea of Christian and I mind-melding.

"And I can read people's feelings. Sometimes an image or a thought or two, but mostly feelings."

It feels better, confessing. I feel something. "And there's more, of course."

He blinks, startled. "Okay, shoot."

Funny that he should phrase it that way, when what I say next is like a bullet, traveling at the speed of sound straight from my mouth to his heart. I don't know why I do it. I only know that I don't want any more pretense between us. It's against my nature.

"My purpose isn't over. I don't know what it is exactly, but I know that it involves Christian. It's like we're meant to be two sides of the same coin. I don't . . . love him the way that I love you, but we're the same, him and me. We make each other stronger."

Storm clouds in Tucker's blue eyes. He stares at me. He doesn't want to know this next part.

But I tell him anyway. Because part of me realizes that, as much as I love him, as much as I want to grab on to him now and never let him go, he'll be better off without me, safer, away from my crazy world of rogue angels and mysterious duties that are going to pop up all my life, happier without me having to lie to him or withhold stuff from him for our entire relationship. I know that telling the truth right now, and especially this next part, will probably ruin things forever for us and as much as I don't want that, I think it might be the only way to ensure that I don't wimp out.

So here goes.

"I kissed Christian." My voice breaks on his name. "Well, actually, he kissed me. But I let him. He said it was part of his purpose, and I let him. Because we're connected. Because in my dream, when my mom dies, when we're at the cemetery, it's him who holds my hand and comforts me and supports me. Because you're not there."

Tucker's expression has gone stony. The muscles in his back are tight. He flexes his jaw.

"When?" he asks huskily. "When did he . . ."

"Two days before my mom died."

He stands up. "I have to go."

"Tuck."

He closes his eyes. His fists clench by his sides, then release. When he opens his eyes again, I see a hint of tears. He lets out a ragged breath. "I have to go."

What have I done? I think dazedly. I follow him out of my bedroom, down the stairs. "I'm sorry, Tuck," I say. Like that can fix anything.

My words don't faze him. He blows right past the group of sympathizers in the living room, past Wendy and Angela, who are sitting together on the couch.

"Wendy, let's go."

She jumps up.

"Tuck," I call again. But then I stop. I resolve to let him go, even if he never talks to me again. The ache in my chest doubles, makes me feel short of breath. I lean against the living room wall and watch Tucker helplessly as he nearly runs out of my house.

He stops at his car, fumbles in his pocket for keys. Wendy catches up to him, grabs his arm, says something, and flicks her head back to the house. He nods. Then he looks back and sees Christian standing on the front porch, and everything seems to slow down.

"You." He shakes Wendy off and takes a few slow steps toward the house.

"Tucker," Christian says quietly.

"What kind of person are you?" Tucker practically growls, advancing on him. He ignores Wendy as she pleads to go home. "You wait until she's at her most vulnerable and then you make your move?"

"Is that what she told you?" Christian asks, not in any threatening sort of way, but also not backing down one bit.

I want to get out there, stop this before someone gets hurt. I have the feeling that someone could really get hurt about now. But as I take a step toward the door, Angela grabs my arm.

"Don't," she says. "You'll make it worse."

"She told me you kissed her," Tucker says.

"I did."

"It doesn't matter to you that she has a boyfriend? That she loves me?" Tucker is close to Christian now, climbing the steps to the porch. He stops a few feet in front of Christian and stands with his hands in fists, waiting for the excuse Christian is going to give him to hit him.

I can't see Christian's face from this angle. His back is turned to me. But somehow I know that his face is impassive, his eyes cool green emeralds that glitter unnaturally in the light. There's no warmth in him at all when he says, "I always liked you, Tucker. I think you're a decent guy."

Tucker laughs. "But what, I'm not worthy of her? She's out of my league, just because—"

"She and I belong together," Christian interrupts.

"Right. Because of your purpose," Tucker says in a low voice.

Christian glances around, irritated that Tucker knows this word, that he would dare to say it here in front of all these people. "That and about a hundred other reasons, none of which you'd be capable of understanding," he says.

"You smug bastard." And that's when Tucker punches him. Right in the face. Christian's head snaps back and a river of blood instantly starts to stream from his nose. He wipes at it, looks at his blood-sullied fingers. It's possible that he's never seen his own blood before now. His eyes narrow. He wipes his hand on his jeans. Then the porch erupts in a flurry of motion, people scrambling to get out of the way, women shrieking, fists flying. I tear loose from Angela just in time to see Tucker push Christian back against the house wall so hard it cracks the glass in the front window. I watch Christian's dark brows draw low over his eyes, a genuine fury rising there, about to be unleashed. He puts a hand in the middle of Tucker's chest and sends him sprawling, striking the porch rail with a sickening crunch as he flies backward onto the driveway. Gravel scatters everywhere. Tucker springs to his feet, wiping a smear of blood off his chin, hair all disheveled, eyes blue fire.

"Come on, pretty boy," he taunts. "Show me what you've got."

"Stop!" I scream.

Christian jumps over the fractured porch railing so lightly he almost seems to float. Next to Tucker he has a slender grace, not the muscle from roping calves and working hard every day, not the grit of being a farm boy from Wyoming, but I know that he is incredibly strong.

Tucker swings at him, and Christian ducks away. He lands a punch to Tucker's side that again sends him crashing back into the dirt. He grunts, straightens up to go at Christian again.

"Stop it!" I scream.

Neither of them pays any attention. Tucker feints another punch, then almost gets one into Christian's gut, but one more time Christian moves away before the blow can land. Tucker makes a frustrated noise in the back of his throat as Christian hits him again, this time in the jaw.

This isn't fair. There's no way for Tucker to win this fight. Christian will always be faster, and stronger, and harder to hurt.

Please, I send to Christian with all my power to speak in his mind turned up full blast. *If you care for me at all, stop.*

He hesitates.

I stumble down the porch stairs toward them. I'm not

thinking anymore. I need to get myself between them. "Christian, don't hurt him," I say out loud.

This stops them both cold. Tucker gives me this incredulous, offended look. How could I think that he'd be beaten by this fancied-up city kid, no matter what kind of blood runs through his veins? His lip actually curls in disgust. You don't believe in me, his eyes say. Why don't you believe in me?

At the same time, Christian drops his fists, turns to look at me with a hurt expression.

I wasn't going to hurt him, he says in my mind. *You think I would use my powers to do that?*

I don't have an answer for either of them.

"Okay, that's enough!" a voice rings out. Billy makes her way down the front steps. She walks up beside me and glares at Tucker and Christian.

"What are you two doing here acting like elk in rut? This is a time of mourning. You should be ashamed."

"I'm going," Tucker says. He doesn't look at me again. He must be hurting all over, but he keeps his head high, his back straight, as he walks to his car. Over his shoulder Wendy shoots me a look that's half murder, half apology. She gets in the driver's seat. I can see her talking, possibly yelling at Tucker as they drive off.

Christian wipes blood off his face. His nose has stopped bleeding, but the blood's still there.

"My uncle's going to kill me," he says.

"He can get in line," I shoot back.

He looks at me, startled. *Clara, I'm—*

Don't you dare tell me you're sorry. Just go.

I was only—

Go. I send again. *I want you to go away, Christian. I don't want you here. I don't need you.*

He swallows, stuffs his hands in his pockets, and looks at me hard. He doesn't believe me.

"Get out of here," I say out loud.

He turns and tromps off into the woods, where shadows are stretching out through the trees.

"Girl, you have a knack for drawing trouble," Billy says, clapping an affectionate hand on my shoulder.

Don't I know it.

After darkness falls the people all go home. The house gets brutally empty. Jeffrey comes home, from wherever it is that he disappears to every day, retreating into his room without a word to anyone. I go to the door of Mom's office and push it open. Part of me expects her to be there, hunched over her computer, writing code. She'd look up and smile.

"Tough day, sweetie?" she'd say.

I swallow. I try to remind myself that she's in heaven. But I can't picture it. I can't feel it. All I know is that she's gone, and she's never coming back.

That night I can't sleep. I'm not even sure I want to. I stare up at the ceiling and watch the shadows flit across it, the outlines of leaves from the tree outside my window, moving back and forth.

Around midnight, the phone starts ringing. I wait for someone to answer it, but no one does. Where is Billy? I wonder. When will Dad come back?

The phone keeps ringing its lonely song. I pad sock-foot into the kitchen, take it out of its cradle, and look at the caller ID.

CLARA, it reads.

Huh?

I'm getting a call from my own phone.

I click TALK. I'm suddenly wide awake. "Hello?"

Silence.

"Hello?" I say after a few seconds of nothing on the other line.

"Hello, little bird."

It's such a strange thing, hearing Samjeeza's voice without the accompanying sorrow. Almost like talking to a normal person, having an ordinary conversation where I don't have to fear for my life or wonder if I'm about to be dragged to hell. Strange, like I said.

"What do you want?" I ask him.

Silence.

"Well, it's been nice talking to you, but I've got to go. . . ." I start to lay the phone back down. "I have to bury my mother in the morning."

"What?" he says, sounding truly shocked.

He doesn't know.

"Please," he says after a minute, real desperation in his voice. "What happened?"

"You knew about the one-hundred-and-twenty-years rule, didn't you?"

He hisses out a breath. "Is that how old she was? I knew she was nearing that, but . . . it's hard for me to keep track of human time. When?"

"Three days ago." I feel a flash of anger, which actually feels good. Any emotion besides crushing sadness feels good at this point. "So now you won't ever be able to hurt her again."

Again, there's silence. I think he might have hung up. But then he says, "I didn't feel her pass. I should have felt it."

"Maybe you weren't as connected as you thought you were."

"Oh, Meg," he says.

That's when I blow a fuse. He has no right to grieve, I think. He's the bad guy. He tried to kill her. He wanted to bring her down to hell with him, right? He doesn't deserve my pity.

"When are you finally going to get it?" I ask him furiously. "My mom's name is not Meg. Whatever you had with her, whatever was between you, was over a long time ago. She doesn't love you. She never did. She was always meant for someone else, from the very beginning. And there's nothing you can do about it now because she's dead."

The word rings in the air. I sense the presence of someone behind me. It's Billy. She catches me by the shoulders, steadies me when I wasn't even aware that I was swaying, about to fall. Then she slowly takes the phone out of my hand and sets it down in the cradle.

"Well, now we know why he's mad at *you* tomorrow in the cemetery," she says. She shakes her head at me. "I would feel a lot better if you didn't go around antagonizing Black Wings." Then, without me even having to ask her, she walks me back to my bedroom and lies down beside me in the dark, sings a low song that matches the cadence of the wind outside, like I'm a kid again. And she holds my hand until I fall asleep.

20

LOVING MEMORY

There are a lot of things the dream didn't prepare me for. Like seeing Mom's body so still and waxlike lying in the casket. They put too much makeup on her. Mom hardly ever wore more than mascara and lip gloss. In the coffin she looks like a painted doll. Beautiful. Peaceful. But not her, you know? It's hard to look at her like that, but I also find it hard to look away.

Or for the line of people who file by to look at her, and then expect to talk to me. It's like a reverse wedding reception. First, see the corpse. Say your good-byes. Then say hello to the family. They all think Mom died of cancer, so they keep talking about pain. "At least she's no longer in any pain," they tell me, patting my hand. "She's beyond the pain now."

At least that's true.

Or the actual funeral. The church part. Sitting in the front row with Jeffrey and Billy, a few feet from Mom's coffin. Dad's still a no-show, and part of me feels betrayed by that. He should be here, I think. But I know he's in a better place, literally. With Mom.

"He *is* with Mom, right?" I'd asked Billy as she braided my hair this morning, a long clean plait that miraculously stays in place all day. "He has been all this time?"

"I think so. Funerals are not really for angels, kid. Your dad would unsettle everyone if he came. He knows that. So it's best if he stays away. Plus, he wants to be with your mother now, help her through the transition."

Tucker's at the church. He comes up to me after the service, stands in front of me with his hands folded together, looking lost. I stare at his black eye, the cut on his cheek, the scrape on his knuckles.

"I'm here," he says. "You were wrong. I'm here."

"Thank you," I say. "But don't come to the graveside. Please, Tucker. Don't come. Samjeeza will be there, and he's angry, and I don't want you to get hurt."

"I want to be there," he protests.

"But you won't be. Because I'm asking you to stay away," I whisper. I would say the same thing to Wendy, ask her not to come to the cemetery, but I already know she won't listen.

Because she's there, every time, in my vision.

"Please," I say to Tucker. "Don't come."

He hesitates, then nods and files out of the church.

So finally, after a day that seemed longer than any other, like it could really have stretched a thousand years, I get out of the car at Aspen Hill Cemetery. I blink in the sunshine. I take a deep breath. And I start walking.

I thought I knew how this day would go, this day that finds me at last standing in a black dress in the grass at Aspen Hill Cemetery. I have seen it so many times. But this time, the real time, it doesn't feel the same. I'm future-Clara now. There's an ache in the middle of my chest that makes me want to cut my heart out and chuck it into the weeds. But I bear it. I walk. Because there is no other choice but to put one foot in front of the other.

I see Jeffrey ahead of me, and I say his name.

"Let's just get this over with," he says.

The color of his tie didn't matter, after all.

Everyone's here. The entire congregation, every single one of them, that I can tell, even the Julia lady. No one chickened out.

Funny that it turned out to be a self-fulfilling prophecy, my dream. I drive myself crazy trying to figure out why Tucker isn't there. Thinking he's dead. Thinking there shouldn't be a force on earth that would keep him away. But in the end, he's not there because I asked him not to be.

That's what we call irony.

The ache really gets me then. This is it. My destined time. My gauntlet to run, and I was meant to do it without Tucker. It gets so bad I have trouble breathing. I stop to catch my breath.

Someone takes my hand. Christian, as I knew it would be. I take in the sight of him, his neat black suit, pressed white shirt, silver tie. His gold-flecked eyes are red-rimmed, like he's been crying too. In them, a question and an answer all in one.

And this, I realize, is the moment of decision, what my vision has been warning me about all this time. I could break away now, pull my hand from his, tell him again that I don't need him. I could hold on to my anger, my frustration at this hopeless choice. Or I could accept him. I could face what's between us, and move on. It's such a big decision to ask of me now. It's not really fair. But then, it never has been fair, this entire fiasco, from start to finish.

The thing is, with him holding my hand, touching my skin, the ache in my chest eases. It's like he has the ability to take on some of my pain. I feel so much better around him. Stronger. And he is willing to take my pain. He wants to bear it with me.

I can see it shining in his eyes. I'm more than a duty to him. I'm more than his literal dream girl. I'm so much more.

I think back to that morning in November, in my kitchen in California when I first saw him standing there in the trees, waiting for me. My heart pounding, my mouth opening to call his name, even when I didn't know it yet, that irresistible need I felt surging through me to go to him. It all plays out in my mind like a movie reel, every moment I've spent with him since then, him carrying me to the nurse's office on my first day of school, Mr. Erikson's history class, the Pizza Hut. Riding the chairlift together. Prom. Sitting on the front porch looking at the stars. Him coming out of the trees the night of the fire. Every night he sat on the eaves, the meadow, the ski hill, this cemetery where he kissed me, every single moment that's passed between us, I felt this force pulling me toward him. I've heard this voice, whispering in my head.

We belong together.

I don't realize I'm holding my breath until I let it out. I gaze down at our joined hands. His thumb strokes slowly over my knuckles. I look up again, at his face. Has he heard all this, the babbling of my heart? Has he read my mind?

You can do this, he says. I don't know if he's talking about Mom, or something else.

Maybe it doesn't matter.

I meet his eyes, tighten my hand in his.

Let's get up there, I send to him. *People are waiting.*

And together, we keep walking.

I expect the circle of people, the gaping hole in the ground with my mother's coffin poised over it, but the shock of seeing it has worn off some. I know the words Stephen will say. I expect to sense Samjeeza there. But I didn't know that I would feel sorry for him in that moment. I didn't plan to go to him afterward, after the prayers are said and the coffin lowered into the ground, dirt layered over it, after the crowd scatters and leaves Jeffrey and Christian and Billy and me standing there. I feel Samjeeza, his sorrow that doesn't come from being separated from God or going against his angelic design, but from finally accepting that he's lost my mom for good. And I know so clearly what to do.

I let go of Christian's hand. I walk off toward the fence at the edge of the cemetery.

Clara? Christian calls after me, alarmed.

Stay there. It's all right. I won't leave hallowed ground.

I call to Samjeeza.

He meets me at the fence. He comes up the hill in the form of a dog, then changes, standing silently on the other side of the chain-link with mournful amber eyes. He can't cry—it's not part of his anatomy. He hates that he hasn't been given the dignity of tears.

This is awkward, him being evil and all. But I've finally moved beyond mad.

"Here," I say.

I fumble to take a bracelet off my wrist, Mom's old charm bracelet. I thrust it through a hole in the fence.

He looks at me, face slack with astonishment.

"Take it," I urge.

He holds out his hand, careful not to touch me. I drop the bracelet into it. It tinkles as it falls. He closes his fingers around it.

"I gave this to her," he says. "How did you . . . ?"

"I didn't. I'm just playing it by ear, here."

Then I turn and walk back to my family, and I don't look back.

"Baby girl, you nearly gave me a heart attack," says Billy.

"Let's go," I say. "I want to go home."

Samjeeza is still standing there, like he's been turned to stone, a marble angel in the cemetery, as we drive away.

What I really don't expect is the police to be waiting for us when we get home.

"What's this about?" Billy asks as we get out of the car to gawk at the police car parked in the driveway, the two officers poking around outside the house.

"We need to have a few words with Jeffrey Gardner," one of them says. He looks at Jeffrey. "You him?"

Jeffrey goes pale.

Billy, as always, is the picture of calm.

"Regarding what, exactly?" She puts her hands on her hips and stares them down.

"Regarding what he might know about the Palisades fire

last August. We have reason to believe that he may have been involved."

"We'd also like to take a look around, if you don't mind," the other officer says.

Billy's all business. "Do you have a warrant?"

The officer's face grows red under her intense stare. "No, ma'am."

"Well, I'm Jeffrey's guardian. He's just been through his mother's funeral today. Your questions can wait. Now you two gentlemen have a pleasant afternoon."

Then she takes me by the shoulder with one hand and Jeffrey by the shoulder with the other and ushers us into the house. The door bangs shut behind us. She lets out a breath.

"Well, this could be a problem," she says, staring at Jeffrey.

He shrugs. "Let them question me. I don't care. I'll tell them. I did it."

"You *what*?" But part of me isn't really so surprised. Part of me suspected it, even from the first moment when I saw him flying out of the forest that night. Part of me knew.

"It was my purpose," he says. "I'd been dreaming about it since we moved to Wyoming. I was supposed to start that fire."

Billy frowns. "Now, see, that's a problem. You two stay inside for the evening, okay? I have to make a few calls."

"To who? The congregation has a lawyer?" Jeffrey asks sarcastically.

Billy looks at him with no humor at all in her usual twinkly dark eyes. "Yes, as a matter of fact."

"Do we have an accountant, too?"

"Mitch Hammond."

"Whatever," Jeffrey says. Any vulnerability I saw in his face earlier today, any hint of the little boy who wanted his mom, is completely absent. "I'll be in my room."

Off he goes, roomward. Off Billy goes, to Mom's office, and shuts the door. Which leaves me alone. Again.

I wait for a few minutes, until the silence of the house starts to feel like a buzzing in my head. Then I figure what the heck and head up to Jeffrey's room. He doesn't answer when I knock. I stick my head in just to make sure he hasn't gone out the window.

He's there, messing around with stuff in his dresser. He stops and glares at me.

I sigh. "You know, it might be easier for both of us right now if you would stop hating me for like ten minutes."

"That's your sisterly advice?"

"Yeah. I'm older and wiser too. So you should listen."

And Mom wanted us to be there for each other, I don't quite dare to say out loud.

He snorts and goes back to counting out pairs of socks.

"What are you doing?" I ask.

"Packing my gym bag for this week."

"Oh."

"I'm busy, okay?"

"Jeffrey . . ." I move a pile of dirty clothes from his desk chair and sit on it. "What'd I do to make you hate me so much?"

He pauses. "You know what you did."

"No. I mean, yes, I guess I was pretty selfish last year, about my purpose and stuff. I wasn't thinking about you."

"Oh really," he says.

"I'm sorry. If I ignored you, or took the attention away from you because I was so focused on my purpose. I didn't know about yours, I swear. But don't you kind of owe me an apology too?"

He turns to me incredulously.

"What for?" he demands.

"You know . . ."

"No. You tell me." Suddenly he tugs off his tie and flings it on the bed.

"You started the fire!"

"Yeah, I'll probably go to juvie. Is there even a juvie in Wyoming?"

"Jeffrey . . ."

But now that he's talking, he doesn't plan to stop. "This is pretty convenient for you, right? Because now you get to blame me. If I hadn't started the other fire, Tucker would have been safe and your thing with Christian would have gone off without a hitch, and you'd be a good little angel-blood who fulfilled her purpose. Is that right?"

"Are you sure it was your purpose?"

"Are you sure about yours?" he counters.

"Okay, true enough. But seriously, I don't get it. It doesn't make sense. But if you say you had the visions about it, and that's what you were supposed to do, I believe you."

"Do you have any idea how hard it was?" He's almost shouting now. "The crazy stuff that went through my head, like I could have been murdering people, starting that fire. All those animals and all that land, and the firefighters and people who risked their lives to put it out. But I still did it." His lip curls in disgust. "I did my part. Then you had to go and bail on yours."

I lower my eyes, look at my hands. "If I hadn't, Tucker would have died."

"You're so wrong it's pathetic," Jeffrey says more calmly. "As usual."

"What?" I glance up, startled. "Jeffrey, I was there. I saved him. If I hadn't shown up when I did, he would have . . ."

"No. He wouldn't have." Jeffrey looks out the window like he can see it happening all over again. "He wouldn't have died. Because I would have saved him." He starts packing his bag again, underwear this time. He laughs, a mean, humorless sound, shakes his head. "God. I was frantic that night, looking for him. He didn't show up where he was supposed to, where he always did, in the visions. I thought I'd messed up somehow. I thought he was toast for sure. Finally I gave up and came home. I saw you on the porch with Christian and I was like, well, at least she did it. At least she fulfilled her purpose. Then I spent all night agonizing over how your face would look when you found out Tucker was dead."

"Oh, Jeffrey."

"So you see," he continues after a minute. He grabs a stick of deodorant and tucks it into his duffel bag. "You thought I screwed up your purpose, right? But the truth is, if you'd followed your vision, if you'd just trusted the plan, then you and Christian would have done your thing in the forest, and Tucker would have been perfectly safe, and everything would have worked out fine. But instead you had to go and screw it up for the both of us."

I don't say anything. I just slink out of his room and shut the door. In my own room I lie down on the bed and stare up at the empty ceiling wide-eyed, dry-eyed, and it feels like the ache opens a huge gaping hole in my chest.

"I'm sorry," I gasp, although I have no idea who I'm apologizing to, Jeffrey or my mom, who believed in me so much, or even God. I just know that it's my fault, and I'm sorry.

Don't beat yourself up, Christian says in my head. I sit up and glance at the window, and of course he's there, sitting in his normal spot.

I messed things up for you too, I remind him.

He shakes his head. *No, you didn't. You just changed things.*

I go to the window and open it, step outside into the cool night air. It feels like summer now, a kind of shift in the way the night feels, the way it smells.

"You've got to stay out of my head," I say as I hunker down awkwardly next to Christian. I'm still in my mom's nice black pumps. My toes hurt. "It can't be very fun for you, always finding out my deep dark secrets."

He shrugs. "They're not so dark."

I give him a hard look. "My life is a soap opera."

"A really, really addictive soap opera," he says. Then he puts his arm around my shoulders and draws me into him. And I let him. I close my eyes.

"Why do you want me, Christian? I'm hopelessly screwed up."

"We're all screwed up. And you look so cute while you're doing it."

"Stop."

The back of my neck feels hot where his breath is touching me, stirring the wisps of my hair that managed to escape my braid. "Thank you," I say. We sit there for a while, not talking. An owl hoots in the distance. And suddenly, miraculously, there are tears in my eyes.

"I miss my mom," I choke out.

Christian's arms tighten around me. I lean my head onto his shoulder and cry and cry, my body shuddering with sobs.

It's one of those loud, probably unattractive kind of sobfests, the kind where your nose runs and your eyes get all huge and swollen and your whole face becomes this messy pink swampland, but I don't care. Christian holds me, and I cry. The ache empties itself out on his T-shirt, leaving me lighter, a good emptiness this time, like if I tried I might be light enough to fly.

21

HIGH COUNTRIES

At graduation all the girls have to wear white robes and the boys wear black. When the band plays "Pomp and Circumstance" we file two by two into the gym at Jackson Hole High School, which is filled with chattering, cheering, frantic-picture-taking friends and relatives. But it's hard to look up into the bleachers and not see Mom. Or Jeffrey, even. The police showed up at our house the next day to question him. This time they even brought a warrant. But he wasn't there. All we found in his room were a bunch of clothes and toiletries missing—and here I'd believed that lie he'd fed me as I watched him pack it up that night—and a single yellow Post-it stuck to his window.

Don't look for me, it read.

He didn't even take his truck. We've been frantically searching for him for days, but there's not a trace of where he might have gone. He's just gone.

I spot Dad in the audience next to Billy. He gives me a thumbs-up. I smile, try to look happy. I am graduating, after all. It's a big deal.

When someone dies in the movies, there's always that scene where the main character stands in the dead person's closet and fingers the sleeve of the favorite shirt, the one she remembers from so many happy moments. That was me, this morning. I went into Mom's closet for this white eyelet dress she used to love. I thought I'd wear it, under my gown. That way, maybe a part of her would be there. Sentimental, I know.

In the movies, the main character always presses her face in to get a whiff of that last, lingering hint of the person's smell. And then she cries.

I wish I didn't know this, how real those scenes are, how unbelievable it was in that moment to stand there looking at all the dead can leave behind. How can the shoes still be here? I thought. How can the clothes survive, when the person did not? I found a hair on the shoulder of a flannel shirt and held it gently between my thumb and forefinger, this hair that was once attached to a person I loved so much. I held it for a long time, unsure of what to do with it, and then I finally let it go.

I let it float away.

It hurt.

But right now she's with me, her vanilla perfume rising off the fabric, and somehow it makes me feel stronger.

This is officially torture, Christian says in my head. *How many speeches are there?*

I consult my trusty program.

Four.

Mental groan.

But we get to cheer for Angela, I remind him. *Angel Club sticks together, right?*

Like I said. Torture.

I turn slightly and cast a subtle glance in his direction. He's sitting a couple rows behind me, right next to Ava Peters. Just down the row from him, Kay Patterson smirks at me.

I know, I know, I think. *I'm still looking at him.*

He lifts his eyebrows.

Never mind, I tell him.

One speech ends and it's time for Angela. The principal announces her as the class valedictorian. One of Jackson Hole High's best and brightest stars. One of the three students who will be attending Stanford University in the fall.

Applause, applause.

Stanford must be lowering its standards, remarks Christian.

I know. Wait, did he say three students?

I think so.

So who's lucky number three?

No answer.

I turn around to look at him again.

No.

He grins.

Now I get it, I tell him. *You're stalking me.*

Quiet now. Angela's about to talk.

I shift my attention back to the podium, where Angela stands stiffly, a stack of note cards in front of her. She pushes her glasses up on her nose.

When did Angela get glasses? Christian asks.

She's playing Studious Straight-A Angela today, I answer. *The glasses are her costume.*

O-kay.

Angela clears her throat lightly. She really is nervous, I can tell. All these eyes on her. All this attention, when she's usually the one in the corner with the book. She looks at me. I smile in what I hope is an encouraging way.

"I know how these speeches typically go," she begins. "I'm supposed to get up here and talk about the future. How great it will be, how we'll all pursue our dreams and make something of ourselves. Maybe I should read a children's book about the places we'll go, and talk about how bright our futures are, out there, waiting for us. That's inspirational, right?"

Murmuring from the crowd.

Uh-oh, says Christian.

I know what he means. It sounds like there might be a very good chance that Angela's going to pull one of those anti-inspirational graduation speeches, the kind that calls the school cheerleader a vapid Barbie doll or a favorite teacher a creepy perv.

Angela glances down at her cards.

Don't do it, I think.

"I know that when I think about my future, I'm usually overwhelmed, knowing how much will be expected of me. I know the odds are that I'll fail many of the things I try. And it's a big deal. What if I figure out what my purpose is, my reason for being on this planet, only to fall short? What if I don't pass the test?"

She looks at me again. I hold my breath. One corner of her mouth lifts—she's laughing at me. Then she goes back to serious.

"But then I think about what I've learned here in the last year, and I don't mean in my classes, but what I've learned from watching my friends face their futures and search for their purposes. I've learned that a storm isn't always just bad weather, and a fire can be the start of something new. I've found out that there are a lot more shades of gray in this world than I ever knew about. I've learned that sometimes, when you're afraid but you keep on moving forward, that's the biggest kind of courage there is. And finally, I've learned that life isn't really about failure and success. It's about being present, in the moment when big things happen, when everything changes, including yourself. So I would tell us, no matter how bright we think our futures are, it doesn't matter. Whether we go off to some fancy university or stay home and work. That doesn't define us. Our purpose on this earth is not a single event, an accomplishment we can check off a list. There is no test. No passing or failing. There's only us, each moment shaping who we are, into what we will become. So I say forget about the future. Pay attention to now. This moment right now. Let go of expectations. Just be. Then you are free to become something great."

She's done. The crowd claps and claps, mostly I think because her speech was pretty short. It's in one ear and out the other for most of us at this point. But not for me. I heard her loud and clear.

"Okay, that was, I have to say, about the cheesiest thing I ever heard in my life," I say to Angela as we're milling around afterward. We hug, so Billy can take our picture. "I mean, seriously. Just be? You should write ads for Nike."

"That was good stuff, I'll have you know. Wisdom from the heart and all that."

"So you're going to be all relaxed about your purpose from now on, then?"

"Not relaxed, exactly. I'm trying to be Zen about it."

"Good luck with that."

"Hey." She looks the tiniest bit offended. "You really didn't like my speech? Because I kind of wrote it for you."

"I know. I did like it. I just don't have a lot of room for philosophy these days. I'm still doing the breathe in/breathe out thing."

"Did you talk to Tucker yet?" she asks.

The girl sure knows how to spoil a good time.

"No."

"Well, you're about to," she says, staring off over my shoulder. "I'll catch you later."

Then she's gone, lost in a sea of black and white gowns. I turn around to see Tucker standing right behind me. He looks uncomfortable.

"Hi, Carrots," he says.

"Hi."

"Some crazy thing, isn't it?"

"What is?"

"Graduation." He gestures around us. "Finally blowing this Popsicle stand."

"Oh. Yes. Crazy."

His eyes narrow on my face. "Can we go outside for a minute and talk?"

I follow him out the back, into the grassy area behind the school. It's quieter here, but we can still hear the buzz of conversation from the gym. Tucker stuffs his hands in his pockets.

"I'm sorry. I was a jerk that day. I don't know, I was surprised, and then I saw . . ." He stops, takes a deep breath. "I think a caveman took over my body. I'm sorry," he says again.

I can't think of anything to say that doesn't involve me bursting into tears.

Tucker clears his throat. "How are you doing?"

"Right now? I've been better."

"No I mean—" He sighs. "God, I'd forgotten how frustrating you can be."

It's an insult, but it comes with a begrudging smile, the admiration in his eyes that sends me back to those days when we used to drive each other crazy.

"And I'd forgotten what a rude hick you can be," I throw in for good measure.

"Ouch." He shows his dimples this time. My heart aches, wanting to make everything better between us again. It must show on my face because his expression suddenly sobers. He steps closer to me, puts his hand on my arm.

"So I take it you're still going to Stanford this fall?"

"Yep," I say without enthusiasm. "Go Cardinals."

"But you're going to be around this summer, right?"

The look on his face is suddenly hopeful, and the summer we could have together unrolls itself in my mind, something like that magical time last summer when I was falling for Tucker hard, falling for Wyoming and all its wonders. I wish we could live it all over again, those lazy days fishing on the lake, hiking up into the mountains to pick huckleberries, swimming the Hoback River, rafting the Snake, marking each place with a kiss or a touch, making it ours. But this time I know it's not meant to be. Because we can never go back.

I glance down at our feet, my strappy white sandals, Tucker's boots. "No. Billy thought it would be a good idea if I got away this summer, you know, away from all the sad stuff."

"Sounds like a good plan," he says quietly.

"So I'm going to Italy with Angela."

"When?"

"Monday." As in, the day after tomorrow. I've already packed.

He nods like it's something he should have expected. "Well. Maybe that's for the best."

Silence.

"I'll be back for a couple weeks right before school starts. You'll be here then, right?"

"I'll be here."

"Okay."

He looks up at me, his blue eyes so mournful it makes my heart feel like it's being squeezed.

"How about tomorrow? Are you free?"

Sometimes the word *free* can have so many meanings.

"Um, sure."

"Then pick me up tomorrow morning," he says. "We'll go out one last time."

Even now, I can't say no to that.

Tucker decided it would be nice to take me to the Grand Canyon of Yellowstone, not so grand as the real Grand Canyon, he said, but close. There's a place where you can stand on the brink of a waterfall that he said I would love. (I did.) On the way home from the Lazy Dog, after dropping Tucker off, I have to stop and pull over. I want to go back, I want the afternoon to last forever, but all I have is the memory and already it's fading. So I sit in my car on the side of the road and I remember him looking at me as we stood against the railing on the edge of the waterfall, the water casting rainbows in the air around us, and him saying, "Oh man, I want to kiss you," and me saying, "Okay."

Then he looked deep into my eyes, and put his lips on mine. It was the sweetest kind of kiss in the world, intense but undemanding, gentle. But it sent a roar of feeling through me louder than the torrent of water dropping away under our feet.

I opened my heart to his. I felt what he felt coursing through me. He loves me so much that this was killing him, the way this kiss felt like good-bye. He never wanted to let me go. He wanted to fight for me. Every part of him was telling him to fight, but he didn't know how. He thought maybe the purest form of love is letting me go.

My own heart soared, feeling that, knowing that he still loves me, in spite of everything that's happened. I struggled to hold the glory at bay, because it wanted to fill me, wanted to shine out with all that I was feeling in that moment.

Then, too soon, much too soon, he pulled away. Stepped back.

Wait, I wanted to tell him as he turned and walked back up the trail. Come back here.

And I could've convinced him, I think, not to let this be good-bye. I could've told him that I wanted him to fight for me. That I love him too. But something inside me was whispering that he was right, when yesterday he said this is for the best. Tucker deserves something better than I can give him. He deserves a regular human girl, one like Allison Lowell. He deserves happiness.

So I let him head off, and we drove back to his house in silence, trying to convince ourselves that we're doing the right thing, for both of us.

Dad's waiting for me on the front porch when I get home. He stands up as I pull into the driveway.

"Don't get out," he says. "There's somewhere I'd like to

go with you."

I slide back into my seat and unlock the door for him. He gets in on the passenger's side and fastens his seat belt. I get this weird sensation like I'm back in Driver's Ed, nervous, because I don't know what he wants. All this mixed with his own special cocktail of joy.

"Okay, where to?" I ask.

"Let's go toward town."

"Okay." I drive. I don't know what to say to him. The last time I saw him was at graduation, but he didn't stick around after. We didn't get the chance to talk. And before that it was him sitting on Mom's bed as she died. I have so many things swirling in my brain right now, questions, mostly, but it feels weird to ask.

Like: Is she okay? Where did she go, exactly? Were you with her this whole time? What's it like, where she is? Does she miss me? Can she hear me, if I try to talk to her? Is she watching over me?

I'm driving too slow. The car behind me honks, swerves to pass me, narrowly missing an oncoming car.

"Crazy California drivers," I say, gesturing to the guy's CA license plates before he screeches off. "Always in such a rush."

When we get to town Dad has me turn off on the road to Grand Teton National Park. It's a road I've been down a million times before with Tucker.

"How much will we need for admission into the park?" Dad asks.

"I've got it, Dad. I have a season pass."

Dad looks pleased, like he's proud to have produced a kid with a respectful appreciation of nature. We come around a long, curving corner, and suddenly the mountains open up in front of us, washed in red and gold. The sun has just gone down behind them. Soon it will be dark.

"Right here," he instructs as we approach a scenic turnout. "Pull over."

Obediently I turn in and park. We get out of the car. I follow Dad as he takes a few steps past the paved part of the road, into the tall grass. He stares off at the mountains.

"Beautiful," he says. "I've never seen them from this angle before. It's quite something, isn't it?"

"Yeah, it's pretty, Dad." But I'm confused. Why would he want to come here?

He turns to me with an arched eyebrow. "Patience is not your strong suit, is it?"

Heat rushes to my face. "I guess not. Sorry. I just thought you had plans, or somewhere you wanted me to see. I've kind of seen this before."

"You haven't seen this," he says. "We're not there yet."

Before I have time to process this, he puts a hand on my back, right below the nape of my neck. Something shifts around us, like a quick change in air pressure. My ears pop. I get the sudden sensation of lifting, the kind you feel when an elevator starts to rise, followed by a rush of light-headedness. Then I notice that there's something different about the color of the grass; it's greener than it was a second ago. I look up at the mountains, and I notice a difference there too, in the light, where before it was fading, night falling on the land, shadows starting across the plains that stretch to the foothills, now the shadows are receding. The air is growing brighter.

It's almost like a perpetual daybreak. The sun didn't just go down. It's coming up.

I sway dizzily, almost fall, like I just stepped off a merry-go-round. I clutch at Dad's arm.

"Are you all right?" he asks. "It might be better if you hang on to me until you regain your equilibrium."

I take a deep breath. The air is almost heavy in its sweetness, like green grass and clover, a hint of something I recognize as the smell of clouds. To say it's beautiful here, wonderfully, impossibly beautiful, wouldn't do it justice. I turn to Dad.

"This is heaven," I say. No question; I know. Maybe the angel part of me recognizes it. I can't help the giddy feeling that floods me. Heaven.

"The edge of it, yes," Dad says.

No longer dizzy, I let go of his arm. I try to take a few steps away from him, but there's something strange about the grass under my feet. It's too hard. My feet don't sink into it or crush it down. I stumble and look back at Dad.

"What's wrong with the grass?"

"It's not the grass," he says. "It's you. You're not meant to be here yet. You're still not solid enough for this plain, but if you were to walk in that direction"—he nods toward the growing light in what, on earth, was due west but here seems a different direction entirely— "you'd grow more solid with every step, until you reached the mountains."

"What would happen when I reached the mountains?"

"Well, that's for you to find out when the time comes," he says mysteriously.

"You mean when I die."

He doesn't reply. He looks off toward those mountains and lifts a hand to point. "I brought you here to see."

I squint toward the light, shielding my eyes with my hand, and then my breath catches. I can make out the figure of a person out there. A woman in a white, calf-length, sleeveless dress. It looks like the eyelet sundress I wore under my gown at graduation yesterday. She has her back turned to us, walking, almost running, it seems, toward the mountains. Her long auburn hair is flowing free down her back.

"Mom," I breathe. "Mommy!"

I try to run toward her, but I can't handle my feet on this stony grass. It hurts, like picking your way across a gravel road with bare feet. I only make it a few more steps before I give up, panting.

"Mom!" I call again, but it's clear she doesn't hear me.

Dad comes up beside me. "You can't reach her, sweetheart, not now. I brought you here because I thought it would do you good to see her. But that's all."

It's not enough, I think, but it's all I have. It's a gift that he's giving me, the best kind of present there is. Proof of my mother, that she is somewhere safe, and warm, and bright. That she still exists out there.

"Thank you," I whisper.

Dad holds out his hand, and I take it. Then together we stand and watch her, this ethereal figure who is my mother, making her way toward those high countries. She's walking away from me for now, but she's walking into the glory. Into the light.

ACKNOWLEDGMENTS

This book was like riding a bucking bronco to write, and I couldn't have held on without the help of so many good people.

My first shout-out goes to Katherine Fausset. I am so fortunate to call you my agent, my cheerleader, my mental bodyguard, my expert on all things writerly, and my dear friend. Thank you for reminding me that the book moved you to tears (I will forever carry around the image of you sobbing on the couch and freaking out your husband), and that you believed in me, especially during those times when I was having a hard time believing in myself. You are the best. Seriously. The best.

Big thanks to Farrin Jacobs, my editor, who pushed me past "good enough" into something I can truly be proud of and kept such a keen eye on how many times I used the word "just" (only one in this entire acknowledgment—aren't you proud?). I also owe high fives to Catherine Wallace, for all your hard work and smart ideas, to my publicist, Marisa Russell, for taking such good care of me schedule-wise, and to the entire awesome team at HarperCollins, including Kate Jackson, Susan Katz, Melinda Weigel, Susan Jeffers, and Sasha Illingworth, who created another gorgeous shiny cover to match my first gorgeous shiny cover.

Thank you to the students and staff at Jackson Hole High School, especially Principal Scott Crisp, Julie Stayner, and Lori Clark-Erickson, for welcoming me back to the school for round two of research and interviews. I appreciate how graceful and enthusiastic you were about this project from the beginning. Clara's world truly came alive for me in the halls of JHHS.

Thanks to my friends: Amy Yowell, Melissa Stockham, Kristin Naca, Robin Marushia, Joan Kremer, Wendy Johnston, and Lindsey Terrell, for being my biggest fans and supporters, each in your own way. Y'all make me feel so loved.

Thanks to Shannon Fields (and Emily!), for taking such good care of my son and for so often being the real-person, adult conversation I had at the end of the day. I needed that.

Thanks to my family:

My dad, Rodney Hand, for listening to all my problems and then gently reminding me that I had problems other people would kill for. And for taking Will on long tractor rides so I could work.

Julie Hand, for being so eager to read the latest drafts and giving me such insightful, honest feedback, even though you worried that I'd be furious.

Carol Ware, my mom, for being my Idaho publicist and for always being there when I needed you. I don't know how I would have survived this year without your help. Maggie is a great mother, but she ain't got nothing on you!

Jack Ware, for being my mom's knight in shining armor, the epitome, in my mind, of a good husband and a good man. Thanks for all the support, the sound tax advice, and always being so eager to help on any level you could.

My own husband, John Struloeff. I said it all last time, but I have to say it again. You are one amazing, talented man, and I'd be lost without you. I'm so glad that you assigned yourself to me all those years ago, my partner and my friend.

Will, my little man, for enduring so many movies so Mommy could work, for always making me laugh, and for reminding me of what's important in life.

And last but not least, Maddie. My sweet girl. Who was with me every moment I was writing this book, growing as it grew, through tears and edits and Braxton-Hicks contractions. Thank you for being a mellow baby who slept like a rock through all those signings and readings.